Chaos

Brian L. Jackson

Following a deadly firestorm, the world erupts in violence as a population, long weary of tyranny, rises up against an oppressive police state. As the world collapses into civil war, a rouge Lightwarrior emerges from the shadows, leaving a trail of bodies in her wake and stirring the rebelling public to a deadly frenzy.

After being outed as a pyrokinetic and blamed for the death of a prominent Resistance leader, Charlie finds herself once again the target of deadly violence. Together with her adoptive parents David and Catherine, Charlie is forced to go on the run once more or face extermination at the hands of a public driven to hatred and rabid violence by fear, misunderstanding and too many years of oppression.

ISBN:

DEDICATION

To my wife Melanie, and my children Heyger and Danielle. The world turns on so long as I can share life with you.

ACKNOWLEDGMENTS

I would like to thank my friend and former law partner, Judge Joseph M. Gardner for his feedback and suggestions; and my mother and sister for their encouragement and advice.

I would also like to express special thanks to Miss Sasha Figarella of Chrissha's Art for her breathtaking cover illustration. You have truly brought my characters to life.

To my loving wife and children; I appreciate your support, encouragement and patience. I am blessed to have you in my life to share this moment.

Lastly, I wish to express my deep and heartfelt appreciation to my father, Dr. Barry L. Jackson, this has been a long and sometimes arduous journey and I would not have gotten this far without you.

Those who would give up essential Liberty, to purchase a little temporary Safety, deserve neither Liberty nor Safety.

-Benjamin Franklin

Civilization is hideously fragile and there's not much between us and the horrors underneath, just about a coat of varnish.

-Carrie Snow

The human species does not necessarily move in stages from progress to progress ... history and civilization do not advance in tandem. From the stagnation of Medieval Europe to the decline and chaos in recent times on the mainland of Asia and to the catastrophes of two world wars in the twentieth century, the methods of killing people became increasingly sophisticated. Scientific and technological progress certainly does not imply that humankind, as a result, becomes more civilized.

-Gao Xingjian, Nobel Lecture, 2000

All civilization in a sense exists only in the mind. Gunpowder, textile arts, machinery, laws, telephones are not themselves transmitted from man to man or from generation to generation, at least not permanently. It is the perception, the knowledge, and understanding of them, their ideas in the Platonic sense, that are passed along. Everything social can have existence only through mentality.

-Alfred L. Kroeber, The Superorganic

"Anger is like flowing water; there's nothing wrong with it as long as you let it flow. Hate is like stagnant water; anger that you denied yourself the freedom to feel, the freedom to flow; water that you gathered in one place and left to forget. Stagnant water becomes dirty, stinky, disease-ridden, poisonous, deadly; that is your hate. On flowing, water travels little paper boats; paper boats of forgiveness. Allow yourself to feel anger, allow your waters to flow, along with all the paper boats of forgiveness. Be human."

- C. JoyBell C.

Prologue

Civilization...claimed by men and women as that which separates them from the beasts, and yet it is but a lie, a fragile set of covenants, expectations and duties; a mere contract among groups of the like-minded to provide the illusion of security and peace. In truth, civilization is a glass house, easily shattered by the slightest blow.

Over my many years walking this dark, mortal plain I have watched many a people, kingdom and nation smashed to a thousand shards by war, plague, the awakening of a population of bleating sheep, or the promises of a leader publicly put to the lie by a moment's misfortune. Tragic and yet predictable, for mankind's hubris and foolishness know no bounds.

To mankind, civil society is both the promise of security and the promise of power whether it be power over others or power over one's own fate. And when those promises are broken... then the glass house shatters and men are left to bleed.

On one seemingly auspicious day, indistinguishable from all the others, ambitious men, stumble across the one child with the power to change the fate of men and seek to take their destiny into their own hands. Not knowing that which they do, these men open Pandora's box and unleash the horrors within.

As the box opens, this child, once innocent, now a victim of tragedy, begins to embrace the great power with which she has been cursed. In pursuit of the promise of a reckoning, she takes her fate into her own hands...

I

Men and women, one hundred in all, filed into a chamber deep beneath the ground somewhere in Europe. Each was chosen for his or her wisdom, scholarship, influence, and lack of corruption. Some were famous, others unknown, but in this darkest of hours all were equal. Each remained as silent as death for their business was grave. Only their footsteps echoing off the chamber's high ceiling broke the solemn stillness.

Each had seen this chamber many times before, but none could help being awed by its beauty. The vast marble pillars, mirror polished marble floor, backlit stained-glass windows and elaborately painted ceiling rivaled the beauty of the Sistine Chapel.

Twelve of the one hundred crossed the perfectly mirrored floor to the long oak judges' bench. Each was chosen to speak for one or more of the delegations.

The remaining eighty-seven members of the secret conclave filed into the large, semicircular jury box that ran along the perimeter of the chamber spanning nearly from floor to ceiling.

When everyone was seated, the presiding officer struck his gavel bringing the meeting to order.

"You all know why you have been summoned here. The *Sigilla Praevaricator* has purportedly been born." The presiding officer addressed the conclave in Latin, the spoken language of all its meetings since the ancient days when it was first convened. As he spoke, his heart began to race with combined excitement and fear. "This information was brought to us by Father James Lenox, a member of the Society of Jesus, and the Order of Light. Father Lenox further claims that he knows the identity of the *Sigilla Praevaricator*."

This drew a number of whispers, which the presiding officer rapidly silenced with his gavel. "These are incredible claims, particularly given that the date of this girl's birth is two years beyond the prophesized time but other than the year the girl does have the correct birthday and the astrological configuration for that date appears correct. Father Lenox has made this claim before without any evidence to support it, but now he has given us a name: Charlene MacLeod. Through our connections, we have been able to establish that Miss MacLeod is a powerful Enlightened and that she is a rare pyrokinetic."

The hushed whispering began anew, forcing the presiding officer to bang his gavel several more times to silence the chamber.

"You all know the implications if Father Lenox is correct. Thus, we must come to a decision tonight as to how we will proceed. In a few moments, I will relinquish the floor to the first of our twelve speakers. When they have finished, I will open the floor to the assembly at which point all members of the conclave may be recognized. There will be no limits set on the duration of discussion nor will I recognize any motion for cloture. All voices must be heard so that the conclave will be fully informed in making this most crucial decision."

Each of the speakers that followed had his or her own take on the meaning of young Charlene MacLeod's birth and how they should proceed; their views were as varied as their religious views. Still, the conclave basically divided into three distinct viewpoints. The first argued that the girl was dangerous and had to be killed before the enemy could obtain her cooperation. This was the viewpoint of the reactionaries and the certainty in their voices both disturbed and angered the presiding officer. *Righteous fools.* The second group, comprised of the most liberal members of the conclave, argued that they should aid the girl but allow her to go free. The presiding officer found this viewpoint equally foolish, and its proponents stupidly idealistic. It was the third viewpoint, held by the realistic members of the conclave, that the presiding officer agreed with. This position argued for finding and detaining the girl for her own protection. To his great relief the majority of those who spoke before the conclave held this third view and, in the end, it was this view that won out.

When the final vote was taken many hours later, the conclave overwhelmingly supported finding the girl and holding her at the conclave's headquarters in Edinburg, Scotland where she would be safe. The conclave also decided, over the presiding officer and several others' objections, that the girl's existence would be kept secret. Many of the members of the conclave felt that the world was not ready to be confronted with the reality which the girl represented.

For his own part, Ogastes felt that while some people would be frightened, and others would refuse to believe, most people would accept her existence and the coming cataclysm of which she was the harbinger. Time was short, and this child could save many. Who were they to say that those people did not deserve to be saved? The people of the world deserved to know the truth about what was coming so that they could make an informed decision about what to do. But this was not to be. The conclave had ruled, and he was bound by their decision.

Chapter 1
Tinderbox

I

The city was like a dream; buildings illuminated in blue, green, pink and red hues; pinpoint lights shimmering through the darkness. It was night and bitter cold, but the streets were still teeming with people of all sorts. Fashionably dressed men and women, teens and young adults dressed in trendy clothes, and wealthy gentlemen and ladies crowded the sidewalks while numerous trucks, cars, buses, and limousines jockeyed for space on the roads. This was the fairyland nightlife that exists in every city around the world.

Beneath this, lying barely unseen in the shadows was the much darker world of the street. Homeless men and women; scrawny, dirty children huddled in doorways and alleys, drawing filthy clothes and tattered blankets around themselves in futile defense against the cold. Hookers wearing cheap makeup and tawdry clothing traded their flesh for its ten to fifty-Euro market value while keeping an ever-mindful eye out for trouble from the police or the many flamboyantly dressed pimps who would beat or kill them for being so much as a Euro short of expected profit.

Other men and some women sporting branded streetwear and gang colors hawked every conceivable variety of street drug, always watchful for the occasional true innocent for whom a free sample would mean a lifetime of addiction.

These were the predators and exploiters of the street profiting from others' misery while all the time fooling themselves into believing they were wiser and better than those who paid for their illicit wares. In truth though, the hookers were no better off than the hopeless, lonely men who paid for their services and the street pushers were no better off than the sad, pathetic wretches to whom they sold daily fixes; all resided in bondage to their own desperation.

Among the bustling crowd walked a brown-haired man with mysterious wolf gray eyes; a green-eyed and red-gold haired woman of slender, athletic build; and a young, slim girl of middle childhood years with waist-length, golden blond hair, and wideset perfect blue eyes. All three wore understated and nondescript clothing and walked with purpose intending to blend in rather than stand out.

Since escaping the Black Empire, David had become much more aware of this world, the real world beneath the cheap plastic veneer of glitz that was the city most people saw. David saw this world more clearly now that he understood certain truths about the way of things, truths that many people never understand.

As he thought of these things David glanced down at Charlie feeling both grateful and frightened for her at once. It was three months to the day since she had been released from the hospital. She was still weak and had much recovery ahead of her, but then it was a miracle that she had survived her injury at all. Her doctors still could not explain it. They had never seen anyone, child or adult, survive a burn as severe as hers. Even more miraculously she had not lost her arm despite having her entire left shoulder burned away down to the bone. She was, in fact, regaining the use of her left arm in small increments, though it remained weak and caused her much pain. And so it seemed that the greatest miracle of all might happen and she would fully recover from her burn without disability. She indeed was exceptional, a miracle come to life.

Charlie smiled back up at him her wide blue eyes twinkling. In her heart, he sensed genuine happiness. "Where are we going?"

He smiled back. "You'll see. It's a surprise."

"Ok." She chirruped.

In his heart, David allowed himself to feel happiness, and for the first time in a long time, contentment. He was with his family, his wife, Catherine, and his adopted daughter, Charlie. They were together again, and they were safe. He knew they could not stay here forever. Sooner or later the Black Empire would figure out where they were, but for now, they were safely anonymous.

David, Catherine and Charlie were on their way to dinner at *der Jagerhund*, after which they would go to the IMAX Theater to see the entire *Lord of the Rings* trilogy, Charlie's current favorite movies. The night promised to be glorious, a wonderful celebration of Charlie's miracle recovery.

The restaurant was crowded, but they had reservations, so the *mater de* seated them almost immediately. After taking their drink orders, the *mater de* informed them that their waiter would arrive shortly before imparting this information to the overweight bartender.

After a few minutes, their waiter, a thirtyish looking man with jet-black hair and Mediterranean features appeared carrying their drinks on a bar tray. All three of them had decided on what they wanted so after the waiter had placed their glasses on the table, they gave him their orders. The man rapidly scrawled their choices on a pad, then just as quickly disappeared into the kitchen.

Sometime after the waiter left, an older looking man approached their table. David recognized him at once.

"Dad?"

"Hi, David."

He had aged considerably and looked much more harried and careworn than David remembered, but it was him.

Catherine smiled. "Hi, Jim. It's good to see you."

"It's good to see you too, Catherine."

He smiled down at Charlie. "Hi, Charlie."

Charlie looked up at him with uncharacteristic reticence. "Hi."

David was incredulous. "What are you doing here, Dad? I mean…How did you find us?"

"The chaplain at the hospital you took Charlie to is an old friend of mine from seminary. He recognized you and told me where I could find you."

There was something he was holding back, David felt it at once. "I wanted to find you, so I can help you."

David studied his father carefully. The feeling that he was holding something back grew stronger with each word he spoke. "I've spoken with some people, and you've been offered asylum."

Now David was very suspicious. "What are you saying?'

"You've been summoned to Edinburg, Scotland by the White Conclave," Dad replied simply.

David sat in silence, unsure of what to think. *The White Conclave ... Who are they and what do they want?* He already knew of course. They wanted the same thing the Black Empire wanted: Charlie. Someone had finally decided to believe Dad's story. The question was could the Conclave be trusted, and to this, David had no answer. Their intentions could be honorable, but he had no way of being sure, and it was very likely that they were just another pawn of the Black Empire.

Even if they weren't that was no guarantee that they didn't have an agenda of their own. Did he really want to place his family at their mercy?

On the other side though, this was his father. If he couldn't trust Dad who could he trust? He didn't know what to do. He wanted to believe his father's intentions were honorable, but he couldn't bring himself to put Charlie and Catherine in the hands of strangers whose motives were unknown.

"Let me think about this, Dad. Sit down. Have dinner with us."

His father smiled. "Okay, David."

And so, David's father joined them for the remainder of the evening out.

II

Upon returning to their motel room the following morning, David put Charlie to bed, then sat down with Catherine and his father to talk.

"What do they really want with us, Dad?"

"The Conclave wants to protect Charlie. They understand as we do the important role she will play in the upcoming battle."

David gave him an annoyed look. "Yeah, I figured that much but what's their real reason."

Dad shook his head. “I don’t know David.”

“Well, I’d like to know before I put my family in their hands.”

“Something doesn’t feel right, but it doesn’t feel like the NSA, or the Black Empire is behind it,” Catherine interjected.

David was silent for a moment. Something *wasn’t* right, but he didn’t sense that the NSA or Black Empire were involved. Still, he was unwilling to trust.

“You’re right, but I’d still like to know what these people want from us before I trust them.” He glanced at his father as he spoke the last few words.

Dad’s expression was neutral, but David could feel his unease. He too was suspicious of the Conclave’s true intentions.

“I wish I could tell you more, but I don’t know any more than you do about this. All they told me was to bring you to Edinburg. I can’t promise anything, but I can tell you that if this is a trick, I will do what I can to help you escape.”

David was silent. He knew his father was sincere, but he doubted there would be much Dad could do if this was some kind of trap.

“What else can we do David?” Catherine said matter-of-factly. “We don’t have anywhere to go, and the Black Empire is still looking for us. At least we’ll have someplace to rest and hide for a little while.”

David turned to her, knowing she was right but not wanting to admit it. “And what happens if they turn out to be just as bad?”

“I don’t know David, but we can’t keep running forever. We have to go somewhere.”

David was silent for a long time. Catherine was right. They had nowhere to go. They had been surviving off of cash stolen from ATMs, changing no-tell motels by the week. He knew they couldn’t keep it up much longer.

David slowly turned to his father. “I don’t trust this White Conclave, but I trust you, and I know you would never deliberately put us in danger. We’ll go back to Edinburg with you.” As he spoke the words David’s heart rebelled and he found himself incredulous at his own words.

“Thank you, David.”

III

The following morning David, Catherine, and Charlie packed up their meager possessions and boarded a direct flight to Edinburg with David’s father. After landing and clearing security with the usual bribes, they got into an armored limousine that took them to a massive castle just outside the city limits.

Upon arriving David, Catherine, and Charlie were shown to their suite and offered food. After eating they, together with David's father, were taken to a throne room deep within the Castle. This was a spacious chamber that spoke longingly of a distant past. Massive white marble pillars topped with lifelike effigies of knights in white armor supported a vaulted ceiling adorned with beautiful, full-color paintings of silver-white armored men and women battling black armored Dark Knights across the open green hills and mountains of the Scottish Highlands. More of these same images decorated the enormous stained-glass windows that opened the walls to their right and left as well as to the rear. These gave the chamber a light airy feeling despite its dim candle and oil lamp illumination.

At the head of the chamber stood a massive, ornately carved gold leaf and mahogany throne upon which sat a tall and slender, elderly man. Despite his age, the man was well built and had an air of strength. Charlie stared in awe for a moment before glancing down at the mirror-polished white marble floor. Her own reflection greeted her in return.

Upon sighting Charlie, the man rose and approached her. ["Hello Charlene MacLeod, Breaker of Seals."]

The man's voice was soft and gentle, and he spoke with a strange accent that Charlie did not recognize. His actual words sounded alien to her ears though she instantly knew them to be Latin.

["Hi, who are you?"] To her surprise, her reply was also in Latin though she had never studied or ever spoken the language before. Charlie felt intimidated and was unsure of why.

The man smiled. ["My name is Alexi Ogastes. I've been looking forward to meeting you."] Charlie understood at once that he was not to be trusted. Ogastes wanted to use her to bring the world under the White Conclave's control.

Charlie met Ogastes's gaze steadily. ["It won't work. They'll never believe it. They don't want to."]

Ogastes returned a confused expression. ["What are you talking about?"]

Charlie's gaze was unchanged. ["You think you can use me to get the Outsiders to follow you. It won't work. They won't believe you no matter what you show them. You'll only make things worse."]

Ogastes's expression became troubled. ["You are mistaken, my child. I only want to help you and your friends."]

He was lying, but she said nothing further.

Ogastes addressed David and Catherine in English. "You are David and Catherine McAuliffe, correct? My name is Alexi Ogastes. I trust you have been well taken care of. Yes?"

"Yes, thank you." David bowed his head slightly, a gesture of respect rather than deference. "We appreciate your kindness."

Ogastes renewed his smile. "It was nothing. I am delighted to see you three. I have some friends who would very much like to meet young Charlene."

Charlie sensed David's suspicion at once. "Ok. And who are these friends of yours?"

"You will meet them tomorrow. Tonight, I ask that you enjoy my hospitality, relax, and rest." He turned towards Charlie once more. "Goodnight Charlene."

Charlie glanced back at him without replying.

IV

When they were out of Ogastes's earshot, David turned to her. "I didn't know you spoke Latin."

"I don't." She replied simply.

"But you were able to understand Ogastes perfectly and answer him in Latin."

Charlie was silent. She was not frightened, only mystified and intrigued. *How am I doing this? I've never heard Latin before, but I can understand it. Why?*

"What did you say to him?" David inquired with more than a hint of concern.

"I told him it wouldn't work," Charlie replied matter-of-factly.

"What wouldn't work?" She could feel David's confusion. He had not yet felt it.

"You'll see."

David's expression became deeply confused and frightened. "Charlie, what's going on?"

"It's ok, David. Everything's going to be ok." This was a lie. She did not know why she was lying, only that she could not tell David what she knew. He had to find out on his own.

But what if he finds out too late?

V

Charlie slept poorly that night and awoke early the next morning. After eating breakfast, she was again taken to the throne room with David and Catherine.

"You have been summoned before the White Conclave." Ogastes was looking right at her as he spoke.

"We'll be happy to cooperate as soon as you tell us what's going on," David replied.

“I don’t think you understand. The Conclave does not wish to meet you and Catherine. They only want to see Charlene.”

“She’s not going anywhere without at least one of us.” David fired back. “I don’t trust you, and I want to know what’s going on before we go any further.”

Ogastes’s expression resembled that of a teacher correcting a stubborn, foolish child.“I cannot tell you that, but I assure you Charlene will not be harmed. We only wish to help.”

“You’re asking us to trust you without any idea of what we’re getting ourselves into. I won’t do that. Not with my daughter, and not with my family.”

“You don’t have a choice,” Ogastes replied coldly. “You’re under my power now. If you will not cooperate willingly, I will summon an Asset to bring Charlie before the conclave.”

Charlie had to stop this. There wasn’t time to fight. The Black Empire would find them again soon, and she couldn’t stand to hear any more fighting. “Stop it! I’ll go with you, just please don’t fight.”

David looked down on her visibly frightened. “You don’t have to go anywhere with them. You don’t have to do anything you don’t want to.”

“I know.” She replied gently. “Don’t be afraid. They won’t hurt me, and I won’t let them take me away.”

David started to argue, but she cut him off.

“It’s ok. Everything’s going to be alright.” Charlie turned towards Ogastes. “I’m ready to go.”

Ogastes smiled. “Thank you, Charlie.”

Charlie sensed genuine friendliness and concern behind his smile, but still, she knew what Ogastes really intended and was distrustful. He thought he was doing the right thing, but he was actually taking the worst possible action other than what Eric had desired. Ogastes would inevitably cause a disaster if he revealed her existence to the world.

So why don’t I tell David? Why am I lying to him? Charlie didn’t know. She knew only that she could not tell. Something was holding her back.

Ogastes led her from the throne room and through countless vaulted corridors decorated with ornate paintings and statuary similar to the throne room. It felt like walking through a dream. The beauty and wonder of it all was too much to be real. No real place could be this spectacular. Charlie gazed at the mirrored marble floor and gleaming gold and silver trim, and the jeweled ornamentation of the many lifelike sculptures and imagined herself standing in heaven once more.

Sometime later they passed through a door and descended a long and narrow spiral stairway to another world.

The narrow, low ceilinged corridors here were forged of cold granite blocks, unadorned save for thick mold and mildew spawned by the damp, musty air. Unlike the brightly lit castle above, these corridors were choked with shadows broken sporadically by the dim flicker of a burning torch. This was a place of secrets, a place unchanged for many centuries and untouched by the changing world above.

Charlie unconsciously strained her ears to catch the horrified screams of torture victims locked behind the many heavy oak doors they passed. She heard nothing save for the drip of condensation and the echo of Ogastes's and her own footsteps.

Many secrets lay here, hidden from the world's eyes, secrets better left undisturbed. Indeed, she was one of them.

They were descending far beneath the castle now. Inside Charlie felt deeply afraid. She was in danger, David and Catherine were too. She felt it in her bones. The feeling was everywhere, surrounding her like a terrible choking mist. She had to do something, but what? What was she going to do?

Charlie couldn't hurt these people. They weren't evil, just selfish and stupid. Charlie wanted to tell David what she felt, but something had kept her from doing that, and now it was too late. Something terrible was going to happen, and there was nothing she could do about it. Charlie felt like crying, but she managed to bite back the tears.

VI

They had arrived at a massive, heavy iron-clad oak door. Ogastes produced a long black skeleton key from within his robes and slid it into the door's ancient lock. There was a loud thud followed by a haunting creak as the door fell open.

Beyond lay a cavernous chamber reminiscent of an old courtroom Charlie had seen in a movie once.

Charlie stood frozen in the doorway for a moment before Ogastes prodded her forward. While more brightly lit than the corridor outside the courtroom was permeated with deep shadows, set to dance by flickering oil lanterns suspended from the ceiling.

Many men and women sat within, their faces hidden in darkness. A select few sat behind the judge's massive bench at the head of the chamber, the remainder were within the large horseshoe-shaped jury box. All gave off a powerful sense of anticipation and fear. Charlie could have learned more if she wanted, but she held back, frightened of what she would find.

Ogastes stopped at the center of the chamber and turned her to face the jury before addressing the courtroom in Latin.

["Here stands the child, Charlene MacLeod."]

The gathered men and women looked her over silently. Though she could not see their faces, she could feel their eyes piercing the darkness.

["I have brought her before you so that we may determine if she is indeed the Breaker of Seals."]

The courtroom remained silent.

["I will begin by interviewing the child."] He turned towards Charlie. ["Please state your full name for the conclave."]

[„Charlene Danielle MacLeod."] She replied automatically in perfect Latin.

["Do you swear to tell the truth, the whole truth and nothing but the truth so help you, God?"]

["Yes."]

Now Charlie was sure she was dreaming for this was the exact same oath she had heard taken many times on TV court shows. Except Charlie knew this was no dream. Her sense of danger was too strong, as was the unquestionable knowledge that what she saw before her was truly happening.

["Now Charlie, do you mind if I call you Charlie?"]

["No."]

["Charlie what is your birthday?"]

["April 30th."]

["Do you know what time you were born, Charlie?"]

Charlie paused to think. ["Umm eleven fifty-seven I think."] She seemed to recall her father or her mother, she wasn't sure which, telling her that she was born three minutes before midnight, but the memory had become a faded photograph and so she could not confirm its accuracy.

Ogastes turned towards the court. ["As you can see, the date and time of her birth are correct."]

He turned back towards Charlie. ["You were born an Enlightened, were you not?"]

["Yes."]

["Describe your powers to the conclave please."]

["Ummm, I can start fires, and I can move things and sometimes, when something bad is going to happen, I can feel it. I can also tell what people really want and what they are feeling."] Charlie could not believe her own words even as she spoke them.

Ogastes nodded. ["So you can light fires and move things with your mind, and you have some clairvoyant and empathic abilities. Will you demonstrate your powers for us?"]

Charlie was silent as she considered his request. Was she going to cooperate with these people who wanted to use her? She knew what they intended. In a way, they were no better than the NSA men, no better than Eric and his Black Empire.

Both the NSA and Eric had manipulated Charlie and used her for her power. Eric had wanted her to *Hate!* Outsiders, to hurt them and kill them.

Maybe these people did not intend to use Charlie to hurt anyone, but what they had in mind would be every bit as dangerous as what the NSA and Black Empire desired. Charlie could not cooperate with them. She couldn't.

["Yes."] *What...What the hell are you doing? You can't give them what they want. They're going to hurt just as many people as the Black Empire would have.*

["Thank you, Charlie. I'll be right back."]

Charlie silently cursed herself in disbelief even as she watched Ogastes leave and return a moment later wheeling a cart laden with a large block of wood. Why was she doing this? She didn't want to. She knew it would lead to trouble. Why was she cooperating with them?

Ogastes parked the cart in front of Charlie and then turned to address the court. ["This is a block of solid mahogany."] He turned towards her. ["I would like you to try to set it on fire."]

Charlie glanced at the block for a moment, still questioning why she was doing this. Then she flicked out with the power. Instantly the block exploded throwing miniature flaming comets in all directions. One of these struck the far wall and shattered in a bright orange starburst.

The courtroom gasped audibly. Their fear was palpable. Someone banged a gavel. Charlie did not look to see who.

Charlie's heart was racing with terror as the power blazed within her mind. She bit down on it hard. Flaming, blood-soaked, shrapnel tore through her skull. Still, Charlie would not let go. She could not.

Stop it!!

Stop it now!!

After several minutes of silent suffering, the power broke. Charlie heaved a great sigh of relief.

The gavel banged again bringing the courtroom to dead silence. ["I think we've seen enough."] The voice was that of the young man in a white robe seated at the center of the judge's bench. ["You may return young Charlene to her guardians."]

["Certainly."] Ogastes turned towards her and addressed her in English. "Come along, Charlie. You're done here."

Charlie went with him silently, heart still racing with fear. What had she done? What had she started?

As Charlie followed Ogastes through the labyrinthine underground corridors and grand hallways of the castle above, her heart filled with dread for she knew she had made a grievous error. She had cooperated with them, and now they knew. Ogastes and his people would surely try to use her to build their own power and in doing so would kill many people.

It was beginning again; the running, the fear, the misery. Charlie could feel it, like a dark shadow closing over her heart. It was starting again, and it was all her fault. She could have stopped it if she wanted to and she didn't. She had cooperated with them willingly.

VII

After being reunited David, Catherine and Charlie were returned to their suite to await the Conclave's decision. Charlie sensed that they felt it now too. Something terrible was about to happen.

The time seemed to pass at a crawl, and with each ensuing hour, Charlie's fear grew stronger as did her certainty that they were all in grave danger.

Several days passed uneventfully. During this time, David, Catherine and Charlie were treated like royalty. Servants waited on them hand and foot. They were fed extravagant meals and given gorgeous clothing. Every luxury was theirs for the asking.

Still, Charlie could not enjoy these lavish indulgences for she knew this was but a gilded prison. Charlie and her adoptive parents had free run of the castle and total command of the servant staff, but they could not leave. The three of them were prisoners, just as Charlie had been a prisoner of the NSA and of the Black Empire. She and David and Catherine were at Ogastes's mercy.

VIII

Within a few weeks, Ogastes revealed his intentions.

It began as a knock at the door to their suite. David answered and was greeted by a pair of Assets. "You and your wife and daughter are required to appear before the conclave in two hours."

"Ok. What for?" David's voice was neutral, but Charlie could feel the fear and suspicion in his heart.

"You'll find out when you get there."

David's suspicion deepened. "What's going on? I want to know before we go anywhere with you."

One of the Assets shrugged. "Don't really know. They didn't tell us what they're up to they just told us to come get you."

"I guess we don't have any choice then."

The Asset did not respond.

"Fine. Give us a few minutes to get ready."

IX

The evening had grown late, and Charlie was already in her nightgown. She knew even before David spoke what he would ask of her and thus turned and went into her bedroom shutting the door behind her.

Charlie's heart raced for she knew what was to come. It was beginning again, and the she and her adoptive parents would soon have to run. It would be worse this time too. Of this Charlie had no doubt.

Charlie knew she could speak up. She could warn David and Catherine, and Charlie knew she should, but something held her back, some force she did not understand. This was the way it had to be Charlie supposed, though she did not understand why. God or someone had determined that it would happen this way and that course could not now be altered.

Charlie was surprised to find that she understood this. As she quickly threw on the clothes she had worn only hours earlier: GAP blue jeans, silk blouse, pink cashmere sweater, black Sketchers, Charlie wondered what would happen next.

Charlie knew they would have to run again, and she knew it would be bad, but she had no sense of specific details. Maybe it was better that way, but Charlie doubted it. If she knew exactly what to expect she could better protect herself and David and Catherine.

As it was Charlie had no way of knowing that David and Catherine would not end up like Mommy and Daddy. But could she really do anything? Charlie had tried to protect David and Catherine before, and they were still captured. She had not even been able to save herself from being taken. What could she do now that she hadn't tried before?

A short time later, Charlie finished dressing and headed out into the living room where David and Catherine waited with the two guards.

"Are you ready?" One of the Assets asked.

The man seemed much taller and more imposing up close. His hard, large olive-toned face and muscular arms suggested that he could easily enforce his will on most anyone he pleased if refused.

Charlie nodded fearfully. She could have escaped if she wanted. She could have burned this man where he stood, and she and David and Catherine would have been able to escape.

That thought brought a moment of cheek burning shame. It was bad to have thoughts like that. The olive-skinned Asset had done nothing to deserve being burned.

It didn't matter. The block remained, invisible and strong. She could not resist its influence.

"Let's go then." As he spoke, the olive skinned Asset turned an expectant gaze on Charlie and her adoptive parents.

David and Catherine silently took Charlie's hands, and together they headed towards the door. The two Assets fell into line in front and back of them.

The corridors flowed by rapidly as if in a dream. Sharp daggers of light flicked out at her from every inch of gold trim and mirror polished marble causing her head to throb painfully and her eyes to run. David must have mistaken the watering for tears for he gently squeezed her hand and softly whispered: "It'll be alright."

Charlie did feel like crying though she managed to resist the urge.

They were beneath the castle now. Their footsteps echoed deafeningly in the dead silence of the dark corridors. All three of them walked in silence for there was nothing to say. In her heart, Charlie knew that David and Catherine felt it now too. And like her, they too were restrained by that same invisible force. They were trapped, adrift in a black storm that they were powerless to resist, knowing in all certainty that it would bring their destruction.

X

Now Charlie and her adoptive parents had reached the great door. The tall, olive-skinned Asset produced an iron key as Ogastes had done before. Then he led the three of them into the council chamber. The silence within was more profound than that of the corridor outside. As she crossed the floor of the conclave, Charlie could feel everyone's eyes on her, piercing out from the darkness. Their intentions were clear. They believed she was the *Sigilla Praevaricator* and meant to keep her here. Charlie was to be kept here for her own safety, but she would still be a prisoner, just as she had been a prisoner of the Black Empire. They would allow David and Catherine to stay with Charlie, but they would not be allowed to take her from Castle Bruce. Charlie would not be allowed to leave until the final battle began.

As they neared the judge's bench Ogastes rose and addressed Charlie in Latin.

["Hello Charlie. We have come to a decision."]

She was silent.

["We have decided that we will grant you protection from the men who are chasing you. You will be allowed to live here in the castle where you will be safe from the NSA and its employees."]

["I don't want to stay here."] Charlie replied already knowing what the answer would be.

["You'll be safer here than you will be outside."] Ogastes said gently.

Charlie remained resolute. ["I don't want to stay here. I want to be free."]

["I'm sorry you feel that way, Charlie but I cannot let you leave. It's for your own good."]

Ogastes's voice was apologetic. Behind it, Charlie felt his true intentions. She was property to him, a tool to be used. Ogastes cared about her only because she was the *Sigilla Prevaricator.* He would never let her out of his control.

Charlie glared up at him defiantly for a momen,t before dropping her gaze. There was no point in arguing. It would make no difference. She was a prisoner unless she used the power and she would not hurt these people. They were not evil; they just didn't understand. They were selfish, but they were not truly evil.

Ogastes turned to David and Catherine and addressed them in English. "You may remain here with Charlie if you wish, but she cannot leave."

"She's *my* daughter," David stated coldly. "You can't do this."

"You don't have a choice," Ogastes replied. "I run this castle. You're lucky I'm letting you stay with her."

"And you're lucky I don't kill you where you stand."

Charlie's heart exploded with shock. *What are you doing?* This wasn't David. He was always so gentle and kind. He would never hurt someone unless he was forced to.

"My father must have told you that I have the power. Are you sure you want to have this fight?" David's voice was low and threatening.

"David wait…" Catherine interjected. The force of her concern struck Charlie in an invisible wave of ice water.

"No. I'm sick of this shit!" David snapped. "These people think they can just come along and lock us up." David turned back on Ogastes. Charlie could feel the force of his anger. "Who the hell do you think you are? All of you. You're no better than the NSA and the Black Empire! You think you can just sweep in and start treating us like property! You stay away from my daughter. I don't care if Charlie is the *Sigilla Praevaricator* she's not your property!" He forcefully grabbed Charlie's shoulders, hurting her a little. "If you don't I'll kill all of you and to hell with the consequences!"

Charlie turned and looked up at David with pleading eyes. "Please don't hurt them, David." Ogastes's intentions, while self-serving, were not evil. She could not let David harm him. She turned towards Ogastes. "I'll stay here. Just please don't fight."

David bent down to her level. "Are you sure, Charlie?"

"Yes."

Charlie couldn't stand anymore fighting, and she didn't want David to hurt these people. She knew he would do anything for her, even if it meant harming an innocent and she couldn't bear the thought of that. Ogastes and his people were assholes, but they didn't deserve to die, certainly not because of her, and Charlie didn't want David to damn himself for her. She wasn't worth it. Charlie didn't want to stay there but she would to prevent a tragedy.

David stood up and closed to within two feet of Ogastes so that the two men, one young, one old, were eye to eye. "I guess we'll stay here then." He dropped his voice, hoping that Charlie would not overhear. "But I swear to God if you hurt my daughter, I'll kill you."

Charlie's heart chilled anew for David's voice was so calm and certain. She knew without the need for psychic senses that he was speaking the truth. His tone of voice and steady eyes told the tale with absolute certainty.

Please don't hurt anyone, David... Charlie reached out with her mind as she thought this, hoping that David would hear. She had not allowed David to listen to her thoughts since that night in the Chicago hospital when she sensed his fear of her.

Charlie could not bear the thought of David fearing her. Not after everything she had been through. Oh, there were many people who feared her, but David's fear of her brought the point home. David had the power too, and he was still afraid. No doubt this was because he had felt for a moment what she felt every day. David had felt the change, the sense that something terrible had begun and the certainty that it was because of her.

Charlie knew that whatever was happening was connected to her. Somehow, she had started something, pushed some enormous boulder down a hill and now it was tumbling wildly out of control, knocking smaller stones loose as it went. She had caused this somehow, and she was vital to its final outcome. This knowledge would burn in her heart in the coming days.

XI

Like the NSA and the Black Empire, Ogastes put Charlie through a battery of tests. Some of the tests were the same as ones she had done before, but some were new. Charlie was asked to light several objects on fire including a large block of wood, a brick wall, and a minivan. She was also required to demonstrate her telekinetic abilities by levitating a series of wooden blocks of increasing size and weight. This later progressed into building structures with the blocks. In yet another test, this one intended to measure her psychic senses, Charlie was shown playing cards and asked what was on the face. She scored perfectly every time to the amazement of the man and woman conducting the tests.

Along with the experiments on her power came other tests. Ogastes's doctors took blood from Charlie and samples of her hair, skin, saliva, muscle tissue, bone marrow, and spinal fluid. These were nothing new, Charlie had endured them at the hands of both the NSA and the Black Empire, and as usual, she was not told of the purpose or results of the tests.

David was right. She was an object to them, just as she had been an object to the NSA and to Eric's Black Empire. Eric had sort of seen Charlie as a person, but his interest in her was because of her power. Otherwise, Charlie would have been just another child, a thing to be used and discarded. She was not a person; she was the *Sigilla Prevaricator*. That was how they all saw Charlie, everyone except her parents and David and Catherine.

Ogastes and his people said they cared for her and that they wanted to protect her, but Charlie knew better. It would not take them long to show their true intentions.

XII

About a week after the tests began, Ogastes came to the suite Charlie shared with David and Catherine. She was alone. David and Catherine had left to have dinner. Charlie didn't blame them for not bringing her. They hadn't had any time alone since being captured by the Black Empire four years ago.

It was around eight-thirty when Ogastes knocked softly on the door. To Charlie's surprise, he was alone and dressed in regular street clothes rather than the raiment of his office. He greeted her with a friendly smile.

"Hello, Charlie."

She returned a nervous smile. "Hi." She knew already what he wanted. A slow chill crept its way up her spine.

"I see David and Catherine left you here alone."

"Yeah, they wanted to have dinner together." Charlie kept her voice calm despite the gnawing fear in her heart. "They haven't had any time alone since we were taken away."

"I'm glad they're finally getting a chance to be alone, but what about you?"

"I'll be alright." Charlie replied matter-of-factly. "I can take care of myself."

Ogastes inclined his head. "That's very understanding of you Charlie. Have you had your dinner yet?"

"Yes." Charlie could feel her pulse in her head. Time was running out. It would soon begin again.

"That's good. Can we talk for a little bit?"

"Ok." She was terrified.

"You're a very special little girl, Charlie. Do you know that?"

She was silent. These were words she had heard before.

"What do you want?" Charlie asked despite already knowing the answer.

"You know the end is coming. You can feel it. But most of the world can't. We have to warn them so that they have a chance to save themselves."

Charlie stared at Ogastes silently waiting for him to tell her that which she already knew.

Ogastes became uncomfortable as if Charlie were accusing him with her silence. "I would like to put you on television so that we can demonstrate who you are and what you can do. Hopefully at least some people will do the right thing."

Charlie remained silent. *The feeling was right, and so was David. You just want to use me, that's all. You're just like everyone else.*

He offered a smile. "Would you be willing to do that for me?"

Charlie did not respond. She knew what it was that he was really asking, and she knew what she had to do. She just couldn't bring herself to do it. The cost was too high. Charlie couldn't face it.

Ogastes looked at her expectantly.

Charlie remained silent. She couldn't face this, not again, not after everything she had already been through. She couldn't go through it all again. But she had to. Somehow, Charlie knew that. This was how it had to be, and there was no escaping it.

"Yes."

The word fell from her mouth like a faint drop of acid burning its way through her heart. There was no hope. Charlie understood that now.

Ogastes smiled. "Thank you, Charlie." Then he turned and left.

Charlie sat and stared into space for several minutes as the gravity of what had just happened sank in. She had agreed to let Ogastes hold her up before the world as proof that there was a God. He believed that this would somehow change things, that people would suddenly stop whatever bad or evil things they were doing and start believing, but she knew better. Ogastes meant well, but he was a fool. All he would accomplish would be to make things worse. There would be no great repentance. There would only be more horror. Charlie felt it deep in her heart and was afraid.

XIII

David was furious when he found out but cooled down a little when he learned that Charlie had willingly agreed to go on television. Still, he had trouble understanding why.

"Why do you want to go on television? Ogastes is using you."

Charlie nodded. "I know, but I don't have any choice."

David couldn't accept that. He thought that this was a needless risk. Charlie agreed with him, but she knew she had no choice. This was how it had to be.

Except nothing happened as Ogastes had planned. On the second night after she had agreed to Ogastes's request, Charlie awakened suddenly, her heart racing. Something was very wrong. She felt it deep in her heart. Without pausing Charlie quickly got out of bed and went to the adjacent bedroom to awaken David and Catherine. By the time Charlie had reached the door, her hands trembled and a thin sheen of sweat coated her skin. Charlie carefully opened the door and entered to find that David and Catherine had also awakened.

"Something's wrong." Charlie was disturbed by the tremor in her voice.

"I feel it too," David replied. "Let's hope the feeling is early."

Charlie was silent. She knew the feeling was not early. Someone had come for them.

Oh no…

Sudden terror exploded within her as she realized who had come for them.

Death Troopers!

The words clanged in her head as memories of her time as a captive of the Black Empire flooded her consciousness.

No please…not again!

The power flared within her, awakened by her fear. Charlie forced it down quickly.

Stop it!

The power quieted down but remained active within Charlie's mind. Suddenly an alarm sounded. A moment later there was a deafening boom in the corridor outside their suite. Charlie ducked instinctively. A scream escaped her throat before she could stifle it.

"Charlie, Catherine stay down." David's voice was terrified. His face as white as a sheet. He had drawn *Deus Irae* and held it in his right hand. "I'm going to try to get us out of…"

Before he could finish, the bedroom door exploded in a hail of splinters. In the same instant, Charlie felt a familiar, cold sensation.

Riyadah?! She recognized the icy touch of the female Dark Knight's mind. Riyadah strode across the threshold and over shattered wood fragments, sword drawn.

"Hello, Charlie." Riyadah's voice was almost conversational. "It is a pleasure to see you. It's been a while. Now, I suggest you surrender. The Emperor instructed me to bring you back alive. He said nothing about your friends here. It would be a shame if I were forced to kill them."

As Riyadah spoke, she extended her left hand, and Charlie felt her strike out with the power. Purple lightning leapt from Riyadah's outstretched fingers and splashed against the bed frame where David and Catherine had taken cover behind, setting it aflame and blasting it apart in the same instant.

Before Riyadah could follow up with a second attack, Catherine stood up and locked eyes with Riyadah. "I challenge you to fight to the death."

Riyadah smiled. "I accept."

Catherine drew a long, silver-steel sword seemingly from nowhere her eyes never leaving Riyadah's. "Get out of here, David. Take Charlie and go."

David started to move towards Charlie. Suddenly Riyadah struck out with the power again. A second blast of purple lightning leapt from her fingertips and slammed into David's chest, knocking him back.

"Not so fast." Riyadah chided. "You're not going anywhere with that girl."

Sudden anger flashed within Charlie's heart, bringing the power up with it. Charlie glared at Riyadah intending to incinerate her as she had done to Orson Tarken. Before she could strike, Catherine called to her.

"Don't Charlie. I will deal with her. Just get out of here with David."

Charlie slammed the power down.

STOP IT!

Twin chromium bolts of pain slammed through her skull, bringing tears to her eyes and causing her to waver on her feet. Charlie stumbled to where David lay in a crumpled heap. His breathing was shallow, and he wasn't moving. Thin tendrils of smoke curled up from the charred remains of his shirt. The flesh beneath was seared black leaving muscle and bone exposed.

Charlie touched David's chest with trembling fingers. "David? David, are you ok?"

He did not respond. Tears flooded her eyes. "Oh, David…"

David groaned softly and began to stir. "Charlie?" His voice was little more than a hoarse whisper.

"David, you're burned…she…she burned you." Charlie was sobbing, not with sorrow but with rage.

"I..I'll be ok," David whispered. "Just help me up."

Charlie slipped under his arm and helped David steady himself as he struggled to his feet with a groan.

"Does it hurt bad?" Charlie asked, fearful of the answer. She did not feel that he was suffering, but her senses were clouded by fear and anger.

"No, it's not bad, I'm just tired," David replied weakly. As he spoke, David stumbled and fell to one knee.

"David…" Charlie sobbed. The power was a living thing within her mind, flowing in rivers of hot magma.

STOP IT!

STOP PLEASE!

Fresh, blood-soaked pain slammed through her skull as she fought desperately against the power that she badly wanted to turn against Riyadah. The Dark Knight must have sensed her intent for she turned her hard smile on Charlie.

"Go ahead if you think you can little girl." She gloated. "Use your power! Burn me!"

Charlie bit back the power setting off a fresh explosion of pain throughout her body.

STOP IT!

The power continued spiraling upward, heedless of her pleas.

STOP IT NOW!

Charlie fought the power back with all of her will. The pain was excruciating. It burned and scourged her from head to toe. She wanted desperately to let go. Riyadah had hurt David; she could have killed him. She deserved to die. But David, David was hurt. She had to get him to safety.

Charlie struggled with the power for what felt like hours but was probably only minutes before she was able to bring it back under control. Even after the power became silent, her head throbbed and her body smoldered with pain.

By this time, David had made it to his feet and had taken Charlie's hand. "Catherine..." He groaned. "Be careful Catherine."

"GO David!" She cried back. "Take our daughter and get out of here!"

For a moment, David stood in silence. Charlie could feel him struggling with his emotions. Then he began to lead her from the room. In the same instant, Catherine charged Riyadah, blade raised.

XIV

Catherine watched David and Charlie flee from the corner of her eye as her blade collided with the female Dark Knight's.

The female Dark Knight ground her sword against Catherine's forcing Catherine to take a step backward to keep her balance. Catherine responded with a low kick to the female Dark Knight's left shin. The female Dark Knight suddenly stepped back and brought her sword around in a high slash targeting Catherine's neck. Catherine ducked under the blow and responded with a low slash that she intended would take out the female Dark Knight's legs. The female Dark Knight gracefully jumped over Catherine's sword landing in a low crouch. As Catherine moved in to press her advantage, the female Dark Knight quickly rose, bringing her blade up suddenly in a sweeping uppercut. Catherine quickly sidestepped and managed to avoid the worst of the blow. Nevertheless, the tip of the female Dark Knight's sword drew a thin line of fire up her left leg to her torso.

Catherine cried out in pain, and the female Dark Knight laughed.

"You were a fool to challenge me." The woman mocked. "You are no Lightwarrior, only a half-trained Enlightened. You will pay with your life for your stupidity."

As she spoke, the female Dark Knight smoothly changed her grip and brought her blade around in a wide arc targeting Catherine's abdomen. Catherine staggered backward. This time the woman's sword point sliced a thin, neat line across Catherine's belly. Hot blood spilled from the wound and stained her jeans. Catherine suffered no pain, but she could feel her body beginning to weaken. The power began to stir within her, spurred on by adrenaline. Catherine struck suddenly, pushing the female Dark Knight backward with an invisible bolt of force. Before the woman could catch her balance, Catherine lunged forward impaling the female Dark Knight through the abdomen. The women let out a cry of combined pain and anger and brought her sword down hard on Catherine's left shoulder. It was only by pure luck that Catherine did not lose her arm. More blood spilled down Catherine's back. Still, she felt no pain. Catherine pulled her sword free of the woman quickly and swung hard at the female Dark Knight's neck. As she did the woman brought her sword up in a massive uppercut. Catherine's sword bit deep into the female Dark Knight's neck at the same instant as the other woman's sword point cut deep into Catherine's cheek and forehead, narrowly missing her right eye.

Catherine's vision went red with blood. The female Dark Knight had collapsed to her knees. Blood coursed from a deep gash in the woman's neck. Still, the female Dark Knight had not given up the fight. Without pausing, the woman lifted her sword and swung wildly at Catherine. Catherine effortlessly sidestepped the blow. She made no attempt to strike back; the duel had ended though the female Dark Knight had not yet acknowledged this fact. Again, the female Dark Knight attempted to raise her sword, this time her strength failed her, and the blade slipped from her hands, clanging off the castle's stone floor. As Catherine watched the woman shuddered and gagged audibly. Then her head dropped forward, and she was still. Catherine could no longer sense her presence. The woman was dead.

XV

A hail of green blaster fire greeted Charlie and David the moment they stepped into the corridor outside of their suite.

"David lookout!" Charlie screamed as she dove to the ground. The power awakened within her once more. Something exploded directly above her head showering her in white-hot sparks. "Oww! Fuck!" Charlie cried out. Anger flashed within her heart.

"Keep your head down," David called to her in a hoarse voice.

Charlie ignored him. *I'm sick of this shit! Why can't you just leave us alone!!!* Charlie stood up slowly, power blazing, brought to the fore by her anger. The darkened corridor made it impossible to see the source of the blaster fire, but Charlie did not need her eyes to identify the location of the Death Troopers who had fired upon her. Charlie reached into the power and suddenly lashed out. There was a blinding flash of light and an instant later, the corridor was bathed in white flames. Charlie heard no screams but knew the men who had fired on her were no more.

"Jesus Charlie…" David's voice sounded weak and very far away against the din of the power as it continued to spiral upward. Charlie focused her mind and fought to keep the power balanced, suspended.

Charlie slowly walked down the corridor, absently pushing the flames aside with her mind. She could feel David's eyes on her.

"Charlie?" His voice was very far away now, but the fear in his tone was unmistakable. Guilt welled up within her, tamping down her anger slightly.

I'm sorry, David…I…I didn't mean to frighten you.

It's ok, Charlie. David's voice replied in her mind. *It's just…How did you do that?*

I don't know. Charlie replied feeling the first edge of fear adding itself to her swirling anger and guilt. *Can't you do it too?*

No. David replied. *I can summon lightning or move things with my mind, but I can't do anything like that.*

Charlie had reached the end of the corridor where it descended into a spiral staircase. David was limping behind her. She could hear his ragged breathing.

"Charlie..." He called to her. "Wait for me."

Charlie slowed her pace slightly but continued down the stairway without pausing. There was a fire door at the bottom. Without hesitation, Charlie pushed it open and stepped out into the castle courtyard and another hail of green blaster fire. She would have to protect David. He had been wounded and was in no condition to fight.

"David, watch out!" She called behind her. Then without pausing Charlie slowly walked towards the source of the blaster fire. Directly ahead stood row after row of Death Troopers. As she approached them, the Troopers spread out to positions of cover throughout the castle courtyard. Again, Charlie reached into the power, preparing to strike. Before she could one of the Death Troopers stepped forward and called out.

"Hold fire!"

"That's enough, Charlie." The man's voice was calm and authoritative.

Charlie could have incinerated him where he stood, yet she held back.

"We have the castle surrounded. Stand down now, and I promise your friends will not be harmed." He gave a slight bow. "I give you my word."

Who is this guy? Charlie thought incredulously. *Doesn't he know I could burn him up where he's standing?*

"You're powerful." The man continued. "But I have over a hundred men here. You can't fight us all at the same time. And your father is wounded. He can't go far without medical treatment."

Before the man could say another word, a red blaster bolt struck him in the chest, silencing him forever in a cloud of charred bits of flesh and red mist. In an instant, the air was alive with green and red blaster fire.

David was screaming at her to get down. Charlie ignored him. A green blaster bolt streaked silently by her head, missing only by inches. Charlie barely noticed. She was once again immersed in the power. Charlie reached deep into the power and lashed out at a group of seven Death Troopers who had crouched behind a nearby stone tower. In an instant, a wave of white fire swept across the courtyard flagstones and swallowed the men whole. Their screams echoed in the late-night air for but a moment before being silenced forever.

Charlie turned and sent the power out again, this time targeting a second group of seven Troopers who were scrambling to find cover. A massive blue-white fireball swallowed the men before they could scream.

Without warning, Charlie's left leg suddenly went numb. She collapsed to her knees and turned her head to the source of the blaster bolt that had struck her.

A female Death Trooper lay prone on the flagstones approximately twenty yards away. Without pausing Charlie sent the power in her direction.

In the same moment, a red blaster bolt lanced out, forcing the woman to duck her head as it shattered the flagstone directly in front of her.

An instant later she was swallowed by Charlie's flames. The woman let out a single, high pitched cry of agony before death silenced her forever. Her armor blazed on in blue-white sheets of fire.

As she looked around for something else to destroy, Charlie felt David lash out with the power. A moment later a massive lightning bolt arced down from the top of the northern parapet and smashed into a group of a dozen Death Troopers who had gathered near the castle gate, exploding in brilliant purple and white.

The Death Troopers had scattered now. Some sought to flee through the castle's front gate while others fired wildly in the David and Charlie's direction. Charlie ignored the fleeing troopers, instead turning the full force of her power on the Death Troopers who continued to fight.

This time there was no fire. For a moment, the air between Charlie and the Death Troopers shimmered. Then there was a massive explosion.

The world went white and silent at once. Charlie felt intense heat on her skin but could neither see nor hear a sound.

Charlie was peripherally aware that the danger had passed but paid little attention to this fact. The power was spiraling madly within her mind, barely within her control. In a moment it would blow loose and destroy everything. Charlie clamped down on it suddenly, sending two chromium bolts of pain rocketing through her body.

STOP IT! STOP IT NOW!!

The power continued to spiral upward. Charlie felt as she had the day she had destroyed the Fallow Point compound. She could not hold on for much longer. She had to expend the power somehow, but there was no water here. She would have to fight it back some other way or let it fall in on herself. She would not allow it to do any more damage. Charlie searched frantically with her mind but found nowhere to expend the power. Panic set in.

STOP IT NOW!! PLEASE!

Wave after wave of hot agony washed through her body as she fought back the power. Slowly but surely, she felt it begin to slow. The pain was excruciating, almost beyond feeling. Something warm spilled down over her lower lip. Searing agony danced over her skin, and yet she continued to fight the power to force it to be silent.

STOP IT!!!

After what seemed like an eternity, the power finally slowed to a dead stop. Charlie collapsed landing hard on her back and banging her head. She was bleeding from her nose and inside her mouth. Her skin was hot and feverish and felt almost as if it had been sunburned. David stood over her, Catherine at his side. She could not see them as her eyes remained obstructed in a field of pure white, but she could *feel* them with her mind.

Charlie! Oh God Charlie are you ok?

David's voice was frightened and weak. She heard him with her mind as her ears remained closed to all sound. She became aware of arms closing around her body and lifting her. Suddenly Catherine's face swam out of the field of white. She was badly cut, an angry red gash scrawled from the base of her jaw, across her left cheek and eye, and ended at her hairline. Thick, red blood ran from the wound and dripped down Catherine's cheek.

"Oh, God…" Charlie moaned. She wanted to cry, but she bit back the tears. "Catherine your face…"

"I'll be ok," Catherine responded. "Are you ok, Charlie? You're bleeding."

Charlie wiped the blood from her upper lip and nose. "I'm ok. I guess." She was afraid, but she managed to keep her voice steady.

Charlie's vision was slowly returning. She could see an outline she knew to be David. As he came closer, his face came into sharp focus. He was very pale. Thick, oily sweat coated his skin. Riyadah's lightning had seared away David's shirt together with all of the skin and much of the flesh on his chest leaving the remaining tissue and bone blackened and scorched. A strong, acrid, burning odor emanated from the wound. David's breathing was shallow and ragged, and he struggled to keep his feet.

The sight of him broke her completely. Charlie sobbed uncontrollably. She had brought this upon them. David and Catherine were both badly hurt because of her. Catherine hugged her tightly.

"It's ok, Charlie. Everything is going to be ok."

"No, it's not!" Charlie spat with bright, self-loathing. "You and David are both hurt because of me. Riyadah…that Dark Knight cut you Catherine and she b…burned David because she was trying to take me away! It's all my fault."

"None of this is your fault, Charlie." David soothed. "You didn't ask to be born with the power, and you didn't do anything wrong to deserve to be chased."

"This is the Black Empire's fault," Catherine said gently. "Not yours."

Charlie said nothing further. She was not comforted for she knew deep inside that this was *all* her fault. Were it not for her, David and Catherine would be happy together instead of frightened, wounded and on the run. She should have remained alone.

"We need to get out of here before anyone else shows up." Catherine's voice was strained and frightened. "Can you walk David?"

"I think so." David's voice was exhausted. "We need to find a place to go."

"We should be able to find a car to steal," Catherine replied. As she spoke, Catherine carried Charlie towards the gate. David followed her in a slow limp.

Several minutes later they had left the castle and were headed towards the city.

XVI

As David, Catherine and Charlie made their way back to Edinburg the survivors of the disaster at Castle Bruce fled into the night. Among them was a prematurely graying thirty-something man in a charcoal gray suit and navy pea coat. This man was a reporter from the BBC and had been invited to Castle Bruce by Alexi Ogastes on the promise that he would be permitted to observe something that would change the world.

From the start, the man harbored serious doubts. He was far too jaded to take Ogastes at his word, particularly since Alexi Ogastes was a member of the Russian Duma. Since the collapse of the Soviet Union, the Duma had been populated by Russian gangsters and corrupt oligarchs. Moreover, in the man's experience when someone claimed to have news that would change the world, it rarely panned out as promised.

On this night though, disappointment was far from what the man felt now. Dinesh Raj had been deployed to cover riots, natural disasters, even war zones. He had been attached to a front-line unit during the second Iraqi war. Still, nothing in his life had prepared him for what he had seen this night, and it wasn't the violence that frightened him. Instead, it was the realization that this changed everything he had thought he understood about the world.

Ogastes had given him a large file on the girl known as Charlene MacLeod. There were DNA records, various test results, photographs, even video but none of it had seemed real when he had read it. It was too fantastic to believe, and he told Ogastes as much. Ogastes, undeterred, had invited him to Castle Bruce to meet the girl and observe her power first hand.

Dinesh had expected to meet a more or less ordinary little girl who was maybe more intelligent and precocious than her peers. What he had found instead terrified him beyond words.

Dinesh had arrived at the castle at approximately 9 pm and was greeted by two security guards who escorted him across the castle courtyard to the main keep. Once inside the two guards led him to the great hall and instructed him to wait for Ogastes who would be arriving momentarily. Fifteen minutes passed, then twenty.

Dinesh heard footsteps ring on stone floors. Then, a door on the far left-hand side of the great hall opened, and Ogastes entered with a woman Dinesh recognized as Senator Hailey Suire, a leader in the American Resistance Party.

Ogastes greeted him. "Hello, Mr. Raj, I thank you for coming this evening."

"I could hardly say no," Dinesh replied. "The file you gave me piqued my interest and your promise to show me real pyrokinesis was too tempting to pass up. So where is this girl?"

Ogastes smiled. "You will meet her soon enough. First, I would like to introduce you to my friend, Senator Hailey Suire."

Senator Suire extended her hand. "A pleasure, Mr. Raj." Dinesh recognized what he thought might be a Creole accent.

Dinesh shook the Senator's hand firmly. "Indeed, Madam Senator, the pleasure is mine. You are well known even on this side of the Atlantic."

Senator Suire offered a slim smile. The senator was indeed well known as a vocal advocate for tearing down the police state that currently ruled America and most of the western world and a hated political enemy of the current American president.

"Before we proceed I wish to lay out some ground rules," Ogastes said. "First, the girl is just a child and should be treated as such. You must not react to anything you see in a way that will upset her. She is, after all, just a little girl." He paused. "And upsetting her is very dangerous."

"What else?" Dinesh asked patiently.

Ogastes regarded him coolly. "You will report on this girl honestly. Do not make a monster of her."

"I will do my best," Dinesh replied. "As you know, I do not have control over what my editor decides to do with the story."

"Yes, we are well aware." Senator Suire replied. "Nevertheless, you *will not* make a monster of this child."

Before anyone could say another word, an explosion shook the keep, followed a moment later by the sounds of battle. Dinesh reacted instantly by grabbing Ogastes and Suire and pulling them to the ground. "Get down before you get shot!" He barked.

That was how it began. A few minutes later, Dinesh found himself outside in the courtyard amid a war zone. Armor-clad soldiers clashed with the castle guards and quickly slaughtered them. Then minutes later, a shirtless man and a little girl appeared from a side door in the keep. Without thinking, Dinesh took out his smartphone and began filming.

One of the soldiers instructed the girl to surrender. A moment later, a red energy bolt cut the soldier down. Dinesh watched in amazement as the little girl slowly advanced on the black armored soldiers, wading through green tracer fire as if it were fireflies on a summer night. The girl's face was amazingly calm, and for a moment Danish thought he saw a smile of pleasure. Then the courtyard erupted in flames and Danish was genuinely terrified. Though there were no outward signs from the girl, she was clearly the source of the massive firestorm that consumed the black-armored soldiers. Danish could feel power in the air, her power, and with each successive fire, he felt it growing.

The armored soldiers were retreating now and with them the surviving occupants of the castle. Suddenly the air became alive with invisible energy. In the same instant Danish spotted Senator Suire running across the parapets towards the front gate. There was a large formation of soldiers gathered between her and the girl. As Danish watched the air around the soldiers and the senator began to shimmer with heat. Then the whole world went white.

Danish's next clear memory was of running down the road leading up to Castle Bruce. He ran for an unknown period of time before his fear had subsided enough to allow coherent thought. Somehow he had managed to hang onto his phone. With trembling fingers, he dialed the office, and twenty minutes later a car arrived to pick him up.

After that, things happened very quickly. The firestorm at Castle Bruce made the news before David, Charlie and Catherine had fled the castle grounds. In less than an hour, the initial reports were supplemented by the video taken by Danish Raj. As it turned out Danish had been able to successfully capture the entire firestorm including the apparent death of Senator Hailey Suire by incineration at the hands of Charlene Danielle MacLeod. Within minutes of the first broadcast of Danish's footage and the announcement of Senator Suire's death, people all over the world took to the streets. One hour after the video first aired, massive riots broke out in cities around the globe, buildings were burned, businesses and homes were looted, people were beaten, raped and killed.

XVII

As the first broadcasts of the firestorm at Castle Bruce aired, Charlie was using her power to start a Ford Fusion in the castle parking lot. Fifteen minutes later, Charlie, David, and Catherine were entering the outskirts of Edinburg. Twenty minutes after that they were pulling into the parking lot of a ratty motel in the city slums.

Charlie found a nearby ATM and quickly emptied it to cover the costs of their room. She hated stealing, but after everything else that had happened that long, horrible day, theft seemed comparatively minor. Catherine went into the office alone to pay for their room. She emerged ten minutes later with an old-style room key. Fifteen minutes after that, David and Catherine had climbed into bed in room 112 of the King's Arms Motel and were dead to the world.

For her part, Charlie could not sleep. She felt exhausted, but her frightened, horrified mind would not allow her rest. After a few minutes of lying still with her eyes shut, Charlie slid to the edge of her bed and flipped on the television. The news came on with footage of the firestorm at Castle Bruce.

As she watched, her terror growing with each ensuing moment, Charlie saw herself setting Death Troopers ablaze. She saw massive explosions that *she* had made. Then she saw something that filled her with renewed guilt.

There was a woman standing on the castle parapets near the main gate. She was directly behind a large formation of Death Troopers. A moment later the woman and the Death Troopers vanished in a blinding white flash of *her* power.

The woman, her name was Hailey Suire, was from the United States, and she was a senator. Hailey Suire had been an accident. Charlie had not even realized what she had done until she saw it on the news. The knowledge that she had killed an innocent tore Charlie apart inside. She sobbed for hours after learning what she had done.

She had killed this woman for nothing more than being in the wrong place at the wrong time. It didn't matter that Charlie hadn't meant to harm the woman. The end result was still the same. She had burned that woman alive.

Sharp, bright self-loathing burned within her for she knew without a doubt that all of this was her fault. David and Catherine would not have been wounded, were it not for her. Hailey Suire would not have died.

I should have let them kill me.

As she continued to watch the news, Charlie felt worse and worse.

They painted her as a monster. A dangerous laboratory accident that had to be captured and destroyed. Hearing this was almost as bad as the knowledge that she had killed an innocent. She wasn't even a person to them; she was a dangerous freak, a monster that had to be put away. What made it worse was that Charlie agreed with them.

I am dangerous. I only hurt and kill people. Daddy and Mommy wouldn't have died if it weren't for me. David and Catherine wouldn't have been hurt if it weren't for me. They would be happy. Hailey Suire wouldn't have died it wasn't for me.

She was no longer crying hard, though silent tears still spilled down her cheeks.

It's all my fault…

XVIII

The day began like any other for Larry Markowski; out of bed at six, shower by six-thirty, newspaper over breakfast at seven. The headlines were nothing special; terrorism in the Middle East, rising crime rates in Los Angeles, the usual politicking in Washington. Nothing out of the ordinary.

By seven-thirty he was brushing his teeth, and by eight he was waiting to catch the bus downtown.

It was Monday, and the bus was unusually crowded. Men and women of varying ages jostled for space in the all too small interior. Larry paid the ten-dollar fair and stood between a middle-aged business suit and a lard bucket in a floral pink muumuu. Larry hated standing next to fat people. They always took up more space than they had a right to and squashed everybody else out of their way. This one was no exception. Her ass alone took up three people's space, and she would lean into him every time the bus accelerated or broke. Larry felt like he would drown in her cheap floral perfume.

After too much time had passed, Larry's stop came up, and he gratefully got off the bus. The streets were bustling as was typical for a Miami Monday. Men and women, school kids, babies, and nannies crowded sidewalks too narrow to accommodate half of them.

Up ahead Larry spotted a pair of Mexicans up ahead standing on the street corner arguing, in broken or more like butchered English and felt a wave of contempt as his lips curled into a faint sneer.

A block later, Larry came upon his favorite coffee shop. The owner was Oriental, and Larry could barely understand the man, but at least *he* knew how to work.

Larry went in and ordered his usual listening to how the man, Chan or something or other, could barely pronounce English and wondering how it was that people could get into the country without learning to speak the language. Still, this man could brew a good cup of coffee, and he worked hard. He was at least good for that much.

A few blocks later, Larry arrived at Mount Sinia, where he made twenty an hour as an ER nurse.

Shit job. Larry thought bitterly.

All day long and some nights he got to deal with the worst of the worst horrors. Kids shot, women raped, babies beaten and starved by drug-addicted mothers.

Valerie Gold was standing outside the nurse's entrance smoking a cigarette. Larry greeted her with a smile.

"Hey. What's it like in there?"

"Crazy. I've been here for four hours, and this is the first chance I've had to catch my breath."

"Great." Larry glanced down at his watch. *Nine forty five.* He had fifteen minutes before his shift started. Larry reached into his pocket, took out a Pall Mall, and lit it with the cheap Bic lighter he kept in the pack. He took a long drag off the cigarette and blew it out into the cool morning air. "Sounds like a blast."

She nodded somberly. "Yeah. Some kid came in here this morning with a bullet in her back. Couldn't have been older than eight."

Larry took another drag off his cigarette. "Mother?"

"Yeah, probly."

"She gonna make it?"

"Nope. Died on the table at six."

"Oh." Larry's heart chilled as he took yet another drag off his cigarette. The smoke was acrid with a bitter flavor reminiscent of stale cigarette butts. He hated Pall Malls, but they were all he could afford right now. Another dead child, another murdering mother and there was nothing anyone could do about it because the goddamned law valued parents more than their children. Larry took one last long puff of smoke and stubbed his cigarette out on the hospital's stone wall before flicking it into the flowerpot to the right of the door. "See ya later Val."

She nodded as she puffed the last of her own cigarette, flicked the still-burning butt into the grass and lit up another. "Later." She was smoking Camels, more his speed but out of his price range.

The day went downhill from there. Less than five minutes after he had punched in, a multiple stab wound rolled through the doors. This was followed by a stroke, two heart attacks, a poisoned five-year-old boy and a particularly nasty car accident. By three thirty Larry was ready for the end of his shift. Instead he settled for a cigarette on the rooftop during a lull. Just as he was lighting up a siren sounded in the distance. At the same moment, the PA beeped.

"All personnel return to the ER. All personnel return to the ER. Multiple patients are inbound."

Within minutes the emergency room was flooded with victims. Stabbings, shootings, beatings and burnings and half a dozen other injuries besides. After six, Larry stopped counting the number of casualties. It was all mind-numbing in its suddenness. One minute he was dealing with the typical emergencies of a Monday morning, the next he was a medic in a war zone.

What the hell is going on? The question whispered in his mind, accompanied by a rush of fear. Something was very wrong; he felt it deep in his heart.

"Give me fifty ccs of epinephrine stat."

Larry prepared the syringe rapidly then injected its contents into the IV line. The man on the table was young, little more than a kid really. He couldn't have been older than twenty, and he was dying, bradycardia as a result of being bludgeoned. The man, one Thomas Hardy had been on his way to class at Florida State when he was accosted by a large mob and beaten with baseball bats. Hardy's heart rate continued to drop.

"No good." Dr. Wong barked. "Charge paddles to fifty joules."

Larry responded automatically, all the time thinking what a shame this was and wondering what the hell was going on.

"Clear!!"

Larry stepped back as Wong applied the paddles to Hardy's chest. There was a sudden ***–zap-***. In the same moment, Hardy's body tensed and arched up off the table. No good. Hardy's heartbeat continued to slow.

"Charge it to a hundred."

Again, Larry rapidly responded. Again, it did no good.

"One fifty!"

As Larry prepared the paddles for the third time, Hardy's ECG gave off a steady low ***–bleeeeeep-.***

"He's flatlining. Hurry it up with those damned paddles."

"Got em." Larry thrust the paddles into Wong's hands.

"Clear!!" Wong slammed the paddles down on Hardy's chest. Still no good. Wong peeled back Hardy's eyelids and looked down into his eyes. "Pupils fixed and dilated. He's gone. Time of death." She paused to glance at her watch. "four pm."

"Shit!" The word passed Larry's lips almost unconsciously. This was such a waste. A young man in the prime of his life beaten to death by a bunch of street thugs.

"No time for grief we've got another one coming in. Twenty-two-year-old female, raped and stabbed."

And so it began again, and again. Patients continued coming in steadily for the next two hours. It wasn't until three o'clock that Larry was able to take a break. That was when he learned what had happened.

Fox News was on the TV in the break room. They were playing footage of a massive fire.

"..unbelievable footage of a nine-year-old girl attacking and killing a large detachment of British soldiers at Castle Bruce just outside the Scottish city of Glasgow. We don't have a lot of details, but it appears that there were a number of foreign and American dignitaries present at the castle during the attack. Among them was Senator Hailey Suire who is confirmed dead at this time. The footage we have here shows the girl, we have confirmed her name is Charlene Danielle MacLeod, attacking the soldiers using a psi talent known as pyrokinesis, a talent that until today was believed to be purely science fiction."

Larry didn't hear any more. The television was still on, but he wasn't paying attention. His mind was lost in combined terror and anger. He would have never believed such a thing possible. That any human being could cause such destruction purely by force of will seemed beyond absurd and yet here was the evidence before his eyes.

She's only a little girl. Nine years old...how the hell is this possible? Somebody must have done something terrible to her to make her into such a monster.

Except she wasn't really a monster. Larry could not accept that a child so young could be capable of creating such destruction out of malice. There had to be more to the story.

XIX

A knock on the classroom door interrupted Carla Garafini mid-sentence. It was seven thirty in the evening and she was lecturing two-dozen freshmen on Charlotte Perkins Gilman's *The Yellow Wallpaper.*

She generally hated teaching gen ed literature. Hand holding, a bunch of vapid eyed, couldn't care less, eighteen and nineteen-year-olds through basic literary analysis and writing skills was hardly her idea of nirvana.

And she generally hated that dirty bastard, Gerald Meir. *"Doctor* Meir" he would always insist in that same mixture of condescension and contempt. The old fucker had been department chair for better than ten years now and he always, without fail, gave her the freshman literature classes.

Gerald was a huge fan of the classic dead white males. Shakespeare, Homer, Dickens, Chaucer, Milton, the deader, whiter and manlier the better. Though he never said so, Carla suspected that Gerald would have preferred that women not be writers at all, and instead confine their activities to the kitchen or the bedroom.

For her part, Carla preferred feminist writers and was pleasantly surprised when the old fucker agreed that she could add Gilman, Sylvia Plath, and Virginia Woolf to her syllabus.

The Yellow Wallpaper was one of Carla's favorites. Even several lifetimes later, its commentary on the attitudes of men towards women seemed directly on point.

-rap, rap, rap-

Carla wrinkled her nose in annoyance and then paused to answer the door.

"There's something on TV you have to see." Her friend, Hannah Neilson's expression was frightened. "Dr. Meir wants the news on in every class."

Carla's interest was piqued. "What's going on?"

"There's been some kind of terrorist attack in Glasgow. They're saying that twenty or thirty people are dead, including Senator Suire."

"Really?" Carla's first reaction was pure shock. This couldn't be right. "What the hell was Hailey Suire doing in Scotland?" She turned to the class. "Ladies and Gentlemen there's been a disaster in Glasgow, Scotland. At this time, I am going to interrupt our class to turn on the news."

That said she crossed the classroom to the corner opposite the door and flipped on the television. CNN came on with footage of a blond hair girl of no more than nine or ten staring down several dozen black armored British soldiers. As Carla watched flames radiated across the ground from where the girl stood and consumed the soldiers. This was followed moments later by a series of massive explosions, the last of which incinerated Hailey Suire who had been unfortunate enough to be caught on the castle parapet.

Carla's first reaction was cynical disbelief. This had to be a trick. CNN had presented it as though the girl had somehow *willed* the fires and explosions into existence, but that was impossible. No human being was capable of such acts. Psychic power was merely a popular myth in modern fiction, one set off by the writings of a certain horror author whose name she chose to deliberately forget. This had to be a trick.

The girl was lovely and though she was on television and not actually present in the classroom she had a strange air about her. Something about her was different and disturbing. That she was allegedly pyrokinetic disturbed Carla still more. The logical part of Carla's mind rebelled against what she saw and had been told. Yet, though the girl was not present in the room, Carla felt strongly that what she was seeing was genuine. The girl had truly caused the firestorm at Castle Bruce with her mind.

As the video footage of the girl continued, CNN presented a series of documents it had obtained from a source that Carla considered beyond reproach. These records detailed the girl's power and the fact that she was genetically unique. Everything appeared to be on the level.

But it can't be! It can't be true! Nobody has power like that! It isn't possible.

Carla could not accept what she saw. This had to be some kind of trick. Carla had long held the view that belief in the paranormal was no more than a modern version of religion and that all religion was just an invention of convenience. She had always believed Lenin's precept that religion is the opiate of the masses.

Still, it was hard to simply discount the records on this Charlene MacLeod. The men and women who had compiled them were some of the most brilliant and respected minds in the scientific community. Moreover, although she did not want to believe, Carla felt that what she saw and had been told was true.

The girl *was* indeed unusual, to say the least. She was also a monster bred out of a lab and very dangerous. Below her conscious awareness, Carla's heart slowly filled with cold hate. The girl's pyrokinesis made her a weapon. She had to be eliminated.

As she was thinking this, the footage of Charlene MacLeod was replaced by images of rapidly escalating violence around the world. Then the screen went black for a moment before a white legend reading "Emergency Broadcast System" flashed across the screen, followed a moment later by a familiar buzzing tone

"This is an emergency action notification. All stations shall broadcast this emergency action notification message. This station has interrupted its regular program at the request of the White House to participate in the Emergency Broadcast System. During this emergency, some stations will remain on the air broadcasting news and official information to the public in assigned areas. This station is CNN for the Ann Arbor market. We will remain on the air to serve the Ann Arbor area. If you are not in this area you should tune to other stations until you hear one broadcasting news and information for your area. You are listening to the Emergency Broadcast system serving the Ann Arbor area. Do not use your telephone. The telephone lines should be kept open for emergency use. The Emergency Broadcast System has been activated to keep you informed. Ladies and Gentlemen, please stand by for a message from the Office of the President."

The black screen changed to an image of the presidential seal, in front of it stood the white house press secretary, his face harried and aged, brows knit with concern.

"My fellow Americans, as you may already be aware, terrorists have attacked a high-level diplomatic meeting at Castle Bruce killing twenty Americans including Resistance Party Senator, Hailey Suire. In the wake of this tragedy riots and armed rebellion have broken out across the United States. The President has already directed the Attorney General and Secretary of Defense to dispatch federal law enforcement and military forces to areas experiencing violence."

Carla switched off the television and glanced out at her class. They were staring blankly in terror. No one made a sound. A pair of girls in the back, Terry Housier, and Rachel Marshall sat with hands folded, and heads bowed in a gesture of prayer. A guy in one of the middle rows, Kyle Bryce, was trembling and mumbling to himself. Several students suddenly stood up and fled the room without even bothering to gather up their stuff. Carla watched her students and saw in many of them the same feelings that filled her own heart. Slowly, in groups of two or three, her students fled until she was left standing before an empty classroom. Part of her insisted that she should be leaving too, going to gather supplies before running and hiding, but she would not allow herself to be afraid. She would not run out of there in terror as her students had.

There's nothing to be afraid of. Nothing. Except, deep inside, Carla knew better.

XX

Charlie watched the news reports of growing violence around the world through the remainder of the night. She was deeply frightened. What had begun as rioting had quickly exploded into armed rebellion and insurgency. Heavily armed men and women were forming armies and attacking anyone who would not join them. A smaller group of people had emerged as leaders. These men and women gave incendiary speeches calling for the destruction of the dangerous freak child to the gathering crowds or offered inflammatory words to any news reporter willing to listen.

At first, law enforcement attempted to break up the rioting, later they were replaced by military forces, but ultimately these efforts failed for no uniform, badge or military insignia can change human nature. By three o'clock all civil control had collapsed in most major cities, and by dawn, much of the world was plunged into anarchy.

People were badly frightened, and she was the object of that fear. Now they were braying for her blood.

As she was thinking this, a realization began to take shape in her mind. It wasn't just fear that was driving these people. Many of them had built their lives around the idea that technology was power and that such power could be confined to the hands of those who would handle it most wisely, the elected or appointed leadership of society. The sudden revelation of her power had utterly shattered that illusion. Rather than accept this and go on these people reacted with violence as is typical human nature. Still, Charlie found this hard to understand.

Why are grownups always so mean?

She understood intellectually. Adults became frightened just like children, and when they were frightened they frequently turned to violence to feel safer. Attack the thing that they feel threatened by. But intellectual knowledge did not translate into visceral understanding. She had knowledge of why this was happening, but her heart could not fathom it.

Why? Why would anyone want to be so mean?

The questions continued to mount as her young mind tried to understand the harsh realities of a cold and brutal adult world.

Around nine in the morning exhaustion finally overtook her and Charlie drifted off into darkness. Her sleep was not restful. Charlie's mind continued to race. Endless questions echoed through her subconscious and rather than bringing answers her superior intellect, and psychic senses only generated more questions and fear.

XXI

As Charlie and her adoptive mother and father slept in room 112 of the King's Arms Motel, the streets of Edinburg exploded in violence. The death of Senator Hailey Suire combined with the sudden revelation of *how* she had died proved to be the final straw for many. The American Resistance Party had many allies around the world who agreed that the police state imposed across much of the allegedly free world had gone too far, that freedom should be returned to the people. Hailey Suire was considered to be the leader of this movement, and her death at the hands of Charlene MacLeod was seen as an assassination.

Although the US government officially denied any involvement in human bio-genetic experimentation, it was well known that such activities were ongoing under the authority of several federal agencies. Nevertheless, no one believed that any of this experimentation would ever produce a creature as terrifying as this Charlene MacLeod. Until one day ago psi powers were thought to be pure science fiction. That illusion was shattered the night before in a brilliant, terrifying firestorm that culminated in the murder of Senator Suire.

Large segments of the population were both terrified and outraged at once for there was no mistaking who was responsible for the attack. The senator had been threatened with prosecution by the American political establishment. She had all but been accused of treason by the sitting American president. Nevertheless, he dared not move against her using the criminal justice system for the potential fallout would have been dangerous. Thus, many concluded that he had unleashed one of his laboratory abominations to do the job for him. The president could then feign outrage and vow to hunt down the terrorists responsible as he had predictably done after the senator's demise. Unfortunately, no one believed that the senator had been killed by terrorists. Instead, everyone blamed the president and his police state, for no one else stood to gain as much from Hailey Suire's death.

Furthermore, the fact that the president had targeted Senator Suire, a high-profile leader of the Resistance Party, with a pyrokinetic meant to many that no one was safe. Thus, for many, there was no reason not to rebel. There was nothing left to lose.

James Lenox searched the streets of Edinburg with growing fear. He had been staying at a nearby pub after being banished from Castle Bruce for expressing his disagreement with Alexi Ogastes's plan to declare Charlie's existence to the world.

I should have known better than to trust him. Alexi was always so ambitious.

Some part of James had been leery of trusting Alexi from the beginning because of the latter's desire for power. Alexi was not an evil man, but he had always aggressively sought to amass power and influence. He had doggedly campaigned to become president of the White Conclave and upon his nomination and election had sought to parlay the position into one of worldwide authority.

Alexi believed he was acting in the best interests of mankind. In Alexi's view, the White Conclave could better govern the world than the puppets of the Black Empire, who currently held power. James disagreed.

The White Conclave was founded for the purpose of guiding those who would fight against the Black Empire, both the Order of Light and the Lightwarriors who the Order would instruct. Originally comprised of only the wisest and most benevolent of mankind, the White Conclave served as an advisory body whose sole purpose was to protect those fighting the true evil from becoming corrupt..

Later, the White Conclave's membership changed, as did its role. No longer was the Conclave made up merely of benevolent wise men and women. Instead, the Conclave slowly became populated by powerful and influential men and women who were excluded from the Black Empire and its shadow government. These men and women were neither good nor evil but rather avaricious and megalomaniacal. Under the influence of these new members, the White Conclave began to amass power and influence in its own right. Thus, it became a rival to the Black Empire. Alexi was among those who believed that the White Conclave should rule the world. In his mind popular rule and democracy were a failure because the average citizen was far too stupid to be trusted with his or her own destiny. In Alexi's view the world needed to be ruled by those who had the wisdom to judiciously wield the reins of power. It was in pursuit of this belief that Alexi had decided to reveal Charlie's existence in the hope that he could use this revelation to bring the public under the influence of the White Conclave.

For his own part, James believed that, while popular rule had its problems, mankind was entitled to freedom and self-determination. Moreover, he doubted that anyone was so wise as to be beyond corruption if permitted too much power. To allow the White Conclave to rule the world would be to trade tyranny for tyranny.

Furthermore, James believed it would be dangerous to make Charlie's existence public. Although publicity would make it harder for the Black Empire and its minions to target her, it would also create a new danger. Charlie's power would certainly terrify a public who believed that such abilities existed only in the imaginations of authors and movie writers.

If only he had known how right he was, James could have acted sooner to protect David, Catherine and Charlie. Instead, he had stupidly tried to reason with Alexi. Last night's firestorm and today's riot had been the result.

The center of Edinburg was totally inaccessible due to military barricades. Thus, James was reduced to searching the streets of the outskirts. The radio blared on with accounts of clashes between soldiers and armed rioters in the city center. James hoped like hell that David, Catherine, and Charlie were somewhere safe. Though James lacked the ability to use the power and thus could not sense his son's presence, he did have some idea of what he was looking for.

The city was awash in violence, so David and Catherine would most likely take Charlie and go to ground nearby. In Berlin, they had drifted between the many cheap motels of the city's red-light district and Edinburgh too had a booming flesh trade that supported many cheap motels.

Still, it was possible that David, Catherine, and Charlie had been killed by the Death Troopers who had attacked the castle or by the rioters who had later taken to the streets. With each passing moment James's fear grew for he found no signs of David, Catherin, and Charlie.

He was headed north on Salamander Street in a section of Edinburg known as Leith. The sidewalks here were flooded with men and women of all ages. Many of them brandished bats, clubs, and knives. Others carried stolen shotguns and pistols. By some miracle the street itself was mostly clear of people, thus allowing him to continue unhindered. James drove his 2012 Fiat slowly, carefully scanning the crowds for a familiar face. He saw nothing.

Directly ahead he spotted a ratty motel, its parking lot was mostly empty save for a pair of crotch rockets and a sub-compact Nissan. The sidewalk mobs were becoming increasingly restless. Suddenly someone threw what appeared to be a Molotov cocktail. The flaming bottle arched through the air and smashed against a nearby one-story home in an orange fireball. Several other Molotov's followed, and after a few moments, the house was ablaze. Gunfire rang out. In an instant a bullet shattered James's rear windscreen. His leapt in terror, not for himself but for his family for he feared what might become of them.

This is all my fault. I should never have brought them to Alexi. I should have known better…

Despite the danger, James pulled into the motel parking lot, got out and headed for the office. His only concern now was for finding David, Catherine, and Charlie before someone more dangerous could. Nothing else mattered. Though he lacked the use of the power, James felt deep in his heart that something terrible had happened and he was afraid of what he would find.

Chapter 2

Wounded and Hiding

I

Somewhere deep in sleep, a sensation of danger came to Charlie, penetrating the darkness in which she drifted. She did not feel that they had been found. Instead, she felt some nagging threat creeping from the shadows, turning her flesh to ice. The sensation gradually built in intensity, pulling her from sleep as it grew.

Something's wrong...

It was the only coherent thought she could manage against the overwhelming exhaustion that had taken her. Slowly Charlie forced her eyes open. The motel room was dark and hushed. Charlie turned over and glanced at the clock radio.

9:30 pm.

Charlie slid to the edge of the bed and stood up. The sense of wrongness grew as she made her way over to the other bed where David and Catherine lay deep in slumber. Except they weren't just sleeping. The moment she saw her adoptive parents Charlie knew they were in trouble. Both had become deathly pale, and their skin was soaked in thick oily sweat. The cut on Catherine's cheek had turned an angry red and was badly swollen. The air had become fetid with the smell of rot. Charlie drew back the blankets to find that David's burn had also become horribly inflamed and was oozing thick yellow and white puss.

Charlie gasped "Oh God..."

Without thinking, she took David by the shoulders and shook him hard. "Wake up David. Please wake up." He moaned but remained unconscious. Charlie tried Catherine. "Please wake up." She begged. "I don't know what to do."

Catherine too remained unresponsive.

Cold terror welled up within her chest, bringing the power with it. Charlie had to fight to keep from panicking.

"What do I do?" She begged. "Please David...Catherine tell me what to do."

The power spiraled upward, fueled by her fear. Charlie bit it down quickly.

STOP IT!

I have to get them medicine. The thought came to Charlie at once in a calm and authoritative tone. *Antibiotics...they need antibiotics.*

Fresh fear cropped up in Charlie's heart, for she understood at once the risk of going outside. Still,

David and Catherine were sick. They might die if she didn't get them medicine. Charlie went to the motel room's single window and carefully drew back the heavy gold drapes.

The air outside was hazy with smoke. The electricity had been cut off leaving the streets cloaked in darkness. Charlie saw no one, she sensed no one. Yet she was still afraid for she knew that the quiet outside was an illusion. Edinburgh was ablaze with violence. If there was no one fighting outside right now, that could and most likely would change very soon. Still, she had to help David and Catherine. Charlie let the curtains fall back into place and quickly went to the ratty looking faux white oak dresser where Catherine had left the room key. Then she paused for a moment to steel herself before heading into the night.

II

The streets outside were indeed deserted, as were the businesses. Numerous cars had been abandoned by the side of the road. Everyone had picked up in a big hurry and just left everything. Charlie looked around carefully. There was a BP station directly across the street from the King's Arms Motel. A little grocery stood to the left of the BP station while a bookstore stood to its right. To her immediate right was a McDonald's restaurant, and to her immediate left was a little movie theater. The dingy, off-white marquee, indicated this was the Royal Pink Theater. Only one movie was playing, *Booty Land*. Charlie had never heard of this move, but she had a pretty good idea of its type. She wrinkled her nose in disgust and continued sweeping the street with her eyes. There was a darkened pub beyond the Royal Pink Theater and beyond that a Days Inn. To the right, beyond the McDonalds stood an Adult World and beyond that an empty storefront. Nothing. There was nowhere she would find antibiotics for David and Catherine.

What made it worse was that she had no idea which way to go. The road was equally populated by businesses to the right and to the left. Either way might lead to a drug store or supermarket with a pharmacy, or it might not. She had no idea. For a moment, Charlie hesitated. Then instinctively she reached into the power, hoping that she would sense which way was correct. At first, Charlie felt nothing. Then, after a moment, she was certain.

Charlie turned left and began walking. She was headed west. A nearby street sign indicated that this was McAlester Street. Charlie walked quickly, passing the McDonalds, the little movie theater and the Days Inn.

All of the businesses were dark and showed no signs of human activity. Still, Charlie felt a growing sense of danger. She was not alone, of that much, she was certain. The power moved within her, a restless wolf growling and pacing about at the scent of a threat.

There was a scattering of cars in the Days Inn parking lot. Charlie briefly considered searching these but decided against it as she did not feel that she would find anything useful and she knew time was short.

Beyond the Days Inn, Charlie came to an intersection. The cross street, Donnelly Avenue, was broader than McAlester. A collection of abandoned cars sat in the middle of the road. This time Charlie turned right.

The businesses lining Donnelly Avenue promised to be more helpful. Here was a collection of small businesses. There was another bookstore, a convenience store, several clothing stores, and a Right Medicine drug store.

Charlie picked up her pace. The sense of danger had grown. Suddenly she felt watched though she still saw no evidence of human presence. Like McAlester, Donnelly was deadly silent. Still, something felt wrong.

Charlie approached the Right Medicine with care. The store was dark and looked undisturbed. Its front display window was unbroken, and the front door remained locked. A quick flick of the power and the deadbolt fell open.

A minute later, Charlie found herself standing inside the darkened store. She fumbled for a moment before discovering a rack of disposable flashlights near the front registers. The store was relatively small and consisted of four ten-foot aisles leading to a single pharmacy counter that ran the length of the back wall. Charlie headed for the pharmacy first.

Her short life had taught her very little about medicine beyond the general knowledge shared by most non-medical professionals. All she did know for sure was that she would need antibiotics to cure David and Catherine.

Charlie found the pharmacy desk locked up tight. A roll-down security gate had been lowered over the entire counter, and a keypad lock secured the only door. The door itself was heavy steel although it didn't really make a difference. She could have easily blasted the door off its hinges with her power. Unfortunately this was not an option as she feared using the power to obliterate the door would undoubtedly result in the destruction of the little drug store and any medicine in the pharmacy.

Instead, Charlie reached into the power and carefully explored the inside of the door with her mind. The lock itself was fully electronic and consisted of a powerful electromagnet on the inside of the door. She would not be able to manipulate this using the power. She could sense which buttons had been pressed on the keypad, but this would not tell her the order in which to enter the numbers. On the far side of the door, a motion sensor controlled the magnetic lock, effectively rendering it always unlocked from the inside.

And just like that, she had an idea. A fire extinguisher hung on the wall just inside the pharmacy. Charlie reached out, grabbed it with her mind, and slowly levitated it through the air in front of the motion sensor. There was a low thud as the magnetic lock released. Charlie carefully grasped the door handle and pushed down. The latch clicked open, and she stepped inside.

The pharmacy was much larger than Charlie had initially anticipated. Here were row after row of white boxed medicines and drugs with names that were mostly alien to her. Charlie did recognize the names fentanyl and oxycodone and intentionally avoided those bottles as she knew both were illegal drugs that people took to get high. After some consideration, Charlie decided upon several bottles marked, ciprofloxacin, digoxin, phenelzine, and moxifloxacin respectively. Charlie couldn't remember for sure the name of the medicine she had been given to keep her burns from becoming infected but these names seemed familiar. On her way out of the store, Charlie also took several boxes of gauze, six rolls of surgical tape and six boxes of Neosporin.

III

As Charlie walked back to the King's Arms motel, Emperor Eric Kane summoned his generals, Vic Garling and Nicole McDermott to the Grand Observation Lounge.

Kane was dressed in his usual black button-down shirt and cotton slacks. His short, black hair was parted neatly at the center. Though his handsome face remained calm, his intense, deep-set, sky blue eyes flashed with anger as he addressed Garling and Nicole.

"This is a major disaster. I cannot believe you allowed Riyadah to lead an unsanctioned attack on the girl and the McAuliffes. I sent you two to earth to control things, to keep the people under our thumbs, *my* thumb, and you let everything go to shit."

Garling was dressed in an immaculately tailored black business suit with a white button shirt and black satin tie, his dark hair slicked back with wet gel. Garling was a tall and slender man with youthful features, close-cropped jet-black hair, and a robust muscular frame. He was very handsome, but he had a cold and cruel air about him. From his hard-chiseled features to his icy blued steel eyes he exuded power and brutality.

Beside Garling sat Nicole McDermott. In her black business suite she cut a youthful and strikingly beautiful figure. Nicole was a slim and athletic woman with pale porceline skin, tapered legs, intense blue eyes and long blond hair. Nicole was also Kane's daughter though this was a secret he kept even from his closest lieutenants.

As usual, Garling was puffing at a Camel. "The situation is unfortunate, but it may not be as bad as it looks." Thick clouds of acrid smoke billowed out of his nose and mouth as he spoke. "The surviving Death Troopers report that both David and Catherine McAuliffe were badly wounded in the attack and are effectively out of commission." He paused to take a long drag from his cigarette. "It's possible the McAuliffes may be dead within a few hours. For all intents and purposes, that girl is on her own, and with all the fighting, we may have the cover we need to grab her."

"No," Kane replied sharply. For a moment, he could feel dark power rising within him. He could destroy them if he wanted to, but that wouldn't accomplish anything. Though he was angry, Garling and Nicole were both bright and trustworthy. While the current situation was a particularly egregious mistake it did not justify wasting two of his most valuable generals. Kane took a slow sip of water from the crystal glass on the table in front of him. "Watch them but don't make any moves unless it's absolutely necessary. I don't want another firestorm, and I don't want the girl harmed. If she's in trouble pick her up, but only if she's in trouble. Otherwise stay out of sight." Kane took another sip of water and set his glass down roughly. "How bad is the damage?"

Garling took another drag from his cigarette. "We've been able to retain most of our essential personnel within the NSA and the rest of the global intelligence community. We have also been able to retain core personnel within law enforcement and organized crime around the world. Unfortunately, we lost control of two divisions of the US Army, a pair of US Air Force fighter bases each containing a full complement, and half of the US Pacific Fleet as well as a large portion of the Russian military."

"You what?" Kane's anger was kindled anew. "Do they have any nukes?"

"No." Garling drew another long drag from his cigarette. "We were able to lock down all nuclear weapons around the world before the worst of the violence started."

"And the remaining military forces?"

"They've all been confined to base indefinitely." He stubbed out his cigarette and lit up another. "We've sealed off the bases and cut off all information from the outside."

"Well, at least you got something right." Kane picked up his glass and threw back the remainder of its contents. "I want you to brick all the nukes. Then divide the remaining military forces evenly among both sides. Make sure neither side can prevail over the other. Dissolve the NSA and bring anyone who knows anything to Ifrinn."

"Of course." Garling took another long drag and blew the smoke out of his nose.

"You can go now."

Garling and Nicole both scurried from the room without further comment.

As they departed, Kane's mind flashed back to the day of the Trinity shot, the culmination of years of research under the code name Manhattan Project. As that ominous black mushroom-shaped could of radioactive particles drifted into the sky, a lone man in a black suit and trench coat stood behind Oppenheimer and the other scientists. The red eye of a cigarette winked malevolently in the shadows surrounding the man's face. On that day the Outsiders had become powerful enough to actually threaten Enlighteneds, and so Kane had personally directed that all nuclear weapons be constructed with a brick code that would not only disable the electronics in the warhead but would totally destroy the physics package so that the components inside could never be used to build another nuke. That decision had been prescient, though, at the time, he had not known of the World Civil War that would come eighty-some years later.

"This may play to our advantage." Lord Beathach rumbled from the shadows beside the largest of the chamber's massive picture windows. "Much of the conflict is over the girl. Thus, the rebels will pursue her to ends of the earth. We need only infiltrate their leadership and then wait for them to capture her my master."

Beathach was a nightmare of a man, standing at seven feet tall and weighing over three hundred pounds, all of it muscle. He was clad in heavy, black, Renaissance-style plate armor and wore a long black silk cape. Armored, black leather gloves covered his hands, and his feet were encased in knee-high black armored riding boots. A massive black steel helm crowned with three long, slender spires shrouded his head, and a black steel death's head mask concealed his horribly mutilated face.

Kane nodded. "You are correct, but what purpose would it serve to retake the girl? We had her once before, and she would not join us. I doubt that she will turn now if we recapture her. No, we need to take a different approach and quickly. These people are frightened and dangerous, they could easily kill the girl."

IV

Charlie stood over David and Catherine in silence. She had the medicine (or so she thought), but she was unsure which bottle to give them, and a powerful sense of danger gave her pause. She looked over the four bottles again carefully.

Ciprofloxacin

Digoxin

Phenelzine

Moxifloxacin

As she read the names to herself, she no longer recognized any of them. The sense of danger was growing, she felt that at least one of these drugs would help, but she didn't know, couldn't be sure of which one. She knew only that she had to do something and if she gave David and Catherine the wrong medicine then they could die. Charlie hesitated a moment longer and then picked up the bottle marked Digoxin and walked over to the bed to wake David and Catherine.

As she approached the bed, Charlie's heart suddenly began to thunder. Something was very wrong. Charlie glanced again at the bottle of digoxin, then placed it on the bedside table and picked up the bottle marked ciprofloxacin. The sense of danger abated slightly. Before she could lose her nerve, Charlie went to David and Catherine and shook them awake. Both came around enough to swallow pills, but neither was lucid. After giving each two ciprofloxacin pills Charlie carefully bandaged David and Catherine's wounds and made them each drink two glasses of water before letting them go back to sleep.

V

The world had become a confusing mess of jumbled fragments punctuated by excruciating pain. David slipped between sleep and delirious wakefulness without knowing the dividing line between dream and reality. His chest was on fire, and his body had become immobile lead. David was uncertain of Catherine's fate beyond a vague knowledge that she too was incapacitated.

Some distant fragment of David's mind understood that he had placed Charlie in danger again. He and Catherine were both severely wounded and could not take care of her. Charlie would have to take care of them. David feared for his daughter but could do nothing to help her. His body was too badly damaged and would no longer obey him.

VI

For Charlie, the time passed in a slow nightmare of days and nights bled together. After getting medicine and bandages for David and Catherine, Charlie's next concern became finding food. At first, she used the power to steal food from the vending machines at the motel. Then later she broke into the little grocery store across the street and took what little canned food remained. Charlie was not proud of this, but she felt she had no choice. Her only options were theft or starving to death with David and Catherine.

It was difficult to get David and Catherine to eat. They were both delirious with fever and pain and would sometimes fight her when she offered them food. Still, somehow, she was able to get them to eat and drink enough to stave off dehydration and starvation.

For a while, David and Catherine deteriorated further, frightening Charlie deeply. She could not bear to lose her adoptive parents as she had lost Daddy and Mommy. She couldn't go through that again, and she didn't know what she would do if she were left alone. Things had gotten so much worse since she had escaped from the Fallow Point compound.

Electrical service had been turned off for weeks, and the streets were becoming increasingly dangerous. Several times Charlie was awakened at night by gunfire outside. One night a flurry of bullets shattered the front window before embedding themselves into the floor and walls. Charlie hid between the beds, pulling David and Catherine to the floor beside her without really considering how she would get them back onto the beds. Nevertheless, she somehow managed to get it done when the gunfire ceased a few minutes later.

After another week, David and Catherine began to show signs of improvement. Both of their fevers broke, and Catherine had regained enough strength to allow her to get out of bed. David remained weak and dehydrated, but now Catherine could help Charlie care for him.

The violence in Edinburgh continued to intensify over the prevailing weeks. Two and half weeks after the firestorm at Castle Bruce, widespread arson broke out in the city center. The random gunfire that punctuated the night a week ago had escalated into a series of pitched battles. And these battles were between groups of survivors. Law enforcement and the military had long since departed.

Fortunately, most of the worst of the violence was close to the city center and thus far away from the motel where David, Catherine, and Charlie were hiding. However, one night, that changed.

VII

Charlie awakened, feeling a sudden and intense sensation of danger.

Something's wrong!

She pushed back the covers and scooted to the edge of the bed. As her feet hit the floor, a gunshot rang out. The sound came from somewhere in the motel parking lot. Charlie hit the floor on her knees, heart thundering in her chest.

More gunshots followed. These were not the dull bangs of pistol fire, but rather the sharp, ear-splitting crack of rifle shots.

"David! Catherine wake up!" She screamed.

David groaned. "Wha…what's…" He was cut off by a second volley of rifle shots.

“Stay down, Charlie!” Catherine called to her over the din.

Charlie crouched between the beds, her heart thundering in her chest. The power moved within her, awakened by her fear. Charlie forced it back.

STOP IT! NOT NOW!

Despite her fear, she understood that it would be unwise to attack the shooters outside. At the moment, none of the gunfire was directed towards them. If she used the power, then they would inevitably be targeted.

Another volley of rifle shots rang out, followed by several screams. A fourth volley of rifle shots followed in answer before the night lit up with gunfire.

Several bullets slammed into the far side of the double bed nearest the window. Charlie screamed.

“David? Catherine? Are you ok?”

For an agonizing moment, there was no reply. Then David’s voice came to her over the din. “We’re ok Charlie, just keep your head down.”

Charlie called out to David. “What are we going to do?”

“I don’t know.” He replied.

As David spoke, several more bullets came in through the broken front window and slammed into the floor less than a foot from where Charlie crouched.

“David we can’t just hide here waiting to be shot.” Catherine’s voice was calm but betrayed fear.

“I know.” He replied. “But we’re pinned down.”

To this, Catherine had no reply.

Charlie remained perfectly still not daring to move a muscle.

The gunfire intensified. Suddenly a man’s scream came from just outside the motel room door. A moment later, the same man collapsed through the broken window and landed on the carpet mere feet from where Charlie crouched. He gasped for breath and managed to crawl a few feet closer to Charlie before collapsing and dying. The man was young, about the same age as David. He had sandy brown hair and pale skin. Two gaping, ragged bullet holes leaked blood from his chest onto the tattered remains of his white undershirt and blue jeans.

Charlie bit her arm to suppress a scream. *That could have been David or Catherine.*

They were closer to the window than she was.

The gunfire had died out. A moment later, a man’s voice filtered in from outside.

“I think that was the last of them. Fan out and search the buildings for supplies. If you find anyone else, kill them if they’re male. If they’re female, it’s your call.” The man’s voice was hard and brutally unremorseful. A few seconds later a hand closed on the motel room door and began jiggling the knob. The door was locked, though the broken window made the precaution somewhat useless.

A moment later, a tall, slender figure appeared through the window, silhouetted against the faint moonlight from outside. Standing only inches from David and Catherine, the figure made a slight movement, and a moment later a narrow flashlight beam penetrated the motel room’s darkness.

The figure approached the young man’s body slowly, and as it did, Charlie made out the features of a tall, middle-aged man of average build. The man gripped his flashlight in one hand and a large Glock pistol in the other. His shadowed features betrayed a look of contempt. Charlie sensed annoyance from him as if he had been minorly inconvenienced by killing this young man.

The tall man swept the room slowly with his flashlight. He stood closer now, his feet only inches from where Charlie crouched between the beds. She held her breath, heart trip-hammering in her chest.

The man’s light played across the bedside table between the two double beds, then slowly traced its way down to the floor where Charlie crouched. In a moment, the man would spot her, and it would be all over. Sheer terror exploded within her. The power renewed its restless movement. Charlie bit it back fearfully.

STOP IT! NOT NOW! PLEASE NOT NOW!

She could have killed this man if she wanted. It would be easy to lash out with the power and end him in a fountain of her flames, but there were more men outside. She could feel their presence. They would rush into the room and attack the moment this man went down.

And David and Catherine can’t fight back.

They were still both severely wounded and weak from illness. Charlie doubted they could survive another battle like Castle Bruce. So, she held the power back despite her fear and despite the pain that had begun to radiate through her body. A moment later the man’s flashlight beam fell on her face. Charlie shielded her eyes from the bright light with her left hand.

“Well, hello.” The man’s voice was amused. “What do we have here?”

A frightened sob escaped Charlie’s throat. She steeled herself for what she knew she would have to do. Before she could strike out with the power, the man tensed. His mouth opened as if to scream but he was silenced when his flesh peeled back, and his skeleton ripped free from his body. Charlie felt Catherine’s power alive in the air. She was horrified but also somewhat impressed despite herself. She would not have imagined Catherine to have such a capability.

Using the power, Catherine flung the man’s bloody skeleton across the room where it shattered against the wall. “Let’s go. We can’t stick around any longer.” As she spoke Catherine appeared from behind the far side of the double bed near the window and helped David up. Charlie scrambled to her feet and followed Catherine to the door.

“What about those other men outside?” Charlie asked, still deeply frightened.

“They will be busy searching for supplies,” Catherine replied. “We should be able to sneak by without them noticing if we’re careful.”

“Ok.” Charlie wasn’t convinced, but she was glad to have an adult take charge. She had taken care of David and Catherine out of necessity, but that was scary. It was a relief to not have to make decisions on her own anymore.

Charlie followed Catherine from their room at the King’s Arms Motel for the last time. The parking lot and streets were indeed deserted as Catherine had predicted. Charlie followed David and Catherine across the parking lot to an abandoned Fiat. Catherine stopped at the driver’s side door, placed her hand over the lock and flicked out with her power. The door suddenly fell open. Charlie could feel Catherine fighting against the power, struggling to keep it balanced. A moment later, Catherine flicked out again with the power and the Fiat’s engine grumbled to life.

“Come on, Charlie. We’re getting out of here.” As she spoke Catherine opened the rear driver’s side door and helped David inside before motioning to Charlie to get into the front seat. Charlie complied wordlessly. She could feel Catherine’s pain as she struggled against the power that was now alive within her mind. “It’s going to be ok.” She was saying.

As if in answer a gunshot rang out and the rear passenger side window exploded in twinkling shards.

Fresh terror erupted within Charlie. Her heartbeat thundered in her ears.. The power moved more rapidly within her, an angry wolf begging to be let out. Charlie bit it back.

GO AWAY! STOP IT NOW AND GO AWAY!

The power, fueled by her fear, continued to build in intensity. Charlie fought against it resolutely. Blood soaked shards of pain ripped through her skull. Charlie was vaguely aware that the car had begun to move. She looked through her window and saw two men with rifles chasing after them on foot and firing wildly. Charlie could have easily killed both men in an instant, but there was no need to use the power, they were far behind and no real threat. Instead, she forced it down aggressively.

GO AWAY!!!

A fresh wave of sharp, burning pain swept her from head to toe and then the power settled back into restless slumber. Charlie heaved a sigh of relief and then closed her eyes in exhaustion. They were safe for now.

Charlie fought against sleep for a few moments longer before surrendering to its embrace.

VIII

Catherine drove until dawn that terrible night. She had no plan, no idea of what to do. All she could think was that she had to get her family to safety. To Catherine, it all seemed unreal. Only a month ago they had been safe in Castle Bruce. Perhaps they weren’t free, but they had warm beds, good food, shelter and at least a measure of security. Then it all fell apart suddenly in a massive firestorm that Ogastes had somehow managed to get televised. Now they were on the run again, her husband was wounded, and her family was in danger. Ogastes had really set this up perfectly.

Piece of shit!

As she thought that her eyes fell on her adopted daughter. Charlie lay curled up in the front passenger seat of the stolen Fiat fast asleep. Her skin was ashen, and her slight body trembled with what could only have been fear. Charlie didn't deserve this. Whatever else she might be, at the end of the day she was an innocent child.

Cold anger flooded Catherine's heart. *How could anyone be so cruel to a little girl?*

The countryside was eerily quiet. It was as if they had traveled to another world, one far removed from that of the global rioting. The rural lands remained as they had been for endless ages past untroubled by the violence surrounding them.

At some point during the night, it occurred to Catherine that she would need to find a new place for them to hide. David was still weak from his burns. He had overcome his illness, but she feared that he could suffer a new infection if they remained on the run. She had to find someplace for them to go.

As she thought that, Catherine became aware of the pain from her own wounds. Dull heat radiated from her stomach, back and left leg. The gashes in her cheek and forehead had almost completely closed although it had occurred to Catherine that she would probably have scars there for the rest of her life.

Sometime just before dawn, Catherine came upon a deserted warehouse and decided to stop for the day. She had little trouble getting past the warehouse's security measures, and within thirty minutes, she had pulled the little Fiat into the warehouse parking lot.

She gently shook her daughter awake.

Charlie groaned. "Where are we?"

"Somewhere in northern England," Catherine replied. "I'm not sure exactly where. Can you walk for a little bit?"

"Ok," Charlie replied softly. "Do you need help with David?"

"I think I can handle him myself," Catherine replied.

She got out of the car and went to the back seat where David was snoring softly. Catherine gently shook him awake. "David, wake up."

"Catherine?" He was still more asleep than awake.

"Come on we're going to stop for the day."

David groaned. “Ok.” He slowly slid into a sitting position. Catherine helped him to his feet and slid under his arm to balance him.

Slowly they limped their way to the warehouse office. Inside Catherine found a small apartment with several bunk beds.

No doubt intended for overnight security.

Catherine helped David into one of the lower bunks and then tucked Charlie into the other before climbing into the bunk above David. Fifteen minutes later she was dead to the world.

IX

On the morning following their arrival, Catherine and Charlie searched the warehouse for supplies. As it turned out, they had chosen their hiding place well. The massive warehouse was stocked full of canned and dried food, enough to last them for several months by Catherine’s estimation. She also stumbled across a small cache of firearms and ammunition as well as a fully stocked first aid kit and a pharmacy’s worth of medicines. Charlie also managed to locate an extensive collection of board games, a library of young reader books and several decks of playing cards.

The days that followed passed quietly. As Catherine and Charlie passed the time by playing games together and reading. David remained weak from his wounds. Though David’s infection had cleared up before the three of them took up residence in the warehouse, his burns were deep and thus healed slowly. For her own part, Catherine too suffered from her wounds though she kept this fact hidden as she did not wish to worry her husband and daughter.

Although the warehouse was well stocked, Catherine would periodically venture from its safety, not to look for supplies but rather to keep track of events outside. All commercial television and radio stations had ceased broadcasting a week before the three of them fled the King’s Arms Motel and the warehouse had no exterior windows. Thus, periodic scouting had become a necessity.

Catherine left with trepidation as she knew David and Charlie were vulnerable alone in the warehouse. Charlie’s power was great, and she was undoubtedly more than capable of defending herself and David, but she was young and did not have full control. David, on the other hand, remained weak and partially bedridden. If anyone came to the warehouse while she was away, then her family would be in danger. Still, they could not remain blind to the outside world.

As she scouted around, Catherine learned that they had settled into a warehouse belonging to 3PL Warehousing in the McGill Industrial Park on the northern edge of Gateshead. In addition to the 3PL Warehouse, there was also a CR England Trucking Depot, a DHL Warehouse, and a Vodaphone call center. Although all of the facilities *looked* deserted, Catherine shied away from exploring any of the other buildings for fear that they might be occupied by someone hostile. Instead, she merely checked periodically for signs of human activity of which she saw none.

Beyond the industrial park lay several housing subdivisions. Catherine explored these carefully, again refraining from entering buildings out of concern for the possibility of encountering dangerous people.

As the days went by, Catherine observed more and more evidence of a rising tide of violence. Although she was on the edge of the city, Catherine still heard intermittent gunfire as well as the occasional scream of fear or pain. The air grew thick with heavy, black smoke from numerous buildings that had fallen victim to arson.

Deep in her heart, Catherine felt a growing sense of danger and knew that they could not hide here for long.

X

Catherine's sense of danger was more accurate than she could ever have imagined. Unbeknown to the three survivors hiding out in the 3PL Warehouse, the city of Gateshead had become a battlefield. Soldiers representing the British Government (now know as Loyalists) and the rebellion (known as the Resistance) engaged in brutal urban warfare for control of the city. Meanwhile, desperate groups of survivors fought each other over rapidly dwindling supplies of food and other necessaries.

Both sides of the conflict were evenly matched, thus preventing either from seizing full control. The Resistance forces faced an additional problem in that the Loyalists had successfully gained possession of both the city's seaport and airport thereby allowing them to bring in an almost unlimited supply of troops and material to continue the battle. In addition, the Loyalists had recently gained control of the city's northern industrial district where the McAuliffes and their adopted daughter had taken up residence. Thus, the tide of battle threatened to turn against the Resistance.

Approximately four weeks after the firestorm at Castle Bruce, Resistance leadership decided that it was time to play their trump card against the Loyalist forces in Gateshead. At 0200 hours three wings of Russian SU-35s scrambled from their base near Moscow. Each fighter was heavily laden with penetrator bombs and extra fuel. Their target was Gateshead, England, more specifically the airport, seaport, and northern industrial district.

By 0600 the SU-35s were within striking distance of Gateshead. The flight commanders of each wing issued the command to arm weapons as the pilots fanned out to their assigned targets in preparation for final approach.

XI

Charlie awoke early that Saturday morning feeling an intense sensation of impending danger. She knew not what the threat was or when it would occur, but she was sure that something was very wrong. Charlie got up and found David sleeping peacefully in his bed. Catherine's bed was empty. Charlie sensed that she had gone outside and exited the office to search for her.

Charlie found Catherine standing in the parking lot slowly sipping a glass of Scotch and looking up at the sky.

"Something's wrong." As she spoke, Charlie's heartbeat picked up slightly. The sense of danger was growing.

"I know," Catherine replied. "I can feel it too."

Far off in the distance, at the very edge of perception, Charlie heard a faint roar that she associated with a jet engine. In the same moment, her blood chilled, and she shuddered involuntarily. A slow breeze stirred the cold night air. The jet engine sound was growing closer, building from a faint roar to a louder rushing sound. Twenty seconds later the sky lit up bright as midday as a giant orange-yellow fireball erupted from near the center of Gateshead. This was followed moments later by a second and then a third blossom of brilliant flame. A few seconds later the air filled with a frightening roar and the ground came alive beneath her feet nearly causing her to pitch forward.

Still, Charlie stood frozen, her mind too shocked and frightened to permit action. Somewhere in her mind, she understood what had happened and what she needed to do, but fear, shock and the unreality of what she had just seen made all action impossible.

Catherine's voice came to her through the growing fog of terror. "It's an air raid! We have to get inside!"

A hand closed over Charlie's. It was good that she knew the hand belonged to Catherine or in her fright Charlie would certainly have incinerated the hand's owner. As she allowed herself to be led back into the warehouse office, Charlie realized that the sound of jet engines was growing louder, closer.

She was inside the office now. Catherine was frantically trying to awaken David. Although his infection had mostly cleared up, he remained weak and slept deeply. Finally, out of desperation, Catherine slapped David across the face hard. He awakened suddenly.

"What the fuck?"

The moment David's words left his mouth, the air filled with a sound so intense as to be beyond hearing. At the same time the ground bucked hard beneath Charlie's feet tossing her onto her side. The bunk beds in the office pitched forward onto the floor as several of the office's steel file cabinets tipped over, spilling their contents in a flutter of papers. Glass skittered across concrete striking a high, tinkling note. Beneath it all, barely detectible against the din, was the sound of a single scream. It took several minutes before Charlie realized that it was her own.

All at once, the south wall of the warehouse office disappeared in a blinding flash of white and orange. This time there was no sound but rather a mighty gale that hurled her into the air. Charlie landed hard on her side and for a moment was winded. She could not see David and Catherine, could not hear them and could not feel them with her fear blunted psychic senses. Charlie tried to cry out their names but found she could make no sound.

A fresh wave of terror swept through Charlie, bringing the power up with it. Where were David and Catherine? The power was spinning wildly, just within her ability to control it. Charlie clamped down hard before the power could get out, sending blood-soaked shards of pain tearing through her skull.

STOP IT! STOP IT NOW!

The power slowed but remained active. Charlie could not tell if David and Catherine were safe. Fear continued to build within her. With a great effort, she forced herself to be calm. She had to find David and Catherine. They needed her help.

XII

Fifteen minutes after entering the airspace above Gateshead the SU-35s were bugging out after a successful bombing run. Both the airport and seaport had been destroyed, and the northern industrial district was heavily damaged. Initial radio chatter indicated that the Loyalists had suffered heavy losses. Resistance forces on the ground were quickly mopping up the survivors. Gateshead would become a Resistance city.

XIII

The gentlemen in white and black slowly reset their chessboard. Pawns rooks, knights, bishops, kings and queens line up in formation ready to do battle on the finite black and white plane of the chessboard.

A disturbance near the front of the bar draws both gentlemen's attention. Two young men have begun an argument. The first man is dressed in a red European cut suit with a solid black dress shirt underneath. The second is wearing a blue denim work shirt. Between them is a young woman dressed in a green cocktail dress. Her long coppery hair hangs in loose curls upon her shoulders.

The young man in the red suit grabs the young woman's arm. "Come one, it's time to go." He speaks with a tone of undeserved arrogance.

The young man in the blue denim work shirt steps between the young man in the red suit and the woman in the green dress. "She's not your property. She doesn't have to leave with you if she doesn't want to." The young man in the blue denim work shirt's words communicate concern for the woman in the green dress, but his tone is one of possession.

"How about you just shove off, mate." The young man in the red suit replies. "This doesn't concern you."

"I believe it does." The young man in the denim work shirt shoots back. "I'm making it my business."

The young man in the red suit pauses for a moment before throwing a haymaker. The young man in the blue denim shirt ducks and responds with an uppercut. He manages to catch the young man in the red suit off guard and strikes him square on the chin knocking him to the floor. The punch is far from a knockout, and in a moment the young man in the red suit is back on his feet and swinging. As he winds up, the young man in the red suit shoves the woman in the green cocktail dress aside. She is wearing spike heels. The young man in the red suit's shove instantly puts her off balance causing her to fall forward and smack her face off the bar top on her way to the floor.

Chapter 3
Surviving the Inferno

I

A man and his young son stood in one of many ration lines that cropped up daily across the globe since the beginning of the Great Civil War. This line was in St. Louis, but it might as well have been anywhere in the world.

As he waited, the man, Cody Rochefort, recalled the events of the past four weeks with something like disgusted amazement. It had begun with the firestorm at Castle Bruce and the death of Senator Hailey Suire, Chairperson of the Resistance Party. Except that really wasn't the beginning at all, it was merely the spark that ignited the powder keg that had been building around the world for decades.

The United States government, together with the leadership of much of the rest of the world, had been slowly developing a police state for as far back as he could remember.
The changes were small at first; intrusive background checks and loyalty oaths. Later came restrictions on items that could be carried through ports of entry and onto planes, and increasingly aggressive airline passenger searches by TSA. Small indignities that people would tolerate for the illusory promise of increased safety from the Communists, and then when the Soviet Union collapsed, from Muslim terrorists.

Later, war came, and with it further restrictions. Renditions and secret trials of supposedly dangerous persons became the norm, followed by drone strikes, and then assassinations. All in the name of protecting the homeland. More recently, the federal government had imposed a universal biometric ID system along with checkpoints at state lines and along the borders of certain major population centers. Together these systems allowed State and Federal authorities to track the movements of citizens, and in many cases to restrict those movements. Still, while many grumbled no one did anything to halt this slow erosion of freedom.

Ironically enough, it never occurred to anyone that they were at a higher risk of being killed getting behind the wheel of their car than ever being harmed by a Communist or terrorist. People were frightened, and fear is illogical and unreasonable.

Then New York City disappeared in a fiery mushroom cloud, and everything changed.

The nuclear attack on lower Manhattan provided a potent object lesson to the general public; that police state tactics did little to reduce the threat of terrorism. On the other hand, the gradual encroachment of government authority on personal liberty *had* effectively stripped the general public of much of their freedom. Before the New York City nuclear bombing, people grudgingly accepted the invasion of personal liberty in exchange for the promise of improved safety. When faced with the threat of death most people will willingly trade their freedom in exchange for the promise of security. Old Maslow had that much right. But, if the said promise of security turns out to be a lie, well then, the victims of the scam will demand their freedom back in a hurry and in a less than kindly manner.

And so, following the destruction of New York City, the Resistance was born. At first only a protest movement, much like the Tea Party and Occupy, within a year, the Resistance grew to a full-fledged political organization comprised of many groups around the world. Over the next two years, the American Resistance Party grew both in registered members and influence. Eventually, it became a legitimate rival to both the Republican and Democrat Parties; even nominating a presidential candidate in Senator Hailey Suire.

Senator Suire had been a vocal critic of police state tactics for years. She would publicly invoke Benjamin Franklin and Thomas Jefferson. Senator Suire was, in a word, compelling. People genuinely believed in her and to many, she represented the last ray of hope that real freedom could be restored.

Then in an instant, hope was snatched away. The fact that a freak girl from some federal government laboratory had killed Hailey Suire after the Senator had tried to protect the girl from rendition had all the appearance of an intentional assassination. The Senator's death was the last straw. Within minutes of the news report on the Senator's death, people around the world took to the streets *en masse* to riot. Within hours the riots had organized into an armed rebellion.

Cody remembered that day well.

II

The alarm on his cell phone began playing *Bad Company* at 5 am, pulling him from a deep and dreamless slumber. Cody reached for the phone and silenced it. Beside him, Stephanie, his wife of fifteen years, groaned softly and mumbled something inaudible.

Cody glanced down at her and smiled. She had curled up on her side and pulled the blankets over her head so that all was visible was a small tuft of her chestnut brown hair. She was as beautiful as the day he had met her in college.

Cody slowly stood up, crossed the bedroom, and exited through the bedroom door on his way to the bathroom. Once inside he turned on the shower and used the toilet while he waited for the water to get hot. As Cody showered, he felt the remaining sleepiness drain from his body. He was not much of a morning person, which was unfortunate given his current assignment. Cody had much preferred his old night patrol. As he thought that, Cody stepped out of the shower and went to the sink to shave.

At forty years of age, his hair had begun to gray, giving him a look that could be described as more than salt and pepper but less than full gray. The hair on his face was still his old natural black. He had the suggestion of a receding hairline and more than the suggestion of stress lines around his eyes. He grinned lopsidedly showing several crooked incisors.

After shaving, Cody exited the bathroom and crossed the living room to his apartment's little galley kitchen to fix breakfast. As he warmed up the Keurig, Cody listened to the soft rushing sound of his wife in the shower. A few minutes later, the sound of the shower was joined by the faint notes of *Lose Yourself* from his son, Blake's bedroom. Then, five minutes later, Blake appeared wearing a pair of blue jeans and nothing else. He held a t-shirt in his hand and as Cody watched he pulled it over his head.

"Good morning Blake."

The boy smiled. "Good morning Dad."

"You sleep good?" Cody asked.

"Uh-huh," Blake replied cheerfully.

As he spoke, Blake sidled behind Cody, opened the fridge, and took out the milk. He then carried it over to the table and set it down beside the cereal bowl and box of Fruit Loops that Cody had put out only moments earlier.

The rich smell of coffee wafted through the kitchen. Cody returned to the Keurig, took his coffee mug, and set it down in front of his place at the table. Then he poured himself a bowl of raisin bran and sat down to eat.

About halfway through breakfast, Stephanie wandered in, fixed herself a cup of coffee and a plate of scrambled eggs, and sat down at the table beside Cody. The little family chatted and ate breakfast for approximately forty minutes before Cody had to leave for his patrol and Blake had to catch the school bus at the corner.

Cody's shift was mostly uneventful. He took a few calls for suspicious activity in Fairground and another for an armed robbery of a store in Fairground Park. Nothing out of the ordinary.

At twelve-thirty Cody took his lunch break at The Deli, ordering a Rueben sandwich, a bag of fries and a Coke. Lunch was followed by three hours of tedious, nothing before he was summoned to the corner of Lee and Obear for suspected drug activity. As it turned out Cody caught a couple of street dealers with two grams of methamphetamine and an eight ball of heroin.

After transporting one of the suspects to the county jail and completing his report, Cody headed back out on the street. It was six o'clock in the evening. The sun had already disappeared beyond the horizon, leaving the city of St Louis shrouded in night.

Within an hour of the start of Cody's second shift, things began to change. Without reason or warning the radio lit up with 10-15 and 10-34 codes from across the city. The streets outside were quiet, almost too quiet. Sudden gunshots pierced the night. Instinctively Cody flipped on his emergency lights and siren and headed in the general direction of the gunfire. As he did, Cody grabbed his radio mic.

"10-78 Shots Fired! Shots Fired!"

The only reply was a burst of static followed moments later by:

"No units available."

A trickle of fear formed in Cody's chest. Rioting and civil disturbance calls from all over the city, something was seriously wrong. Cody accelerated as more gunshots echoed in the air. He was headed north on Kossuth towards Hull. Another shot rang out. This one seemed to be coming from an alleyway directly ahead and on the right. Cody slammed on the brakes and got out. Before leaving his squad car, he grabbed the AR-15 he kept in between the front seats. Two more shots rang out followed by a woman's scream.

Cody hurried to the source of the screaming and found a gang of African American male youths attempting to rape a young African American woman who couldn't have been older than eighteen. The gunshots that had brought him there had been fired into the air by one of the youths in an attempt to intimidate the woman. The tactic had failed. Cody racked the bolt of his rifle.

"Everybody freeze!"

He had expected the young men to scatter. Instead, all four youths drew pistols and opened fire on him. Each of them missed, having chosen to hold their weapons in a side cock manner. Cody returned fire instinctively, dropping two of the youths with his first pair of shots. The young woman began screaming even louder as the threat to her life came home to her. The sight of their two friends lying in the street, leaking crimson from multiple little, round holes, changed the priorities of the other two youths who rapidly fled. Cody went to the young woman and helped her to her feet. She had stopped screaming, but her face still registered deep fear. Her mocha skin was dotted with sweat despite the cold night air, and her deep brown eyes were wide. The soft scent of strawberries, intertwined with cigarettes, and body odor wafted from her trembling form. It was a scent Cody associated with mortal terror.

“Are you ok?” Cody asked.

She shook her head. “They tried to make me…” Her voice dissolved into sobs.

Cody took the woman’s hand and led her towards the mouth of the alley. “Come on, it’s not safe here. Do you live nearby?”

The woman could not respond. Cody walked her to his car, intending to drive her to the nearest hospital. Upon entering, the radio once again came alive.

“10-34! 10-34! All units return to station immediately. Repeat, all units return to station immediately.”

Cody hesitated for a moment. Something was very wrong. Code 10-34 was reserved for situations in which there was danger at the station. This was a likely scenario given the earlier civil disturbance alerts over the air.

But why would they recall everyone?

If there were indeed city-wide civil disturbances, then command would keep as many officers on the streets as possible to avoid further spread of violence. They would recall however, many units were needed to handle whatever trouble was going on at the station, but that number would be kept to a minimum.

As he thought that, the sky above the city center lit up in bright orange and yellow. Thick black smoke filled the air, and yet there were no sirens. The only sounds that broke the night’s silence were the pop and crack of gunfire underpinned by the roar of fire.

For the first time, Cody thought of his family and became frightened. His wife and son would be at home in their apartment in Central West End. It was around dinner time. Stephanie had promised to make beef Stroganoff. Blake would be working on his homework.

They were about four miles from downtown, and he had not heard a report of civil unrest near his home, but doubt had already begun to take root in his mind. What if their neighborhood had exploded in violence and no one had reported it? Perhaps the cops in the area had been recalled to their station.

The recall code repeated over the radio. Cody looked at the young woman he had rescued feeling torn. His sense of duty to his fellow officers demanded that he return to the station. The part of Cody that was a husband and father insisted that he should hurry home to protect his family. And then there was this woman he had saved. She needed to go somewhere safe. His first instinct was the hospital, but now that he had more time to think about it he decided that the hospital might not be secure. As the various demands of loyalty and duty fought within his mind, Cody spoke to the woman.

“What’s your name?” He asked this in his best professional tone.

“Autumn.” The young woman replied. She was no longer crying and had calmed. Cody enjoyed the rich, smoky timbre of her voice.

“Where do you live, Autumn?”

“Fairgrounds Park Place.” She replied softly,

“Do you have any family there? Anyone, to protect you?”

She shook her head. “No. It’s just me. My mama died last year from cancer. My daddy was shot by a robber when I was seven.”

“I can’t just leave you off then. The whole city is going to hell, and this neighborhood isn’t safe.” He paused as he tried to think logically. He had just met this woman, and she could very well be dangerous. “Do you have any family in the area?”

“My sister lives in Kingsway East. The neighborhood sucks, but she keeps her house locked up tight. If you can get me there I’ll be alright.”

In that moment, he decided. It would not be until later, when he learned of the fate of his fellow officers, that Cody would feel guilty for abandoning his duty as a law officer.

Despite his fear for his family, Cody agreed and kept to his word, delivering Autumn directly to her sister’s doorstep. During the five-minute drive from the Fairgrounds to Kingsway East, the streets began to fill with people. Men and women armed with everything from baseball bats to semi-automatic rifles streamed from homes and businesses. Cody was fortunate that the crowd seemed mostly indifferent to his presence and allowed him to pass unhindered. Still, he knew that would not last. He had to return home quickly before returning home became impossible.

Cody found Autumn’s sister’s home without any trouble, and let Amber off on the doorstep.

“Be careful.” He admonished her. “I don’t know what’s going on, but something is very wrong. Keep your doors and windows locked and the lights off.”

Autumn nodded. “I will thank you, Officer…” She paused. “I don’t even know your name.”

“It’s Cody Rochefort ma’am.” He replied.

“It’s nice to meet you, Officer Rochefort,” Autumn replied.

“Just Cody ma’am.” He replied.

“Thank you, Cody,” Autumn said with a slight smile. “I think I will be ok from here. Be careful going home.”

And with that, she turned and went to the door of her sister’s home. She knocked, and for a moment, just stood there before the door opened a crack, and a large, black woman poked her head out. Autumn’s sister recognized her at once and hurried Autumn indoors before shutting the door tight.

This was the last time Cody saw Autumn. Later he would learn that Kingsway East fell victim to arsonists during a battle between Loyalist and Resistance forces over the neighborhood. Not a single building was spared.

On a typical day, the drive from Kingsway East to Central West End takes ten minutes. On that night, it took Cody two hours. By now the streets were impossibly clogged with rioters and debris. Cody found several roads outright blocked by burning cars. Worse still, the crowds had begun to take notice of his status as a cop and attacked him. Cody quickly abandoned his squad car in favor of a "borrowed" 92 Jeep Cherokee that someone had conveniently abandoned with the keys in the ignition. At any other time, he would have found this highly suspicious, but under the circumstances, he was far beyond being bothered.

Cody switched on the radio in the hopes that he might learn something about what the hell was going on. An emergency alert indicated widespread civil unrest throughout the United States. St. Louis was one of many hot spots. The radio reporter warned against any attempt to traverse the city as the streets were mostly impassable and filled with armed rebels clashing with National Guard troops.

Interstates 44, 70, 55, 64 and 170 were all closed, effectively shutting down all major routes out of the city. The radio reporter advised all citizens to remain indoors and keep all doors and windows locked. Cody suspected that this advice was somewhat futile for those caught in the immediate vicinity of the fighting. A locked door would keep out neither bullets nor determined attackers.

About one hour into the drive, Cody encountered a huge, pitched battle between armed rioters and a large detachment of what appeared to be National Guard in riot gear, and fatigues. While the Guardsmen were better armed, the rioters were far more numerous and very determined making the battle fairly even. From his position, Cody could see that the Guardsmen were in danger of being overrun, and hoped like hell that their leadership would be wise enough to have them withdraw before something terrible could happen.

As that thought crossed his mind, a bullet shattered his windshield, and another zipped through the front passenger seat. These were strays, but he had to leave immediately before someone noticed, and opened fire in earnest.

The battle was directly ahead, so Cody turned the Jeep around, and headed up a side road for several blocks until he found a relatively quiet street that was headed the way he wanted to go. An hour later, Cody was standing outside his apartment building, feeling both relieved and frightened at once. He was glad to be home but frightened of what he would find. The streets surrounding Castle Gate Apartments were alive with angry, armed rioters. Gunfire rang out in the night, while several bonfires blazed in the street filling the cold night air with thick, acrid-smelling smoke.

Cody found the security desk abandoned, and the lobby dark. He pulled the flashlight from his belt and headed for the stairs. Ten minutes later, he was carefully sliding his key into the lock on his front door. As the deadbolt slid open, his nose detected the faint odor of diner.

Cody found his wife and son sitting in the dark, watching the news on Blake's iPad. In his relief to find his family unharmed, Cody took only peripheral note of the news story.

A girl about Blake's age had somehow managed to assassinate Senator Hailey Suire. According to the reporter, a middle-aged Indian man, this girl was a mutant gifted with a talent called pyrokinesis.

A talent that made it possible for her to light fires by merely thinking about fires. This girl was believed to be a genetically modified human, bred in an American laboratory for some unknown reason. Although no one knew for sure, it was strongly suspected that this girl had been deliberately released for the purpose of murdering the Senator. Despite the girl's power, no one believed that a nine-year-old child would ever be able to escape US custody on her own.

The reporter went on to discuss the import of the girl's existence. She represented proof that paranormal abilities are real and that humans with such powers could be laboratory-bred. For his own part, Cody doubted that second part. That girl may indeed have originated in a laboratory somewhere, but he suspected that she had arisen from an accident.

Still the combined news of Senator Suire's assassination and the nature of the Senator's killer struck a match in a tinderbox that had been building up for many years and now the world was aflame.

III

The Senator's death had occured two months ago. Cody still marveled at how quickly things had gone to shit. The power was off. Within seventy-two hours all commercial radio and television broadcasts had ceased, and before long, food and water supplies became dangerously scarce. Cody felt grateful that he had the foresight to maintain a cache of dried and canned food and bottled water for his family.

During this same time, the world degenerated into a state of total civil war. Resistance forces clashed with police and military forces that remained loyal to national governments around the world.

In the ensuing weeks St. Louis became a battlefield before eventually falling to the Resistance after a devastating airstrike by F-15Es. Under Resistance control, all supplies were tightly rationed. Each household would be allotted a specific quantity of food and water based on the number of occupants. Household provisions were issued at assigned distribution centers throughout the city. Ration lines were long. Thus someone would have to go to the center early each morning to pick up the household supply of food and water for the day. Cody had volunteered that morning.

Now he was nearing the front of the line and from what he could see supplies were growing exceptionally thin. Today he was given exactly one pound of food and two gallons of water. Barely enough for his family to survive on.

As he picked up his family's daily allocation, Cody noted that the warehouse behind the distribution desk was mostly empty. There were a handful of crates and maybe a half dozen drums of water. These would be depleted by the end of the day, and there did not appear to be any reserves for tomorrow. Fresh supplies were shipped in by truck, but the city had not seen any new shipments for at least two weeks. Food and water were about to dry up, and Cody knew the consequences that would inevitably follow.

IV

The emergency room continued to flood with patients as the situation on the streets of Miami continued to deteriorate. Burns, gunshot wounds, stabbings, beatings, all arriving in greater and greater numbers. Larry found his heart thundering and his mind racing with growing terror. Mount Sinai was well equipped to deal with large numbers of casualties, but this was beyond anything anyone could have planned for. Miami had become a literal war zone, the demands of which were taxing the hospital's resources to their limits.

By seven o'clock in the evening, the hospital had reached its capacity, and the directive went out that they could not accept any new patients. Larry was in room one with a ten-year-old gunshot victim when the code echoed over the PA.

Oh shit...

This was followed a few minutes later by Loretta William's deep twang. "Code Silver, ER, we have a Code Silver in the ER." Her normally jovial voice had grown sharp with terror.

-BOOM-

The sound of the pistol shot slammed through his head, setting his ears to ringing. The little boy on the table, only semi-conscious, twitched and went as white as a sheet with raw terror. Then, in that moment, Larry did something he would forever feel ashamed of. He ran. He ran from Room One of the Mount Sinai emergency room and never looked back.

"We have a Code Silver in...."

-BOOM-

The second gunshot was further punctuated by Loretta's shrieking wail of combined pain and terror. Larry understood she had been shot, but he did not turn back. Instead, he let the steel fire door at the rear of the emergency room snick shut behind him leaving his co-workers and yes, his friends behind forever.

V

On that strange day, Carla remained in her classroom until the time her class was scheduled to end. Never mind that all of her students had fled within fifteen minutes of the news report on the firestorm at Castle Bruce. Never mind the news reports on the growing violence in the streets that followed. She would not dignify any of this by panicking and fleeing like a plebian. She had not spent the better part of her twenties earning her doctorate in English literature just to spook like a stupid animal at the first report of trouble.

Still, this girl, this Charlene McLeod was troubling. Carla found the news reports on her alleged powers incredible, but the evidence was too strong to deny. The girl was indeed powerful and a pyrokinetic.

Pyrokinesis

It was a term Carla found so fantastically unbelievable that she refused to even speak the word or acknowledge it to herself consciously.

The girl is dangerous, and she is a murderer. She had killed Senator Suire, no doubt at the behest of the US federal government.

Carla was old enough to remember what it had been like in the nineties, before the rise of the Patriot Act and the Security and Interdiction Acts that followed. She had been a sophomore in college at the time of the 9/11 attacks and like pretty much everyone else she was outraged. Still, Carla was never in favor of the legal regime that followed. She had watched as the federal government took the public anger that followed the attacks that destroyed the Twin Towers in Manhattan and used it to build a regime that had, over the subsequent years methodically stripped the people of the United States and the world at large of their rights as citizens.

Many people on both the left and the right enthusiastically embraced these changes as they were sold as "common-sense national security measures". People grumbled but accepted the small, incremental invasion of their liberties because they believed it was necessary to protect them from the omnipresent threat of Islamic terrorism. Never mind that the statistical risk of being killed by a terrorist was far smaller than the risk of being killed by a drunk driver. Never mind that more than a decade had passed without a major terrorist attack against the US homeland. These people were frightened, and hard-line security laws made them feel safer. Oh, they weren't happy about having their privacy invaded and were even less thrilled about having to show ID to move between states, but they would tolerate these measures just as they endured being groped by TSA agents at the airport. Fear is a powerful motivator.

Then Manhattan disappeared in a five-megaton nuclear blast, instantly laying bare the lie of safety. Over the subsequent four years, public discontent and anger slowly smoldered as people began to realize the true nature of the ruling class's deception. Terrorism had afforded the excuse that both political parties had needed to subjugate the public. Unfortunately, they had not bargained for the fact that a nuclear warhead would fall into the hands of these very same terrorists. Nor had they expected that those same terrorists would be able to smuggle that same warhead into the United States and detonate it in the middle of one of the most heavily guarded cities in the world. Thus, the people of the world received a harrowing and potent object lesson.

In the aftermath of that disaster, the American Resistance Party was born. Carla had supported the ideals of the Resistance Party from the start. She had never been in favor of the policies underlying the Patriot Act and the subsequent Security and Interdiction Acts. In her mind, freedom was far more valuable than security. Nevertheless, she had never actually joined the Resistance Party or the underlying Resistance Movement. The cost would have been far too high. She had watched several tenured colleagues lose their positions at the university for supporting the Resistance Movement. Instead, she had chosen to quietly bide her time.

Still, Carla had seriously considered voting for Senator Suire for president in the fall. Carla doubted that the Resistance Party candidate would be able to successfully roll back the police state that had infected the United States, but she saw no harm in supporting Senator Suire.

As that last thought passed through her mind, a wave of anger followed. The US government and the ruling class that controlled it had tried every method available to them to stop the Resistance Movement. At first, they relied on negative propaganda. When this tactic failed, they escalated to punitive measures against open supporters of the Resistance Movement. Many found themselves suddenly unemployed, subject to audits by the IRS, unable to obtain credit, subject to nuisance civil suits and trumped-up criminal charges. No law was ever passed officially banning the Resistance

Party or the Resistance Movement but to support or join either was certain to bring one trouble.

Carla had worked hard to get where she was and was unwilling to risk her career for a political cause that in all likelihood, would ultimately fail.

Now, as she stood looking over her empty classroom it occurred to her that she no longer had anything to lose. On the television beside her, the CNN newscaster was reporting massive rioting around the world.

Today in resorting to assassinating Senator Suire, *They* had crossed a line from which there was no return.

Carla looked over her classroom once more, knowing that this would be for the last time. Then she gathered up her personal effects and left, locking the door behind her. She found the exterior corridor stood empty, Benjamin Franklin Hall having been abandoned.

Outside, the campus grounds of the University of Michigan were deserted. Distant sirens rang out on the silent evening air.

That girl though... She thought with more than a hint of anger. *She murdered Senator Suire.* But it was what the girl represented more than what she had done that drove Carla's fury. She was outraged with the government's police state policies, sure. And Senator Suire's assassination served as a potent symbol of those same tactics. Still, the fact that the US government had intentionally bred a monster, a laboratory horror in the shape of a little girl, was beyond atrocious.

That little girl personified everything that Carla had fought against as an environmentalist. She was a human GMO, an abomination, and a crime against nature.

As she walked to her car, Carla contemplated what she would do. She felt as though everything had suddenly changed. Still, she knew not what she would do about it.

In her mind, Carla felt she was too intelligent to be out rioting, and in any case, she did not own any weapons with which to fight. Being a firm believer in gun control Carla had never touched a gun in her life. Still, she felt she had to do *something*. As Carla started the engine of her 2012 Acura RL the wail of sirens grew closer. Carla switched on the radio only to be greeted by the irritating buzz of the Washtenaw County emergency alert system. A moment later an artificially calm reporter announced rioting in Ann Arbor and the surrounding communities. Residents were advised to remain in their homes with the doors locked.

"Thanks," Carla said sardonically to no one in particular. "I'll do that."

Instead of heading home, Carla went to the supermarket. If she was going to be stuck in the house, she would at least have a good supply of food.

Carla headed to Whole Foods only to find it in a state of utter chaos. Cars were scattered across the parking lot while a massive hoard of humanity fought to gain access to whatever provisions the store might have had on hand.

"Fuck that!" Carla exclaimed as she beat a hasty retreat.

Several blocks down the road she found a Seven-Eleven that appeared deserted. Carla pulled into the parking lot and carefully shut off the car engine. She was at the corner of Washtenaw Avenue and Golfside Road. It was quiet here. She heard no sirens and no cars. Still, the gas pumps were turned on, and the Seven-Eleven store was brightly lit. From where she sat she could not see if there was a clerk, but the store looked open.

Carla took a moment to look around her car for a weapon. She settled on the tire iron and popped the trunk to retrieve it. After removing the slender piece of tubular steel from its place underneath the carpeting, Carla slowly approached the Seven-Eleven. She tried the front door and found it unlocked.

As she stepped across the threshold, Carla heard the distinct racking sound of a pump-action shotgun and turned to her right just in time to see the clerk behind the counter aiming a gaping barrel at her head. Carla dove to the ground as he fired. The blast narrowly missed, blowing apart a potato chip display and showering her in bits of Lays.

What did the battery say to the bag of chips? If you're Eveready, I'm Frito Lay!

The absurd joke had popped into her head unbidden, and now that it was here she couldn't help but giggle stupidly.

The clerk racked his shotgun again and called to her.

"Freeze!"

Yeah no shit! Carla thought contemptuously. She hated idiots with guns. Carla raised her hands and stood up slowly. "I don't want any trouble. I'm just looking to buy some groceries."

The clerk was not persuaded. "Bullshit, lady! The whole city is going to shit, and you're in here trying to buy groceries?!" The clerk's voice was young, and he spoke with a slight accent that she couldn't place.

"I swear I'm telling the truth," Carla replied. She was not yet frightened. She felt more annoyed than anything else. Who was this asshole waving a shotgun around? "Look all I want is a couple of groceries. The Whole Foods is a bloody mob scene."

"Turn around slowly, lady." The clerk responded harshly.

Carla turned to face him with her best friendly smile. As it turned out, the clerk was only a kid, maybe fifteen or sixteen years of age at most. He held his long brown and black pump action with the assured authority of one who is familiar with weapons.

"Now, back away." The clerk said as he gestured with his weapon. "Get out of my store and don't come back." His green eyes flashed as he spoke.

"Look, kid." Carla began slowly. "I have money. I just want to buy some groceries, and then I'll leave."

The clerk hesitated for a moment, and Carla imagined she saw a thoughtful expression cross his face for an instant. Then he leveled his shotgun and began to take aim.

In that moment time slowed. Carla made a move to dive out of the way but her body was frustratingly sluggish.

There was a bright flash, but she never heard a gunshot. Something warm and wet splattered across her face.

For a moment, Carla was sure she had been shot and waited to die. The store was deadly silent, she thought at first that she had gone deaf from the blast of the clerk's shotgun. But then her ears caught the distinctive sound of sirens in the distance. Still, the clerk made no sound. After several more minutes had elapsed, Carla slowly stood up.

The ground in front of her was splattered with blood. None of it was hers. Carla went to the counter and found the young clerk lying face down in a pool of his own blood, his head mostly gone. Bits of skull and brain dotted the floor and wall behind the counter.

The sight was horrifying beyond her ability to comprehend. Carla turned away quickly and busied herself with gathering up supplies. Here was a box of cereal, there a can of Campbell's soup. She was very calm and felt nothing. The fact that she had just witnessed the murder of a young boy was far from her conscious thoughts. All of her attention was focused on gathering up as much food as she could carry. As an afterthought, she also grabbed up some first aid supplies, several quarts of motor oil and an empty gas can. It did not even occur to her to take the dead boy's shotgun. Nor did she pay any mind to the location of the boy's killer and it was this last oversight that would ultimately come back to haunt her.

As Carla left the Seven-Eleven several men armed with Glocks approached her. Their apparent leader, a massive, dark-skinned man of indeterminate age, approached her, pistol leveled.

"I'll take those." He said in a business-like tone.

Carla was nonplussed.

The man's expression immediately became aggressive. "I said, drop the fucking bags, bitch!"

Carla remained frozen, unable to react. She was not so much frightened as just straight out shocked. This couldn't be real. This day had been just too weird.

"You deaf bitch?! Drop the fucking bags!" The man's voice boomed like boulders falling down a mountain.

Carla 's mind reeled, and her body stood motionless. It did not even occur to her that she was in mortal danger. All she could think was how impossible this whole situation was. *There's no way this could be happening...*

The man approached her, gun still leveled, and snatched her bags from her hands snarling "Cunt!" as he did.

Carla remained stunned, standing and staring like an idiot for a full twenty minutes after the gang of men had scattered before finally wandering back to her car. She drove away in a state of total shock, still unable to comprehend what had just happened to her. It wasn't until she had arrived at her home in Burns Park and closed the door behind herself that Carla broke down sobbing.

VI

A red-haired woman lurked in the shadows outside a seedy nightclub checking her watch.

Three a.m. *Almost time for close.*

A steady stream of drunken clubgoers began to shamble out the front door. The chilly night air filled with the sounds of their alcohol-fueled revelry. The red-haired woman watched them patiently, waiting until the crowd dispersed.

As she stood in silence, the red-haired woman's mind retreated into memory, drifting back to happier times.

VII

Kira Morozov had never had an easy life. She was an accidental pregnancy arising from a one night stand between two Russian university students who had met at a party. She had never known her father or mother as she was placed for adoption in America while still a baby.

She was also born an Enlightened and was thus an outcast. Still, though her adoptive parents were deeply frightened by the power, they had accepted and loved her. They were among the few who did.

Dell and Linda Bennett had given her a happy if not carefree childhood. She had grown up in Stringtown, Oklahoma, the very epitome of small-town, middle America. Stringtown boasted a single, small grocery, a gas station, a McDonald's and not much else. Her childhood home was a two-story, white clapboard farmhouse situated on eighty acres of ranch land six miles east of town.

Even now, as she stood watching the last of the patrons of *The Black Adder* trickle out onto the sidewalk, Kira could still clearly picture her parents' little white farmhouse with the big oak tree in the front yard. There was an old tire swing in that tree. As a little girl, she had spent countless hours swinging from that tree and laughing, enjoying the warm breezes of Oklahoma spring and early summer.

Throughout her childhood, Kira had few friends. Though she was careful to keep the power a secret, other children always seemed to sense something odd about her. Thus, she was mostly shunned. The one or two friends she had were kids who were also outcasts for one reason or another.

By the time Kira reached her teenage years, she had become a full-fledged introvert and kept mostly to herself. She had no friends and considered dating to be more than she could ever realistically hope for. Sure there were boys Kira liked, but none of them would ever notice her. She was the strange girl with the Russian last name. She was that girl with the eerie air. And then there was the power. Having the power had always made her feel separate from those around her. The need to protect the secret meant she could never open up to anyone. She would forever stand apart for fear of how people would react if they knew the truth about her.

And so she remained alone throughout high school, not daring to entertain even the thought that she might meet someone, boy or girl, that could accept and understand what she was.

Instead, Kira poured herself into academics. She had always found learning and school work easy if not necessarily fun. In elementary school, Kira participated in the gifted program. By the time she had reached high school, she was in honors-level courses. These eventually gave way to advanced placement classes in her senior year. She had given herself over so completely to academics by this point that she spent the night of her senior prom studying for college admissions tests.

Kira graduated Salutatorian from high school and was admitted to Yale. However, before she could enroll, her father died suddenly of a massive heart attack and her mother was diagnosed with cervical cancer. Thus, Kira turned down Yale in favor of OU in order to be closer to home.

Kira could still remember the day she left for college clearly as if it had happened just yesterday. Her mother had helped her pack her shit box F150 as best she could and then stood in the front doorway wiping away tears of pride as Kira drove away. It had been uncharacteristically blustery that August day. The sky was a solid blue blaze, unmarred by even a single cloud. The air smelled of newly mown hay and cattle. Kira had kissed her mother goodbye before climbing behind the wheel and driving away. This would be the last time she saw her mother alive as Linda Bennet would be found dead in bed two weeks later.

Linda Bennet's funeral was small and poorly attended. Besides Kira, a few of the neighbors turned up along with the pastor from the local Methodist church the Bennets where the Bennets had been parishioners for years. Everyone told Kira how sorry they were but remained distant. For her part, Kira didn't care how sorry they were. By the end of the funeral, she felt that if one more person told her how sorry they were she would knock their teeth down their throat. Especially since she could feel how disingenuous their sympathetic wishes were. In truth, they would miss Linda Bennet for a few weeks before they forgot her entirely and none of them gave two shits about Kira. To them, she was Linda's odd-ball daughter, someone to be politely avoided.

And so, Kira was left truly alone. Rather than allowing grief and crushing loneliness to destroy her, Kira again poured herself into her studies. By the end of her freshman year she was an honors student, and by her senior year, she was in line to graduate summa cum laude. Following graduation, Kira applied for her first supervised engineering position and quickly found employment.
It was also during this time that Kira's life began to change in ways she could never have imagined. During her Junior year, Kira met a sandy-haired, freckled man named Terrel Blackhawk, Terry for short. She had literally bumped into him in the student union, spilling his coffee with cream down the front of her blouse. He had offered to buy her dinner at O'Connell's to make it up to her. She had at first taken his gesture as one of pure guilt until she took a moment to listen to her psychic senses and realized that he had used the coffee spill as a pretext. In truth, he found her quite attractive. Her reserved nature, rather than being off-putting, intrigued him as it offered a challenge which he would gladly accept.

Still, Kira remained cautious. This was partly because she believed Terry was too good to be true and in part because she feared what might happen if he should learn of the power. Nevertheless, that first date at O'Connell's went well, and before long, he had asked her out on a second date and then a third and a fourth. Rather than finding her *otherness* off-putting, Terry seemed to find it alluring as if she were some mystery for him to figure out.

Kira remained distant from him for a long time for she feared what Terry would think if he learned of her true nature. Still, he remained patient with her. Slowly, Kira's resistance broke down until she found herself contemplating telling him of the power. At first, she dismissed this idea as wishful foolishness. But then, as time went on, she found herself *wanting* to reveal the power to him. She had fallen in love with him, and she hated to have the barrier of this secret between them.

And yet the logical portion of her mind told her she must keep the power a secret. There was no telling how this man might react if he should learn that the woman he was dating was a psychokinetic. At a minimum, he would almost certainly reject her, and he could do far worse as well. She had lived her entire life in fear of being dragged off and locked away in some laboratory if it ever got out that she had the power. No one knew about her, save for her adoptive parents and they had told her again and again as far back as she could remember to never, never tell anyone. To reveal that she had the power would be perilous.

Still, Kira loved Terry, and she wanted to believe that he would understand as her parents had. She desperately wanted to believe for she felt so alone. And so, after many months of contemplation, she finally decided.

VIII

Kira remembered that night as clearly as if it had happened just yesterday. It was a balmy Friday evening in early April. Terry had surprised her with an impromptu road trip to Tulsa's Blue Dome District.

Dinner at Kilkenny's was followed by dancing and drinks at Woody's. The night felt magical. As she danced with Terry to their favorite song, Kira knew she would tell that night. She was well aware of the risk and yet felt unafraid. She trusted this man, more than she had trusted anyone. They were meant to be together. The song ended, and Terry leaned in to whisper in her ear.

"Let's get out of here."

Something warm tricked through her chest. "Ok."

Terry took her hand and led her out into the night. The street outside glowed in bright colors from numerous neon signs. Kira followed Terry to his silver Chevy Silverado. She knew not what would come next, but she did not care. All that mattered was this moment with this man.

A short time later they had arrived at the Hard Rock in Catoosa. Fifteen minutes after that, they were checked in and headed for their room. Once inside the elevator, Terry leaned in and stole a kiss, electrifying her body with ecstasy. Kira kissed him back fiercely, not wanting to move from that spot and that moment. The spell broke a few seconds later when the elevator door fell open to reveal an empty hallway. Terry took her hand once more and led her down the hotel corridor. His touch was enchanting, sending her heart leaping within her chest. Now they were inside their room, the door snicked shut and locked.

Terry began slowly, making his intentions clear but remaining respectful. Before things got too far, Kira stopped him.

"Can we talk first?" She asked, forcing herself to speak normally over her quickening breath.

"Ok." Terry's voice was a bit confused. "Is something wrong?"

Kira smiled and nearly burst into tears. He was so sweet. She hated to spoil the moment, but now she was decided. She needed to tell him. "Nothing's wrong. I.." She paused for a moment and sucked a slow breath over her lower lip. "I need to tell you something, and it won't be easy for you to understand."

Terry's expression changed, and for a moment she thought she detected fear.

He thinks I'm about to break up with him. The realization nearly broke Kira's heart for this was the very antithesis of what she wanted. *I love you, baby. I..I don't ever want to lose you.*

"There are some things about me that you need to understand. Some things that I have kept from you because I was afraid of how you would react."

"Whatever it is it's ok," Terry said with emotion in his voice. "I love you, Kira. That's all that matters to me."

Then, before she could change her mind, she told, *everything.* To her surprise, when she had finished, Terry did not reject her as she had feared. Instead, he looked her deep in the eyes with such love and compassion that she nearly burst into tears and told her the one thing she had not dared to hope for.

"It doesn't matter. I love you for who you are."

He was not afraid of her or put off by her differences. Instead, he accepted and loved her just as any man would love any woman. It was at that moment that she allowed herself to fully fall for Terry and in that moment that she knew they were meant to be together.

Six months later Kira and Terry were married, and a year after that Kira was pregnant with her first child, a girl she would name Aria.

The birth of her daughter was the second time Kira remembered feeling true love. For a while, life was idyllic, a dream she prayed she would never awaken from.

Regrettably, the dream lasted but a few short years before the darkness that permeated her bleak existence reasserted itself.

IX

The last of the drunken club crowd had stumbled off into the chilly night air. With an effort, Kira pushed memory aside and focused her mind on the task at hand. Now was the time. To her surprise, Kira no longer felt the anger she had expected. Instead, she felt only cold contempt and a terrible resolve to destroy the man who had taken her daughter from her.

Gary would be working late, as he did every Saturday night, counting the evening's take and carefully recording it in the black ledger book he carried with him everywhere.

The power stirred within her restlessly as she stepped from the night's shadows with deliberate slowness. There was no reason to rush, Gary would not expect her, and she wanted time to plan before acting.

The Black Adder consisted of a single main room with a dance floor at its center and a bar along the southern wall together with a small block of offices in the rear. Kira bypassed the main entrance in front, choosing instead to head for the darkened ally on the south side of the large brick building that housed the *Adder*.

As she entered the alley, the combined stench of rotting garbage, urine and stale vomit assailed her nose. Towards the rear of the club, a heavy steel security door provided direct access to the business office. Kira approached the door with deliberate strides. A quick strike with the power and the door fell open as if unlocked by its key.

The corridor beyond was dimly lit by naked flickering fluorescent tubes. Somewhere in another room, a stereo thumped out the muffled bass tones of some sort of techno. Kira reached under her long coat and carefully drew her sword. The blade gave off a muted silver glow in the poorly lit hallway.

Gary's office was at the end of the hallway. He had left the door partway open. Soft, pink incandescent and neon light crept from within.

Kira reached out with the power, and the door slowly drifted open as if by its own will. Gary stood with his back to the door carefully stacking bundles of cash inside a wall safe.

"Gary."

Gary Volkov turned at the sound of his name. Upon seeing Kira, only his steel-gray eyes registered surprise.

Before her stood a man of average build and slightly above average height. His dark, shaggy hair came to his shoulders and held more than a trace of gray. His face, though not old, was weathered and hard as granite.

"Kira." He spoke her name in a voice that was soft and melodious. His accent, while clearly western Russian was but a subtle coloring as he spoke with a clarity reserved to native English speakers.

All at once she brought her sword up and severed both of Gary's hands in one swift and terrible motion

Gary screamed and collapsed to his knees, clutching his wrist stumps to her chest. Blood sprayed across the room in a magnificent crimson fountain.

Kira bent down to Gary's level until they were literally eye-to-eye. "You sold my daughter to be pimped out and die."

"Do you expect me to be sorry?" Gary bit out.

"I don't care what you do." She replied with soft sincerity as she slowly raised her sword.

"An eye for an eye," Kira intoned as she changed her grip on her sword and thrust hard putting all her strength and weight behind the blow. The blade flashed under the soft incandescent office lamps trailing red spray behind it. Gary screamed again and fell on his back, the sword still embedded in his belly. Kira pulled hard, ripping her blade loose and spilling Gary's entrails onto the white shag carpet.

Chapter 4
Fugitives Once More

I

The air smelled of acrid smoke from dozens of burning buildings. Everything had become deadly quiet. Even the wind had gone mute, though she could feel it tugging at her clothing. Charlie's eyes stung from the thick, sooty air. She called to David and Catherine and found that though she could feel her throat vibrate, her voice made no sound.

Icy fear gripped her chest.

David!!

Catherine!!

Are you guys ok?

She could not tell if she had screamed the words or only thought them. Charlie reached out with the power but could sense neither of her adopted parents.

Charlie began to panic. *I can't be alone! Please, God, I don't want to be alone again!*

Big tears welled up in her eyes and rolled down her sooty cheeks. The power stirred within her, awakened by her growing desperation. Charlie fought it back fearfully.

STOP IT! STOP IT PLEASE!

Flames licked across the ground at her feet.

Charlie clamped down hard, sending an explosion of nails ripping through her head.

STOP IT NOW!!

She did not want a firestorm. Everything was already bombed-out, she did not want to make it worse. But her fear made it hard to hold on, and it hurt so much to stop.

Charlie forced herself to be calm despite her growing terror, despite the swirling power in her mind. She forced herself to focus and reached out carefully with her mind. At first, Charlie felt only a general sense of danger. Then she slowly became aware of a faint but familiar sensation.

Charlie followed the sensation to a nearby pile of twisted metal and broken cinderblocks. The thick, oily smoke in the air made her eyes burn. Tears ran down her cheeks both from fear and from the toxic air. Still, she thought she could make out a familiar crop of dark hair. Without thinking, Charlie ran towards the pile of rubble.

"David!" Her ears detected no sound, yet she knew she had called out. The crop of dark hair stirred slightly. Charlie climbed over debris to find David lying in a crumpled heap. A cruel gash skidded across his forehead. Blood slowly leaked from the wound and tricked down into his eyes and over his cheeks. Chunks of concrete block buried him up to his waist. As she approached him, his wolf gray eyes flicked open, and his lips mouthed something unintelligible.

A moment later, his mind touched hers.

Charlie! Thank God you're ok!

David, you're bleeding!

I'm ok, Charlie. It's just a cut.

Can you hear anything? His mind asked hers with more than a hint of concern.

No. Charlie replied. *Everything is so quiet. I think the explosion did something to my hearing.*

Charlie your ears. You're bleeding. David's voice was frankly frightened now.

He reached for her. As he did, Charlie saw the blood running from David's ears.

No. I'm fine but David... Before she could finish her thought, she noticed for the first time the thick, warm liquid running down the sides of her neck and understood its import. Her eardrums had burst in the explosion. So, had David's. In that same moment, Charlie also became aware of a nagging ringing noise that she had not noticed before. Her entire head buzzed with its cadence.

Charlie instinctively closed her eyes and made the sound silent. Or rather she pushed it beneath her consciousness.

David, where's Catherine?

I don't know Charlie? I can't feel her.

Again, Charlie reached out with her mind. As she did, Charlie felt David reaching out as well. After a few moments of blind fumbling, Charlie felt the familiar sensation of Catherine's consciousness. As she had with David, Charlie followed the sensation to find Catherine lying face down on what remained of the warehouse's concrete floor. She too bled from her ears together with several nasty looking wounds in her arms and on her chest.

Charlie touched Catherine with her mind. *Are you ok?*

For a moment, there was no response. Then, *I...I think so.* She turned over and staggered to her feet. *My ears are still ringing from that blast.*

Where is David? Catherine's voice echoed in her mind with more than a little concern.

Over here. Charlie replied as she motioned to Catherine to follow.

Charlie helped Catherine dig David out of the heap of rubble by hand all the time hoping that David was not seriously injured.

As it turned out, David was mostly unharmed beyond some bruises and shallow wounds.

After extricating David from the heap of rubble, the three of them carefully picked over the bombed-out remains of the warehouse in search of their car. The front fifty feet or so had been completely obliterated, leaving only the concrete pad and heaps of rubble behind. Going further back portions of the wall stood between blazing piles of debris. Among these, they found the flaming remains of the Fiat.

And so, David, Catherine, and Charlie began to walk. No one had any idea where to go, only that they had to get away before any more fighter jets could arrive.

II

After walking for an indeterminate distance, they stumbled upon an abandoned Dacia Duster that had only suffered superficial damage in the air raid. A quick flick of the power and Charlie had the engine running. Five minutes later, David, Catherine, and Charlie were on the road, on their way out of Gateshead.

Despite his still-healing burns, David volunteered to drive first. Catherine offered Charlie the front passenger seat, electing to stretch out across the back seat and sleep.

The three fugitives drove south all day until the sun had become a copper coin upon a sky of deep, crimson blood. That night they took refuge in an abandoned roadside motel. There was no electricity, but the water taps still worked. The worst problem was that there was no food. Charlie had been hungry when they stopped and awoke feeling ravenous. David and Catherine both searched the motel for food in vain before eventually admitting that there was nothing and that they had to move on before someone noticed their presence.

Golden sunlight had already begun to peek over the horizon of a royal purple sky when the three of them left their room at the Sheffield Inn, outside of Doncaster. The sky was both beautiful and haunting at once.

That day Catherine volunteered to drive, and though the area appeared deserted she scrupulously avoided the city proper.

As they drove, David explained to Charlie that they would leave Britain and head into France. After that there was no specific plan, only to keep moving to avoid being caught by rioters.

He had not told her with words as all three of them remained unable to perceive sound following the airstrike on Gateshead. Instead his voice spoke directly in her mind. It was in this way that Charlie, David, and Catherine communicated until it became natural and they hardly noticed any difference from the spoken word.

The drive went slowly as they were obliged to avoid the major highways in favor of back roads to avoid strangers. As the miles wore on, Charlie had time to think. It had been only a little over a month since they had escaped Castle Bruce and yet it seemed like an eternity. Everything had changed with dizzying speed.

For Charlie, life had always been cold and cruel, and yet she had never seen anything like this. The entire world was at war with itself. Neighbor against Neighbor. Friend versus friend. And all because of that one terrible night. Except that wasn't true. Not really. This had been building for many years. Charlie understood that. The firestorm and the death of Hailey Suire had been the final straw.

As she thought that last part, Charlie's face flushed with guilt for she knew she had, had a role in that final straw. She had started the fire that had killed Senator Suire. Charlie hadn't meant to harm the senator but that was no excuse. She had killed an innocent.

Charlie felt like crying but would not allow herself. She did not want to worry David and Catherine.

Charlie gazed out the car window and watched skeleton trees silhouetted in harsh white morning rays race by. Then she quickly closed herself off before David or Catherine could sense the sadness and remorse in her heart. For a long time now, a part of her had wished she had never been born. Now, that part of her lamented her existence with a voice as keen and biting as a sharpened razor. Though she would not allow herself to shed a tear externally, in her heart, Charlie wept bitterly for she knew all of this was her fault. Everything bad that had happened to her parents, to David and Catherine, all of the riots, the death, the war, the horror; all of it had happened because she was born a firebrand.

Because of me. Charlie thought bitterly and with intense self-loathing.

Charlie slowly turned away from the window and glanced at the men's gray steel Seiko on her left wrist.

It was February; two months from her tenth birthday, and it was late. As she glanced at the watch she had taken…

-stolen, you stole it from the warehouse-

Ok, yes, fine stolen.

Charlie had stolen the watch because it was the same as the one Daddy wore. The watch that was taken from Daddy the day that the NSA took them both away.

Oh, Daddy, I miss you so much...

In that moment, the pain of losing her father was as bitter as it had been on that terrible day when Robin shot Daddy dead. David and Catherine had become mother and father to her, but they could never replace Mommy and Daddy; instead they were her other mother and father, in addition to Daddy and Mommy.

Charlie had taken the Seiko watch because it was identical to Daddy's watch and somehow that made her feel close to him again.

Now, as she looked at the watch she had stolen, Charlie's left arm began to shake as searing pain radiated out from the still healing burn on her shoulder. She had mostly ignored her shoulder wound while caring for David and Catherine but now that they had healed enough to take charge…well, the pain was still impressive.

As that last thought crossed her mind, Charlie glanced at David. He had stretched out across the back seat and was sleeping soundly.

Snoring, Charlie imagined though she could hear nothing and thus could not be sure. David's expression was deeply peaceful and relaxed. More so than she had seen from him since the first day she had known him.

Charlie felt a rush of combined guilt and love so intense that it brought tears to her eyes. David and Catherine had been so kind to her. They had made her their daughter and…they were her second Mommy and Daddy; the only Mommy and Daddy she had now. She loved them more than she could find words to describe. Charlie stole a quick glance at Catherine and felt a resurgence of that same combined feeling. Catherine looked tired and badly frightened. Charlie gave her a weak smile as she touched Catherine's mind with her own.

It's ok. We're safe for now. Charlie told her, repeating the words she had heard many times from both David and Catherine and knowing that they were an utter lie.

Catherine's voice laughed in Charlie's mind. *Shouldn't I be the one telling you that everything's going to be ok?*

Charlie giggled momentarily because in some strange way the whole thing did seem funny. Here she was comforting her adoptive mother despite being only a child herself.

Charlie offered Catherine a brief smile and then turned over and closed her eyes. As she drifted in darkness, Charlie's mind returned to the past. The memories it presented were not happy ones for they revisited her captivity with the Black Empire.

Unwillingly, Charlie found herself dragged back through torment and temptation as her memory rebelled against her conscious control. She remembered everything, felt everything, and beneath it all lay the old, familiar bloodstain of *Hate.*

III

Charlie awakened many hours later when Catherine stopped for the night. By this time, the sky had become a palette of rich golds, reds, and purples, as if painted by an invisible hand. They had arrived in the outskirts of Dover on the shores of the English Channel.

This time they spent the night in an abandoned stone cottage. It would be the last time she would sleep in a real bed for many weeks.

Charlie's sleep was fitful and plagued by nightmares. She awoke ravenous, and as with the roadside motel of the previous day, the stone cottage contained no food. David went out in the early evening to look for food and returned sometime later with a pair of rabbits. The sight of the poor, dead bunnies made her sad but only for a moment. Charlie was too hungry to worry about them for long.

As it turned out, the rabbits were mostly skin and bones. David and Catherine gave her the lion's share of what little meat there was and made her eat it. Charlie finished the stringy meat quickly feeling mostly unsatisfied.

Still, she worried more about David and Catherine who had split half of a rabbit's breast between them. They both looked ravenous and exhausted. Charlie knew they could not go on like this for long.

IV

After eating, David and Catherine went into the cottage's master bedroom and shut the door.

Once inside, David turned to Catherine. *We're going to have to get a boat from here.*

For a moment, she did not reply. Then: *What do you have in mind?*

He shook his head, unsure of what to do. *I don't know. But we can't very well take the Chunnel train.*

David thought for a moment. They were outside the port of Dover. Even with the riots, there had to be ships carrying goods across the Channel. Surely someone would be willing to ferry three passengers for the right price. Money would not be an issue, he could steal it from an ATM quickly enough. The problem was the risk of approaching a stranger to ask for transport. There was an equal chance that any ship's captain would either accept David's offer or simply rob him and contact the authorities, or worse the rioters.

There have to be ships still operating, even in this mess. David ventured slowly. *I can find an ATM and get some money. Somebody should be willing to take us across the Channel for enough cash.*

Are you sure it's safe? Catherine replied cautiously.

No. David responded flatly. *But I don't see any other options. We have to keep moving.*

I know. Catherine answered softly. *But David…I'm scared. You almost died at Castle Bruce, and you're still recovering. I don't want to lose you.*

I'll be careful. David replied.

In truth, he was afraid too. After everything he had been through; all the times he had nearly lost Catherine and Charlie; he did not want to take yet another risk that might take his family away from him forever. Still, he knew there was no other way, and he certainly had no intention of asking Catherine to take the risk.

Keep Charlie safe while I'm gone.

I will. Catherine's voice remained soft. *Just…hurry back.*

I will.

And with that final word, David impulsively leaned in and kissed his wife, relishing her lips for a few moments before leaving.

V

David found an ATM without too much trouble. A quick flick of the power and he was twenty thousand pounds richer. David quickly packed the money into a large garbage bag as it rapidly spilled out of the ATM. Once the machine was empty, David closed the garbage bag, tossed it over his shoulder and carried it to the car. He was genuinely surprised by the bag's weight. He would never have imagined that paper money could be so heavy. A few minutes later he was back on the road on his way to the Port of Dover.

He found both the City and Port of Dover a shattered remnant of their former glory, devoid of all human presence their buildings lying in burned-out ruins. Whatever happened here caused all of the residents to leave.

Well, most of the residents…

He detected a slight scent of burning wood and searing meat. Someone was cooking. There was also a faint odor of diesel fumes. As he neared the port, David's pulse began to quicken. Something was wrong. David saw no one, but there was an intense sensation of extreme danger; the same feeling he had felt that terrible night at Castle Bruce.

In that moment David was glad that he had left Catherine and Charlie behind at the abandoned cottage.

He found the port mostly destroyed. Heaps of shattered concrete and cinderblock marked the graves of buildings. Scattered amongst the ruins lay the twisted metal corpses of heavy cranes, forklifts and shipping containers. The water surrounding the port was black with oil and littered with the torn remnants of countless sunken ships. To his dismay, David realized that the port must have been bombed from the air.

I'll be lucky if there's anyone left alive here.

As he drove further, David realized that the destruction was not as complete as he had initially thought. Several smaller boats remained afloat. All of them appeared abandoned, but as he grew nearer still David observed signs of human activity. Several of the supposedly abandoned boats sported fresh diesel soot, while a nearby tugboat showed signs of someone's recent attempt to remove many years of caked on rust.

David elected to approach a fishing trawler. While nothing about this boat distinguished it from any of the others, David's instincts told him that he should try here.

As it turned out, the boat belonged to a tall and stocky man in his sixties. He introduced himself as Wil.

At first, Wil was suspicious of David and greeted him with the muzzle of a pump shotgun. David found communication difficult as he was still mostly deaf and had only lip reading as a means to try and understand Wil's speech. Despite this, David easily persuaded Wil to lower his shotgun and connected with him enough to obtain passage for the cost of £4,000.00.

After negotiating with Wil, David returned to the little stone cottage without incident to find Catherine and Charlie playing Texas Hold 'em at the dining room table.

Looks like we're going to be here another night. As he touched Catherine and Charlie's minds, he fought to keep his tone as cheerful as possible.

Did you find someone to take us across the Channel? Catherine asked cautiously.

Yes. David replied. *He says the Channel is very dangerous and he will need a day to prepare.*

Ok. Catherine met his eyes steadily. David could feel her concern. *What time do we meet him?*

Eight o'clock tomorrow evening. David answered.

As his mind spoke the words, it occurred to him that he too should be concerned. This man Wil was a total stranger and could be capable of anything. David had sensed no malice in the man, but his psychic senses had failed him most spectacularly in the past. It had been one such failure that had led to the capture of his family by the Black Empire.

And as he thought that, his heart flooded with guilt. His wife and daughter had suffered terribly at the hands of the Black Empire. Charlie still had not regained the full use of her left arm. They had *tortured* her. All because he had failed to recognize a threat.

Charlie must have sensed something troubling him, for she came over and hugged him tightly. *I love you, David.* Her voice whispered in his mind with great sincerity. *And it's going to be ok.*

David ruffled her hair. *I love you too, Charlie. And I know it's going to be ok.* As his mind spoke the words David forced a smile for Charlie and Catherine's sake. *Everything is going to be fine.*

David would come to deeply regret that last lie in the days to come. For things were far worse than he could ever have imagined.

VI

The remainder of the evening went by uneventfully. This time Catherine went out to find food and returned carrying a few cans of Spam. Once again, David and Catherine insisted that Charlie eat the majority of the food. For her part, Charlie found the Spam less than appealing, but she was hungry enough not to care. So, she wolfed the greasy, tasteless meat down quickly. When Charlie had finished she was still hungry but said nothing as she did not want to make David and Catherine worry.

After dinner, the three of them played cards for a while before Charlie decided to go to bed. She was exhausted, though she doubted that she would be able to sleep. She had not had a restful night since arriving at Castle Bruce, and when she did sleep she was plagued with nightmares and flashbacks to her time with the Black Empire.

Tonight, was no exception. Charlie fell asleep as soon as her head hit the pillow, but her sleep was not restful.

VII

Before long, Charlie found herself standing in that same golden forest she had visited in her dreams so many years ago. Once again, she was with David and Catherine, just walking and chatting about nothing in particular.

For the first time in a long time, she felt happy. They were approaching a clearing, she recognized its sun-kissed grass and soft trees. A gentle breeze tugged at her clothing. The scents of pine and field grasses filled her nose.

Charlie smiled. *It's so beautiful. It's like heaven.*

David touched her shoulder gently. *I'm glad you're having a good time. Come on, we're almost there.*

This is the best place for picnics. Charlie turned and saw for the first time a large picnic basket in Catherine's right hand.

Charlie ran ahead, calling to David and Catherine to hurry. As she neared the clearing, the sunlight grew warmer and brighter. Charlie's smile widened, her heart filling with indescribable joy. As she entered the clearing, the sky began to darken. Big black storm clouds began massing on the horizon and pine, and field grass gave way to the harsh metal of ozone. Thunder rumbled in the distance. Charlie stopped short, frozen in place by sudden fear. Within a few seconds, the sky went from blue to haunting green and then pitch black. Purple-white lightning forked directly above, followed a moment later by an angry peal of thunder. Charlie cried out in fear and whirled around to see that David and Catherine were gone. A panicked sound, half moan half sob, escaped her throat.

Charlie tried to call to David and Catherine; heeding the advice of the remaining logical part of her mind that insisted that they couldn't be too far away but found that her voice had deserted her. Panic began building in her chest. A second bolt of lightning slashed through the air, illuminating the entire world in brilliant purple for an instant. This time there was no peal of thunder but rather a furious roar that nearly took her off her feet. Charlie screamed in terror for she knew what was to come next.

And sure enough, the dark man reappeared. Purple lightning outlined his tall, powerfully muscular frame. Charlie turned to run only to discover that the forest had disappeared behind a horde of faceless black shadows. The air rang with their angry shouts. Before she could react, the horde charged. Charlie froze in place. The dark man's iron grip closed upon her shoulder and drew her back. In the same movement, he produced a massive, black sword and brandished it at the charging shadows. Charlie wanted to struggle, oh how she wanted to struggle, but she could not. Her body remained frozen. She reached for the Power only to find that it too had abandoned her. The shadows were closing now. Steel flashed before her eyes, and the nearest figure in black collapsed in a cloud of red mist, its head landing at her feet with a dull thud. Instinctively, Charlie recoiled in horror and suddenly found herself free of the dark man's grasp.

She backed away as the dark man continued fighting. Though the shadows posed no threat to him personally, the dark man was losing. Black figures streamed by him on both sides as he cut his way through the center of the horde. Charlie turned to flee and was seized by both arms. Before Charlie knew what was happening many hands dragged her away even as her desperate cries echoed on the stormy air.

VIII

Suddenly everything went dark. A voice was screaming. It took Charlie a full three minutes to realize that the voice was her own. The bedroom door opened, and someone came in. It took Charlie another three minutes to recognize David and Catherine. Their frightened voices echoed in her mind, but she could neither understand their words nor could she stop herself from screaming.

The power was a living thing inside her. She bit it back as best she could.

STOP IT! STOP IT NOW!

Fueled by terror, the power continued to spiral upward. She held on as best she could. David had taken her into his arms and was gently stroking her sweat streaked hair. She wanted to scream at him to get away before she set him on fire, but she could not make her mouth or mind form the words.

The room had become explosively hot. Then suddenly Charlie felt the power go out and a wastebasket in the corner erupted into flame. David let her go for a moment, turned and thrust out with his own power. In an instant, the wastebasket was swallowed in a cloud of white. At the same time, the temperature inside the bedroom dropped precipitously. Goosebumps rashed out on her skin, and Charlie began to shiver. She was no longer screaming. Instead, she sat in dead silence feeling terrible guilt for what she had done.

It's ok. David's voice whispered in her mind. *It was just a dream, Charlie. That's all. Just a bad dream.*

Charlie stared past him towards the trashcan she had torched. It now sat frozen solid, like brittle crystal. She had lost control of the power. Thought it was only for a moment she could have burned the stone cottage to the ground. She had placed David and Catherine in danger because she couldn't control the power.

She didn't cry. Rather Charlie sat gazing intently at the frozen remains of the wastebasket feeling like a piece of shit.

Her behavior was not lost on David. *It's ok.* His voice repeated in her mind. *It was an accident. It's ok.*

Charlie did not say a word as David and Catherine tucked her in and kissed her goodnight. David had promised to stay with her for a while. She was grateful, but remorse kept her silent. She had let the power out. It had been an accident, but that didn't make her feel any better. She could have hurt David and Catherine.

IX

Charlie did not sleep, so David sat with her all night. Neither of them spoke a word, and by the time the sallow sun finally peeked over the horizon both father and daughter were exhausted.

Charlie wanted desperately to sleep but could not. So, she spent the day in bed alone with her thoughts, getting up only briefly to eat when David called her to dinner.

This time dinner consisted of squirrel meat. Charlie found it less than appealing but ate anyway. Then after finishing, she went back to bed.

David followed her into her room. *Are you ok, Charlie?* His face demonstrated genuine concern. *You've been quiet since last night.*

I'm fine. Charlie replied flatly. *I'm just tired. I couldn't sleep last night.*

David studied her carefully. *Are you sure you're ok? You look like something's bothering you.*

Charlie drew a deep breath. *I lost control of the power. I don't know why. It hasn't happened in a long time.*

David gave her a look of deep compassion. *It's ok, Charlie. Sometimes accidents just happen, and you were pretty upset.*

She was not placated. *That's no excuse.*

Charlie, you don't need an excuse. I know you didn't do it on purpose. And nobody was hurt. So, don't worry about it. As he spoke that last part in her mind, he offered her a warm smile.

Charlie hugged him tightly, nearly bursting into tears. David always seemed to know the right thing to say. She loved him deeply.

Try to get some sleep, Charlie. David's voice was saying. *We have a long trip ahead of us tonight.*

Ok, David.

For the first time, Charlie felt like she could sleep. She no longer felt guilty or afraid. In that moment she felt at peace.

Charlie laid back in her bed and closed her eyes. David drew the covers up to her chin and kissed her on the forehead.

Sleep well.

X

Charlie finally did sleep, deeply and restfully. This time she did not dream, and when she awoke, it was dark outside.

Charlie glanced at her watch. *Six o'clock.* It was time to get up. Charlie got out of bed and walked out of her bedroom for the last time. She found David and Catherine in the living room gathering up what little supplies they had.

Instinctively she reached out to them with her mind. *Can I help?*

Sure. David's voice replied in her mind. He gestured towards a pile of blankets. *How about you carry those out to the car.*

Ok.

Charlie gathered up the blankets and carried them out to their little gray Duster. She easily opened the trunk with her mind and placed the bedding inside.

As Charlie silenced the power she felt a renewed sense of extreme danger. A short time later, on the way to the Port of Dover, Charlie shared her fears with David and Catherine. Both reassured her that everything would be fine. Charlie knew they were lying, not out of malice but out of a desire to comfort her.

It didn't take long for them to arrive at the boat that would carry them across the English Channel. A man named Wil greeted them. Though he was imposingly tall and stout, Charlie was not intimidated. She felt at once that this man was not a threat, and in truth was not even interested in their money. Instead, she sensed concern and compassion in him. Wil had once had a family of his own and…

She decided not to probe further for she sensed that she would find only sadness. This man had recently experienced tragedy. She did not need to know the details.

The trip across the Channel went by mostly without incident. Wil told them of a few radio contacts reporting submarine activity, but nothing close enough to be a significant threat.

Two hours after disembarking, they arrived in Calais, France.

The city was mostly deserted save for a few homes where candlelight flickered from boarded-up windows. The sensation of danger was stronger here. Something was very wrong. David and Catherine must have felt it too for they wasted no time in driving out of town in a stolen Fiat.

The French countryside was littered with burned-out husks of vehicles, smoldering wreckage of homes, and numerous dead bodies. The remains of a recent, bloody battle. Even from within the car's controlled environment, Charlie could detect the pervasive, rancid, and cloying smell of death.

For the first time, she understood the magnitude of what had occurred. This was more than a rash of rioting, more than a civil war in Scotland and England. This was world war.

As they drove through the blasted remains of what had once been northwestern Europe, Charlie's sense of danger grew and grew. She began to understand, something terrible had happened. The darkness was spreading. That thing that had begun so many years ago was metastasizing. Charlie was deeply afraid. She sensed that David and Catherine too understood the import of what they were witnessing. She could feel their fear and horror.

The night went slowly and with little conversation among David, Catherine, and Charlie. As the cold amber sun began to peek over the horizon, David pulled the car into a ramshackle barn. Charlie felt exhausted, having not slept at all that night.

Once inside, David and Catherine laid out bedrolls with the blankets and pillows they had taken from the little cottage in Dover.

Five minutes after her head hit the pillow, Charlie was dead to the world.

XI

David awoke to find himself shivering fiercely. The air had grown frigid, and the old barn gave no protection from the elements outside. Late afternoon sunlight shone brightly through the spaces in the slatted walls. He was alone. Catherine and Charlie were gone. For a moment panic welled up within his heart before he felt their presence outside. He groaned softly and eased himself up. His back crackled and his muscles complained. This wasn't the first time he had slept on the ground, but his body objected just the same. David rubbed his eyes and slowly stood up. As he did, his stomach grumbled for food that would not be forthcoming. Once on his feet, David headed out of the barn and found Catherine and Charlie sitting together under a nearby tree.

He reached out to them with his mind. *You two ready to move on?*

Yeah, but David, I'm hungry. Charlie's voice answered plaintively in his mind.

I know Charlie. I am too. We'll see if we can find someplace along the road. He bent down and picked her up. *Come on, kiddo. The sooner we get on the road, the sooner we can get some dinner.* He was lying through his teeth and Charlie had to know it, but she gave no sign. Catherine gave him a look as she passed him on the way to the car but said nothing. She didn't have to; the message was clear.

They had to find something to eat. David was hungry, Charlie was hungry, Catherine was hungry. They couldn't go on like this.

David drove for two hours before stopping in a small farm town near the border between Germany and Poland. There were no restaurants here, but there was a small market, and he still had over ten thousand Euros left from an ATM he had ripped off on the outskirts of Dunkirk. David bought a large bag of apples and another of oranges as well as a big bunch of grapes and several bunches of bananas.

The fruit was delicious, but that didn't matter that much. David was more concerned with feeding Catherine and Charlie. They were all that really mattered.

After David, Catherine, and Charlie had each eaten their fill they returned to the road to run once again. Over the next three days, they traveled through Poland, Lithuania, and Latvia before entering Russia.

During this time, David found his hearing slowly returning. Likewise, Charlie and Catherine too recovered from their blast-induced deafness until, by the time they had entered Russia, the three of them could talk normally.

Since the withdrawal of American forces from Iraq and Afghanistan and the subsequent collapse of the Middle East, Eastern Europe had become a modern-day old west. Anarchy and mob justice ruled. While the governments of the Eastern European nations remained intact, they were no more than figurehead institutions. The real power lay in the hands of criminals and rogue military forces. Nowhere was this more true than in Russia. Ruled by its powerful criminal underworld and a handful of corrupt generals and former KGB insiders, Russia had become a genuine gangster's paradise. Thus, it was perhaps the last place on earth where David, Catherine, and Charlie would be expected to hide. Still, this was not the reason David had chosen to flee there. His choice was one born of desperate grasping rather than even momentary consideration. He had taken his wife and daughter east because there was nowhere else to go.

XII

It was late, and they had arrived in the outskirts of an unknown Russian city. Charlie was ravenous. It had been three days since she had last eaten. David had tried to find food, but there was none to be had. There were a few restaurants, but David said it was too dangerous, someone might recognize them. So, they had gone hungry rather than risk being discovered. Her stomach grumbled angrily, reminding her of the urgency of its demand. As if she needed reminding.

"David, I'm hungry." The words passed her lips before she could stop them. She hated to complain. She knew it would only make David and Catherine feel bad.

"I know Charlie. So am I." He turned back towards her and gave a forced smile. "We'll get something soon. I promise."

"Ok." She looked out of the car window and saw nothing but abandoned storefronts and burned-out shells of buildings. A sign some ways back along the road had indicated in strange letters that this was Saint Petersburg, but it didn't look like they would find any food here.

This place was like no other city she had seen. There were no lights in the windows of the buildings, and most of them appeared long abandoned. The streets were littered with garbage, and empty save for a few scattered street people dressed in rags who ran like rats at the approach of their car. This was no city at all, but a ghost town long forgotten.

As they passed deeper into St. Petersburg, the city began to change. The abandoned buildings were replaced by gaudy neon signs advertising "girls girls girls" and "XXX movies". Outlines of scantily clad women flickered in red against the darkened sky. Other signs advertised all manner of alcoholic beverages and drugs while still others took on the shapes of dice, roulette wheels or playing cards. There was even a gigantic neon cowboy, looking decidedly out of place among the snow-covered rooves and sidewalks of Saint Petersburg.

The scattering of ragged street wretches was replaced by streetwalkers, pimps, dealers and gangsters each sporting their own variant of flamboyant garb. Beat up old cars crowded the curbs and streets interspersed on occasion by sleek sports cars and swanky Mercedes Benzes or BMW limousines. As they continued towards the city center, the buildings continued to grow more decadent and the people on the street wealthier and more corrupt. It occurred to her that she had been wrong about this place, this was not a ghost town but a city of the damned, a place not of the forgotten but of the lost.

The feeling here was much like that of the Black Imperial capital world of Ifrinn, though perhaps not as strong. The evil in the air was palpable, like an intensely cold draft. Charlie shivered slightly and drew her coat more tightly around her body.

"Are you alright, Charlie?" David asked from the front seat.

"I'm fine." She wasn't really fine, but she did not wish to frighten him.

“We’re almost there, Charlie.” He spoke as though he knew where “there” was though she felt strongly that he had no more idea of where they were going than she did.

Eventually, David turned onto a side street and parked the car. “Are you guys up for a little walk?”

Charlie nodded.

“Sure, David, but where to?” Catherine inquired.

“We’re going to look for something to eat.”

“Ok.” Catherine’s voice was unpersuaded.

The air outside the car was bitterly cold, much worse than Charlie had imagined. Gusts of wind sliced through her clothing as though she were naked. David must have seen how miserable she was for he draped an arm over her shoulders and pulled her tight against him even as he did the same for Catherine on the other side. They walked for several blocks like this without speaking. It was strange, no one on the streets seemed to even take notice of them. It was as if the firestorm at Castle Bruce had never happened. Charlie found this both comforting and frightening at once for she had to wonder whether these people truly did not recognize or care to recognize them or if this was some kind of trap. She did not sense a trap, but she felt a powerful sense of danger none-the-less.

Eventually, David stopped in front of a large and brightly lit building. A sign on the front indicated its purpose.

The Devil’s Pit. Again, the words appeared in strange letters she did not recognize yet could read as if she had known them all her life. Below this sign was another less brightly lit one reading: *Food and Drinks served 24/7. Nightly entertainment. Live Nude Girls. Professional MMA.* This place, whatever it was, exuded an electric sensation of excitement and corruption.

“This looks like as good a place as any to get something.” David’s voice was overly upbeat.

Catherine glanced at him and whispered. “Are you sure this is a good idea? What if someone recognizes us?”

“Do you have a better idea?” David replied. “We can’t keep going without eating.”

To this, she had no answer.

Charlie knew what sort of place this was but somehow didn’t think she would see anyone taking off their clothes tonight. Something else was going on here though she did not know what.

A large man in black jeans and a black t-shirt greeted them at the door. “What do you want?”

“How much to get in?” David asked in reply.

“Tonight is special night. Championship fighting tournament. Two hundred American dollars each.”

"Do you take Euros?" David inquired.

"Four hundred Euros each then." The man replied in an annoyed tone.

David quickly counted out the money and paid the man.

"You and woman may come in, but girl must wait outside."

"I just paid for all three of us." David's voice remained reasonable, but Charlie could sense his annoyance.

"I told you, girl must wait outside. We do not allow children in club."

"Look," David said tiredly. "We're just looking for someplace to eat. We won't stay long. My daughter's well behaved. You can seat us somewhere in the back. You won't even notice she's here."

The man looked disposed to be obstinate, but then his face softened. "I have daughter of my own her age. All right I let her in, but she must be silent, or I throw all three of you out. Understand."

David nodded.

"Good. Wait here while I look to see if boss is watching." He disappeared for a few minutes then returned to hustle them inside.

The door led into a long corridor lit in red. At the end of this corridor was a second door that opened onto a stairway lit in red that led down. The stair ended in yet another door on the other side of which was the main club room. The air inside was thick with stale cigarette smoke and cheap booze. Heavy metal rock boomed from old speakers with enough force to make her stomach vibrate. The club was packed with an even mix of men and women of varying ages. Most were young, but there were some older people as well. Their dress was an eclectic mix of formal and anything but formal. There were some cocktail dresses and three-piece suits, some halters and jeans, a few ripped t-shirts, even a group of goths gathered in one corner drinking red wine.

Down here, the lighting was darker and more intensely red. The floors were carpeted, and the walls were padded with leather, topped with red satin wallpaper and accented with chrome buttons and trim.

The room itself was laid out like a miniature Coliseum. At the center, the room dropped down, forming a concrete pit. Dried blood smeared the bottom of the arena telling the tale of many recent fights. About a foot above the floor of the pit was the first of a series of graded concentric circles containing narrow black wood tables and chairs. A steel retaining barrier provided the only separation between spectator and spectacle.

Someone here has the power. The realization came to Charlie all at once, though she had known since arriving at the club. *There's someone here like us.* She could feel it in the air.

The doorman led them to a corner table near the bottom of the entrance ramp. Not long after they were seated, a waiter appeared to take their drink orders before vanishing into the kitchen. A few minutes later, he returned and set three Cokes on the table in front of them before taking their orders and disappearing into the kitchen once more.

Suddenly, the lights dropped, and the room fell silent. A moment later tinny strains of *Crazy Train* began flowing from the ancient speakers, followed a moment later by an over-enthusiastic male voice.

"Ladies and gentlemen. This is the final matchup of tonight's tournament. Introducing first, from Vladivostok, Siberia, weighing in at four hundred and ten pounds, Ivan Dimitrivitch." The words were spoken in Russian, but Charlie understood them perfectly.

As the name was spoken, a massive blond-haired man strode into the room from a hidden door and headed towards the center pit. Charlie stared at him in combined awe and fear. Dimitrivitch was huge, more monster than a man. Standing next to him, she would have only come up to his hips. Dimitrivitch was not slender, but his girth was anything, but fat for the man's pale skin was pulled taut to the breaking point by layer upon layer of rippling muscle. Dimitrivitch might have been handsome, were it not for his freakish size. To Charlie he was terrifying.

Upon entering the pit, Dimitrivitch removed his blood-colored robe and tossed it over the retaining barrier leaving him naked save for his boxing trunks and wrestler's boots.

Suddenly the music changed to a heavy metal rendition of *Turn the Page.*

"And his opponent, from Moscow, weighing in at two hundred pounds even, the undefeated Stephen Wolf." At the sound of his name, a second man appeared. This one was much smaller and quite ordinary looking when held against the freakishly massive Dimitrivitch. Wolf's hair was jet black, and his face was a soft cream color. He was dressed in old Soviet military dress black complete with knee-high steel-plated riding boots, and he had the power. She could feel it in the air, pulsing and throbbing. A slight smile came to her face for she knew this man was not a Dark Knight. He was a friend or rather a potential friend. This man could be trusted or, so she hoped.

Dimitrivitch did not move or blink as he watched his opponent slowly approach the pit. His emotionlessness was indeed very intimidating, and Charlie feared for Wolf. Though she did not know him, she did not wish to see him hurt.

Wolf approached the pit slowly with an air of supreme confidence. It was almost as if he had already won, and this was but a mere formality. Upon reaching the retaining barrier, Wolf stopped. For a moment, he was perfectly still. Then suddenly his body tensed and in one smooth motion Wolf leapt up to the top rail of the retaining barrier. He balanced there for a moment before somersaulting into the pit.

"This is the last fight of tonight's tournament ladies and gentlemen. The winner of this bout will walk away with five million US dollars. If you have not yet placed your bets, ladies and gentlemen now is the time."

There was a brief shuffle at one end of the room as several of the Goths made their way to the betting window opposite the door. The voice waited patiently for them to return to their seats before continuing.

"All betting is now closed. Fighters to your positions."

Wolf and Dimitrivitch slowly approached the center of the pit. When they had closed to within approximately two feet of each other, they stopped and slid into fighting stances.

"Shake hands and come out fighting."

The two men extended their hands and shook quickly. Before Wolf could fully withdraw his hand, Dimitrivitch swung hard. Wolf swiftly moved out of the way, countering with a punch of his own. Wolf's fist connected with Dimitrivitch's left cheekbone with a sharp smack. Dimitrivitch didn't even blink.

The power was flowing in the air like invisible electricity. The hairs on Charlie's arms stood on end.

Dimitrivitch swung again and missed. Wolf replied with another sharp right hand to the face. Again, there was no effect despite the power of the blow. Dimitrivitch responded by attempting to grab Wolf by the throat. Wolf sidestepped, grabbed Dimitrivitch's arm and hurled him across the pit. Dimitrivitch landed hard on his back, but in a moment was once more on his feet, and on the offensive. Again, Dimitrivitch moved to grab Wolf but this time when Wolf attempted to counter Dimitrivitch slipped out of Wolf's grasp and locked him into a bear hug. Wolf struggled against the larger man for a few minutes, his air nearly cut off.

Then, to Charlie's amazement, Wolf somehow managed to break free. Before Wolf could counter-attack, Dimitrivitch grabbed Wolf and hurled him across the pit. Wolf struck the retaining barrier hard and landed on his stomach with a dull thud. Without a moment's rest, Wolf got up and leapt at Dimitrivitch, extending his right leg as flew through the air. The jump kick leveled Dimitrivitch. Unfortunately, he didn't stay down for long. As Wolf moved in to follow up, Dimitrivitch grabbed his legs and pulled him off his feet. Then he grabbed Wolf by the throat and slammed him to the ground. This was followed by a second chokeslam, and then a third. Charlie looked on in horror, certain that Wolf would be seriously injured. To her surprise, he managed to break free and counter-attack with a throat punch. He followed this a moment later with a low thrust kick and a roundhouse to the side of the head. Dimitrivitch staggered backward but did not fall. Wolf somersaulted forward into an inverted scissors kick. Blood sprayed from Dimitrivitch's shattered nose, splashing across Charlie's face. Still, Dimitrivitch did not fall. Wolf then spun around and backhanded Dimitrivitch across the face with a closed fist. This was immediately followed by a backward somersault kick that sent Dimitrivitch flying across the remaining distance of the pit. He struck the retaining barrier hard and fell flat on his face. This time he did not get up. Charlie sat calmly, as Dimitrivitch's still warm blood trickling down her left cheek. She watched Wolf with combined awe and fear as he walked to the center of the pit and stood at attention, waiting for the voice to acknowledge the obvious.

"And the winner and still undefeated tournament champion, Stephen Wolf!"

Wolf remained stoic, without even a slight victorious smile. A fat, balding man in a black tuxedo appeared from the same hidden door through which the two fighters had entered earlier and approached the pit. Upon entering, he took Wolf's arm and raised it in victory.

Wolf's expression remained fixed for a few seconds before suddenly changing to something suggestive of combined confusion and surprise. In that same moment, his eyes fell directly upon Charlie.

Charlie met his gaze with an equally surprised one of her own. He had recognized her, or actually all of them to be more precise. For a moment the two locked eyes, then they broke away. No words were spoken, but something had passed between them, an understanding of sorts. Without speaking or even acknowledging his
victory, Wolf left the pit and headed back towards the hidden door from which he had emerged.

Charlie's heart raced. *He has it too...*

The words echoed again and again in her mind. She was trembling slightly though she was not aware of this. While she did not know Wolf, Charlie felt a connection to this man, a connection much like the one she had felt with David the day they had met.

As she was thinking this, the waiter returned with her order, a bowl of borscht. She wasn't exactly thrilled by red beet soup, and it was precisely as tasteless as she had expected. She had only ordered it because it was one of the few items on the menu she recognized and was willing to trust. Still, it was food, and she was too hungry to care all that much.

Charlie ate absently as her mind was still focused on Wolf. She could feel his power in the air, flowing and pulsing in invisible waves. About halfway through the bowl, Charlie felt him approach. She didn't look up. She didn't have to. Charlie knew at once that it was Wolf because she could feel his power grow in intensity.

Wolf addressed them in perfect English, with only a slightly Russian accent.

"Hello."

David and Catherine both looked up quickly, visibly startled.

"Hi. Who are you?" David's voice was not challenging, only curious.

"My name is Stephen Wolf," Wolf replied directly. "I couldn't help noticing you and your family."

This elicited a slight smile from David. "Yeah, I suppose we're not exactly the kind of people you usually see around here."

"No." Wolf dropped his voice. "Look, I know who you are. I recognize your daughter from the news reports." He turned towards her. "You're Charlene MacLeod."

She nodded. Normally she would have been terrified. She should have been terrified, but she knew deep inside that this man meant them no harm. He was concerned for them and wanted to help. But perhaps the real reason she was not frightened was that he had the power. He understood what they were going through and would not betray them.

"I know all of you have the power. I can feel it. And I know you're in trouble, more trouble than you probably realize. Things are rapidly going to shit around the world."

"Now what's happening?" David asked though he already knew at least part of what was going on.

“See for yourself.” Wolf stood up and motioned for David to follow.

“Hold on a sec.” Charlie could sense David’s immediate suspicion. “I’m not leaving my wife and daughter alone out here.”

“Bring them,” Wolf replied.

Wolf took them back through the hidden door from which he had emerged. Beyond was a narrow, poorly lit, concrete corridor with many doors. Wolf took David, followed by Catherine and Charlie through the second door on the left which opened into what was almost certainly his personal dressing room. The room was small but very plush, having been outfitted with red shag carpeting, matching silk wallpaper and ebony and leather furniture. There was a large mirror polished ebony bar along one wall and a massive entertainment center set into another. A woman clad in an elegant black ballroom gown waited patiently behind the bar.

She looked up as they came in. “Hello, Stephen. Can I offer you or your guests something to drink?”

“No. Just leave us.”

“Of course.” She replied before rapidly departing.

Wolf motioned them over to a black leather couch before flipping on the radio behind the bar.

After a few seconds of static, a young woman’s voice came on. “Five more Russian towns were destroyed today in a second series of airstrikes by rogue Russian fighter jets bringing the total to twenty-three towns destroyed in the past two weeks. American radio broadcasts report an additional six airstrikes over the midwestern United States bringing their total to approximately forty.” The woman’s voice was tense with fear.

Wolf flicked off the radio. “You three have managed to really fuck things up. A group calling itself the Resistance has seized control of a large portion of our military including several divisions of the army, eight naval capital ships, and six wings of MiG-29’s and SU-35s. They also have control of a chemical munitions dump in Siberia. Radio broadcasts from America are saying that they have had similar success over there.”

“Shit.” The word passed David’s lips as little more than a terrified whisper.

Charlie shook with terror. Her superior intellect had already filled in all the details of what she had just heard. They were killing each other because of her. The death of Haile Suire had been the final straw. After decades of having their liberties slowly stripped away, Haile Suire had been their last hope for a reprieve. When she died, it became painfully clear that freedom would never return. This realization combined with the sudden revelation that there were people out there with god-like power left only violence as an answer. Charlie suddenly felt great sadness and fear.

Wolf continued. “Everyone’s looking for you three, and here you are on my doorstep.” His tone was more than slightly angry but behind it, she sensed concern and fear. “You put me in danger just by being here. If I recognized you, someone else will too, and those Resistance morons will be here looking for you. If they find out about me, then everything I have will be ruined.” He paused. “I spent *years* building what I have here, working my way up to the big money fights, getting people’s trust and you three are putting it all at risk."

Sudden anger flashed in Charlie's heart. He wasn't supposed to be like this. He was supposed to understand, to care.

"I want to help you three. Hell, I don't really have a choice, do I? But I need you to leave before somebody else recognizes you." Wolf went to the desk in the corner, opened the top drawer, and took out a large roll of money which he then thrust into David's hands. "Here, take this and get lost. You can finish your meals back here. I'll take care of the bill. But then I want you to get the hell out of here. Tonight. Right away before somebody figures out who you are."

David glared at Wolf but said nothing in response. There really wasn't anything to say. Charlie understood that. What she didn't understand was why this man was sending them away. She realized intellectually that he had a lot to lose by joining with them. Wolf had a comfortable life as a pit fighter that would be gone if they were discovered with him. But this was all in her mind. In her heart, she could not understand. He had the power too. He had to know what they were going through. How could he turn them away? Charlie sat pondering this question as she finished her dinner.

Wolf sat and watched silently as they ate. When they had finished he stood up.

"Do you need anything else? Dessert perhaps?"

David and Catherine both looked at Charlie.

She shook her head. She wasn't hungry for sweets. In fact, she felt a little nauseous.

"Then take the money and get the hell out of here." His tone was neutral. There was no hostility or malice, only a simple request and yet Charlie was furious with him for not joining them.

As they stood up to leave, there was a sharp bang on the door. Wolf turned to answer, but before he could, the door flew open to reveal a large, heavily armed, and irate crowd. The man at the front of the crowd addressed them in English.

"You're the McAuliffes, I assume." He drew a Makarov from within his sports jacket. "You'll come with me now." The weapon's nickel-plated exterior gleamed menacingly under the soft lights.

Charlie froze in terror. The power was already alive within her.

Stop it, please!

She tried to fight it back, but it would not be silenced. Over the roar of the power, she could feel the cold malice of the gathered crowd.

"Let's go." The man demanded.

No one moved for an instant. Then David stepped between the man and her. "We're not going anywhere with you."

"You will come with me now, or I will shoot you where you stand." The man snapped back as he leveled his gun.

"You know who we are." Behind David's calm tone, Charlie could sense his growing fear. "And you know what Charlie can do. I suggest you leave us alone before something happens."

The man glared menacingly. "I'm not going anywhere."

Before any of them could do anything, Wolf suddenly struck from the side, knocking the man's gun from his hand with a rapid flick of the power. Before the man could react, Wolf followed up by slamming him up against the wall and holding him there. The remainder of the crowd scattered in terror at this unexpected development. Wolf approached the man slowly.

"She's just a little girl Uri, not the monster they made her out to be on the news. Leave her alone. She was just leaving."

"Fuck you!" Uri snapped.

"Listen to me." Wolf continued in a surprisingly reasonable tone. "You know what I can do, Uri. I could break you in half. I have the power too, just like the girl, and I'm a hell of a lot more vicious than she is."

"Fuck you, Wolf!" Uri barked. "You're dead! You and your friends are all dead!"

Wolf glared at him. "You're dead if I want you dead Uri." His tone remained reasonable. "But you're not worth it. I'm going to let you down, and I want you to run away and not turn back. If I see your face again, I'm going to peel it from your skull. Do you understand?"

"Fuck you!! I'm gonna have you and your friend's balls in matching jars on my desk! I'm gonna make you watch while I fuck both of your little girlfriends until they beg me to cut their throats!"

Wolf struck out with the power. As Charlie watched Uri's face went taut and then began to stretch to absurd proportions. A slow gurgling gasp escaped his bruised and bloody lips.

"Don't fuck with me Uri," Wolf replied calmly. "I can splatter your brains all over this wall. That would be a real pretty sight, wouldn't it? A nice brain omelet. You want me to do that?"

"No." The word was barely discernable and sounded more like 'Mo.'

"Then I suggest you leave." Wolf suddenly clamped down on the power dropping Uri to the floor in a heap. "Now."

Uri wasted no time in scurrying from the room.

"Thanks," David said with genuine gratitude. "But what are you going to do now?"

Wolf smiled wryly. "Looks like we're stuck with each other now. Come on, we'd better leave before Uri finds his balls again."

David grabbed Charlie's hand and led her from the room. Charlie followed him mutely, feeling both frightened and grateful at once. She was right about Wolf. He understood. He was just like them, and he understood. And she had gotten him in trouble. Sudden guilt washed through her. Wolf was involved now. They would come after him. They would try to kill him. And it was all her fault. Charlie's cheeks flushed with shame. What had she done now?

I ruined his life.

Sudden hot tears spilled down her cheeks. Everyone she touched got hurt. If it weren't for her, Daddy and Mommy would still be alive, and David, Catherine, and Stephen Wolf would be happy instead of running scared. This was all her fault.

They were getting into a car now. A small, black, two-door Fiat. David was holding her trying to comfort her. It didn't matter. There was nothing he could say to change the fact that she had caused all of this. She had ruined all of their lives. She had ended her parents' lives. And because of her, the world was ending. She was the *Sigilla Prevaricator*. Her birth had begun the end. Everything was falling apart, and it was all her fault.

Chapter 5
Into the Lion's Den

I

We have to get away.

It's beginning again.

We have to get away.

The words echoed over and over in David's head as he raced through the streets of Saint Petersburg in the back of Wolf's car. Charlie and Catherine were beside him. Neither spoke a word. The cold of their fear radiated in the air adding to his own terror. They had been found again, and now they had to run. But where? That was the question. Where could they go? If even Russia was not far enough, where could they go to be safe?

David pondered this question as he hugged his family to his chest and tried to comfort them. "It's alright." He was saying. "Everything's going to be okay."

It was a lie, told for Charlie's benefit, though he sensed she probably knew the truth.
He hated lying, but there was nothing else to say, only the old lie that adults always tell children when they are frightened or upset, that everything will be all right. They tell this lie despite its terrible fallacy for in truth nothing is ever really all right, not in the cruel world that they lived in.

"Everything's going to be fine." He hated himself for telling this lie, but what else could he say? That things were worse this time? That he didn't think they were going to escape? He couldn't tell her that even though he felt very strongly that she already knew.

Something was wrong. David felt it as certainly as he felt his own hands and feet. Angry shouts intermixed with scattered, terrified screams filtered in from the outside. David slowly looked up from Charlie's small tearstained face to see a war zone erupting all around them. A riot had broken out. Huge crowds filled the sidewalks and street, enveloping the car in a sea of angry, frightened faces. Hands and fists pounded at the windows and doors accompanied by militant shouts and chanting in Russian.

David quickly turned to Catherine and Charlie. "Get down!" They hadn't been recognized yet. If no one got a good look at Charlie, they might have a chance.

"I'm scared, David." Charlie's voice was slightly muffled.

David put an arm over her back. "It's ok, Charlie. I don't think they know who we are." He said this as if it mattered but it really didn't. The crowd was hysterical enough that they would attack anyone not recognized.

“What are we going to do, David?” Catherine’s voice was obviously frightened.

“Just keep your head down.”

Wolf suddenly leaned hard on the horn, nearly causing David’s heart to stop. Charlie let out a little squeak. This accomplished nothing other than further enraging the crowd. Wolf leaned on the horn again.

“What the hell are you doing?” David cried heatedly. “You’re just pissing them off.”

“Shut up,” Wolf replied calmly as he leaned on the horn once again. This time the crowd began to thin, granting them a narrow passageway through which to drive. Once the car was clear, Stephen turned to face David. “People around here know to get out of the way when someone honks their horn ‘cause that’s the only warning you get before they speed up. No one around here gives a shit about hit and runs.”

David turned to Catherine and Charlie. “I think it’s ok to sit up.”

They straightened up slowly. Both were wide-eyed with fear.

“Where are we going to go now?” Charlie’s voice was soft and deeply frightened.

“I don’t know. Just away.” In truth, David really had no idea. They had run out of places to go. Where could they go when the whole world was looking for them?

II

They drove all night and through part of the next day before arriving at a small airfield.

“We fly from here,” Wolf stated simply as he pulled the car off the road near the tarmac.

David said nothing in reply, though he wondered, and sensed that both Charlie and Catherine wondered as well, where they were going to fly. There was nowhere to go, no safe haven, no hiding place. The world was ablaze with hate and rage. Anywhere they ran they would undoubtedly be recognized and hunted like vermin. Ogastes had ensured that they were no longer anonymous. The world now knew their names and faces (or rather Charlie’s name and face) and would hunt them to their deaths.

As the four fugitives fled Saint Petersburg, the fires of violence continued to grow. Atrocities abounded around the world. Towns and cities were bombed and burned from the air; riots erupted in cities; men, women, and children were beaten, raped and brutalized; innocents were murdered. All in the name of resisting tyranny.

III

Four people huddled in an abandoned barroom in Geneva, a bottle of cheap liquor passed among them as they talked in frightened, hushed voices.

"Radio broadcast says they found the girl again." The man who spoke was young but appeared old beyond his years. His face was scratched and bruised, and he was missing one of his front teeth where he had been struck in the face with a baseball bat. He went only by Rick, his real name forgotten by necessity.

"Where?" This was an older man who was comparatively less battered, sporting only a black eye and a cut cheek. His name was Gary, nothing more complicated.

"Saint Petersburg." Rick took a slug of cheap gin. "Russia."

"Her parents are smart." A young woman interjected. "They took her to about the only place in the world where she might be safe."

The young woman was also bruised and battered from having weathered many riots. There was black soot on her face and a blistered burn on one cheek where someone had put out a cigarette. Her long red hair was streaked with dirt and ash. She was known only as Kay.

The fourth person, a middle-aged woman, took the gin bottle and drew a long draft. "Does anyone know where she is now?"

This woman was somewhat chunky, though not truly fat and was missing an eye. A crimson-stained bandage covered the still bleeding socket. Below this, her face was as hard as steel, the face of a survivor, the face of one who has been violated. She was called Susan.

"No." Gary took the bottle from Susan and swallowed two mouthfuls of foul liquor. "They've vanished again."

She's dangerous, but the girl is not our problem." As he spoke, Rick took out a cigarette, lit up and took a long drag. "Sales and production are up, but it is getting increasingly dangerous to ship our product.

"That will only benefit us," Gary responded. "Scarcity will drive up the price, and our product is far too desirable to be priced out of the market."

Rick smiled slightly for he knew Gary was right. The drug, known on the streets as *Reaper*, produced a high like a combination of high-grade meth and acid, but the drug's most interesting effect was the psychic powers it gifted its users. These powers were most potent when the drug's high was strongest, ensuring that users would always come back for more. Rick had acquired the formula, and a small sample from a former American intelligence agent right before everything went to shit.

While Rick, Gary, Kay, and Susan sat drinking in Geneva, a group of three, two males and a female, sat discussing the same matter in Moscow. All three were virtually unknown, but to the followers of the Russian Resistance movement, they were gods, for they were the leaders of the insurgency that had seized control of a large portion of the Russian military.

“The girl has escaped us.”

The man who spoke was young and quite handsome. His face was still more boy than man, and his blond hair had been cut into what had once been called a flattop but was now popularly known as a stump. His name was Captain Ivan Stephenov. Stephenov had been in the Russian Army for three years now. In that time, he had advanced quickly to his present rank. By all appearances though he more resembled one of the young buck enlisted men.

“She has to be killed. She’s too dangerous to be left alive.”

As he spoke the older man, one Colonel Uri Nikitakoff, fingered the many decorations on his army uniform. Nikitakoff was a tall and very imposing man of approximately fifty. His iron-gray hair, saddle leather skin, weather-beaten features, and deep-set dark eyes combined to give him a truly fearsome air.

“Yes, I know that,” Stephenov replied, suddenly annoyed. He didn’t need Nikitakoff reminding him of how dangerous the girl was. He had seen the news reports too.

“Well, what exactly do you plan to do about it, Captain Stephenov?”

Now he was pissed. “They have to go somewhere where there’s an airport or at least a large open tract of flat land, or they won’t be able to land that thing. It’s a Leer jet for Christ’s sake, not a damned chopper. So, the only question is where would they run to?”

“Why don’t you just dispatch some MiGs to shoot the damned thing down.” Nikitakoff’s tone of voice was reminiscent of an adult, suggesting an obvious solution to an obstinate and particularly stupid child.

This only served to anger Stephenov further. “Well, I would if I knew where the hell they are. Damned jet must be flying in the grass or something cause none of our radar stations have been able to sight it. I suppose I *could* dispatch a couple of wings to sweep for it, but that would be a big waste of time and fuel. But by all means, if you want me to launch them.”

“Watch your tongue, soldier.” Nikitakoff snapped back, suddenly angry. “Do not forget who you are addressing.”

“Remind me,” Stephenov replied with a sneer.

“I am a superior officer! And you are my subordinate.” Nikitakoff suddenly whipped out his sidearm. “And if you don’t fancy a bullet in the brain I suggest you remember that.”

“Yes, sir.” Stephenov’s tone was anything but serious for he knew Nikitakoff was bluffing. The two of them had been friends for years, but even without that, he knew Nikitakoff couldn’t afford to shoot him. He was the one who had organized the coupe. It was his intelligence connections that had made the whole thing possible. Killing him would only ensure that Nikitakoff lost control of the military and probably wound up dead.

After a moment Nikitakoff’s anger passed and a smile broke through his rocky exterior. “You are right, of course, my friend. It would be foolish to dispatch fighters without knowing the location of our target."

Stephenov nodded, accepting his friend's apology. "It should be no problem to find them anyway. That jet of theirs can only fly so far without refueling. All we have to do is figure out all the places within its flight radius where it could land and have them watched. We should have the girl within forty-eight to seventy-two hours."

"And what exactly do you plan to do with this girl once you find her?" Both men turned at the sound of Ariana's soft, musical voice.

Beautiful, young, fire-haired Ariena. Stephenov's girlfriend of nearly two years. Though perhaps girlfriend was not exactly accurate as all they did most of the time was screw.

"She's a pyrokinetic, and from what they're saying on the radio she's killed before. How do you plan to handle her once you find her?"

Stephenov smiled and slowly drew his sidearm from its belt holster. "How do you usually handle vermin?" He leveled the weapon and fired a single shot at a rat that had been creeping up to a nearby garbage can. The bullet went true, splattering the rat's guts all over the street. "Terminate with extreme prejudice." As he spoke, Stephenov's blood ran cold with fear.

IV

Once they were in the air, David went to the cockpit to talk to Stephen. He found the Russian lying back in his seat with his eyes closed. To anyone else, Stephen would have appeared to be sleeping, but David knew better. He could sense the man's alertness. He was very relaxed, but even in this state of relaxation, he was more wary than a cat stalking its prey.

David stood in silence for a moment before speaking. "Where are we going?"

"Siberia," Wolf answered without opening his eyes.

"Siberia," David repeated dumbly. "Ok."

He didn't really know what to make of this. They would be way out in the middle of nowhere. Except that they would have to find an airstrip to land on which would inevitably be located someplace at least slightly populous, and any city they traveled to would be dangerous.

"Why?"

"I know some people. They might be able to help us escape." Wolf's voice was perfectly neutral, suggesting neither hope nor despair.

David was silent for a moment. "How did you get this plane anyway?"

"I won it." Wolf's voice remained neutral. "Some idiot bet that I couldn't beat him in a fight."

"Oh."

"He lost the jet and three of his front teeth." Wolf cracked his neck with one hand.

David opened his mouth to say something else and stopped as he realized that he didn't really have anything to say. Instead, he turned and walked out of the cockpit.

He found Catherine and Charlie fast asleep in the main cabin. David carefully slid into his own seat, taking pains not to wake them. It didn't take long for him to drift off as well.

V

When he awakened, the plane had grown quiet. A quick glance out the window told him what he already knew: They had landed. The sky had grown lighter, though the sun had not yet peaked over the horizon. Heavy white snow blanketed the ground. David groaned and slowly stood up. Catherine and Charlie were still sleeping. They both looked so peaceful, curled up in one another's arms. A stranger could have mistaken them for vacationers rather than the sad fugitives they were. David sighed and turned away, as sorrow sharp enough to draw blood suddenly welled up within him.

I'm so sorry. I should have never let this happen. I should have done something.

And he knew what he should have done.

Should have learned to use the power. Should have listened to Dad. Should never have trusted Ogastes. Shouldn't have let this happen. Should have fought harder, tried harder, done something...

Slowly, David crossed the cabin, heading towards the cockpit door.

There has to be something to drink around here.

That was the thought on his mind. He was too tired and frightened to think of anything more complicated than that. He just wanted an out, if only for a short time, an escape from the fear and guilt. If he couldn't be happy, he could at least be drunk. Oh, he knew it wouldn't solve anything, but at that moment he didn't care.

David found the cockpit door open and the pilot's seat empty. Wolf was gone.

Son of a bitch left us!

David's first thought before his psychic senses told him differently. The strange Russian had indeed left, but it was to find them transportation not to abandon them. As this realization came over him, David noticed a small slip of paper taped to the control panel above the yoke.

'Left to find a ride. Be back in a few hours. There's food and drinks in the cabinets in the back of the cabin. Don't leave the plane.'

Stephen

David carefully folded the note and slipped it into his jeans pocket. Then he turned and left the cockpit. David found a full refrigerator and pantry in the back as promised. He also found a fully stocked bar, and it was this that he partook of first. After a quick perusal, David took out a fifth of Glenmorangie and poured himself a double in one of Wolf's crystal whiskey glasses. After a few mouthfuls of bitter liquor, he began to feel a little better, and after a couple of drinks, he was able to make himself not care as much. David forced himself to put down the bottle after this. David wanted more, he wanted to get drunk, but he knew he had to stay sober enough to think clearly.

Catherine and Charlie were still asleep. They would be hungry when they awakened. David began to prepare breakfast, taking care not to make any noise. He found some bread and a half dozen eggs, and so decided to make French toast. As he was finishing up, Charlie wandered over, still rubbing her eyes.

"What smells good?"

"Breakfast sweetheart. I thought you and Catherine would like some French toast."

Charlie smiled. "Oh, goodie." For a moment she became a child again, her face filled with youthful glee, totally devoid of adult concerns and fears. Then it passed, and the old troubles returned. She said nothing, but he could see the fear and misery in her eyes. She knew as well as he did that there was no real escape. They were safe here for but a moment, and that was all.

Still, he managed to force a smile in return. "Why don't you go wake Catherine and then wash your hands and by that time I should have everything all set."

"Ok." Her voice did not hold the same mirth as it had but moments before. She turned quickly and scurried off. She was such a sweet little girl. She didn't deserve this.

Ten minutes later, they were sitting down to breakfast. They ate and talked about unimportant things, just as any family would. For that half-hour, they had become normal. It would be for the last time.

After they had finished eating, Catherine and Charlie retired to the bathroom to clean up, while David cleared the breakfast plates. As he was loading the last dish into the dishwasher under the sink, Wolf returned.

"I got us a ride, but we have to go right now."

"Alright, just as soon as Charlie and Catherine finish cleaning up."

"We have to go now." Wolf's voice was patient but insistent.

There was no point in arguing with him. Wolf was right, they had no time to waste. "I'll see if I can hurry them." David closed the dishwasher and walked over to the bathroom door. He knocked gently. "You two almost finished in there?"

"Give us a couple of minutes." Catherine's voice replied from within.

"Stephen's back with our ride, and there isn't much time."

There was silence for about twenty seconds, and then the door opened, and Catherine and Charlie emerged both looking considerably fresher than he felt.

David started back towards the kitchenette in the back when Wolf stopped him. "Don't worry about gathering up anything, we'll have everything we need where we're going."

David wasn't very convinced. He still didn't completely trust Wolf, but there seemed to be no arguing with the man.

Two days later they boarded a Russian container ship loaded down with weapons bound for the Washington coastline. The temptation to stay in Siberia was strong for David. No one knew them. The people here had only the vaguest knowledge of the happenings of the outside world and were baffled by the growing violence.

It didn't matter anyway. David, Catherine, and Charlie were still being hunted, and sooner or later, they would be found no matter how far out in the middle of nowhere they hid. So, David put his family on a rust bucket container ship on its way to Seattle.

VI

Angela Cacy still remembered the day clearly. It was a beautiful, cloudless day as all days on the island were. The sun burned orange in the sky, and the air was still, yet alive with power.

Angela remembered the face of her liberator. Young, innocent as hers had once been. She had felt the girl's compassion, deep in her heart, she still felt it.

Then the power came. The girl bore it, and it was with her. Angela had felt it pulse through her and the girl. It was the power of God. Of that much, she was sure. Whoever this girl was, she was not human, nor was she an angel.

In her mind, Angela could see the pillar of light, stretching from the earth to the heavens, pulsing with unbridled power. Despite its magnitude, the power was not frightening, but rather comforting, even though she was but a child. The pillar grew in intensity until it reached its peak, then it was gone.

In its place was a broadsword. Plain though it was, the blade bore all the power of the pillar. Its only marking was a strange script of ancient days. A script Angela had never seen before and could not read. The sword materialized in her arms, yet strangely she could not feel its weight. Though Angela was locked in stone, she could still feel, see, and hear things, she just could not respond. But somehow, despite its size, this sword had no weight to it at all. It was as if it weren't there, though Angela could feel its hard, metallic form and the phenomenal power that flowed through it.

The girl took the blade from Angela's arms and gave it to the man that was with her. Then the girl left with the man and his wife, leaving her alone.

It was then that the real miracle happened. Angela felt her flesh warming and *softening*. Rather than being stone, she became surrounded by stone, almost like a skin, a skin that was thinning and breaking away. Within minutes the stone had completely broken away, and she was free.

She remained unchanged. She was the same age, the same size, she even wore the same clothing as the day she had been imprisoned.

Angela was confused. She still did not know for sure how she had gotten there. Her last memory was of that NSA man, Vic Garling. He wasn't like the other NSA agents. He could do things, and he carried a broadsword in addition to his gun. Garling had drawn his sword, and she had felt his power in the air. He raised his sword, its blade glowed deep purple and swung at her head. Then she was here, on this strange cliff side, locked in stone. Angela would remain thus for eleven years before another child would free her.

It was then that Angela realized that she was not alone. There had been many others imprisoned on the clifftop, and the girl had freed them all. Now they were milling about as confused as she felt. Several of them tried to talk to her, but she ignored them and left the island alone.

Angela hated people, they had hurt her and taken away the only person who ever loved her. They killed Kurt.

After an unknown period of time had passed, Angela landed on a beach she did not recognize. She would learn later that she was in northern Scotland. Angela would also come to learn that she had somehow been frozen at age nine, the age she had been when she was imprisoned in stone. Sometime after that, Angela was taken by a man in a black leather jacket, who spoke with a Russian accent. His name was Ivan, and he was from Moscow. Angela tried to escape, but he was too strong even for her. Ivan took her back to Russia with him and beat her until she agreed to serve him.

At first, he just had her fight for him. Angela remembered the first time like it was yesterday. Her opponent was a tall and slender man with blond hair and blue eyes. He was dressed like a boxer but fought more like Jackie Chan. Angela entered the ring, terrified and beat him easily. After that, it became a little easier with each fight, but even now three years later she still felt deeply frightened before facing each opponent.

Ivan was like Vic Garling. He had power. That was why he could overpower her. Angela knew it. She could feel it. There was something about both of them. Something dark and terrifying. They seemed to almost radiate cold evil. A word came into her mind, *Dark Knight*, that was the name for them. They were Dark Knights. Whatever a Dark Knight was.

"Angela!"

She turned at the sound of her name.

"Angela, get your ass in here!" It was Ivan.

Ivan was sitting at the bar in the livingroom visibly drunk. His eyes were dark with malicious intent.

"No." Angela was incredulous at her own words.

Ivan's voice dropped. "What did you say?"

"I said no," Angela replied steadily.

Ivan's face paled, and his eyes widened. "You little shit!" Angela could feel the force of his anger.

An invisible wave struck her, throwing her across the room and into the far wall. Angela landed on the floor in a heap. Before she could get up, Ivan crossed the room and dragged her up by her hair, holding her suspended in mid-air. Sharp pain ripped through her scalp.

"You'll do what I tell you to do! You're mine!"

Angela struggled fiercely against Ivan's sturdy grip. Without another word, he hurled her across the room. She struck hard, punching a large hole in the drywall. Pieces of shattered plasterboard rained down on her as she hit the floor. Without thinking, Angela struck out with her power knocking Ivan off his feet.

"Now, you're fucked!" He growled.

An invisible hand closed around her throat and lifted her into the air. Angela wriggled and gasped for air that her closed throat would not admit. Angela struck out wildly with her power, but it was to no avail. The hand only tightened its grip.

"You think you can fuck with me? Huh?" Ivan's voice was filled with righteous indignation. "You think you're hot shit, bitch? You forget who the man is around here. Me! I'm the man! You're just a little piece of shit! That's all you are!"

Angela gagged in response. Her lungs cried out for air.

"I'll make you beg to what I want." His voice was smug.

Her head was swelling until it felt as though it would explode. Her lungs were screaming. White sparks flickered in front of her eyes. She began to panic. She was going to pass out. She was going to pass out and die. The sparks were turning purple and growing into a mist. She could no longer see. She was dying. Then just as she was about to lose consciousness, the hand released her, and she collapsed to the ground gasping.

Suddenly the door exploded. Heavily armed soldiers streamed into the room. The first wave was instantly frozen solid in a flash of bright blue energy. In the same instant, Ivan spun around, sword in hand. Gunfire erupted all around him. Angela looked on in fear. She already knew what had happened, what these men intended.

Ivan lashed out with his power again. This time purple lightning forked down from the ceiling, skewering five soldiers. There was a brilliant shower of sparks as the smell of burning flesh filled the air.

"I suggest you help me," Ivan shouted over the din of gunfire. "These assholes aren't here to deliver a package."

Angela instinctively slid into a fighting stance. Power stirred within her. Suddenly the floor cracked and shot upward in a hail of splinters. There was a chorus of screams as half a dozen soldiers were shredded. One man was impaled through the stomach and nailed to the ceiling. Another was decapitated. Still, another was deprived of both legs and lay on the ground shrieking in agony.

Without pausing, Angela sent her power out again. This time the wall around the door shuddered and collapsed outward swallowing more of the soldiers and adding to the cacophony of screams. The gunfire was dying down, but more soldiers were streaming into the building to replace those who had fallen. Bullets whizzed all around her like angry hornets. One painted thin fire across her upper arm while another zipped by her ear. Ivan was walking forward, directly towards the soldiers that were firing on him. Bullets surrounded him in a tunnel.

"You wanna fuck with me?" He was saying. "I'll rip your goddamned guts out."

His sword was out and glowing deep purple. Suddenly he struck, severing one man's head and opening another's chest and stomach. In the same motion, he extended his left hand. Blue lightning leapt from his fingers and laced into another soldier. He hit the floor hard, convulsing for a moment before he became still. Without pausing Ivan spun around again, impaling yet another soldier through the stomach. Ivan kicked the doomed man free from his blade, then grabbed another man and broke his neck in a single smooth motion. As he did, Ivan's eyes caught hers.

"Well? You gonna help me or just stand there like a dumb bitch!"

Angela leapt forward into the fray. A soldier fired on her. She jumped clear and grabbed the man, breaking his neck like a toothpick.

"Fire in the hole!"

There was a low clink as something metal struck the floor.

Shit! Grenade!

Angela instinctively dove for cover. As she landed, there was a deafening boom. The floor shook beneath her, and there were several fresh screams. When she looked up, Angela found herself lying among flaming debris. Half a dozen soldiers surrounded her, guns trained on her head.

"Get up!"

Angela nodded her head and slowly got to her feet, hands raised in a gesture of surrender.

A gun was jammed into her back. "Move it ya freak, or I'll blast ya right here!"

Angela complied mutely. As she was led away, she passed Ivan. He lay unconscious with no visible wounds. A trio of soldiers was struggling to carry him from the room.

Once outside, Angela was loaded into a military truck filled with others who looked every bit as frightened as she felt. Hours later, the truck stopped, and soldiers flooded in. Angela was grabbed by two burly soldiers and dragged away.

They had arrived at some sort of military installation. At first, Angela believed this was just a base. Then she saw the hundreds of other people in civilian clothes and realized the truth. This was an internment camp.

Terror flooded through her as the scent of death wafted into her nostrils. People had died here, people were still dying here. She was taken to the rear of a long line of people.

Angela looked ahead and saw that the line ended at the feet of a man and woman in white lab coats. Each held a clipboard and would scribble notes on it with each new person. Soldiers stood guard on either side. Beyond them, the queue divided in two based on age. The first line, consisting of all the teens and young to middle-aged adults, led into a series of barracks. The other, consisting of the children and elderly, led into a large warehouse.

She knew at once what this building's purpose was without the need for psychic senses. The barracks teemed with activity. Men and women in prison uniforms milled about them tending to the basic needs of survival and attempting to create some semblance of home. By contrast, the warehouse lay still and silent. There were no people outside save for the guards at the door. Though the building had several large chimneys, there was no evidence of fuel of any kind. She supposed it was possible that there were underground gas or oil tanks, but she doubted it. Furnaces of that sort would not need such large chimneys, nor would they produce such heavy, oily smoke as that which was now pouring forth.

After what seemed like many hours, Angela reached the man and woman in lab coats.

The man spoke without looking up. "Name?"

"Angela Cacy." She replied automatically.

"Age?"

"Twelve." Again, her mouth engaged without any involvement by her higher brain.

"Birthday?"

"December first."

The man took some notes on the clipboard and turned to the woman. The two talked inaudibly for a moment before the man turned back towards her.

"Get on the line to your left. You will be provided with a uniform and toiletries in the barracks."

Angela complied mutely.

After waiting in line for another hour or so, she was taken into the furthest barracks building. She was assigned the upper bunk in the far-right corner from the door and given a blue denim uniform, a white plastic toothbrush, a tube of no-name toothpaste and a small bar of soap. Then she was told to remove her clothing and taken to a small shower cubicle. After a cold shower, she was sprayed with anti-lice treatment and then returned to the barracks. Angela dressed quickly, feeling immensely self-conscious doing so in front of the coed and varied age occupants of the barracks. When she was finished, Angela climbed into bed and pulled the blankets over her head.

VII

Charlie awoke feeling thirsty and stumbled her way out of bed still mostly asleep. She crossed the cabin listening to the sounds of slumber. David and Catherine lay in each other's arms, while Stephen slept alone on a nearby bunk. There was a bathroom across the hall. Upon opening the cabin door, Charlie found herself standing at the edge of a long, dimly lit corridor not belonging to the ship.

This corridor was illuminated in soft red and pink hues and featured red silk wallpaper and heavy black steel doors. The floor was covered in black linoleum, and there was a drop tile ceiling. Stale tobacco and weed smoke blended with the stench of alcohol-laced vomit. Suddenly Charlie no longer felt safe or contented. Her heart chilled as if she were about to witness something horrible.

Something's wrong.

Though she did not want to, Charlie stepped into the corridor and began to walk. As she went, the chill intensified, then changed to a hot burning sensation. Charlie continued, now trembling, now feeling energized. The power had come alive within her, but for some strange reason, she felt no pain from holding it down. She was furious. The realization came to her suddenly, like a light flicking on in a darkened room. No, she wasn't just furious; she was totally enraged, and she didn't quite understand why. As she continued down the corridor her anger grew in intensity, chilling and blackening as it did, until it had become a cold black flame of *Hate*. She still did not know what had triggered her *Hate,* she knew only what she felt.

The corridor ended abruptly in a door. Charlie could not help trying the knob. The door fell open to reveal a lavish office. A man in a black suit and purple silk shirt stood up from behind a broad, ebony desk and strode towards her.

Suddenly, a sword not her own, appeared in her hands, and before she knew what was happening Charlie had severed the man's hands and slashed his stomach open, spilling his entrails all over the black, shag-carpeted floor.

The man let out a horrible scream and collapsed, clutching his wrist stumps to his midsection. Hot blood spurted everywhere, covering her in sticky red, and rushing out onto the floor.

Now she was standing outside herself looking on. Only it was not herself that she saw, but rather a woman about Catherine's age. The woman had vibrant, red hair that came down to her shoulders and porcelain skin. Her face was set in an expression of stony hatred, cold and without passion. The woman was beautiful, but to Charlie she was terrifying. Without pausing the woman turned from the bleeding, and screaming man and walked away, disappearing into thin air. In the same instant, the office vanished, and Charlie found herself standing outside the bathroom trembling.

Someone was crying. It took Charlie a full five minutes to realize that it was her and another five to stop. She knew the meaning of what she had seen at once. Charlie reached for the doorknob and stepped into the bathroom. She wanted to run to David and Catherine, but she would not allow herself.

They both looked so tired yesterday. They need their sleep. Besides, they have enough to worry about without this too.

VIII

Ten days after leaving port in Siberia, the *SS Kazakhstan* arrived in Seattle carrying a cargo of small arms, artillery shells and four fugitives.

David, Catherine, Charlie, and Stephen disembarked from the *Kazakhstan* before dawn the day the ship reached port. They found the streets of Seattle in chaos. Massive riots had broken out as rival factions clashed for control of the city. Militia forces under the command of the newly formed Resistance had been dispatched to put down all opposition.

Upon leaving the ship, David noticed the glaring absence of the American flag over the customs office. In its place, a red flag fluttered in the cold morning air. At its center was a great eagle, embroidered in gold thread. In the eagle's claws was a broadsword from which the scales of justice hung with just the slightest tilt to the left. A broken shackle was visible on the eagle's right foot. As he noticed this, David also became aware of the thick hazy smoke that filled the air. There were many fires, but strangely enough, he heard no sirens. The only sounds were a scattering of gunshots and a crash of broken glass. This was followed a short time later by a distant scream. David looked at Charlie and Catherine and was afraid.

"Well, we'd better get going before it gets late. We have a lot of ground to cover today." His own voice sounded alien to him. It spoke as though he knew where they were going. It spoke as though they were about to set off on vacation rather than on the run. In truth, he had no idea where they were going or even how they were going to get out of the city. It wouldn't take long before someone recognized them, and once that happened they would have great difficulty escaping.

Charlie looked up at him without speaking.

Catherine leaned in towards him and whispered in his ear. "Where are we going, David?"

He shook his head. He still couldn't believe they had come back to the states. Stephen's idea to hide in the lion's den seemed even more foolish than it had the day he had first proposed it.

David leaned in towards Catherine. "For now, let's just worry about getting the hell out of here."

Catherine nodded. "I'm scared, David."

The question was how to get out of the city.

It's not like we can call an Uber.

He looked around slowly.

For something to steal. David told himself reproachfully.
ugh the port was deserted, the parking lot outside was still teaming with cars. Some of the vehicles in the lot were new and would have the security features mandated back in two thousand five. Still, there were many with the old key ignition systems. These could be easily bypassed using the power.

David turned to Stephen. Something passed between them silently. The two men converged wordlessly on an old Subaru DL. David carefully placed his hand upon the driver's side door and reached out with the power. Instantly the lock fell open. David looked around carefully before climbing behind the wheel. There was no one.

Ten minutes later they were on their way out of Seattle. The streets were eerily quiet. There were no cars and no pedestrians on the sidewalks. The sounds of ongoing fighting were belied by the emptiness of the streets. Seattle was both a ghost town and a war zone.

Fires burned in collapsed shells of buildings. Massive heaps of rubble lay where buildings once stood. Mangled cars and bodies were scattered through the cratered streets. The smells of burning and death were everywhere.

The four of them rode in horrified silence. The carnage surrounding the car defied all words.

-CRACK-

A bullet ripped through the windshield. Another slammed through the front passenger side door and buried itself in the floorboard.

"Down!" The word escaped David's lips before he had time to think.

There was another roar of gunfire followed by a rapid series of ***–plinks-*** as more bullets pockmarked the car's metal skin.

David ducked down as he floored the gas.

Someone, either Charlie or Catherine, screamed.

"Get us out of here NOW!" Wolf's voice was steady but held more than a hint of fear.

More bullets sliced through the car.

"David, we have to get out of here!" This was Charlie, and her voice was terrified.

"I know," David replied. "Just keep your head down." He was frightened too. His heart was racing madly in his chest. *Gotta get out of here. Gotta get away.* The thought repeated maddeningly in his mind.

Angry shouts filtered in from the outside. They were too numerous to make out individual voices, but the message was unmistakable.

David leaned harder on the gas as still more gunshots ripped into the car. It was only by random good luck that none of them struck the tires.

There was a squeal of rubber on asphalt followed by a crunch of metal on metal. The wheel suddenly pulled hard to the left as another car struck the rear bumper. David floored the gas but not quickly enough to avoid being hit again. This time the Subaru lurched hard to the right nearly spinning out of control. The right-hand front tire impacted the curb with a hard thud.

Charlie screamed.

David cut the wheel hard to the left, drawing another squeal from the tires. All four were thrown forward hard as the car struck their rear bumper for the third time. In the same instant a bullet shattered the back window. Glass rained down on Charlie and Catherine.

“David get us out of here!” Catherine cried in a frightened tone.

“I’m trying.”

-CRUNCH-

The Subaru skidded sideways. David struggled to right it. Before he could, a car slammed into the rear right quarter panel, sending them into a spin. Another gunshot shattered the rear driver’s side window.

“Shit!” David cut the wheel hard to the right and gunned the gas. The Subaru straightened out and lurched forward in one sudden movement. The other car accelerated to keep up. It was no use. The Subaru was no match for the other car’s power and speed. They weren’t going to escape.

-WHAMMM-

Another impact. David nearly lost control again. There had to be something he could do. There had to be a way to escape. That was when he felt it.

The air became alive with power, Charlie’s power. Before he could say anything, he felt her lash out. Suddenly the car behind them vanished in a massive fireball. The shockwave blew out the remaining windows of their car, showering them in safety glass.

More gunfire rang out, followed by an erratic *-plinkety plink-* as bullets rained upon the car’s metallic skin.

“Punch it!” Wolf shouted.

David didn’t need to be told twice. He slammed the accelerator to the floor, driving the car into a sharp forward lurch.

“There’re more coming.” Charlie cried fearfully.

David cut the wheel hard to the left, then hung a right following the signs for the interstate. A huge crowd filled the road directly ahead. Its anger pulsated out at him in waves. Fights had already broken out. Suddenly someone shouted, “Kill the freaks!”, and the crowd charged. Rocks and bottles rained down on the car. One struck the hood and exploded into flames.

Charlie’s power flowed freely in the air. David’s heart began to pulse in his chest.

“No, don’t!” He had to struggle to keep his voice calm for he already knew what was coming.

Suddenly Charlie bit down on her power. He could not sense her thoughts, but her shame was evident on her face. "I…I didn't mean to." She burst into tears.

David's heart went out to her, but he couldn't do anything for Charlie right then. He had to get them out of there alive.

The crowd remained solid. David would have to drive over them to get through. He felt his own power stir. *Not now!!* He had to think, and he had only milliseconds to do it. The crowd wasn't budging. He would have to either kill someone or stop. That was his choice. David kept the gas pedal to the floor. The crowd did not part. The car sped forward. The crowd remained stalwart. At the very last second, David felt his power go out in a great wave. All at once, the crowd was swept aside, as if by a great invisible hand. As he drove through the center of the mob, David could feel people struggling against his power. It was a sensation like nothing he had ever felt before.

After passing through the last edge of the crowd, David let go. In an instant, the mob closed in on itself and began to charge towards them. More bottles and rocks pelted the car. The hood continued to flame where a Molotov cocktail had struck. It was a miracle the engine hadn't overheated. Then it was all over. Just like that, they were out of the city and on their way to…

Where?

David didn't really know. He got on the highway heading east because that was as good a direction as any. Once they were a safe distance from Seattle, David pulled over to check on Charlie and Catherine. He found them looking frightened and dazed. Catherine sat staring straight ahead, a blank expression on her pallid face. Beside her, Charlie sat perfectly still with a similar emotionless gaze. She had placed her hand in Catherine's. Catherine held it tightly squeezing it so the flesh blanched white. There were tears in Charlie's eyes, but she no longer wept. David suspected that were he able to sense her thoughts, he would find her emotionless, neither upset nor frightened nor happy, just blank.

"Are you two ok?"

At first, neither spoke. Then Charlie suddenly burst into tears.

"It's ok," David whispered to her as gently as his frightened mind could manage. "Everything's going to be ok."

She only cried harder.

David took his daughter into his arms. He felt like crying too, for his heart truly went out to her. She was only a little girl. She didn't deserve this. She didn't deserve to be terrorized and hunted like an animal. She didn't deserve to be cursed with a power she had neither asked for nor wanted.

It took a long time for Charlie to calm down, but she eventually did. Or more exactly, exhaustion took precedence over fear and Charlie cried herself to sleep. David kissed his daughter on the forehead and gently laid her down in the car before seeing to his wife.

Catherine too was deeply frightened, though she was not in tears as with Charlie. Instead, she refused to acknowledge that anything was wrong.

"I'm fine," was all she would say. David held her for almost as long as Charlie. Then it occurred to him that it would be wise to move on before someone found them.

IX

They drove on in silence for the rest of the day. Sometime after the sun went down, they came to an abandoned motel. A quick flick of the power got them a pair of rooms at the far end of the building. Inside, the rooms looked like they hadn't changed since the year 1970. The thick, musty air within suggested that they hadn't been opened since the 1970s either. Upon entering the room, Charlie collapsed on the bed and immediately fell asleep. Catherine sat down beside her.

David looked down on her with concern. Catherine's face was pale and wan. Her eyes were wide, bloodshot, and outlined in purple.

"I'm going to go look for some food." The words came out of his mouth sounding alien. It was as if he had not really spoken them.

"Ok." Catherine's voice was drained of all energy.

"Are you ok sweetheart?"

"I'm fine." She replied flatly. She wasn't. He could feel her fear and total exhaustion.

On his way to the door, he stopped to talk to Wolf. "Keep them safe."

Wolf nodded. "Don't worry." His voice dropped to a whisper. "Be careful, there's somebody snooping around nearby. I can feel them. Try to stay out of sight."

David nodded. He could feel them now too. There weren't many, only one or two, but they could easily raise the alarm. He would have to take care not to be seen.

David reached out with his mind. There was a man across the road behind an old barn, and another man taking a dump behind a stand of trees. Neither of them had a line of sight to the room door. David took a deep breath and carefully opened the door.

He found nothing in the motel office, save for a few financial files, an old .38 Chief and a half box of bullets in a locked desk drawer. After a few minutes debate, he decided to take the gun, if only to keep someone else from picking it up and using it on his family. Behind the motel, stood an old ramshackle cabin, and it was here that he hit pay dirt. Inside a cabinet in the kitchen, David found two-dozen cans of Campbell's soup.

Squirreled away for a rainy day no doubt.

Well, today it was pouring. David gathered up the food and hurried back to the room.

After they had finished eating, Wolf retired to his room, and Charlie went back to sleep having barely eaten anything. David and Catherine climbed into the other bed together.

"I'm scared, David."

"So am I." He replied.

„What are we going to do? We can't keep running like this."

He shook his head. "I don't know." Everything was going to shit. The whole world wanted them dead. There was no safe place left for them to go.

"They're going to catch us one of these times." She whispered fearfully.

"No. They're not." He was lying, and she probably knew it. He knew as well as she did that sooner or later they would be cornered. Sooner or later they would land in a situation they could not fight their way out of and then it would be all over. "Not as long as I can still fight back."

"Oh, David…" Catherine's voice was tearstained, her face broken. "You always try so hard, but…"

"I'm not going to let them hurt you or Charlie. No matter what happens. I won't let them hurt you."

"Ok, David." She spoke gently. David knew she didn't believe him. In truth she thought he would try as hard as he could but that he would fail again.

X

As David and Catherine sat talking. Kain and Lord Beathach met in the Grand Observation Lounge.

"We have a problem." As he spoke, Eric unconsciously gripped the sword at his side.

"Indeed, my master." Lord Beathach replied in a flat, emotionless tone.

"This woman, this Kira Morozov is killing Russian mafia left and right and leaving behind a signature that practically screams Enlightened. Her vigilantism is only further stirring up hatred and fear of Enlighteneds. She needs to go away.."

As he spoke, Eric found himself incredulous at his own words. This woman was a Lightwarrior, and thus marked for death for that reason alone, but normally he would never dream of interfering in such a trivial matter. Except, in this case, he had no choice. The wasteful slaughter of Enlighteneds had to stop. He had already lost a dozen Dark Knights in the death camps. This woman was only giving credence to the claims of the Resistance that Enlighteneds were dangerous and had to be "controlled." She had to be stopped before the situation got any worse.

Lord Beathach inclined his head. "It shall be as you wish my master."

Kain's expression remained cold. "Thank you, my friend." He stood perfectly still, gazing out the window until Beathach had gone.

XI

Marcus Reichert entered his security code with some trepidation, for he had doubts about the wisdom of releasing the creature. It had once been human, a youth of about eighteen. It had developed a respectable telekinetic ability following its exposure to the X-22 virus. Unfortunately, the X-22 virus that had gifted the youth with this power also stripped him of all humanity.

X-22 was a virus unlike anything ever seen before, either in nature or the lab. In addition to being a virulent pathogen, it was a potent mutagen. The virus was designed to alter the physiological structure of its host, increasing muscle mass, reducing fat, increasing metabolic rate, changing brain structure and many other unpredictable effects besides. The final outcome of all this would be the transformation of the subject into a horribly mutated creature with bestial intelligence while still keeping their power intact.

As he watched in horrified fear, the containment chamber opened to reveal a massive bone white creature complete with mutated, twisted flesh and freakish size. The creature was fitted with several implants to further augment its power and to keep it under control, as the virus had an effect on the subject's personality similar to rabies.

As the creature emerged, Marcus could hear its breathing, loud, almost growling. Slowly, the creature loped across the room to the armored door, which now stood open to the outside world. The hallways had already been cleared. It was a straight shot to the outside, and the creature had already been programmed with its mission: find and destroy Charlene MacLeod and her adoptive parents.

In a nearby laboratory, a dozen men and women lay secured to gurneys. IV lines dripped saline laced with *Reaper*, a crude, street version of D-13 into their veins. Some wore vapid, drugged-out expressions while others lay wide-eyed with hallucinatory terror. The air inside the laboratory, heavy with the scent of chlorine and iodine blended, was electric with power. A pencil lifted slowly from one steel counter and lanced across the room, embedding itself in a corkboard on the opposite side of the room. The subjects here, bred for a single purpose, would come to be known as Lawgivers. And these Lawgivers would go on to become the most feared members of the Resistance.

XII

Three days after leaving Seattle, David, Catherine, Charlie, and Stephen arrived in Chinook, Montana. Chinook was deserted, and from all outward appearances, the residents had left in a tremendous hurry. Something wasn't right here. Charlie felt it deep inside. Something terrible had happened.

There were few cars. Toys and tools were scattered across the lawns of deserted homes. Many houses stood wide open, their owners not even bothering to close the front door. Windows were smashed, street signs stood at angles. One lay on its side like a dead dog. Another was bent to the left in the shape of a bumper. Further down the road, a fence lay in pieces across a front lawn with tire tracks through the center.

Downtown the damage was worse. Storefront windows were shattered, their contents looted. Trash lay everywhere interspersed with broken glass and blood. Several fires burned out of control blackening the sky with thick smoke. Most terrifying of all was the silence, the dead silence. There was literally no sound at all save for the crackle of fire. Seattle had been frightening with its screams, gunshots and shattering glass, but at least these were sounds of life. Here there was nothing. This place was dead, a graveyard. She could feel it in her bones.

David drove the car into the Chinook police parking lot and stopped outside. He had chosen this place because it was isolated from other buildings and close to the edge of town. After cutting the engine, he turned to Charlie and Catherine.

"I'm going to take a look around. You two stay put." He turned to Stephen. "You mind backing me up." His voice dropped. "Something doesn't feel right."

Stephen nodded silently.

If you see anything, I want you to take Charlie and run.

This was meant for Catherine, but Charlie easily read David's thoughts. She had not yet met anyone strong enough to shut her out.

David and Stephen got out of the car and drew their swords. Charlie was afraid for them both. Something was very wrong here. With each passing moment, she felt the danger increasing.

XIII

As he walked away from the car, David's heart chilled.

We shouldn't be here.

He felt certain of this. Still, it was getting late, and they were exhausted from driving all day. They had to at least find food before moving on. Nevertheless, David could not shake the feeling that something terrible had happened here. Chinook almost felt like a battlefield recently abandoned. David turned to Wolf.

"Something's not right. Whatever happened, everyone tore out of here in one hell of a rush."

The Russian nodded and lifted his sword. "We should not stay long."

David inclined his head in agreement.

Without another word, the two men headed towards a nearby Seven-Eleven. The store had been abandoned recently. Inside the air was dead and still. Everything was completely ransacked. Shelves lay in pieces all over the floor while the remnants of merchandise littered the wreckage. Even the glass coolers had been shattered and picked clean. Behind the counter, the cash register had been broken open. Money lay scattered across the floor behind it. On the back wall, the cigarette display had been smashed, its glass remnants sprayed across the floor like a thousand twinkling stars.

As he stepped further into the store, David saw the clerk. He lay on the floor directly behind the register in a massive puddle of tacky blood. Part of his head had been blown away, leaving a bloody crater in its place. Brains and gore splattered the wall behind him. A cold shudder wormed its way through David's body. The clerk was little more than a boy. He couldn't have been older than sixteen.

"Oh, fuck…" The only words that would come from his lips.

Wolf looked down at the slaughtered boy and shook his head. "Such a waste. There was no need to kill him. He wasn't even armed."

David started to say something else, but before he could, Wolf's hand clapped down on his shoulder. "Come we don't have much time. Whoever killed him might come back."

David sensed as Wolf must have, that this was highly unlikely. Whoever had killed this boy had fled with the rest of the town's residents, never to return.

What happened here?

It was a question that he would repeat to himself many times that evening.

They found little of use in the store, save for a few dented cans of Dinty Moor stews, and a single box of stale doughnuts that had lain hidden behind the counter.

Behind the Seven-Eleven, stood a dilapidated ranch-style house, and it was here that they hit pay dirt. While the convenience store had been ransacked, the house behind it was mostly untouched. Here they found numerous canned and dried foods, and even some edible fresh fruits in the refrigerator.

After some discussion, David and Wolf went back for Charlie and Catherine, having decided it would be safe to rest here for a while and stock up on supplies.

By some stroke of luck, it also turned out that the gas pumps at the Seven-Eleven were still functioning and full of gas. David found two empty gas cans in a shed behind the house. After topping off the car, he filled both cans up and tossed them in the trunk before heading into the house for dinner.

Their meal consisted of fresh fruit along with a can each of beef stew. After everyone had finished, they retired to the living room to relax. This was a small, poorly furnished room that reeked of stale cigarettes and mold. The couch sagged and was ripped in one place. All of the cushions had cigarette burns in them. Beside the sofa stood a ragged vinyl recliner, and a lopsided lawn chair. The television was an old Panasonic with foil festooned rabbit ears. Yet somehow its owners had managed to pay for a DirecTV connection. All television broadcasts had stopped weeks ago, but there were still intermittent radio broadcasts. David found a radio in the kitchen and dialed around the AM band until a female voice broke through the crackling static.

"Great Falls hospitals are swamped following the outbreak of a frightening new hemorrhagic fever now being called the Centennial Virus after the movie theater where the first outbreak occurred." The voice of the speaker, Mara Fields, was noticeably frightened. "Over one hundred cases of the virus have been identified so far. Fifty people have died. Early symptoms of the virus are flu-like with a high fever, cough, headache, muscle soreness, and painful joints. Within six to twelve hours these symptoms progress to bruising, reddening of the eyes, severe stomach pain, vomiting and coughing up blood, bloody diarrhea, and bleeding from the eyes, nose, mouth, ears, genitals, and anus. Liquefaction of the organs quickly follows, leading to multiple organ failure and death. The virus is always fatal, usually within two to four days and there is no treatment or cure. The route of transmission for this virus is unknown, but unofficially experts believe it may be airborne. Earlier today, Resistance General Norman McDaniels dispatched mechanized infantry and airborne units to the Great Falls area to enforce a mandatory quarantine. Travelers are ordered to stay away from the Great Falls area until further notice. Residents are ordered to stay inside their homes and avoid public places if at all possible. If you or anyone in your family have any flu-like symptoms stay indoors and avoid other people." She paused. "In other news violence continues between Resistance troops and Loyalist forces in the Midwest. General McDaniels has issued a statement warning that if the violence does not end soon he will be forced to use airstrikes against Loyalist positions to protect the public."

XIV

Charlie listened to the radio broadcast in horror. So, this was what had happened. This was why Chinook was deserted.

As she was thinking this, a scream rang out. It took several minutes for her to realize who it was. Catherine had gotten up several minutes ago to go to the bathroom. Now she was screaming. Charlie was the first up and running. David and Stephen were close behind her. She found Catherine in the master bedroom and…

Oh my GOD!!

Now Charlie was screaming too. The smell was the first thing that struck her. Pungent and cloying, the smell of death. She felt her gorge rising at once and had to choke it back. The bedroom was a horror show of buzzing flies, blackened flesh and crusting mucus. Two bodies, barely discernible as human, lay in pools of dried blood, one on the bed the other on the floor.

Charlie understood at once the meaning of what lay before her eyes. These two had died of the Centennial Virus. There was no question in her mind. Charlie grabbed Catherine's hand and began to pull.

"We've gotta get out of here."

Catherine went with her without a word.

David and Stephen were standing in the doorway, staring. David spoke first.

"Yes, I think we should be leaving now." His tone would have been laughable if she were not so terrified.

We could have already been infected.

Within minutes they were in the car on their way out of Chinook. Though none of the spoke of it, all of them shared the same fear. Had they been exposed?

XV

Sometime later they pulled onto a dirt road. David, Catherine, Charlie, and Stephen traveled along this road for a while, winding, bumping, and jostling, not really going anywhere but heading out of sight of the highway. When the four fugitives finally reached the end of the road it was dark outside. David cut the engine, and they all piled out.

"We'll sleep here tonight." David's voice was flat and emotionless.

No one responded.

Without another word, he turned away to search for firewood. Charlie followed him wordlessly. When the two of them had gathered up a large pile of sticks, Charlie set fire to them using the power. It occurred to her that this might be dangerous, that Resistance forces might see the smoke and come to investigate, but she didn't care. She was too tired to care, and besides, it was cold out, and they didn't have any blankets.

Not long after settling in, Charlie drifted off to sleep. She hadn't felt tired, she was too frightened, but in truth, she was exhausted.

XVI

Catherine too drifted off quickly, leaving David alone with Wolf. The two men sat together without speaking for a long time before David finally broke their silence.

"Where to next?"

The big Russian sat in contemplation for a moment, a blank look on his face. "We turn north." Wolf gazed deep into the fire for a moment, before producing a cigarette and lighting up.

David met his eyes. "We came back here on your suggestion. I hope you know what you're doing."

The single red eye of Wolf's smoldering cigarette winked in response.

XVII

A creature walked in darkness. Charlie could see it at the edge of the shadows. She could hear its mechanical breathing. She could feel its strange, cold presence and she was terrified for she knew it was close.

Wakefulness struck Charlie like a slap in the face. She found herself sitting up in her bedroll, soaked in sweat and quivering like an autumn leaf. It was still dark out, but the sky had become purple, the first suggestion of the slow arrival of dawn. The creature was close. Charlie knew that much. It did not yet know how close it was to success, but if they did not flee soon it would stumble upon them by pure chance.

As Charlie felt this, a cold wave swept through her, followed by a familiar and very dark presence.

Oh, God...

She knew at once who it was she sensed for this was a presence she knew well.

Lord Beathach...

He had come back for her. He had come to take her away. He had come to make her suffer.

Panic set it at once, making it hard for her to think. Before she knew what was happening, Charlie found herself straddling David shaking him and Catherine awake.

"We have to go! We have to get away!" Charlie was saying. Though in truth her mouth was engaged without her brain.

"What's wrong?" David asked. His concern was like a cold wind in the dark.

"He's here! I can feel him! He's found us!"

"Who?"

"Lord Beathach!"

David said nothing further. In one smooth motion, he was on his feet and rapidly gathering their meager belongings. When he was finished, David kicked Stephen awake. "Get up. We've gotta get out of here."

Wolf groaned. "Why? What's going on?" His voice was thick with sleep.

"I'll explain it later just get up."

Wolf nodded sleepily.

Ten minutes later, they were packed and driving away from their campsite. The un-extinguished remains of their fire still glowed red in the distance.

Lord Beathach was very close now. His presence was a cold knife in Charlie's heart. Yet there was something strange. She could feel him, but she did not sense that he felt her. Not yet at least. Nor did she sense that he was seeking her. Instead, Lord Beathach sought another. Someone he considered a serious threat.

Who?

Who would be so important that Kain and Beathach would seek them rather than continuing their pursuit of the one person they believed could bring them absolute power? Kane and Baeathach had spent five years trying to gain her cooperation. Why would they abandon their pursuit now? She supposed she should have felt relieved, but instead she felt frightened. This was not what she had expected. She had thought she understood Kain and Beathach, but now she found herself more confused than ever.

XVIII

The four fugitives fled throughout the night, not stopping until well after dawn. As they were scavenging breakfast from an abandoned RV, Wolf spoke the question that David had sensed he had wanted to ask since awakening the night before.

"I saw Charlie's eyes. She's terrified of something, something a lot worse than the mindless idiots we've been running from so far. So, tell me something. Who are we running from?"

David was immediately grateful to Wolf for his discretion. They were alone inside the RV, and out of earshot of Charlie and Catherine. Still, he shook his head. "You don't want to know."

Wolf's eyes flashed with immediate anger. "I *do* want t to know. If there's someone after us who you didn't tell me about, I damned well want to know."

Very well. "I wasn't totally honest with you, Stephen," David stated apologetically. "We're in more trouble than you think."

Wolf 's glare intensified, but he remained silent.

"Ogastes is an asshole, but there were people after us long before he even knew our names. The United States government was chasing us on the orders of a group calling themselves the Black Empire." David paused. "This is going to sound crazy. I still can't get my own head around it completely, but it's true. The Black Empire is this…I don't know intergalactic nation of pure evil that has been slowly corrupting the cosmos. They want Charlie because she is uniquely powerful, and because they believe she can unlock an ultimate weapon of evil."

"You're right that does sound crazy. I'm out of here." With that, Wolf turned and headed for the door.

David called after him. "Wait. I know you can sense my motives. Look into me. You'll see I'm not lying, and I'm not crazy."

Wolf turned and closed to only inches. "So, you're not lying. What do you want from me? Am I supposed to throw away my life too?"

David felt his skin flush as anger erupted within. "Look around you. Your life's already screwed up. The whole fucking world is going to shit, and do you think for one moment that the Black Empire doesn't already know you're helping us? You want to go it alone, that's fine. But if you could dig your head out of your ass for one moment maybe you might think about helping someone besides yourself."

Wolf stepped back eyes flashing. In an instant, his sword was in his hand. "You want to fuck with me, David? Huh? I've been pit fighting since I was a teenager. How about you?"

Without a thought, David's blade was out. *Deus Irae* glowed brightly in his hand. He could feel the weapon's power pulsing with the thunder of his heart. "I'll take my chances."

There was a deafening clang of steel upon steel as both men struck at once. David pushed forward against Wolf's parry, forcing the Russian to take a step backward to keep his balance. Then he changed his grip on his sword and swung again. Their blades collided a second time with a tooth-jarring crash as Wolf knocked his blow aside. The inside of the RV was tiny, strictly limiting their maneuvers. Quick as a flash, Wolf thrust out at David. As David sidestepped the blow, Wolf struck out with the power, sending David sprawling as if struck by an invisible fist. David responded by using the power to tear the door from a nearby cabinet and send it whirling in Wolf's direction. As Wolf ducked under the sudden projectile, David leapt to his feet and pressed his momentary advantage with a sudden overhead swing. His blade struck a light fixture, obliterating it in a shower of plastic and sparks. Still, the blow lost none of its power, and Wolf was obliged to sidestep to avoid being sliced in half. Without pausing, Wolf responded with a sideways slash. David parried the blow with a hard, horizontal strike intending to knock the Russian's blade from his hand. The two swords collided with a terrific smash. David threw his weight forward in an attempt to unbalance the Russian. Instead, he received a sharp right cross to the jaw. David staggered backward, mouth filling with blood. Before he could lift his blade, Wolf followed up with a roundhouse kick to the midsection and then brought the hilt of his sword down on the back of David's skull. White light exploded in David's head, momentarily blinding him. When his eyesight cleared, David found himself lying flat on his back staring up the length of Wolf's blade.

"We're finished." He stated flatly.

David lay still for a moment. Blood still thundered in his veins. Reflexively he reached into the power.

Wolf pressed his blade ever so slightly into David's throat, gently parting the skin.

"I *said* we're finished. Don't make me kill you."

David nodded, gritting his teeth against the still boiling anger in his heart. *Who the hell do you think you are? Arrogant prick!*

Wolf held him like that for a moment longer before withdrawing his sword. "You're better than I thought, but you still have a lot to learn. You should never attack out of anger." Before David could retort, Wolf turned and left.

David stood shaking with anger for a moment longer, before gathering up the food the two of them had found and leaving the RV. It would occur to him later how foolish this was. Wolf had a right to be angry. They had not told him the full story.

David was frightened. He too felt the presence of Lord Beathach. What was strange was that David sensed that the Dark Lord was not seeking them. Instead, Beathach was hunting for another. Someone he intended to kill.

XIX

After many hours of travel, David, Catherine, Charlie, and Stephen found themselves outside some tiny, nameless burg in northern Montana. The small gathering of buildings barely qualified as anything at all. There were no businesses other than a small movie theater that had long since gone under. The marquee was blank save for the letters M, X, and R. To the right of the theater stood a boarded-up church. To the left the burned-out husk of a house. A cluster of trailers lay on either side of the road a few miles up. That was all. The rest of the area was nothing but barren brown fields. An eerie desolation hung heavy in the air.

Having no preferable options, they broke into the movie theater. Inside, the theater was dark and filthy. Cobwebs festooned every nook and cranny. After finding someplace where Catherine and Charlie could be comfortable, David and Stephen raided the concession stand and employee lockers for anything resembling food. Behind the front display counter, they found an entire case of Mr. Good Bars. After eating dinner Charlie, David, Catherine and Stephen set out their bedrolls and quickly drifted off to sleep.

XX

Charlie awoke suddenly. Something was wrong. She could feel it in her heart. Something was very wrong. The theater was quiet, save for the soft sounds of sleep.

But something doesn't feel right.

Charlie couldn't put her finger on exactly what was wrong, but she felt it strongly. They were in very real danger. For a moment, she considered ignoring the feeling. She was so sick of running and hiding, and she was tired, so very tired. The feeling persisted. They had to get away.

It's already too late.

The sounds of metal ringing upon concrete came through to her like gunshots. Her heart froze.

Oh no...

A low mechanical whine was followed by the clang of metal and stone. Someone or something was there, but it wasn't Lord Beathach or one of his followers. This was something else, and she was sure now that it was indeed a thing. It was not a person but a thing. A horrible monster straight out of her worst nightmare.

Chapter 6
Terror and Tragedy

I

We have to get away!!

The thought rang in her head even as the clang of steel upon concrete and mechanical whining grew louder.

Before she could move the sounds abruptly stopped leaving only dead silence. After that, everything happened very quickly.

There was a bright white flash followed by a deafening boom. This was followed a moment later by a roar of gunfire. In her mind, Charlie could feel the whirling chunks of steel as they screamed towards her head. Without thinking, she reached out with the power and swatted them away. Another explosion rocked the theater. This one was much closer. Its heat baked her skin, and its shockwave rattled her teeth. She still could not see her attacker, but she sensed its presence. It was not human, at least not anymore. Whatever it had once been, the creature's mind had been obliterated, reduced to a crude, bestial will driven by mere instinctive reaction. There was no consciousness left, only the ability to react to stimuli with single-minded violence. Another stronger will had subjugated this bestial consciousness. This second will was much more focused but was every bit as single-minded as the first. Its purpose became clear to her at once.

KILL CHARLENE MACLEOD
KILL DAVID MCAULIFFE
KILL CATHERINE MCAULIFFE
KILL STEPHEN WOLF

The words echoed in her mind as if in a nightmare. This second will was like a shock of icy water. It almost hurt to touch it. Most terrifying though was its total lack of emotion. There was no anger, hate, fear, or even desire, only cold mechanical determination. Charlie steeled herself for the battle that was about to begin.

There was a low whirring noise. This was followed by more gunfire. Something small and very hot zipped by Charlie's left ear. She lashed out with the power. Fire erupted from the ground enveloping the dark silhouette of the living nightmare that had disturbed her sleep. For a moment she could see nothing save the flames which quickly licked their way up the plaster wall and swallowed the wooden molding above. There was a low ***–CLANG-*** of steel on concrete. This was followed a moment later by a low ***–whirrr-*** and a second ***–CLANG-.*** It was then that she could see it spotlighted by the flames. The creature's skin was pale bone-white and twisted beyond recognition. Its face, barely recognizable as anything but monstrous, was a horrifying death's head visage. The right side was covered by an ocular implant complete with guidance laser. The creature's right arm ended in long, yellow, hooked claws. Its left had been converted into a combination rocket launcher and Vulcan cannon. The creature's feet and much of its torso were clad in reinforced blast steel.

Behind her, Charlie sensed David, Catherine, and Stephen slowly moving from behind cover. She had not been aware of them until now. Their presence had been eclipsed by the fear pulsing in her heart. Only seconds had passed since the creature had first appeared, yet a powerful pang of guilt thrust through her heart. She had forgotten them.

Before she could dwell on that thought any further, the creature raised its arm and unleashed a hail of gunfire. For a moment, time inexplicably slowed around her. Charlie dove to the ground. In the same instant, she reached into the power and swept David, Catherine, and Stephen off their feet. Then time resumed its normal speed, and the creature's bullets stitched a ragged line across the wall behind her, showering her in plaster dust.

Charlie had her sword in hand. She did not remember drawing it. Again, she reached into the power and lashed out at the creature. A massive fireball erupted beneath the creature's feet, swallowing it in bright yellow and orange flames. The creature let out a cry of combined pain and rage and flailed at her wildly with the power.

An invisible fist struck Charlie in the midsection and sent her carooming into the wall. She landed on her chest, winded.

David screamed, "That's my daughter you son of a bitch" and flung the power at the creature.

A massive, blinding blue-white lightning bolt forked from the ceiling impaling the creature on its way to the floor. David followed up suddenly with a second potent thrust with the power. Again blue-white, forked lightning lanced through the creature, this time surrounding it in white coronal energy.

The creature fell to one knee, as a suffering groan escaped its throat. Before the creature could recover, David charged, sword out. As he brought his blade down on the creature's head it raised its clawed arm and deftly parried the blow. In the same movement, the creature shoved David back, nearly knocking him off his feet.

Charlie was back on her feet now. "David get back!"

As Charlie called to her adoptive father, she reached into the power. Blue-white fire licked up the edges of her sword. Once David was clear of the creature she leapt forward using the power and brought her blade down in a vicious overhead slash. Again, the creature brought up its clawed arm to defend itself. This time it wasn't so fortunate for her blade easily severed half the creature's hand and buried itself in the creature's chest. Charlie ripped her sword free and lashed out with the power. This time the creature was swallowed whole by blue-white fire.

Deep, intense pleasure washed through Charlie as she poured the power out upon the creature. At first, her flames merely shrouded the creature in a brilliant white veil. Then its features began to run and blend together like hot tallow. Then flesh flew from bone and forged steel until only a blazing, twisted skeleton remained. A sudden, bright flash blinded her. Charlie continued flooding the creature's remains with the power. When her vision cleared she was standing over a smoldering pile of ashes and fused metal. Burning flesh and ozone hung heavy upon the air. And...strangely enough the power was silent within her.

The little theater was ablaze with Charlie's flames, the air hazy with smoke. They had to get out before it was too late. Without a word, she put away her sword, grabbed David and Catherine's hands, and pulled them towards the nearest exit. As she did her mind reached out to Stephen with a single word: ***RUN!***

II

Outside, the snow and wind had picked up into a full-blown blizzard. Charlie shivered fiercely and with such force that it actually hurt.

Though the swirling snow limited her vision, Charlie could make out the outlines of several people. For a moment, she was frightened before her psychic senses told her that these people meant no harm.

A man's voice called to her. "Is anyone there?"

The distant figures began to move closer and take shape. "Are you ok? Did you just escape from the theater?"

David discreetly placed his hand on Charlie's shoulder and pulled her behind him. *Be ready to run. We don't know what these people want yet.*

She reached out to him with her mind. *They don't mean any harm, David.*

By now the figures had closed to within twenty feet of them. The owner of the voice was a tall man with shoulder-length, gray-flecked sandy hair. His face was tan and weathered with deep, careworn lines. His voice was deep and melodic with a slight western accent.

Beside him stood a woman of approximately the same age. Her face was pale, freckled, and equally careworn. The woman wore her curly black hair short, and somewhat wild. Her deep-set narrow eyes studied Charlie with more than a hint of suspicion.

Next to the woman stood a second man. This man was somewhat shorter than the first man and was a bit more slender. He was dark-skinned with buzz-cut hair and a long oval-shaped face. His features were as hard and intractable as the Rocky Mountains.

All three had rifles slung over their shoulders and pistols at their sides though none of them acted with any particular aggression.

David took a step backward shooing Charlie back with him. "What do you want?"

"We saw the fire at the theater and came to see what was going on." The sandy-haired man replied carefully.

"We had nothing to do with that." David lied. "We just came into town and found the theater burning."

The sandy-haired man was silent a moment as he studied David's eyes. Then he smiled. "You all have somewhere to sleep tonight? This storm won't be moving off anytime soon."

"No. We've been traveling east to Omaha," David replied.

The sandy-haired man's smile broadened. If he had detected David's lie, Charlie sensed no suspicion. "Well, you're welcome to stay with us if you'd like."

Charlie reached out to the three strangers with her mind. She sensed some concern but only because Charlie and her family were unknown to them. Charlie painted a friendly smile on her face and stepped from behind David.

"We would be happy to. Thank you."

David and Catherine both looked at Charlie with more than a hint of surprise.

Stephen shrugged. "It would appear we do not have a choice."

The sandy-haired man smiled. "Great. Come with us. We have enough room in our truck for all of you." As he spoke, the sandy-haired man turned in the direction he had come from. Charlie started off after him. David's hand gently closed on her shoulder.

Charlie wait. These people could be dangerous.

She met his eyes and saw genuine concern. *It's ok. They don't mean us any harm. They're just concerned. I can feel it.*

David did not reply for a moment. Then, *I feel it too, but these people are strangers. And I don't think they know who we are yet. We should take our own car. Just in case.* As his voice spoke in her mind, David led Charlie back to the truck.

He called to the three strangers. "We have our own truck. We'll follow you."

"Ok, sure." The man replied.

Five minutes later, they were on their way out of town on a narrow pair of tire tracks in the snow. Charlie sat in the back across from Stephen, clutching her shoulders as shivers wracked her slight body. It was getting colder, and the storm was picking up. She could barely see out of the window beside her. Snow gathered on her lap and lighted on her hair.

The night was amazingly dark as if light had never touched this place or would never touch it again. Charlie's heart chilled. Everything was falling apart. Here they were, out in the middle of nowhere, and they were not safe. They would never be safe. As they bounced and thudded along that lonely pair of tire tracks in the endless span of white snow Charlie felt the walls closing in around her. *They* were close. It would not be long now. Her family, David, and Catherine would be taken, Stephen would be taken. She would be taken. They would be taken by the Resistance or by Lord Beathach. She was not sure which, she only knew that she and her family would not escape from this place.

After a few miles, the tire ruts turned up a soft hill. At the same time, the darkness lifted slightly to reveal the outline of a tall building. A twisted, half-collapsed metal sign advised that this had once been the Black Hills Hotel.

As they grew nearer, a large, multi-story tower of gold glass and steel loomed above a scattering of smaller outbuildings.

The black SUV pulled up to the front door and David parked the truck behind it.

The three strangers greeted them at the door. The man they had spoken to earlier introduced himself first. "Name's Louis Blackhawk." He glanced towards the woman and the dark-skinned man. "This is Lori Sueden and Frank Greenewood."

Lori and Frank nodded without speaking.

Louis smiled. "Welcome to Black Hills."

Lori and Frank exchanged a glance with Louis that clearly said, *"Can we trust these people?"*

Louis's responding gaze communicated his intention clearly, *"We're helping them. No questions."*

Without another word, Frank pulled open one of the hotel's brass framed glass doors and held it. David led the way into the hotel's opulent lobby.

Here the floors were sand-colored marble with ornate oriental rugs and the front desk was rich red cherry wood with brass trim. The lobby was furnished in deep, brown leather easy chairs and couches. A great crystal chandelier bathed the lobby in gold. Further inside, the hotel opened into a massive twenty-story atrium. From where she stood, Charlie could see floor upon floor of hotel rooms.

Frank led them past the front desk to the glass elevators before hitting the button for the second floor. Charlie marveled at the view as the car rapidly ascended.

After leaving the elevator, Frank led them to a large double door directly above the lobby. Inside was a large and well-appointed office.

Here the walls were adorned in off-white wallpaper with golden threads and the floor was covered in off-white shag carpeting. A small number of high backed overstuffed dark brown leather chairs had been set along the left-hand wall, while the righthand wall opened into a large, off-white tiled fireplace.

In front of the hearth stood a long couch of the same overstuffed brown leather and, at the far end of the office, behind a massive cherry wood banker's desk sat an imposing, dark-skinned man of impressive height and build. The man stood up slowly, his bald head shining in the warm office lights, and smiled earnestly as they entered. As he did, the man studied them carefully. Charlie sensed what she thought was recognition. When he spoke, the man's voice was a low baritone.

"Give us a moment alone, Frank."

"Sure," Frank replied before turning towards the door. "I'll leave you three here with Ken. I'm sure I'll see you around the hotel."

Ken waited until Frank had left before addressing them. "Hello, Mr. and Mrs. McAuliffe."

All at once, Charlie's heart exploded with terror. He had recognized them. Though she sensed no malice from Ken, she nevertheless knew this could not be good.

As that thought passed through her mind, Ken approached her. "And you must be Charlie MacLeod." Though he used a friendly tone, Charlie remained frightened and wary.

Ken turned to Stephen. "And you are?"

"Stephen Wolf." Stephen's voice was steady and emotionless. Charlie could feel caution behind his calm demeanor.

"My name is Ken Greenewood. I am the manager of this hotel…or at least I was until the world went to hell. I recognize the three of you from the television reports. You were the ones who started the firestorm at Castle Bruce."

Charlie flinched at that last sentence for she still felt some guilt for the death of Senator Suire.

Ken immediately detected her reaction. "It's ok. I know it wasn't your fault." His baritone voice held genuine sympathy. "You're a kid, you didn't ask for your power. You just lost control, and things happened. It was an accident."

Ken was trying to be sweet, but he didn't get it. That was probably good, or he would not have been so understanding.

"You're all in a lot of trouble, and you'll need somewhere safe to go. I can give that to you." Ken turned towards his desk. "Come in. Sit down. We have a lot to talk about."

Charlie sensed that David and Catherine were nonplussed. For her own part, she did not know how to react. Her psychic senses told her that this man was genuine, but she remained reluctant to trust him. Ogastes had offered to help too and had managed to place them in greater danger in addition to instigating world civil war.

David approached Ken's desk slowly and sat down in one of the overstuffed leather chairs in front. Wordlessly Catherine took another and motioned for Charlie to sit on her lap. Charlie silently complied while to her right Stephen mutely sat in a third leather chair.

David spoke first. "Why should we trust you?"

"You shouldn't," Ken replied matter-of-factly. "But if you are who I think you are, then you should be able to read my mind and know that I'm telling the truth. I'm just trying to help."

"You may mean well," Stephen replied. "But even the best intentions can end badly. We are deep in Resistance territory. How do you plan to protect us from *them?*"

Ken flashed a wry smile. “The Resistance doesn’t pay much attention to us. We’re way out in the middle of nowhere, there are less than a hundred of us, and we have just enough supplies to keep ourselves going.”

For the first time in a long time, Charlie sensed David allowing himself to hope a little. “So as long as the Resistance doesn’t know we’re here then we’re safe for a while.”

“Yes,” Ken replied. “I can offer you a block of suites on the club floor. No one else stays up there so you should be reasonably safe. I would suggest that you guys keep to yourselves. Not everyone here is as open-minded to people like you as I am.”

“What is this place?” Catherine asked.

“Before the world went to shit, this place was known as the Black Hills Hotel.” As he spoke, Ken took out a crystal decanter of whiskey, poured five glasses and handed one to each of them.

Charlie stared at the amber liquid in her glass for several minutes without imbibing. She had never tasted hard liquor before, and she had bad memories of her father’s past drunken behavior.

“We used to cater to the very wealthy and very private.” Ken continued. “This place was set up as an escape of sorts where the rich could go to get away from everything. The property features horseback riding, archery, hunting, four restaurants, a casino, and a water park. Behind the scenes, we also have our own power plant, vegetable farms, and even a cattle ranch. This place can produce its own power, water, and food without any supplies from the outside.”

Charlie slowly lifted her whiskey glass to her lips and took a tentative sip. The amber liquid tasted intensely bitter and burned her mouth and throat. It also made her chest feel warm and head a little lighter. Slowly her fear receded a bit. Charlie took another sip, coughed from the sharp burn, and felt herself relax a bit more. In that moment, it occurred to her why Daddy and David liked to drink whiskey so much. It took away the fear (if only for a little while) and made everything seem easier.

“After the world went to hell, the employees took shelter here. We also took in a few survivors from Turner.” As he spoke, Ken took a slow sip of whiskey from his glass. “We’ve been lucky enough to be mostly ignored by the Resistance so for all intents and purposes we are neutral.”

David slowly swirled his whiskey before taking a long draw of amber liquor. “So, if we stay here, how long will we be welcome?”

“As far as I’m concerned, you can stay for as long as you want, but there are others here who might have a problem with me taking in the girl that killed Senator Suire and her family. So let’s say you’re welcome for as long as you can keep your presence a secret. Like I said, I can give you a block of suites on the club floor. No one else lives up there so you’ll have the floor to yourselves. And I do suggest that you keep to yourselves. The suites up there have kitchenettes, and I will have food delivered every day. We have communal meals in the atrium three times a day and a happy hour from six until eight at the bar, but I would suggest that you skip those. Keep the rest of the community from getting too close to you.” He paused and renewed his wry smile. “I’m sorry that it has to be this way, but it’s for your own protection. We do have CB radios here, and I don’t want anyone turning you in to the Resistance.” After speaking that last word, he drank down the rest of his whiskey and set his glass on the desk.

David downed the rest of his drink. "Thank you for your hospitality."

"Of course," Ken replied. "Now it's getting late, and your daughter looks tired. How about I show you to your rooms?"

Five minutes later, Charlie stood between David and Catherine staring in awe at the lavish suite that Ken had given them.

The living room floors consisted of dark mahogany with white alpaca rugs, while red silk wallpaper adorned the walls. Directly ahead and to the left a narrow end table separated two deep, high backed, overstuffed dark brown leather chairs. To the right, the wall opened into a large, white marble fireplace over which hung an enormous flat-screen television. In front of the fireplace and television stood a long overstuffed dark leather couch identical to the one in Ken's office. On both sides of the marble hearth stood two large bookcases laden with numerous hardcover books.

Here stood J.R.R. Tolkien, Lloyd Alexander, Tom Clancy, C.S. Lewis, and an entire collection of Stephen King novels. All of her favorites. She smiled for a moment. This was a good place. She would spend many hours here, reading in peace.

Directly across from the bookshelves and slightly at an angle stood a large black grand piano. Charlie examined this with pure wonder for she had never lived anywhere with a piano. For a moment she wanted only to sit down and play with the black and white ivory keys. Then the desire passed, and she slowly crossed the living room.

The back wall of the living room consisted of solid, ballistic glass. Heavy red floor-length drapes covered this, making the living room a private sanctuary.

To her left the wall opened into a narrow alcove inside of which stood two heavy mahogany doors with brushed steel knobs; while to her right and beyond the far bookshelf the wall opened up into a dining area and kitchen.

The dining room table was of the same dark mahogany and was surrounded by matching high backed chairs with black leather seats. A large, crystal chandelier hung above the table, bathing the entire room in its vibrant golden glow. Dark mahogany cabinets with brushed stainless-steel hardware and appliances appointed the kitchen itself while a long black marble countertop separated kitchen and dining room. Three mahogany and black leather bar stools stood in front of this. Like in the living room, the back walls of the dining room and kitchen consisted of heavy ballistic glass. Along the front wall stood a mahogany and black marble bar complete with crystal decanters and barware.

Charlie admired this for a moment before turning left towards what she hoped would be the bedrooms. Now that the danger had passed, she suddenly felt drained. Charlie opened the nearest door in the little alcove and found a large bedroom.

Like the living room and dining room, the bedroom walls were appointed in red silk wallpaper, and the floor was dark mahogany with alpaca carpeting. A smaller fireplace opened up the wall opposite the door, and a huge, king-sized bed sat facing it. The bed was made up with white linens and a white comforter. A door next to the fireplace led into an en-suite bathroom with a glass shower and spa tub.

Charlie crossed the room and collapsed into bed without bothering to undress. Five minutes later she was dead to the world.

III

The wind felt cool and smelled of the sea. The city of Miami was deathly quiet, but Beathach knew better. Although a Loyalist city, Miami was far from under Loyalist control as the city continued to experience violent dissent from several organized crime factions that had taken the Great Civil War as an opportunity to attempt to seize power.

It was here that the last killing had occurred. Sergei Markovic had been found at his brothel with his hands severed, and his entrails spilled out on his office floor. A thirty-something statuesque red-haired woman had been sighted near the scene of the killing.

Beathach had not spoken to anyone but rather had used the power to stay out of sight and observe. Now, as he stood over the massive bloodstain left behind by Sergei Markovic, Beathach sensed the lingering presence of his killer. Chronologically she remained young, but life's experience had aged her well beyond her years. Beathach sensed sadness and a tremendous amount of anger and *yes,* the burning desire for vengeance. Someone had taken something most precious from this woman, and now she was seeking recompense.

Beathach smiled slightly with the good side of his mouth. She might have made a powerful Dark Knight, but he sensed no malevolence in her intentions. Only great, crushing grief and an edge of…

Madness?

She was, indeed, a threat. A rouge and possibly insane former Lightwarrior. Her actions had already stirred hatred for Enlighteneds among the public at large. She would be unpredictable and dangerous to anyone around her. She had to be eliminated.

She also represented a unique opportunity. Beathach was close, he had her identity if not her name. It would not take him long to find her location and finish her. However, if he killed her, he would only gain her death.

But then there were the McAuliffes and the girl. They were still on the run in a world plunged into civil war and they faced a mortal threat from the Resistance. They had to be getting desperate. Beathach recalled that David McAuliffe's primary concern had always been protecting his wife and adopted daughter from harm. Perhaps he could be persuaded to kill this woman in exchange for the promise of safety for his family. Maybe the safety of his family would be reason enough for him to commit an act of murder. And if so, well then, David McAuliffe would have taken the first step in the direction of becoming a potential ally.

After that final thought passed through his mind, Beathach turned and left Sergei Markov's office. As he walked through the dark halls of Markov's brothel, Beathach's mind drifted back to an earlier time. A time when he had been younger and oh so much more innocent.

IV

Beathach awoke to the sound of bird's chirruping in the window. The golden sunlight streaming in through the east window told him that it was still early. He slid to the edge of the bed, stood up, and went to the wardrobe across the room without bothering to summon the chamberlain. The castle's wooden planked floor creaked slightly under his weight.

As he dressed, Beathach detected the slight scent of roasting venison and his mouth began to water. He was starving hungry despite having eaten a heavy meal the night before.

After dressing, Beathach crossed his bedchamber and took the stairs down to the great hall where he found his adoptive mother and father already eating.

Beathach had been born approximately one hundred years after the fall of the Western Roman Empire as the illegitimate grandson of an early Briton king. He had never known his father or mother and was raised by a family of nobles the descendants of whom would be central to the history of Scotland.

He had also been born with the power, he would later come to learn that this made him an Enlightened. Even from a young age, Beathach had understood that he would need to keep the power a secret or risk being branded a warlock and burned alive. Thus, even his adoptive parents did not know that their son was an Enlightened.

As Beathach approached, his father looked up and met his eyes. "Good morning."

"Good morning, father," Beathach replied.

His mother smiled. "Good morning, Lucius."

"Good morning, mother." Beathach sat down across from his parents and began to eat. The salted pork was unappealing, but it satisfied his hunger all the same.

After eating his fill, Beathach went to the stables where the stable hands had his black charger, Storm, saddled and ready to ride. He would head out to the castle of Sir James Stewart, one of his father's vassal knights. Officially he was meeting with Sir James to collect the monthly rents. Unofficially, he intended to meet with Stewart's daughter Alana.

Beautiful, raven-haired, Alana Stewart. If he closed his eyes, he could picture her porcelain skin and honey gold eyes. And when it was silent he could still hear her soft, musical voice.

His hands remembered the soft touch of her skin and his nose, the sweet scent of rose water that lingered about her.

His heart quickened at the thought of her. Beathach knew that she was of a lower social standing, but he didn't care. She was beautiful and made him feel like no other could. He loved her, and that was all that mattered.

The ride to Hemlock Manor would take all day. Thus, he would be joining James and his family for dinner and then taking residence in their guest quarters for the evening.

The ride went by slowly and uneventfully. Beathach crossed farmer's fields and moors that later gave way to vast, old-growth forest. By midday he was deep within the great Byrnwoode forest, that would later be known as the Queen's Forest. The trees here were fantastically tall and thick, leaving the forest floor mostly clear of underbrush. It was late summer, and the forest was alive with the songs of birds, the skitter of squirrels in the trees and the rustle of leaves. Far off in the distance, at the very edge of perception Beathach detected a low snort followed by the faint rattle of deer antlers. His psychic senses told him that a buck several miles north of him had caught his scent.

Beathach smiled, at a different time, he would have urged his horse on in pursuit of the buck, but at present, his interest was with Alana. He still had four to five hours of riding ahead of him. A detour to hunt a deer would only delay him further.

After a time, the path widened a bit and opened into a small clearing. At the center of this lay a small, mirror-smooth pond. Golden sunlight shone down between the trees and gleamed off the water's surface setting it aflame. Beathach slowed his horse and dismounted near the water's edge before sitting down near the water's edge to eat.

He had packed a small lunch of salted pork and a skin of red wine. As he prepared his food, Beathach glanced at his reflection in the water. The young man that gazed back was handsome with cream-colored, smooth skin and intense perfect blue eyes. Beathach wore no facial hair and let his long, golden blond hair hang loose over his broad shoulders.

The salt pork was delicious and quickly sated his hunger. The red wine was his family's own vintage and was his favorite. It's dry, fruity notes cooled his palate and slaked his thirst. After eating and drinking his fill, Beathach mounted Storm and continued along the path.

V

By the time Beathach arrived at Hemlock Manor, the shadows had grown long, and the sun had drifted low in the sky. He was met at the gate by Alexandar, a servant of the Stewart family. Alexandar directed Beathach to the manor house before taking the reins of Storm and leading him to the stables.

A second servant by the name, William, admitted Beathach to the manor house and led him into the great hall. Sir James was a successful knight. Thus, his home Hemlock Manor was both a well-fortified castle and a lavishly appointed mansion. The castle's great hall was a long chamber with a vaulted ceiling supported by great stone pillars. The walls too were stone while the floor had been hewn of massive, red oak beams cut from ancient Byrnewood trees. The chamber was illuminated in flickering firelight and narrow bars of copper sunlight.

Long, red oak tables ran along the right- and left-hand sides of the chamber. Another shorter table sat upon a dais at the far end of the great hall. This table had been set for a dinner of roasted pork and turnips.

Here Sir James sat eating with his wife Kirstin and daughter Alana.

James was a middle-aged man of medium height and more than medium girth. His black hair was streaked with gray and balding in spots. He had a sallow complexion with many scars from a bout of smallpox in his youth. James wore a red fox fur cloak closed with a simple iron broach. Beneath this, he wore a white linen shirt and leather breeches.

His wife was a tall and portly woman of middle thirties. Her face was pale and freckled, and her hair carrot-colored and straggly. She wore a long green linen dress that covered most of her skin below the neck. The dress had once been quite beautiful, Beathach noted, but many years of wear had left it threadbare and stained in places.

Alana looked stunning despite her worn and threadbare blue linen gown. Her raven black hair had been neatly combed and lay loose and shining on her shoulders. She met his eyes wordlessly as he approached.

James stood and bowed his head slightly. "Good evening, my Lord, what a pleasant surprise."

Beathach inclined his head slightly in response. "Good evening, Sir James."

"You are just in time for dinner, my Lord." As he spoke, James nodded imperceptibly to an attendant who silently pulled out a chair beside Alana. Beathach sat down, and a platter was set before him. This was soon piled high with slices of pork and turnips. The attendant then placed a goblet of blood-red wine beside Beathach's plate.

"To what do we owe the pleasure, my Lord?" Sir James asked amiably.

Beathach offered him a slight smile in return. "I am here to collect the monthly rents." Though neither spoke of it, both Beathach and James knew this to be code. Beathach had arrived on horseback alone, and Sir James was to tender payment in pounds of gold which would be both difficult and dangerous to transport without a wagon and a guard.

"Would you care for some music, my Lord?" This too was code. There would be music to allow him to dance with Alana. James was inquiring as to whether Beathach intended to continue to court his daughter.

"I would," Beathach responded.

Both men had long since agreed that they would not speak a word of Beathach's courtship of Alana Stewart following Beathach's father's public declaration of his desire to see Beathach married to a lady of the royal house Wessex of England. Beathach had met several ladies of the said house, and although they were quite beautiful and friendly, none of them were Alana.

For his part, Beathach had no fear of defying his father's wish that he would marry an English princess. He knew that no harm would come to *him.* Nevertheless, he was far less confident of the safety of Alana should his father learn of Beathach's love for her. It was for this reason that he had sworn Sir James to secrecy until after he and Alana had married.

On that night though, Beathach put his fears aside and enjoyed the evening. The two drank together, danced and talked of inconsequential things.

VI

Later that night they decided to take a walk under the late summer moonlight. The night was warm and not especially dark, owing to the great orange full moon. For a while, they walked in silence before Beathach broke the spell.

"It's a beautiful night." He found himself saying, avoiding the topic that occupied his thoughts.

"It is." Alana agreed. "I'm glad we can spend it together, my Lord."

"Yes, but you need not refer to me as 'my Lord.' Just Lucius."

She smiled. "Of course…Lucius."

He stopped walking for a moment and turned to meet her eyes. Without a word, Beathach and Alana closed the distance between each other. Neither broke eye contact. Beathach leaned in impulsively and then they were kissing.

A warm sensation flooded through his body, bringing every individual nerve ending and muscle to life. The hairs on his arms seemed to stand on end. He had never felt so alive and…yes… happy in all his life. Yet he was afraid, not of his father, rather he feared that Alana did not have the same feelings for him as he had for her.

In that moment he wanted nothing other than to spend the rest of his life with Alana. Now he was kneeling and had taken Alana's hand into his.

"I am neither a wise man nor a pious man. All I know is that I want nothing more than to spend the rest of my life with you."

Alana was silent and held his gaze steadily. Then she offered him the sweetest smile he had ever seen. "I love you, Lucius, and nothing would make me happier."

His heart leapt with joy bringing the power with it. Beathach forced the power down even as a deliriously joyful smile spread across his face.

"Then let us be married at once." He found himself saying.

"But my father…" She began to protest.

"I will seek his approval of course," Beathach responded. "He will surely grant his blessing."

VII

Indeed, Sir James did give his blessing. In fact, he arranged for his household priest to wed them that night.

Within two hours, Beathach and Alana stood before the priest swearing their vows. By midnight they were wed and locked inside the guest chambers to consummate the marriage.

They began slowly. Beathach took Alana into his arms and opened her dress with slow deliberation before allowing it to slip to the ground. She now stood nude before him. Her pale, porcelain skin glowed under the flickering candlelight. She leaned in and kissed him passionately, her tongue finding its way into his mouth. Beathach's hands found her pert breasts and gently kneaded them. Her erect, pink nipples slipped between his fingers. Alana's breath quickened, and she kissed him more deeply. As she did, Beathach felt her hands feverishly untying the leather thong that held his breaches closed. In a few moments, she had cast them down around his ankles. He was somehow shirtless, his shirt top tossed upon the floor.

Now they were on the bed, and he was kissing her firm breasts as her hands stroked his erect manhood, sending waves of pleasure through his body. His breathing quickened, and a soft groan escaped his lips. Her breath was rapid and punctuated by soft little moans of pleasure. Her flesh was amazingly warm, almost feverish to the touch. He wanted to be inside her.

"Oh, God." She was saying. "Lucius, I need you."

He mounted her and tried to push inside. She was impossibly tight. He stopped. "It feels too small. I'm afraid I'll hurt you."

He felt her push down against him. A soft moan of pain escaped her throat. "I want you so bad I don't care if it hurts."

He pushed in firmly and felt something break. Then he was deep inside. Alana let out a cry. It had hurt her, more than she had expected, he felt.

Still, Alana did not ask him to stop, to the contrary, she pushed against him, and he began to push back. The sensation was almost hurtful in its pleasure. Without meaning to, Beathach felt himself reaching into the power. His mind touched Alana's, and they became one. Joy beyond measure flooded through their combined consciousness.

Suddenly, Beathach knew her, understood her better than he understood even himself. Her favorite color was green. She loved wolfhounds and riding and the smell of the ocean. Part of her wished she were a man so that she could be a knight like her father. She kept an engraved bastard sword in her chambers below the bed. And she loved him, more than anyone in the world, she… loved… *him.*

And he loved her. She was all that mattered to him now. It was a strange feeling as if he had awoken from a dream. His entire reality had changed in that one moment.

All at once Beathach felt an explosion of joy and then it was over. His mind disengaged from Alana's, and they were lying in bed next to each other, panting and sweating.

"I love you." The words escaped his lips as little more than a gasp.

"I love you too." She replied softly as she laid her head on his shoulder. Beathach slipped his arm around her, and it was in this position that they drifted off to sleep.

VIII

Kira Morozov lay still in her darkened hotel room at the Dorchester, mind racing out of control.

She had found and killed Sergei Markovic only hours earlier. Sergei had bought her daughter, Aria and pimped her out to the man who murdered her.

Sergei deserved to suffer and die, and she had exacted brutal revenge upon him. Yet she did not feel vindicated or relieved. Instead, the pain of losing her daughter felt more keen than ever. And she felt something else, remorse for killing Sergei and Gary. They both deserved to die. Yet she knew that she was wrong to have killed them out of hate and vengeance.

She was a Lightwarrior and had pledged to reject such base instincts as revenge.

Why? Her daughter's voice whispered in her mind. *Mom, why did you kill those men?*

They hurt you, baby. She replied desperately. *Those men raped and murdered you. They deserve to suffer for what they did to you.*

For a moment, Kira imagined she could see her daughter step from the shadows at the foot of the bed. Aria was a tall, slender girl of twelve. Her luxurious, dark brown hair hung straight and loose on her shoulders as her normally cream and rosy pink skin shone bone-white in the moonlight from the hotel window. Aria's wideset, deep, liquid brown eyes met Kira's steadily. *No Mom. Those men hurt me, but that didn't make it ok to kill them.* Aria's words cut through her like razors.

Baby I couldn't just let them get away with what they did to you. Kira responded on the verge of tears now.

I'm ok Mom. I'm worried about you. Aria's voice became soft and deeply sympathetic. *You broke your promise, Mom. You killed those men for revenge. You're still covered in their blood.*

Kira was crying now. *I'm sorry Baby, it… it just hurts so much. I miss you, Aria.*

I miss you too, Mom. Aria replied with a sad smile. *And I love you. But you have to stop. They can't hurt me anymore. If you keep killing, then you're letting them hurt you.*

I'll stop just, please stay here with me Baby. Kira sobbed.

It was then that she realized she was alone again. The darkened hotel room seemed colder than before and lonelier than ever.

Please don't leave me here alone. Kira begged in vain.

She would always be alone. Her husband had died drowning in his own mucus and blood, and her daughter was murdered because of her mother's sins.

IX

Kira lay in silence for an unknown period of time, eluded by sleep. Eventually, she rose and went out into the night.

She left her hotel room without any thought or intention but somewhere deep inside, beneath conscious awareness, her purpose was fixed.

The night air was quiet and still. At this late hour, even the club-goers and barflies had wandered home to sleep off their drunkenness. Only the true night people remained, and these people were nowhere to be found. A cold, stiff breeze tugged at her blue jeans and battered, brown leather jacket.

Kira turned south on Collins Avenue and walked for a block before coming to her car, an unassuming gray 2001 Toyota Corolla. Five minutes later Kira was headed south on Collins with no specific plans as to where she was going.

Kira knew the names and locations of the Russian gangsters who had been involved in Aria's death but the location of the man who had actually raped and murdered her daughter remained a mystery.

She sensed that he remained somewhere in Miami, but that was all. As she continued north, Kira's mind returned to this man. He had been a high-value client of Sergei Markovic. Sergei had refused to say anything more even at the threat of death.

She had reached South Beach and, though she still had no specific plans, she felt strongly that she had neared somewhere important. Impulsively she turned left on 5th Street on her way to the MacArthur Causeway.

Twenty minutes later she was standing outside the gates of a large mansion on Hibiscus Island.

X

For seven years following the birth of Aria, Kira's life was idyllic. Even the loss of her job with Devin Energy, after her department was downsized turned out to be a blessing. Terry's FBI agent's salary provided enough to for them to live on and she was able to be a stay at home mother for Aria.

When Aria was three years old the FBI reassigned Terry to its Miami branch and moved their family to Florida.

Four years later, everything began to fall apart. It began when Terry came home early one afternoon with a cough and a high fever.

It was two o'clock in the afternoon, and she was relaxing on the couch with a cup of Chai. A rerun of *The Tudors* was on the television when she heard Terry's key in the front door.

Kira was more than a little surprised. She had not expected Terry to come home until seven or eight. Her surprise quickly turned to concern when she saw him.

Terry's black hair was sodden, and his normally tan skin was pale and glistened with sweat.

“Are you ok, babe?” Kira asked, making no attempt to keep the worry out of her voice.

“I’m not feeling so great.” Terry’s deep bass voice was weak and hoarse. “But I’ll be ok. I just need to lie down.” As he spoke, Terry staggered into the living room and collapsed onto the couch, still wearing his suit jacket and dress shoes.

Kira went to him and laid a hand across his forehead, her concern mounting. His flesh radiated intense heat. “You’re burning up!” The words escaped her in a harsh, frightened whisper before she could stifle them.

“I’ll be ok.” He repeated in a low, groan. “I just need to sleep.”

“You need to go to the hospital.” She replied as calmly as she could manage.

“No. No hospital. Just let me sleep.” She could barely make out his voice now. Terry had closed his eyes, and his breathing had become slow and labored.

Kira’s heart quickened. Without bothering to argue, she went to the bathroom and got the electronic thermometer out of the medicine cabinet. A quick scan of her husband’s forehead confirmed her worst fears.

“105°! Fuck! I’m calling 911.” Before Terry could contradict her, she took out her cell phone and dialed.

Twenty minutes later, they were rushing into the Mount Sinai emergency room. Kira was on her phone again, this time with her friend, Fiona Weston, to request that she pick up Aria from school.

“How long has he had these symptoms?” The doctor was saying.

“He came home from work today with a fever.” She replied. “Last night he was fine.”

“Has he had any other symptoms besides the fever?”

She shook her head. “No.”

“Has he eaten anything unusual?” The doctor continued.

“No.” She replied.

“Ok, we’ll do what we can to get the fever down and run some tests to find out what’s making him sick.”

“Thank you.” Kira was not comforted. She sensed something horrible was about to happen and was afraid.

That evening Terry was admitted to the quarantine unit diagnosed with an aggressive form of hantavirus.

Kira had been forced to leave her daughter with Fiona as she would not be permitted within the hospital. Moreover, Kira knew not what had made her husband sick and was unwilling to risk exposing Aria. It didn't matter, in truth, even if Aria had been permitted in the hospital without the risk of infection Kira had no desire to traumatize her daughter with the sight of her father in such a state.

XI

By ten o'clock that night, Terry's condition had worsened to the point where he was barely conscious.

Terry lay in a hospital bed surrounded in plastic. A rat's nest of tubes and wires laced into and through his body. Kira sat wordlessly beside his bed, the yellow gown she had been obliged to wear crackled lightly with each movement she made. In her heart, she was frightened. She had always known Terry as a strong man. Now, for the first time since she had met him, Terry looked weak, like a small, vulnerable child.

"Kira?" He croaked barely audibly.

"I'm here Terry." She replied softly. "How are you feeling?"

"Like shit." He responded with a thin smile.

She couldn't help but chuckle slightly. Even as sick as Terry was, he had not lost his sense of humor.

"I think I'm dying. I feel like I'm drowning." As he finished he began coughing furiously, until he spat up a quantity of blood.

"Oh, god…" Kira's fear was growing. Without thinking she hit the call switch on the side of Terry's bed. A nurse appeared a moment later.

"He's coughing up blood." Kira snapped at the young woman.

"It's going to be ok." The nurse was saying. She approached Terry. "Mr. Blackhawk, are you having trouble breathing?"

Terry nodded in between harsh barks. More blood spilled from his mouth. He was struggling to get air in.

"Mr. Blackhawk, I'm going to intubate you. Is that ok?" The nurse's tone was calm and professional but held a hint of concern.

Terry answered with another series of harsh coughs and a barely perceptible nod.

Before the nurse began, Terry turned towards Kira. "I love you, sweetheart." These would be the last words he would ever speak.

Five minutes later, the nurse had inserted a flexible plastic tube down Terry's throat, making speech impossible.

XII

Kira sat up all night with her husband. By midnight he had lost consciousness, and by morning a dramatic drop in his heart rate drove him into a deep coma.

Later that morning, Terry's physician, a Dr. Spender arrived. He gave Terry only a cursory once-over before asking Kira if they could speak in the hallway. Kira agreed knowing already what the doctor would tell her.

"Your husband's condition is deteriorating rapidly," Spender told her in what she sensed was intended to be a sympathetic tone. To her, his tone sounded cold and condescending. "I'm sorry, but it is unlikely he will survive beyond the end of the week."

Spender continued talking, but she was no longer listening. Instead, she simply studied him, wanting to remember the image of the man who told her that her husband would die. Dr. Spender was a tall and slender man in his mid-fifties with iron-gray hair; hard, weathered features and dark eyes. The scent of stale cigarette smoke wafted from his institutional green scrubs.

Spender was saying something about calling Terry's family. She almost laughed. Like Kira, Terry's parents were dead, and he had no siblings. Kira and Aria were his only family.

Kira found herself asking. "Is he contagious."

"No," Spender responded.

"Then can I have our daughter brought here?" Kira asked.

"How old is she?" Spender asked.

"Five." She replied.

Spender looked annoyed. "It's against hospital policy to bring children in here, but we can't stop what we don't know."

Without another word, he turned and left.

Kira took out her phone and dialed her only friend.

"Kira? Is everything ok?" Fiona's voice held compassion and concern.

"No," Kira replied, suddenly close to tears. She took a deep breath. "I need you to bring Aria here right away. It's bad. They're saying Terry doesn't have much time left."

"Of course," Fiona replied. "We'll be right there."

XIII

Thirty minutes later, Fiona arrived with Aria. Both looked bewildered, and Fiona was more than a little concerned.

Fiona Weston was a curvy thirty-something woman of mixed descent with black hair and cinnamon skin. She spoke with a slight suggestion of an Eastern Asian accent that Kira could never place. "How are you holding up?"

Kira met her dark eyes steadily. "I'm ok. I still can't believe this is really happening. I keep waiting to wake up." She felt close to tears.

"I'm sorry…I wish there was more I could do." Fiona responded.

"Is Daddy sleeping?" Aria asked plaintively.

"Yes, sweetheart, he's sleeping." Kira lied. "But he can hear you if you talk to him."

"Ok."

Kira watched as Aria approached her father's bed cautiously.

"It's ok," Kira said gently. "I know he's a little scary looking, but he's still Daddy."

Aria gingerly took her father's hand. "Daddy?" She whispered. "I love you, Daddy. I'm sorry you're sick."

The sight of five-year-old Aria comforting her father brought silent tears to Kira's eyes. Aria had no idea of what was to come and that made it all the more hurtful for Kira knew that there was no hope. Terry was dying.

Though he was unconscious, Terry too seemed to know that his time was short for his heartbeat quickened slightly before becoming erratic and triggering an alarm.

Several nurses and a doctor appeared with a crash cart and quickly shooed Kira, Fiona, and Aria from the room.

Kira stopped just outside the room and watched through the window as her husband died.

Her heart tore apart in her chest, but she would not allow herself to break down. If only for her daughter's sake. She loved Terry, more than she would have thought possible, and she knew in that moment that she would never love another.

XIV

Terry's funeral was ten days later. There were no mourners beyond Kira; Aria; Fiona and her girlfriend; Sharon Dixon.

It all seemed unreal, even as the funeral director closed the lid on Terry's casket for the last time it still didn't seem real to her. Two weeks ago, Terry had been healthy and active. They had made love for God's sake. And yet here she stood watching as her husband was carried from the small Lutheran church they attended somewhat regularly.

Now she was on her way to the gravesite she had hastily picked out. Aria sat beside her, chattering away about SpongeBob, Teen Titans, and God knows what else. It was not real to her either. She was too young to understand, and it had all happened so fast.

A short time later, Kira found herself standing over Terry's casket at the gravesite. The church pastor was reading from the Bible and reciting meaningless platitudes.

This can't be real. It just can't. Terry was fine. He was healthy and active. There was nothing wrong with him.

Now they were lowering him into his grave. Suddenly, it became real to Kira. Terry was gone forever, the man who had understood her like no one else, the man she had confided in about the power, the man she had married; the man who had fathered Aria. He was gone, dead. It had all happened so suddenly. All at once Kira broke. She cried with no force, for any energy she might have had was driven from her. Instead Kira wept softly and bitterly as her husband was slowly lowered into the ground.

At the time she believed that day was the worst of her life. Kira felt a pain like nothing she had ever felt before. Her heart bled, and she was afraid.

How would she support her daughter now that Terry was gone? He had been the breadwinner their entire marriage. Kira never seemed to be able to hold a job for more than a few months. Kira and Terry had managed to accumulate modest savings and Terry had a small life insurance policy through the Bureau, but that money would only support Kira and Aria for a few months. Kira would need to find work, and she knew that would be difficult.

XV

In the following weeks, Kira hunted in vain for work, any work, that would pay the bills. She was not successful and in the ensuing time, sank deeper and deeper into depression. Kira missed Terry, but more than that she needed him. Kira was intelligent but could not easily relate to others. Terry had always been good at getting people to like and respect him. He had been the careerman, while she had cared for their daughter.

It was not as though Kira did not desire a career. She had worked hard to earn her engineering degree. And yet, success always seemed to elude her. Kira had put her own ambitions on hold when Aria was born but now... Now she needed to work to support her daughter, and she was *failing.*

Kira was failing her daughter. As time wore on, Kira was increasingly tempted to give up. Yet she would not allow herself for she knew Aria depended on her.

Fiona and Sharon stopped by the house regularly, sometimes to bring food, other times to take care of Aria while Kira went out to job hunt and still others to help with chores. Kira was grateful for their help and yet she hated them. They had been incredible friends to her after Terry's passing, and yet Kira hated them because they still had each other. Neither Fiona nor Sharon had lost the person they had fallen in love with. They weren't alone. Kira hated them for their good fortune and hated them more for being happy. Each time their eyes met was a dagger in Kira's heart and each time they shared a smile or laugh Kira died a little inside.

Oh, how she hated them.

Two months after Terry's passing, Kira became convinced that things could not get any worse. It would not be until later that she would learn how very wrong she was.

XVI

It began on a Friday night. Fiona called around eight o'clock and asked if Kira wanted to go out that night.

"I don't have a sitter," Kira replied in a faux regretful tone. The last thing Kira wanted was to go out anywhere with Fiona and Sharon so that she could have her nose rubbed in their happy relationship.

"Don't worry about that," Fiona said with a smile in her voice. "Sharon will keep Aria while you and I have a girls' night out."

"I don't know…I'm kinda tired." The fact that Sharon would stay in with Aria made the idea of going out only slightly more palatable. Kira felt deeply depressed and not in the least interested in socializing.

"Come on, you need this." Fiona's voice had become slightly cajoling. "I'm not taking no for an answer."

Kira forced herself to chuckle slightly. "Then I guess the answer is 'yes.'"

Thirty minutes later Kira found herself getting out of Fiona's 2010 Chevy Tahoe at the front door of the Tropical Sands casino. Kira was not a gambler, and Fiona knew it. Still, casinos generally served cheaper drinks than the bar, and they were less tolerant of nonsense from drunken patrons.

Fiona wanted to play slots. While Kira initially abstained, she eventually decided to put a couple of dollars into a James Bond-themed machine. Kira knew before she started that she would lose and sure enough within twenty minutes, her two dollars were gone. Still, she had fun despite herself.

Later that evening, and after a few cocktails, Kira found herself sitting across a poker table from Fiona, two hundred dollars in poker chips lay stacked on the felt in front of her. The game was No-Limit Hold 'em.

Here Kira was in her element. After a few minutes of nervousness, Kira quickly realized that she could sense the other players' emotions and intentions. She *knew* when they were holding good cards and when they were bluffing. She could also quite clearly sense what cards would come off the deck next. And so, she found herself winning easily.

Before long Kira's small two-hundred-dollar stack had grown to a two-thousand-dollar stack and then an eight-thousand-dollar stack when a grizzled looking and uncouth fifty-something man of enormous girth made the mistake of pushing all-in against her with a low pair when she was holding three tens. The man was genuinely shocked when she showed her cards and, in his surprise, managed to drop his smoldering Pall Mall onto his stained wife-beater t-shirt.

"Fuck me!" He snarled as he quickly swept his cigarette onto the floor, stomped it out and pushed away from the table.

As he walked out of the poker room, Kira was left with a clear view of the man's paint-stained dull blue sweatpants.

At around three in the morning, Fiona wanted to leave as she was tired and had spent all of her gambling money. Kira agreed, though she felt energized and more than a little excited. As she gathered up her winnings, Kira could feel the blood in her temples. The money in front of her would keep Aria and her in food, mortgage, and utilities for at least three months.

As she rode home with Fiona that night, Kira considered that she might have found a way to support her daughter. The power had made it impossible for her to hold down a normal job for any real length of time, but now she had found a way to use the power to make money for her daughter.

XVII

In the days that followed, Kira returned to the casino regularly, each time leaving with greater and greater sums of money. Some of the regulars began to become wary and refused to play at the same table as her. Around the same time, the pit bosses began to watch her closely. She sensed that they suspected her of cheating and in a sense, she supposed she was. To use the power to read the emotions and intentions of the other players, and to predict the other cards certainly gave her an unfair advantage. But she would never be caught, and she needed the money.

Furthermore, she felt there was some justice to what she was doing. The normal people, those without the power, had rejected her. They had made it impossible for her to survive with her daughter. It was only fair that she use the one advantage she had to push back, and it was not as though she was robbing these people. They chose to enter into a card game knowing that they risked losing money to her or anyone else that might sit down.

For several months, Kira confined her poker game to the casinos around Miami. Then late one night she was approached by a hard-looking man in his mid-twenties. It was two in the morning, and Kira was standing outside the main entrance to the Magic City Casino waiting for the parking valet to bring her car around when a pale-skinned slender man with close-cropped blond hair stepped out of the shadows beyond the entryway overhang. As he approached her, Kira noted the man's black leather biker's jacket and slender cut designer blue jeans. A smoldering cigarette dangled from the man's left hand. Though she sensed no threat from the man, Kira understood at once that he was dangerous.

"You play well." The man's slow, melodious voice held no accent. After speaking, he slowly raised his cigarette to his mouth and took a long drag.

Kira said nothing.

"I've been watching you for several days, and you always seem to come out ahead." The man's eyes, two chips of ice, met hers as he spoke. "Your skill is wasted here. You play for a few thousand dollars here and there, but you will never make any real money playing low stakes against the tourists."

"I'm not here to get rich," Kira replied.

"No. You are here to support your daughter." The man replied, matter-of-factly. "And I can help you with that. You could be playing one or two games a year instead of playing every week. And you could be making hundreds of thousands instead of a few grand."

"I'm not interested," Kira replied. Just then the parking valet returned with her car. "I have to go. Don't come near me again."

The man smiled, revealing a set of straight, perfectly white teeth.

Shark's teeth. She thought. This man was Russian Mafia. Her psychic senses assured her of that much.

"Very well. I will be around if you should change your mind." He took another long drag from his cigarette, then turned and disappeared into the shadows once more.

XVIII

For the next four years, Kira continued to support herself and her daughter by playing low stakes poker once or twice a week. She was able to pay off the mortgage on her home, settle Terry's medical bills, and send Aria to private school. Her life seemed to be getting better, and for a while, Kira almost felt happy.

During this time, she did not see the blond man though she sensed that he was still nearby, still watching and waiting.

Kira had almost allowed herself to believe that things were going to work out when the darkness closed in once more. It was late in the afternoon on the last Thursday in January four years and eight months to the day Terry had died.

Kira had slept most of the day in preparation for an all-night trip to the Tropical Sands. Fiona had agreed to pick up Aria from school and keep her for the night although in truth Aria hardly needed babysitting. At twelve years of age, Aria knew first aid, could do her own laundry and dishes and even knew a few basic recipes. Still, Kira felt safer knowing that her daughter wasn't alone.

Kira lay in her bed drifting in and out of consciousness when her phone began playing *Hurt* by Nine Inch Nails. Kira groaned and answered the call.

"Hey, Kira." She recognized the voice at once.

"Hey." In the back of her mind, Kira suddenly felt that something wasn't right.

"I'm at Mount Sinai. Aria's had an accident…" Fiona's voice was close to tears. "You should get here quickly. Kira…I'm sorry."

Before Kira could react, the line went dead. Kira felt her heart leap up into her chest and for a moment thought she would vomit. In the same moment, the power stirred within her. Kira instinctively bit it back. Now was definitely not the time for that.

Despite her rapid heartbeat, Kira remained unnaturally calm throughout the twenty-minute drive to the hospital. Upon arriving she headed for the receptionist's desk where she was directed to a private room in the very rear of the emergency room. Here she found Fiona talking to a doctor young enough to be fresh out of his teens. The two were talking in hushed voices, and both immediately shut up upon noticing her arrival.

"What happened?" To Kira's surprise, her voice came out very calm.

Fiona spoke first. "Aria's been hit by a car. She was riding her skateboard in front of the house, and a drunk driver hit her." Before she could say any more, Fiona burst into tears.

"Are you Aria's mother?" The doctor inquired.

"Yes, Kira Morozov." Her exterior was still calm though inside Kira felt the beginnings of panic. "Is she ok? Is my daughter ok?"

The doctor was silent for a moment. "Your daughter has suffered a severe concussion, a fractured hip, several fractured ribs, and an abdominal hemorrhage. We will need to perform surgery to stop the bleeding."

For a moment, Kira had a feeling of *Déjà vu* as she recalled having a similar conversation regarding her husband four years earlier.

"Can I see her?" Kira asked absently as her mind continued to reel with growing fear. The last time she had been here, she had lost her husband. Was she now destined to lose her daughter as well?

"You may visit with her briefly before we take her upstairs. But Miss Morozov I have to warn you…she's in pretty rough shape, and she won't recognize you."

"I understand. But I need to see my daughter." Kira persisted, her voice still artificially calm.

"Of course."

Kira passed through the doorway into her daughter's room to find Aria lying like a broken doll amidst a tangle of wires and tubes. Her face and head were bruised and wrapped in crimson-stained bandages. One of her legs was strapped into a brace while the other had been packed in bloody gauze. Though she was unconscious, Aria's face was contorted in an expression of pain.

The sight of her daughter broke Kira completely, and she began to weep softly. "I'm here baby." She whispered through the tears. "Mom's here."

She carefully took her daughter's hand. "It's going to be ok, Aria."

The doctor's voice came from behind her. "That's all the time we can spare. We need to get her into surgery right away."

Kira stepped back and watched as the doctor and a gang of nurses gathered Aria up and wheeled her away. Kira followed them to the elevator and watched the doors close over Aria's small, broken body. In her heart, she feared that this would be the last image she would have of her daughter.

XIX

Aria was in surgery for over seven hours; seven hours that Kira spent frozen in abject terror that she would end up alone. The power, stirred by her emotions, bubbled menacingly in the back of her mind, begging her to let it out to destroy. Kira focused her waning will on suppressing the power, mostly because she had nothing else to do, for a significant part of her did not care if the power got out and ravaged this accursed hospital.

By default, Kira's power always manifested as some version of psychokinesis. It could be very destructive even if it only got loose a little bit and so she was careful to maintain control.

At some point, before her daughter got out of surgery, Kira was approached by the blond-haired man from the casino. Once again, he was dressed in his black leather biker's jacket and slim-fitting designer jeans. His ice-chip eyes and cold expression were as hard and -intractable as ever.

"I am sorry to hear about your daughter." The man's voice held a hint of genuine empathy. "If she were mine I would have the heart of the man who had run her over on my desk."

Kira glanced at him coldly. "I appreciate your condolences. Now, what do you want?"

"The driver who hit Aria. He hasn't been found by the police, has he?"

Kira shook her head. "No."

A cop had stopped by to talk to her about the accident and advise her that the driver had fled the scene and remained at large.

The man's expression became grim. "We can find him for you and make him pay."

Kira stared at the man coldly. "You mean kill him."

"*Find* him." The man corrected. "Of course, accidents can happen…" He smiled darkly exposing his perfect white shark's teeth.

"And what will you expect in return for this…*kindness*?" Kira responded with more than a hint of suspicion.

"Play for us." The man responded. "Three games. We will stake you one million dollars per game. You may keep half of any money you win."

Kira was silent.

"Your daughter deserves justice, and her medical bills will be substantial. We can help with both." As he spoke the man took out a cigarette and clenched it in his teeth without lighting the end.

Aria did deserve justice. The man was right about that much. "You are Russian mafia, correct?"

The man did not respond.

"Your favors never come free." Kira continued. "If I accept your offer I will be indebted to the *Bratva* forever."

The man smiled slightly. "Is that so bad? We are all slaves to someone. Whether it's a nine to five employer or a gangster, someone owns everyone."

Kira met the man's gaze steadily. "Three games. And you get me the name of the man who hit my daughter first."

"Of course." The man replied unctuously. "As a goodwill gesture." Without another word, the man turned and left.

XX

An hour later, Aria got out of surgery. She remained unconscious and looked even worse for wear, but the surgeon, a Dr. Skinner assured Kira that she would pull through.

Kira sat with Aria for the remainder of that night, finally drifting off to sleep when the sky had turned from black to purple. When she awoke again, Kira found that Aria had regained consciousness and was watching TV and munching on French fries.

Her face remained bruised and swollen, but Aria did not seem to be troubled by this. She smiled when she noticed Kira had awakened.

"Hi, Mom." Her voice was a bit slurred as a result of the swelling.

"Hi, Baby," Kira replied with a smile. "How are you feeling."

"Hungry," Aria replied simply. "Can I have some more fries?"

Kira almost burst out laughing. She was immensely relieved that Aria was doing better, and the simple unimportance of Aria's question suddenly struck her as hilarious. "I'll go find the nurse and see if she'll bring you some Babe."

Kira took the call button from Aria's bed and clicked it. A few minutes later, a nurse in institutional green scrubs appeared. "May I help you?"

"Can I have some more fries, please?" Aria piped up.

The nurse smiled. "Of course, sweetheart. Doctor says you should eat as much as you can."

Aria smiled. "Thanks."

Kira spent the rest of that Friday and all of Saturday with her daughter. Together they watched TV, played cards, and talked. Late Saturday afternoon, Fiona stopped in with a stack of books and board games.

XXI

After Aria drifted off to sleep Saturday night, Kira's phone rang with a blocked number. The voice male voice on the other end was one she had never heard before and spoke only a single phrase.

"Go home."

Then the line went dead.

Though the caller did not identify himself or give an explanation, Kira understood at once. Taking pains not to make a sound, she quietly kissed her daughter on the cheek and crept from the room.

Twenty minutes later, she was standing in the living room of her home. An average-sized, nondescript brown box sat on the red oak floor near the entryway. For a moment Kira was afraid to move for she understood at once what the meaning of this package was. Then she slowly bent down, took the box into her hands, and carefully opened it.

In an instant, she screamed and dropped the box as she recoiled both outwardly and inwardly. Inside she found a man's severed head. He had been young. His dark black hair was greasy and mottled with blood. His hazel eyes stared up at her unseeing, like two cloudy marbles. She could not bear to look, but could not look away either. Beneath the head lay a photograph of a white, Audi R8 coup with a shattered front grill and a dent in the hood stained in fresh blood.

Though she was horrified, Kira carefully moved the head out of the way to find that there was a second photograph beneath the first and a handwritten note. Kira briefly noted that the second photograph matched the plate number from the police report before turning her attention to the note.

Saturday night, two weeks from today. Double J Storage. Overtown.

Without a word, Kira picked up the box again and carried it into the garage where she kept the trash cans. Quickly and without thinking, she closed up the box and buried it in the rotting scraps from dinner three nights ago. Trash pickup was the following morning. Kira made a mental note to come home early so that she could carry the bag directly to the garbage truck.

Whomever this young man had once been he was wealthy. Someone would surely be looking for him, and it would not be good for her or Aria if she were caught with the young man's head. Kira was surprised by how calm she was. She was horrified by what the man from the casino had done in her name. She had only wanted to know the name of the drunk driver who had run over her daughter so that she might turn him in to the law. The ice chip eyed young man had brought her the man's head. Yet it made perfect sense, for now, the *Bratva* owned her.

Or so they think... She thought, feeling very clever.

They could not possibly know who they were really dealing with. Oh, Kira would keep her end of the bargain, and then the *Bratva* would leave her alone. She was a Lightwarrior; she was more of a threat to them than they were to her.

XXII

Over the next two weeks, everything was quiet. Kira spent most of the time with her daughter. The hospital held Aria for the entire time before releasing her with prescriptions for several antibiotics and pain medications. On the Friday before she was to play, Kira's cell phone rang. A young man's voice told her simply to meet them at 11:00 pm the following night.

As it turned out, Double J Storage was merely a meeting place. After she arrived, two men approached Kira, put a black burlap bag over her head, and led her in the dark towards the sound of an engine. Hands grasped Kira's arms and forcibly shoved her into a car. A few moments later the vehicle began to move.

After an unknown period of time, and a dozen or more turns, hands grabbed her again and pulled her from the car. Kira allowed herself to be led inside an strange building. The air inside the building was stale and smelled of cigar smoke, cheap beer, and even cheaper perfume.

The hands led Kira some distance before spinning her around and forcing her to sit. A moment later, the burlap bag was snatched from her head.

Kira found herself sitting in a red velvet wingback chair in front of a massive ebony banker's desk. Behind this desk sat a man of average build and slightly above average height. His dark, shaggy hair came to his shoulders and held more than a trace of gray. His face, though not old, was weathered and hard as granite. She would later know this man as Gary Volkov. Gary was dressed in a black, pinstripe suit and a pastel pink button-down shirt and was puffing away at a fat Cuban cigar. Thick clouds of purple smoke floated around his head filling the air with the rich scent of fine tobacco. Gary looked up at her briefly and met her gaze with penetrating steel-gray eyes.

"So, you're the poker genius that Alexi is so excited about." He said softly.

"And you are?" Kira responded.

"Gary Volkov." As he spoke, Gary extended his hand to her. Kira took it, expecting a handshake. Instead, Gary turned her hand over and kissed the back gently, a chivalric gesture long forgotten by most.

"It's a pleasure to meet you, Miss…Morozov isn't it?"

"Yes." She confirmed softly.

"Can I offer you a drink, Miss Morozov?" He continued. "I have a very nice bottle of Moskovskaya, or if you prefer brandy I have Paul Beau."

Before she could reply Gary turned to the man at her left, a young man of medium height and some noticeable girth with a tattoo of a dagger through his neck and a stylized skull on the back of his hand.

A murderer. She thought absently.

A touch of his mind with the power confirmed the story told by the man's tattoos.

The murderer turned wordlessly and left the room only to return a moment later carrying two jigger glasses of vodka. He placed them both on the desk in front of her.

Kira hesitated, and Gary met her eyes with his. "Please, have a drink with me." As he spoke, he took the glass nearest to him.

Kira paused only a moment longer before taking up her glass as well. As she did, Gary raised his glass.

"Nostravia"

"Nostravia." She repeated back automatically before downing her vodka. The clear liquor tasted spicy and slightly fruity.

Gary set his own glass down with a low sigh. "Very nice." He took a puff from his cigar. "Now then. To business. I want you to play for me tomorrow night at the *Red Star*. There's a high stakes cash game there. One hundred, two hundred, no-limit hold 'em. The minimum buy-in is one hundred grand. I will advance you the buy-in, and you will keep fifty percent of whatever you win." He took another puff from his cigar and set it down in a crystal ashtray on his desk. "Would you care for another drink?"

Kira accepted the second drink even as she sat there trying to think of a way to get out of this. She knew well the risk of gambling with this man's money. If Kira won, she would keep a substantial sum but if she lost she would be indebted to the *Bratva*. Kira had no means by which she could repay a hundred thousand dollars, and they would come after her in any way they could to recoup their money. Even Aria would not be off-limits.

Except it was already too late. They had killed the driver for her. She was already indebted, and she could not say no.

XXIII

And so, Kira did not and found herself sitting at a red felt poker table the following night. One hundred thousand dollars of Gary Volkov's money, now converted to chips, sat stacked before her. The remainder of the table was populated by a relatively even mix of hardened gangsters and whales dressed in trendy club threads.

Instinctively, Kira reached out with her mind as the cards came. The man to her immediate right, a greasy-haired thug, dressed in a black silk shirt and white cotton pants, was holding a pair of threes. In the seat next to him sat a twenty-something in an oversized football jersey and ripped blue jeans. He was holding an ace and a king. Beside him sat a curvy dark-haired woman in an ill-fitting A-line dress. She was holding a pair of queens and nervously sipping a martini. The next five players were all holding garbage, nothing higher than six-seven offsuit. The player to Kira's immediate left, a gray-haired man in a gray satin suit and gold chains, was holding a pair of jacks and the man to his left was holding a ten nine. Kira cupped her hands around her cards and carefully pulled up an edge. She saw an ace and king of spades.

Greasy hair raised the bet to three thousand. Football jersey re-raised to ten and the ill-fitting A-line called. The five players with garbage all folded along with the man with the ten nine. The gray satin suit called. Now it was Kira's turn. Before deciding Kira reached into the power once more. She sensed that the flop would be the queen and ten of spades together with the ace of hearts. A rush of excitement flooded through her causing the power to stir restlessly. Kira forced herself to be calm and disinterested on the outside while slamming down the power. She called without raising, placing her chips into the pot with steady slowness.

The dealer, a black man of middle age and athletic build, swept all of the chips into the center of the table and dealt out the flop. The ace quickly persuaded Greasy hair to check. Football jersey pushed twenty thousand into the pot, and the ill-fitting A-line called together with the gray satin suit. Kira reached into the power once more, sensed that the next card would be a three of spades, decided to raise and pushed an extra twenty into the pot. There was now over a hundred thousand in the pot. Greasy isntafolded, football jersey called, ill-fitting A-line folded and the gray satin suit did the same. Now there were two of them. The next card came out, and Kira now held a spade flush. Football jersey raised again, this time sixty thousand, enough to put Kira all in. Kira already knew she had football jersey beat but pretended to take a moment to think. Almost instinctively she reached into the power and found, to her great surprise that the next card was a jack of spades. She would have a royal flush, and football jersey would probably suspect all spades. It didn't matter. He was already going to max her out. Kira called and turned her cards over.

"Oh, fuck!" Football jersey exclaimed. He was beaten, and he knew it. The jack of spades came out next, and Kira found herself sitting on over two hundred thousand dollars.

The remainder of the night followed a similar pattern. Kira could easily read all of the players and was able to win enough hands to turn Gary's hundred thousand into seven figures. After Gary's cut was taken out, Kira was left with over half a million dollars; easily enough to pay off Aria's medical bills and still leave them comfortable. There was no need for her to play any further, but Kira knew she was not yet done.

XXIV

In the weeks that followed, Kira played for ever-greater sums of money. Gary staked her again for her second game, a one thousand two thousand no-limit table with a two hundred and fifty-thousand-dollar minimum buy-in. This time Kira walked away with over two million dollars.

Before her third and allegedly final game, Gary took Kira to a mansion on Star Island. Here she was taken to a small bedroom where a black, string bikini had been laid out for her. Her escort encouraged her to undress and put on the bathing suit as she would be taken poolside to meet with the "boss."

Kira did as she was bidden and was then escorted to the rear of the mansion where a thirty-something man of muscular build and dark hair lay sunning himself poolside. As she approached, the man sat up and lifted his aviator-style shades to reveal coral green eyes. He met her gaze steadily and spoke in a friendly tone.

"Welcome Miss Morozov." He extended his hand to her. "My name is Ivan Maxim Petrovic. I am pleased to finally meet you."

Kira placed her hand in his, and like Gary, Ivan turned her hand and kissed the back. In another context, she would have found him alluring. But Ivan was a high-ranking crime boss. He did not bear the tattoos of his underlings, but Kira had no doubt of whom she was dealing with.

Ivan motioned to Kira's escort and he disappeared only to reappear a few minutes later with a magnum and two flute glasses.

"Gary tells me you play cards well. You will play for me now." He said matter-of-factly. "I am going to front you five million dollars for a game at the *Red Star*. "You will play heads up against Victor Sharpe. Sharpe is a whale, more money than talent, and he's putting up ten million for anyone who can beat him. You will play by tournament rules."

She nodded silently.

Ivan popped open the magnum, poured two glasses, and handed one to her. "Excellent. Let us drink to your success."

Kira took Ivan's champagne and drank it in silence. For the first time, she felt afraid. Something felt wrong, she did not know what, but something.

XXV

After leaving Ivan's mansion, Kira went home and spent the evening with Aria. They ordered pizza and played video games for hours until Aria began to yawn and asked to go to bed. Kira tucked her daughter in and kissed her on the forehead before retiring to her own room to attempt some rest. Somewhere deep inside some part of her felt that her time with Aria was running out, that this would be the last time she would play video games with her daughter.

Kira lay awake that night and wept softly. She mourned for her husband, her daughter, and most of all, she mourned herself.

XXVI

The following night Alexi picked Kira up from Double J storage in a black Lincoln Navigator. One hour later, she found herself sitting across an oblong poker table from Victor Sharpe. Sharpe stood approximately five feet eleven inches and was a stocky man with a big round head and a beer belly. He sat at the table with the self-assurance of one who has everything under control.

As the cards were dealt, Kira reached out with the power and found, to her horror, that she could not read him. For some reason, she did not understand some people were simply closed to her. This Victor Sharpe was apparently one of those people. And it could not have come at a worse time. Kira could still sense what cards would come off the deck, but she knew not what Victor held and could not sense his intentions either. Victor was an enigma. He was also an excellent poker player. After two hours of play, Kira found herself down to a third of her chip stack.

The dealer set two cards in front of her and Kira nervously glanced at them even as she instinctively reached out with the power. She felt nothing, could not sense what Victor held. Her cards were decent, a pair of queens. Kira quickly decided to make a move and bet a hundred thousand in tournament chips.

Victor immediately raised her all in. Kira called. He flipped over his cards first to show a pair of jacks. She was ahead. Kira's momentary elation immediately turned to terror as she sensed that there would be another jack in the flop.

The cards came down, and Victor was now holding a set. She was significantly behind. Kira needed a queen, and she felt that she would not get one. A seven of clubs came out on the turn, and the river card was another jack. She was down to the felt. She had lost.

Without a thought, Kira stood up from the table and made her way out of the *Red Star.* She was careful to avoid Alexi for she knew she was in trouble. She had lost five million dollars of Ivan's money.

After sneaking out of the *Red Star,* Kira hailed a cab and made her way home. Her car was still sitting at Double J Storage, but that was the least of her worries. She wanted to get back to Aria before Ivan found out she had lost his money.

As she rode home, Kira's fear mounted. She had lost so much money. Would Ivan come after Aria? Or would he just kill Kira when he learned she could not pay him back? Perhaps he would make her play for him until she could pay him back.

Kira knew that last one was a fantasy. Ivan would never ask her to play using his money again. He would expect repayment and would collect his money any way he could. She knew the *Bratva* traded in children. Would they take Aria?

Suddenly, Kira became convinced that she would arrive home to find Aria missing and Fiona dead at the hands of Alexi or some other *Bratva* goon. With each moment her conviction grew, as did her fear, such that by the time the cabbie had stopped in front of her home in Coconut Grove, she was near panic.

Her home was dark and quiet. She approached slowly, terrified of what she would find. As she neared the door, Kira fumbled in her purse for her keys. After a moment, she found the chain and inserted her house key into the front door's deadbolt. The lock slid open with a dull thud.

Still locked. Good.

Inside, deathly quiet permeated the heavy, and still air of late night. She detected a faint alien scent of men's cologne blended with shitty Russian cigarette smoke. Fiona lay dead on the floor by the couch, throat slashed, blood pooling on the ground beneath her body.

"Oh, my God…" The words escaped her lips before she could stop them. Liquid ice flooded her veins, and a frozen iron fist closed upon her heart. Kira had to fight to stifle a scream. Her head thudded with each pulse of thundering blood.

Kira ran to the stairs and ascended them two at a time, feet quickened by explosive terror. Upon reaching the top, Kira dashed down the hallway, turned left into her daughter's bedroom and froze.

"You weren't planning to run off, were you? After you lost all of that money?"

Alexi sat on the bed with Aria on his lap. He restrained her with his right hand while holding a gloss black Smersh 5 dagger to her throat with his left. His ice-chip eyes had become glaciers in the night. The force of his malice struck Kira like a fist. Aria's sat wide-eyed, too frightened to make a sound.

"What do you want?" Kira bit out.

"You owe a debt." He continued, glacial eyes flashing. "And it's time to pay up."

Kira flashed a sardonic smile. "You have no idea who you're messing with. Do you?"

Alexi replied with a malicious grin. "Oh, I know exactly who you are, Lightwarrior. And I doubt that you will use your power on me. Or maybe you'd like to test how precise your weapon is? Is it as precise as mine? All it takes is one little cut here." As he spoke, Alexi made a drawing motion across Aria's throat with his knife. "And you will no longer be a mother."

Aria had begun to hyperventilate, silent tears glistened on her cheeks. Fear radiated out from her in cold waves.

Kira's heart went out to her daughter, and for the first time, she felt stirrings of anger in addition to fear.

How dare you threaten my daughter!?

Anger, in turn, brought the power blazing to the surface. Kira bit down hard on the power but did not attempt to suppress it.

Alexi must have felt the energy building within her for he tightened his grip on Aria, pulling her closer to his chest. "Go ahead. Try it. Maybe you'll be able to kill me before I cut your daughter's throat."

Kira wanted so badly to reach out with the power and crush this man's windpipe or hurl him into the wall. Yet she dared not. The risk of harm to her daughter was too great. Instead, Kira forced the power down, driving iron spikes through her body.

Alexi's smile widened, "Good girl," before it hardened into a glare colder than the Arctic. "Now both of you can get your asses in my car. You both belong to Ivan Petrovic."

Once outside, men pulled black hoods over Kira and Aria's heads before forcing them into what Kira imagined to be a large SUV. Though darkness shrouded her eyes, Kira could feel the distinct touch of leather, and her nose detected the scent of new car.

XVII

The car ride went on for an imperceptible period of time. During this time Kira made several attempts to reach out with the power so as to learn something, *anything* about where they were going and what their captors' intentions were. She detected three men in the car in addition to Alexi and yet she could discern only malice and fear. Kira sensed that Aria was near panic. Her daughter's fright lit up the air like electrified plasma.

Frustration and fear flooded Kira's body and mind bringing the power to the fore again and again. She wanted desperately to do *something,* but she dared not for fear of harming Aria. And so, she forced the power down, sending fresh chromium spikes ripping into her flesh.

Eventually, they stopped, and hands forcibly unloaded Kira and Aria from the SUV before herding them into a strange building. Inside, the building's soundless air smelled stale and musty, like a cheap motel room that had not been opened in a long time.

The same hands grabbed Kira and thrust her forward onto a mattress. Then, without warning the bag disappeared and Kira found herself sitting upright on a dirty motel bed. The room around her was poorly lit, dingy, and windowless. A honey-colored, waist height dresser, matching end table, and ratty looking CRT television served as the room's only furnishings.

Aria sat on the bed next to her, face deathly white and tearstained.

"Mom? What's going on? Why did they take us?" Aria's lips trembled as she spoke.

Tears burned in Kira's eyes. "I..I'm sorry, Baby. This is my fault."

Kira sensed Aria's confusion. "What do you mean Mom? Why did they take us?"

Before Kira could speak, Alexi provided the answer. "Your mother is a degenerate gambler, and she lost a large sum of money that didn't belong to her. Now it's time to pay up."

Suddenly Kira understood and felt a horrified chill. "We are the payment." The words escaped before she could stifle them.

Alexi replied with a sardonic golf clap. "Very good." His voice positively dripped contempt. "You and your daughter will fetch a good price. Hopefully, enough to pay back what you lost, but at the very least, you will set an example."

Kira reached into the power intending to kill Alexi on the spot and found, to her immense terror, that the power had deserted her. Then for the first time, she noticed the needle mark on the inside of her forearm. She had never felt the injection.

Alexi must have noticed her staring at the injection site for he smiled cruelly. "As I told you before, we know who you are, Lightwarrior."

XVIII

The time that followed flowed without measure. Day became indiscernible from night in the little motel room. After some time had passed, Kira could hear gunshots and screams from outside the motel room. Police sirens followed these at first but then later, as the gunfire intensified, the sirens were muted. As more time passed, she also began to detect the heavy smell of burning buildings. As a war survivor, Kira knew this scent well and could not help but feel terror.

Aria too must have understood the grave meaning of these sounds and smells for her already palpable fear grew with each passing hour.

Alexi remained with them during this time, but the other men who had accompanied him began to slowly trickle away until only Alexi himself remained. Alexi had made a particular point of regularly drugging Kira. Nevertheless, she suspected that he had run low on drugs as he acted increasingly nervous and would step out frequently to use his cell phone.

After what Kira imagined to be several days, the worst of the gunfire and burning smell passed, and the exterior streets fell quiet. Then, sometime later, the door opened and several men Kira had never seen before entered.

These men conversed with Alexi in Russian for some time before yanking black bags over Aria and Kira's heads and forcibly carrying them to a waiting vehicle outside.

After some time had passed, hands grabbed Kira, pulled her from the vehicle, dragged her along what felt like a long corridor and forced her into a chair before snatching the bag from her head. When her vision cleared, Kira found herself sitting in front of a familiar desk with an all too familiar and far from friendly face seated behind it.

Gary Volkov met her confused gaze with a glare of pure malevolence. "The boss has tasked me with disposing of you and your daughter in the most profitable way possible, and I believe I have found a buyer." He flashed her a brutal grin. "Really a shame about your daughter. She seems like a sweet kid."

Kira instinctively tried to get to her feet before heavy hands forced her back into her chair. An impotent cry escaped her lips. "You piece of shit!"

Gary laughed. "Am I now? I'm not the fool who gambled away money she had no hope of ever repaying."

He had a point in a certain way. Before she could stop herself, Kira broke. Burning tears of shame streamed from her eyes for she knew Gary was right. She should have turned Alexi away, should have refused him outright. Instead, she had placed her daughter in grave danger, for money and a moment's satisfaction.

I am a fool. Kira thought contemptuously.

Gary gave her another vicious grin. "Don't worry. You won't be separated. Ivan wanted me to make sure you see the full consequences of your actions."

XIX

Kira did indeed witness the horrible price for her error in judgment. Gary sold both Kira and Aria to a gangster named, Sergei Markovic, who took them to a large brothel in Miami Beach named *The Red Room.*

The first two weeks passed uneventfully. Kira and Aria spent the time as normally as possible under the circumstances. Sergei provided them with a little apartment inside the brothel, and they passed their time reading, playing board games, and talking.

Aria wasted no time in asking Kira what they were doing at *The Red Room,* and why Kira had been gambling with these men's money. Kira did her best to explain her actions in a way that Aria might understand without causing the little girl to hate her. (She intentionally withheld the part about wanting revenge on the driver who had run Aria over.) To Kira's great relief, Aria seemed to accept the reasons given without comment or anger. Instead, Aria's expression became compassionate and very sad.

"It's ok, Mom. I know you were only trying to take care of me. But Mom, how are we going to get out of this place?"

Kira bit back relieved tears as she answered. "I don't know baby. We'll just have to wait for the right time."

"Ok, Mom."

That conversation occurred on Monday of the second week. Five days later, an early morning knock at the door awakened them. Kira opened the suite door to find Sergei's madam, Katya standing in the corridor.

"Sergei wants to talk to you both, so shower and dress nice." Without another word, the woman turned and left, trailing the scent of cheap perfume behind her.

Kira felt deeply frightened. Nevertheless, the power remained silent within her as Katya had been careful to keep her drugged at all times.

"What did she want?" Aria asked, voice still thick with sleep.

"I don't know Baby." Kira found herself replying. "I guess we should get up and find out."

"Ok, Mom." Now Aria's voice had become a bit brighter.

Kira had lied as she had a very good idea of what Sergei wanted and felt deeply afraid for herself and her daughter. Kira did not know if she would be able to have sex with a stranger, and she knew what would happen if she disobeyed.

Kira, showered and dressed with growing trepidation, dreading what she knew was to come.

Ten minutes later, Katya returned and escorted mother and daughter to a small, but well-appointed office on the ground floor of the brothel. Red silk wallpaper, together with several prints featuring the Russian countryside decorated the walls in Sergei's office. Here the furniture consisted of ebony wood and red brocade. Sergei sat behind a massive ebony desk with a white marble inlay and a red satin swivel chair. As Kira and Aria entered, Sergei stood and greeted them with a predatory grin.

"Why, hello. You must be Kira Morozov." He turned his evil sneer on Aria. "And you must be Aria. A pleasure I assure you."

Kira glared at him coldly. "What do you want?"

He broadened his black smile until he was positively beaming. "Well, I imagine you know what we do here. And so, you know why *you* are here. Now your daughter is a special case. Very young and very beautiful and most importantly, a virgin. I wanted to wait until I had a client willing to pay an appropriate price. I have now found such a client."

Kira's heart exploded with fury. "You wouldn't dare!" She spat.

"And what do you propose to do about it?" Sergei replied in a calm tone. "You can't even use your power thanks to the drugs Katya has been shooting you up with. Amazing how well good old-fashioned Haldol keeps you people in check. I don't think you will be able to do much of anything without your powers. But don't worry, I haven't forgotten about you. While your daughter earns her keep, you can watch on live video."

Aria had begun to cry as she understood what would come and was terrified. Kira took her daughter into her arms and turned a glare of blazing fury on Sergei. "She's a child for god's sake. Let me do it in her place."

Sergei shook his head. "I don't think so. This client has paid far more than you are worth my dear.

Your daughter will do as she is told, and you will make her available when the client arrives at nine this evening, or I will cut out her heart and feed it to you."

For the first time in weeks, Kira felt the familiar stir of the power somewhere in the back of her mind. She gratefully reached for it only to have the power desert her once more.

Before she could attempt any physical resistance, Kira felt hands grasp her shoulders and forcibly lead her from Sergei's office. Beside her, Aria continued to weep softly.

XX

Once back in their suite, Kira spent the remainder of the day sitting with Aria trying both to comfort her and to find a means of escape. She felt terribly guilty but quickly put this feeling aside in favor of attempting to find a solution.

Kira first made several attempts to access the power without success. Then, after determining that the power would not be available to her, Kira searched the little suite top to bottom for anything that could be used as a weapon. She eventually settled on a dull chef's knife. Kira held the knife in an expert's grasp but recognized that the blade had been forged of weak, stainless steel and barely had an edge on it. She could certainly do some damage to whomever she attacked first, but she and Aria would be at the mercy of the remainder of Sergei's goons. The knife would only bring about their deaths, and Kira was unwilling to sacrifice her daughter in a failed escape attempt. Thus, Kira did the only thing she could do for her daughter and helped prepare her mentally for that which she would later endure.

Terrible guilt flooded her heart for Kira knew that this was all her fault. Her daughter would suffer for her mother's misjudgment.

I never should have agreed to play for them. Never should have let them convince me. I was arrogant. I was a fool to believe that they were no threat to us, that I could handle them and use them just because I am a Lightwarrior. I was such a fool.

In that moment, a burning knife of self-loathing dug into Kira's chest as she understood something that she had refused to admit to herself earlier.

The games, I didn't agree to play to support Aria, or even because we needed the money. I was doing well enough at the casino playing low stakes. I did it because it was exciting and for the money.

At eight o'clock, sharp Katya barged into the little suite carrying a dress bag and accompanied by two tough-looking men in sharkskin suits.

"Time to get dressed little girl,"

As she spoke, Katya unzipped the bag and emptied its contents. Here were a black A-line cocktail dress and black kitten heel shoes. Clothing suited more to a twenty-something woman rather than a twelve-year-old girl.

Aria eyed the outfit nervously. Kira could feel cold fear radiating off her daughter in waves.

"You don't have to do this. Please, I'll take her place. Please don't do this to my daughter." Kira begged.

Katya smiled cruelly. "Customer paid for her, and we're going to deliver."

Kira let her eyes bore into the woman, her face became rock hard with pure hate. Hot blood slammed into her temples and rushed through her cheeks.

In response, Katya's smile faded, and her face became glacial with naked contempt. "Don't look at me as if I were the one doing this. You chose this. You knew the risks of gambling with the *Bratva*."

"I lost money." Kira retorted. "It was *my* debt! *Mine*! Not my daughter's. Aria's innocent in this. She doesn't deserve to suffer for my mistake."

"You're right, she doesn't." Katya coldly agreed. "Which is why it is all the more disgusting that her mother would place her in such a situation." Katya turned to Aria. "Go take a shower and then get dressed. Don't be late."

A single tear spilled down Aria's right cheek as she turned and entered the bathroom, shutting the door behind her. A few minutes later, Kira heard the rush of the shower, then ten minutes later Aria emerged wrapped in a terry white bath towel. Her face had paled, and her eyes had widened, the very picture of terror. She was not crying, but her fear had intensified to the point that it turned the room icy.

The scent of lavender and ivory soap wafted from the now vacant shower. At any other time, Kira would have found these smells comforting, but at that moment, they made her stomach hula hoop around her ass, and her mouth fill with the taste of bile.

Kira felt her throat open, and stomach acid begin to sear her esophagus. She swallowed hard to keep from vomiting.

Katya took out a cigarette and a red Bic lighter. Despite the woman's cold exterior, Kira detected bitter, coppery self-loathing. Katya slowly puffed her cigarette, sending clouds of heavy shitty smelling smoke into the suite's stagnant air.

Aria dressed quickly and wordlessly. Despite the torrent of icy terror flowing from her, she did not speak a word of protest.

When she had finished dressing, Katya took Aria by the arm and led her over to the vanity beside the suite's single, king bed. Aria complied wordlessly, allowing Katya to make her up much like a twenty-something headed to the club to troll for men.

The sight of her daughter caused Kira's heart to drop into her shoe and her eyes to burn and water. She wanted desperately to cry but would not allow herself for she knew it would only make it worse for Aria.

Katya took a long drag from her cigarette and then proceeded to lead Aria towards the door. "It's time to go." She sounded almost regretful.

Both sharkskin suits moved in on her. Kira made no effort to resist and soon found herself being led down the exterior corridor.

Time flowed strangely. After what seemed like both an eternity and an instant Kira now stood within a small lounge.

Here the furnishings consisted of gaudy, overstuffed red velvet couches and lounge chairs and several cast iron, glass top coffee tables. The air reeked of sex and stale cigarettes, while a thin film of filth covered everything. A large one-way mirror occupied the right-hand wall, giving a clear view into the neighboring bedroom.

Kira entered the little lounge flanked by the two sharkskin suits and sat down on the nearest chair. As she did, she noticed that a muscular twenty-something man occupied the neighboring bedroom. He lay spread across the king bed wearing nothing but a pair of black boxer shorts. Kira felt the force of his anticipation.

In another context, Kira would have found this man handsome with his dark, deep-set eyes, flawless, almond skin, messy black hair, strong jaw, and thin lips. But he was here to do…*things* to Aria, her *daughter*. Kira dared not even think the word that would describe that which would soon happen, as if to speak that word would somehow make the inevitable a certainty.

After a few minutes, the bedroom door opened, and Katya appeared with Aria. Twenty-something's anticipation grew, electrifying the air as if before a thunderstorm.

Kira's stomach began to accelerate its orbit while her mouth filled with sour acid. She swallowed hard, fighting the urge to vomit. Kira felt her skin begin to rash out in goosebumps and cold sweat. Each individual hair on her body became electric with horror.

Katya led an ashen-faced Aria towards the bed where it would begin. Aria complied mutely, head hung like a condemned man being led upon his last walk to the electric chair. She sat down on the bed without prompting and allowed twenty-something to place his hands on her shoulders.

Katya took out a fresh cigarette and lit it with her red Bic. "You have all night, Mr. Birch and you are free to do whatever you like as long as there is no *permanent* damage."

Birch flashed a lopsided grin. "And how much if I want to do *permanent* damage?"

Katya took a long drag from her cigarette. "The girl is a valuable asset, so that would be an expensive service and would require payment upfront." Kira could hear thinly veiled contempt in Katya's voice as she spoke.

Birch ran a hand through Aria's hair. "I'm your best customer, and I always pay my debts."

"That you do." Katya acknowledged between drags from her cigarette. "Fine. Do as you like but be prepared to pay before you leave here. Especially if the girl is reduced in value."

Birch renewed his crooked smile. "I always do."

Katya stubbed out her cigarette on her shoe, tossed it aside, and then turned and left. Once the door had snicked shut behind Katya, Birch turned his full attention to Aria.

"Hello, my name is Hunter. What's your name?"

Aria remained silent, cold terror flowed from her in waves.

Kira wanted desperately to stop this but knew not how she could. The power had deserted her, silenced by the drugs Sergei had shot her up with.

"Come on." Hunter cajoled. "I know you can speak. What is your name?"

"Aria." Barely audible.

"Aria." He repeated slowly as if tasting the word. "A beautiful name."

When Hunter finished, Aria lay in a tousled heap, weeping softly. Hunter meanwhile, lay beside her, sleeping peacefully, his arm draped across her as if she were a lover and not a victim.

Black fury, burned through Kira, bringing her heart to a sprint and chilling her flesh. Something moved within her, something familiar.

The power?!

Kira reached into the moving sensation and for a moment thought the power had returned, but she quickly found that the power remained just out of her reach. She had gotten to her feet at some point and had now run towards the door. Before she could reach it through, the two sharkskin suits grabbed her and dragged her back to her seat. Kira fought them with all of her strength until a blow to the back of her headset off an explosion of light in front of her eyes and set her ears ringing.

"Shut the fuck up bitch and watch. The show's not over yet." The male voice seemed to come from everywhere at once.

Kira wanted to stand up and fight her way to her daughter, but the white lights in front of her eyes and throbbing in her head made it impossible. And so, she sat there impotently.

After some time had passed, Hunter awakened and closed his hands around Aria's neck. Aria did not cry out this time, instead meekly resigning herself to her fate.

In an instant, Kira was on her feet and headed for the door. The two sharkskin suits restrained her and dragged her, kicking and screaming, back to her seat once more.

Hunter closed his grip tighter around Aria's neck but not tight enough to fully cut off her air. Instead, he simply made her suffer. After several minutes of this, Hunter produced a small stiletto and gently laid the point against Aria's body. She looked up at him with tears in her eyes.

Without hesitation, Hunter slowly pushed the stiletto into Aria's flesh until he had buried it up to the hilt. Aria opened her mouth and let loose a horrible shriek of pure suffering.

Kira struggled against her bonds, cutting her wrists open and spilling her blood on the red pile carpeting.

The power suddenly awakened within her and leapt out before she could even think. A ripple of invisible force shot through the air shattering furniture, fragmenting the one-way mirror and spraying shards of broken glass through the little lounge. A lengthy shard embedded itself in the neck of the taller of the two sharkskin suits while a second neatly severed the other shark skin's head.

Kira, now free from her bonds, stood up and ran to the new opening in the right wall. She found that Hunter had already fled, leaving Aria lying on her back bleeding and weeping softly. Kira's daughter's breaths came in shallow gasps. Kira gathered her Aria up and carried her out of the bedroom.

She found the corridor deserted and took her daughter from *The Red Room* without any resistance.

XXI

Kira used the power to steal a car with the intention of taking her daughter to the emergency room. As she approached Mount Sinai, Kira quickly changed her mind. She found the hospital bombed out and smoldering. A tangle of derelict cars clogged the parking lot. The air here hung heavy with the acrid stench of smoke and raw gasoline. She would find no help for Aria here.

Instead, she took Aria to a deserted hotel nearby. By this time, Aria had lost consciousness, and her breathing had become slow and ragged. Deep fear flooded Kira's body with cold.

"It's ok, Aria. Mom's here." She found herself repeating. "Mom's here, and she'll never let anyone hurt you again."

Over the subsequent hours, Aria continued to weaken, and her breathing continued to slow. By the time the sun peaked over the horizon, Aria had spiked a fever, and her breathing had become frighteningly shallow.

Kira attempted to awaken Aria, and to her surprise, her daughter's eyes flicked open. "Mom?" Barely audible. "Is it over?"

Hot tears burned Kira's eyes. "Yes, Baby, it's over. That man is gone, and no one will ever hurt you again."

"Okay." Aria took a deep, shuddering breath. "Mom, why did he hurt me. Why did you let him do that to me?"

"I wanted to stop him, Baby," Kira whispered between tears. "I wanted to stop them all. I couldn't. I'm so sorry."

Aria took her Kira's hand in a weak grip. "It's ok Mom. It's not your fault. But Mom…" She began to gasp for air. "Mom… it hurts *so* much. I can still feel it. I don't want to feel it anymore, Mom. I just want it to stop. I want to forget."

"It's going to be ok Baby." Kira soothed. "Somehow, everything is going to be alright."

As she spoke, Kira pulled back the blankets to examine Aria's wound. The bandage Kira had placed earlier had soaked through with black blood and smelled of rot. Aria's abdomen had turned an angry red.

Kira struggled to keep her emotions from showing on her face even as she fought against the power that raged within her. Great rending pain tore through her body as Kira held the power down with all her will.

NOT NOW!!

Aria squeezed Kira's hand. "I love you, Mom." Then her eyes went blank, and she stopped breathing.

A tempest of painful emotions whirled within Kira. Guilt, self-loathing, grief, anger, and most frightening of all hate and a burning desire for revenge. Kira drew her sword, the thing that had been impossible under the influence of Sergei's drugs. In the same instant, she turned the power loose and obliterated the little hotel room, leaving only Aria untouched.

Though Kira understood that she bore some responsibility for her daughter's suffering, her guilt and self-loathing quickly began to fade beneath icy torrents of hatred for the people who had killed Aria.

They had taken Aria away, and she would make them pay dearly. A terrible hunger took her, bringing pangs to hear heart and hollowing out her soul. Only vengeance could satisfy this hunger, and until she could exact vengeance, she would be consumed with terrible, soul-rending famine.

Kira held her sword for a moment longer, eyes trailing along its slender, polished blade. Morning sunlight fell upon the weapon, and it shone like silver. Then Kira sheathed her sword, gathered up her daughter and left the shattered remnants of the little hotel room whose name she could no longer recall.

Kira buried Aria in Lummus Park, under a large palm tree with a clear view of the Atlantic Ocean. After a brief prayer, and a quick, off-key rendition of *Amazing Grace* Kira, said a final goodbye to her daughter before setting off on the grim task of quelling the terrible famine ravaging her soul.

XXII

The sound of a car immediately yanked Kira back to the present. A limousine had arrived at the mansion gate. After a moment's pause, the gate opened, and the limo continued on to the mansion's front door. Several minutes later, the front door opened, and a group of men filtered out. Kira recognized Hunter Birch among them, he had become more haggard and gaunt since that terrible night at *The Red Room,* but this was unmistakably him.

Terrible hunger pangs wracked Kira's heart.

You killed my daughter you son of a bitch. You brutalized her and killed her. You deserve to die for what you did.

She desperately wanted…no *needed* to avenge herself upon this man. She would make him suffer far more than Gary or Sergei. She would hurt him as much as he had hurt Aria.

The hunger pangs had become a deep burning ache within her soul, one that brought the power to the surface. Kira fought back the power, for though she desperately wanted to attack Hunter right there, she knew better. She would have to wait until she could get him alone.

As Kira stood watching Hunter get into the limousine and drive away, Aria's voice whispered softly in her mind. *Mom, don't. I'm ok now. You don't have to do this. You'll only hurt yourself.*

Despite desperately wanting to heed her daughter's words, Kira could not ignore her ravenous heart.

Chapter 7
"Bend the Rule Without Breaking It"

I

Inside the bar what had begun as a scuffle between two young men over a woman has now escalated into a full-scale brawl. Both the gentleman in white and the gentleman in black unobtrusively make their way to the rear of the bar in the hopes of avoiding becoming embroiled in the growing violence.

The young woman in the green cocktail dress remains on the floor bleeding from an ugly gash in her forehead. She is not unconscious and is desperately trying to get to her feet, but the angry rabble continues to knock her down and trample her.

The two young men who instigated the conflict, one in a red European cut suit, one in a blue denim work shirt, continue to fight each other with growing aggression. While they are ostensibly fighting over the woman in the green cocktail dress, the young men mostly ignore her plight as they too trample her in their fervor to dominate one another.

"Should we stop them?" The man in black suggests to the man in white. As he speaks, a series of gunshots echo in the darkened streets outside the bar. "That woman is but a victim. Should we not rescue her?"

"Her plight is tragic, but we cannot interfere. You know well that they must be left to choose for themselves." The man in white retorts. "And we should not abandon our game."

"The game is interrupted." The man in black replies, pointing out the obvious.

"For now." The man in white answers calmly. "When the fight dies down, we will be able to continue."

As the last words leave the man in white's lips, a woman screams out a child's name. Both gentlemen turn to see a woman in her mid-thirties crouched over the crumpled body of a young girl of eleven or twelve. She lies broken, her face bruised from trampling feet, her frozen eyes wide with terror.

Rather than attend to the fallen girl, the woman slowly straightens up, draws a knife and attacks a tough-looking man nearby. This man's shoes still bear bloodstains from the fallen girl. He is no match for the thirty-something woman who kills him with a single knife thrust to the chest. Then instead of returning to her fallen daughter, the mid-thirties woman begins to lash out at random with her knife, wounding several bar patrons unfortunate enough to get in her way.

Both gentlemen, understand the threat this woman poses though neither wishes to act as this woman's actions are understandable if not condonable for one who has suffered such a loss...

II

Deep red rays of twilight from a dying sun streamed through the massive picture windows of the Grand Observation Lounge. The chamber lay empty, save for a single occupant.

Eric Kane sat in a large, overstuffed, black leather chair near the center pane of glass, a crystal tumbler of water in his right hand. As he watched the sky darken to ever-deeper shades of red Kane carefully contemplated each move he had made to get to this far into the chess game.

He'd had Charlie MacLeod and her adoptive parents under his power and had allowed his servants to torture the girl mercilessly before attempting to become the girl's father and eventually offering to make her his empress, and co-equal ruler of the Black Empire. She had opened up to him, and for a while, she had trusted him. Yet in the end, she had resisted his promises of power and revenge.

It was at this point that Kane had decided to take a calculated risk. Though he possessed the ability to use the power to travel through time, Kane generally abhorred tampering with the timeline for the consequences of doing so were both dangerous and impossible to predict. Nevertheless, in this particular instance, he had decided it was worth the risk.

The girl was both rare and valuable, Kane had never encountered an Enlightened with power stronger than his own, nor had he ever before come across a pyrokinetic. Moreover, the girl could potentially unlock *Wormwood.* And despite her resistance to his attempts to manipulate her, the girl had a weakness.

Having lost both of her parents to agents of the National Security Agency, Charlie harbored a great need for revenge. The identity of the agent who had killed Dana MacLeod was lost, but Kane knew that an Asset by the name of Robin Striker had killed Jack MacLeod and in a particularly cruel twist of fate he had also befriended Charlie before doing so. Unsurprisingly, the girl had responded by immediately incinerating Striker. She believed she had killed him. Kane decided that he would put that belief to the lie.

Through the many years of his long life, Kane had dedicated himself to learning every nuance and facet of the power. During this time, he had learned to use the power to do many extraordinary and miraculous things and had found the capabilities and scope of the power almost limitless. Limitless, with only the exception that the power could neither be used to create life nor raise the dead.

Kane suspected that the All Father had reserved these abilities only to himself; that the power to create and the power over death itself were solely the provinces of the divine. Nevertheless, the rule could be bent without being broken.

Kane had developed the ability to use the power to project himself into any moment or epoch he desired and with the ability to travel to any period in time came the ability to manipulate events.

Kane considered the power to change history, both formidable and dangerous. Not long after learning to use the power to transcend time, Kane blundered his way into learning the extreme danger of tampering with the timeline.

Kane learned to use the power to manipulate time in the early years of the High Middle Ages. Following Richard the Lionheart's ill-advised departure on the First Crusade, the English kingdom became embroiled in near civil war as several usurpers vied for the throne. Among them was a Dark Knight of extraordinary power. Given the name Phillip Mark, history would remember him by his title. Mark would ultimately be challenged and defeated by a near-equally powerful Lightwarrior.

At the time Kane had considered Mark valuable enough to warrant his direct intervention, particularly in light of the fact that Mark had come close to seizing the English throne and placing the kingdom within Kane's grasp. Knowing that he could not resurrect Mark from the dead, Kane elected instead to manipulate the events leading to Mark's defeat so as to save the Dark Knight from death.

Kane had intended to preserve his Dark Knight so that he might assume the English throne as Kane's puppet. Instead, by preventing Mark's defeat at the hands of a Lightwarrior, Kane had created a rouge Dark Knight and rival for control of Europe. Mark easily seized the throne and imprisoned both Richard the Lionheart and Prince John. He then embarked on a war of conquest and destruction taking control of Europe from Lisbon to Moscow and slaughtering millions before that same Lightwarrior surfaced again and defeated him.

As a consequence of the rise of King Phillip, who had taken the title of Dark Lord, Europe experienced a near-apocalyptic depopulation followed by mass chaos. This chaos would open the door to invasion and conquest by barbarian Mongols in the east and the Muslim Caliphate under Saladin in the west. While Kane had connections within both the Caliphate and the Mongol Empire, the damage was done. Between Mark's conquest and genocide and the later conquest of Europe by Muslims and Mongols, the population of Europe had been devastated. Moreover, Mark ultimately executed both Richard the Lionheart and Prince John, together with a majority of the nobility within England. Thus England ultimately became an absolute monarchy under the surviving Plantagenet dynasty for seven hundred years before the rise of classical liberalism and self-rule that would open the door to the shadow government and allow Kane to assume the de-facto rule of Earth.

As he reminisced, another memory returned to him unbidden and unwanted. The rise of Mark had also exacted a far more personal cost for Kane.

During the first year of Richard the Lionheart's rule, Kane had met and fallen in love with Margery of Cornwall, daughter of the Earl of Cornwall. Kane never married Margery, but he did father two children with her; a son who they named William and a daughter they named Juliana who would later be known as Nicole. After impregnating Margery for the first time, Kane took her away to the estate of Lord Caithness in northern Scotland.

For the next ten years, Kane and Margery lived as man and wife and raised their children in relative happiness. Life had been good; good enough to make Kane consider settling down with Margery and living something like a normal life. It was not to be.

On the tenth year following the birth of William, the Dark Lord Mark dispatched an invading force of one hundred thousand swords into Scotland. Before the fighting ended, Kane lost Margery and William. Only Juliana survived, and Kane quickly decided to give her up to adoptive parents for her own safety. Mark had killed Kane's common-law wife and son because they were *his* wife and son.

As Kane gazed out from the Grand Observation Lounge at the blood-red sun, a single tear spilled down his cheek. He had truly loved Margery, William, and Juliana. They had brought Kane the only joy he had ever known in his life, and their loss had taken something from him that he would never regain. Kane would ultimately be reunited with his daughter, but by then, she was no longer Juliana, and he was no longer the father she had known.

Manipulating time had ripped his family away from him, and like a fool, he had resorted to manipulating time again to gain the girl's allegience. And he had failed.

Kane had spent a great deal of time with the girl, Charlie MacLeod. She had become almost a daughter to him, though he never lost sight of his real objective. Thus, he placed one temptation after another before her with the aim of turning her young heart. Yet she somehow managed to resist him and the more she resisted his enticements, the more his respect for her grew.

Charlie was indeed powerful and strong-willed. Despite the torment she had suffered at Beathach's hands, despite Kane's having become a surrogate father to her, despite his promises of power and a life of ease; despite the opportunity to use her power freely; even despite having been shown the vile nature of humanity, Charlie refused to adopt the path of a Dark Knight.

Throughout this time Charlie remained closed to him. Nevertheless, Kane did not need to read her mind or intentions to know that his appeals to her darker nature had indeed enticed her. Part of her *wanted* to turn to the darkness and not for the typical reasons of greed, self- aggrandizement, megalomania, addiction, or even hedonism. Instead, Charlie carried inside her a desperate need for revenge; a need that both drew her heart and chilled her all at once. And so, she fought against that soft siren song of vengeance with ever waning efforts.

Here, Kane saw her weakness. She would never adopt the path of the Dark Knight for herself, but for recompense for the murder of her parents, she could be persuaded to embrace the darkness.

Kane had known of Robin Striker's role in the death of Charlie's father from the day he had first learned of her name, and it was here that he saw her weakness. Striker had shot Charlie's father in the stomach and Charlie had burned him alive in retaliation. She believed him to be dead. If that belief were put to the lie, if she were presented with her father's murderer once more; then she would most certainly kill him in cold blood.

There was, of course, one problem: Charlie had killed Striker, and the power could not be used to resurrect the dead. Nevertheless, Kane knew of another means to bring Striker back. He could use the power to manipulate time in such a way as to allow Striker to survive, after a fashion.

Bend the rule without breaking it.

Though dangerous, Kane judged this approach to be worth the risk. He needed Charlie's willing cooperation, and he believed that the promise of revenge would be the way he could gain it.

III

Charlie herself, confirmed Kane's calculation when she unexpectedly opened up to him on the day before her birthday. It was late in the afternoon, and Kane had taken Charlie to the Imperial Water Garden, one of the better water parks on *Ifrinn*. He had done this knowing that a trip to the water park had been the last normal thing Charlie had done with her father before the NSA murdered Charlie's mother and tore her and her father's lives apart.

Charlie and Kane were sitting next to each other, eating ice cream. Charlie wore a sporty blue two-piece while Kane wore a pair of black trunks and an open black terry cloth robe.

As with all foods on *Ifrinn,* the ice cream was mostly tasteless and brought only fleeting pleasure. Charlie spent the day with a wistful smile on her young face; her blue eyes intense and sorrowful. Though she seemed to have gained some enjoyment from the day she appeared haunted by memories of a happier time so many years ago. As she nibbled at her mostly tasteless ice cream Charlie met his gaze with her direct blue eyes and spoke softly and with great sadness.

"The last time I went to a water park was with Daddy, right before the NSA showed up and…" She fell silent. Her eyes intensified and narrowed. "…killed Mommy." She spat those last words out with naked, cold, hate.

Kane met her gaze, and for a moment, felt something almost like empathy for the girl. "I'm sorry those men took your parents from you. You deserve better than what you have been given."

Charlie looked at him silently, her eyes almost accusatory. "I wish I knew who killed Mommy. Robin killed my Daddy, but I never saw who killed my Mommy. I was in the car and Daddy went in the house. He told me later that he found her dead, but he didn't say who did it. I don't think he knew." Her eyes drifted far away until she was almost looking through him instead of meeting his gaze. "I killed Robin because he shot my Daddy. It hurt so much and I was so angry I just burned him up. I shouldn't have done that. It was bad."

Kane gave her what he hoped was a compassionate gaze as he placed a gentle hand around her bare shoulders. "What you did wasn't wrong. He killed your father, it's natural to want revenge, and there's nothing wrong with taking it."

Charlie hung her head. "I killed him, and it doesn't even help. It still hurts, and I feel…" She fell silent for a moment. "…so angry. I think I hate him. I think I hate all of those NSA men and nothing helps."

Kane gently placed his right index finger under her chin and slowly turned her face towards his. "It's ok to hate them." He soothed. At the time, he had been smiling internally. "They took your family away and destroyed your life. You have every right to hate them. It doesn't make you a bad person.

It makes you human."

Charlie remained silent for a moment before softly whispering: "I know it's bad, but I'm glad Robin's dead."

In that moment, Kane understood and decided his course of action. He spent the remainder of that day showing Charlie as good a time as possible under the circumstances. She seemed to enjoy herself though her eyes betrayed her troubled heart.

IV

Late that night, after escorting Charlie to her chambers in the Black Imperial Palace, Kane returned to his own chambers and sealed himself within.

The royal suite offered views unrivaled anywhere on the Imperial capital world. Outside the sun had already retired beyond the horizon, leaving a black satin sky punctuated with a scattershot of white starlight and twin orange oval moons. Kane stood in the royal living room observing the night through massive floor to ceiling picture windows separated by hand-carved serpentinite Roman pillars. He had adjusted the chamber's lighting to a low flickering candle flame that cast long shadows across the polished serpentinite floor and vaulted ceiling.

Furnished in red satins, black leathers and dark hardwoods of Edwardian style, the chamber reflected Kane's personal tastes in every way. From the black bladed swords that decorated the chamber's great pillars and single wall and the large serpentinite fireplace set into that wall to the spiral staircase that opened the center of the living room floor, the chamber exuded Kane's tastes in every way.

As he watched the deepening night, Kane reached far into the power, mustering every bit of focus he possessed. His heart quickened in his chest as indescribable ecstasy washed through his flesh in waves. Following this came a slipping sensation as if he had sidestepped out of his body and out of this reality into some other realm of consciousness. The sensation built and built until he had plunged into a raging icy river to be swept away by its current.

At the same time, the night sky and royal suit began to shimmer and twist as if taken by some great, invisible hands. The river swept on, and the world contorted and flickered until everything had faded to white. And somewhere in that white, the river swept him to a new shore for when his vision cleared he found himself standing on a familiar beach.

Fallow Point...

V

He had arrived precisely twenty minutes before Robin Striker would set foot on the beach. Kane took care to ensure that he would not be visible to Charlie, her father or Striker. He intended to preserver Charlie's memory of killing Striker, and he wanted to remain a stranger to her until after his Death Troopers captured her in Iraq.

Kane cloaked himself in the power and took up a position ten feet from the rock where Striker would seat himself to await Charlie's arrival.

Twenty minutes later and right on cue Robin Striker arrived carrying an antique scoped K98K and dressed in a battered leather bomber jacket, desert fatigues and worn classic leather combat boots. Despite his expressionless face and blank eyes, Kane sensed excitement and…*love?...* in Striker's heart. Kane would not have imagined an Asset capable of excitement or love and yet there was no mistaking the warm, heady sensation.

Yes, Striker loved Charlie as if she were his own daughter and the prospect of seeing her excited him as it would a parent who had been away from their child for a stretch. Kane watched as Striker checked his rifle over carefully, slid the bolt open and deftly loaded five 8 mm expanding rounds into the magazine one at a time before closing the bolt and chambering a round. As he did Kane sensed Striker's sincere hope that he would not need the rifle.

After inspecting his Mauser, Striker slowly reached inside his jacket and withdrew a slim stiletto knife and polished it carefully on his slacks before lovingly tucking it away. This would be his gift to Charlie. It would be an act of mercy and love for Striker understood a painful truth about Charlie that her own father refused to face.

Charlie was never meant for this world. She was a miracle that was never meant to be, and for her own sake, she needed to be put down. Otherwise, Charlie would continue to suffer for her power at the hands of a world that hated and feared her.

As he watched Striker prepare for the girl, Kane became aware of Charlie's approach. She was presently crossing the Fallow Point compound grounds accompanied by an NSA agent by the name of Mike Biggs.

Though Charlie's mind was closed to him, Kane could sense palpable fear from Biggs, who clearly wished that he were anywhere else. He had drawn the short straw and was assigned the task of supervising an increasingly angry and defiant fire-starting little girl while she swam in the ocean.

The MacLeod girl frightened Biggs. He had heard stories of what she had done at the Ephrata police station and had no desire to be anywhere near this hellacious child. Nevertheless, Colonel Atarox, the Fallow Point commander, had made it clear that refusal would be detrimental to his future.

Minutes ticked by and Charlie, followed by Biggs, appeared on the stairway leading down to the beach from the Fallow Point grounds. Biggs wore a cold, blank expression but his rat-like eyes betrayed his fear. For her part, Charlie's face had hardened, and her eyes glittered and widened ever so slightly. She looked not like a child about to go play on the beach, but instead a soldier headed off to a battle that would end a war and probably her life.

Kane felt his heart quicken and steadied his breath. The power moved restlessly within him, awakened by his emotions. A cool breeze stirred air alive with energy, and heavy with the damp scent of saltwater. In the back of his mind, Kane understood that the energy he felt on the salty wind was Charlie's power. This part of him marveled at the sheer blindness and ignorance of Biggs and Striker. They knew not what they were doing. They knew nothing of the hell-storm they would soon unleash.

Charlie had reached the beach. Biggs had caught up with her and walked at her side. She carried a duffel bag over one shoulder and walked with stiff purpose. The wind picked up, electric now with the girl's immense power. Thunder rumbled low in the distance, as far off storm clouds gathered on the horizon.

Charlie stopped approximately twenty feet from the water and turned to Biggs. "I need to get my bathing suit on, could you go somewhere so I can have some privacy." Her tone was friendly, but Kane detected a subtle warning behind it.

Foolishly Biggs shook his head. "Sorry kid I was ordered to keep an eye on you, and that's what I'm going to do."

Kane smiled slightly. *Idiot, you have no idea who you are dealing with.*

"I'm not going to run away or anything I just don't want to take my clothes off with you watching." Charlie continued in a reasonable tone. Her warning had become more pronounced.

Mike remained stationary. "I can't leave." His posture feigned stoic bravery, but Kane easily felt the terror beneath.

"Go away!" Charlie shouted, all pretense now dropped. Kane felt Charlie's power begin to stir.

"Can't do that kid." Biggs reached into his jacket for his gun. His eyes were frightened, narrow, and verminous.

Charlie waited for the gun to appear before striking suddenly with the power. Biggs dropped his weapon with am anguished cry as a fresh crop of ripe blisters appeared across his now angry red palm. The fool had been lucky the Glock had not exploded. It would have certainly served Biggs' right if it had.

"Get out of here you bastard and don't turn back." Charlie barked angrily, then her tone sharpened to an iron threat. "I'll be watching, and if I see you turn around I'll fry you!"

Biggs froze, his terror palpable on the cool, salty breeze. For a moment Kane sensed him considering a move for his Glock, which was lying in the sand a few feet away. Then his long-lost survival instinct kicked in, and he fled in terror.

Striker had been watching this little scene play out with an expression of amusement. Once Biggs had fled, he stood from his rock and called out to the girl in a loving, almost *fatherly* tone.

"Charlie."

The girl instinctively turned at the sound of her name, and her face immediately registered recognition.

"You!" Her voice came out as no more than an angry hiss.

"Yes, it's me, Charlie."

The girl's face and eyes became hard and cold as ice, as her power electrified the air. "You tricked me. You lied. You tricked Daddy and me."

"Yes, I lied. I lied because I had to. I was your father's friend. I did my best to help him. I didn't make him join the program. Hell, I tried to talk him out of it. I took care of you because you're my best friend's daughter. I got you to do the tests because if I hadn't, they would have killed you. What did you think? That they'd say: 'Oops we fucked up.', and put you back on the street. You know better than that. You've seen what these people are capable of. You've seen what they do, what they did to your mother. They ripped out her teeth and shot…"

"Stop!" The girl begged, her voice registering terrible suffering as her power raced through the air with blistering fury.

Charlie turned suddenly and thrust the power into the ocean. The water sizzled, and wisps of steam floated up from its surface. Charlie's power slowed but continued to flow upon the cool ocean air.

As Charlie stood staring at Striker, sudden realization flooded her face. "You shot us. You shot us at the cabin in Indiana."

"Yes, it was me. I shot you." His voice held no shame but rather deep compassion. "And we both know that I had no choice. You're not normal. You're dangerous, Charlie, and you know it."

"That's not my fault," Charlie replied sharply.

"No, of course not. But the fact remains you cannot be let go. Even if we let you go you'll just be grabbed up by someone else. The British maybe, or the Russians, the Chinese, maybe even ISIS. You'll never be safe Charlie."

Charlie's expression was nonplussed, and she made no effort to argue with Striker.

"It's all bullshit anyway. Barrister, the NSA, all they care about is power. They look at you and see armies of invincible soldiers. Telekinetics, mind benders, firestarters, human weapons of mass destruction. They see human breeding farms. Hitler's dream perfected. You're not even a person to them. You're a thing, a monster, an anomaly to be dissected. I don't care about any of that. I never did. All I care about is you."

Charlie's expression changed to one of disbelief.

"I didn't lie about everything Charlie. I was betrayed. The NSA made me an Asset and sent me to Iraq to eliminate rogue insurgents and when I got caught they abandoned me there because they were assholes. Just like Barrister. I won't hurt you like they did. I want to help you. Come and sit down beside me. Let's talk this out."

As if controlled by magic, Charlie began to walk towards him. She remained closed, but Kane saw on her face that she had given up. Striker had offered her a release from suffering and terror, and she had gladly accepted. Her expression held something akin to gratitude to Striker for being her last, loyal friend.

"You won't feel anything." Striker soothed. "I promise. I'll make it quick and clean."

Charlie went to him calmly, gratefully accepting his gift of death.

Jack MacLeod had arrived at the stairs now and descended them two at a time, reaching the sandy beach just as his daughter had closed within five feet of Striker.

"Charlie!" MacLeod's voice held uncharacteristic fear.

The girl spun around suddenly at the sound of her father's voice."Daddy no! Stay away!"

"It's a little late for that Charlie." Robin's voice was annoyed. As he spoke, he methodically raised and leveled his rifle, sighting MacLeod through its antique scope.

Charlie ran to her father and wrapped her arms around his waist. Her face registered combined fear and joy. "Oh, Daddy!"

MacLeod greeted her wearily. "Hi, Charlie."

"Come here, Charlie. Nothing's changed." Robin intoned with a soft, hypnotic voice.

"I'm sorry, but I cannot allow you to do that." Kane sensed tension and anger behind MacLeod's calm, conversational tone.

"Come to me, Charlie, or I'll shoot your father."

Charlie turned slowly, her face had fallen, her joy at having been reunited with her father had melted from her cheeks and eyes only to be replaced by fear and exhaustion. "Why can't you just leave us alone?"

"You know why. Now come to me. Let's end this."

Charlie stared at Striker coldly. "You let us go, or I'll burn you up."

Striker smiled. "I don't think you want to do that because I bet I can shoot your father before you can kill me. And Jack if you try to attack me, then I will shoot your daughter."

Charlie's expression became that of a trapped rabbit. "Please, just leave us alone. Please…"

"It's your choice, Charlie. Your father can go free. I don't care. Or I can shoot him in the head. Freedom, or a bullet in the brain. You decide."

A desperate sob escaped Charlie's throat. Kane felt the girl's power light up the air yet no fire erupted. Instead, Charlie turned towards Striker and slowly approached him.

"Charlie, no!" Her father tried to stop her, but she twisted out of his grasp.

Robin's smile returned. "Good girl Charlie." He lowered the Mauser slightly.

Charlie went to Striker and allowed him to put his arm around her shoulders. He led her towards a nearby rock.

"Come let's sit down."

Charlie went with him mutely.

"No! Don't go with him, Charlie! Don't listen!" MacLeod's fear and desperation flowed on the cool ocean winds in icy torrents.

Tears glistened in Charlie's eyes. For a moment, Kane saw himself in her and felt something close to empathy and sorrow.

Charlie went with Striker without looking back. When they had reached the rock where Kane had awaited Charlie's arrival, Striker sat down and met Charlie's eyes with his own."Come here, Charlie. You can sit on my lap."

Charlie complied wordlessly.

"You know this is the only way."

She did not reply.

"You don't have to be afraid. I promise it won't hurt." Striker reached into his weather-beaten leather jacket and produced his stiletto. "In the days of the Roman Empire, the Sakara Ii used stiletto knives like this to kill their enemies. I'll show you. Bend your head forward."

Though Kane knew the story of Striker's death and Charlie's escape from Fallow Point well, his heartbeat picked up ever so slightly for he knew that the slightest change in events could lead to disaster.

Charlie complied with Striker's request without a word. MacLeod looked on with a horrified expression Kane would not have imagined him capable of.

Striker touched the back of the girl's head where her spine met the base of her skull. "The blade goes in here and penetrates the brain stem. Death is instantaneous. There is no pain."

Charlie shuddered in Striker's arms.

MacLeod had begun to scream. "No! NO!"

"Don't be afraid." Striker soothed. "It will be very fast. You won't feel anything."

Striker's words did not comfort Charlie as her expression remained tight and fearful though she made no effort to escape.

“I won’t do it until you tell me it’s ok. When you are ready, nod your head forward.”

Charlie sat perfectly still for a few seconds. She remained closed to Kane, but he did not need the power to know that Charlie was terrified. Though she did not tremble or sweat her rigid posture and pale, expressionless face laid the story bare.

Wordlessly, Charlie lowered her head. Striker gently turned her face towards his with his left hand while he positioned the stiletto with his right.

“NO!” As the word left his lips, MacLeod struck out with the power, shoving Striker and Charlie off the rock. Nevertheless, Striker deftly managed to maintain his grip on Charlie, and she had already resigned herself to her fate. Charlie positioned herself on Striker’s lap once more, dipped her head and turned her eyes to meet Striker’s.

Striker thrust the blade into the base of Charlie’s skull with sudden gentleness. The girl’s expression registered surprise for half a heartbeat, then relief before becoming blank. Her eyes once alive had become dull blue marbles. A thin rivulet of blood trickled from the back of Charlie’s head and over Robin’s left hand.

A single tear spilled down Striker’s chin as he hugged Charlie to his chest before lowering her to the sand.

Fury and confusion flashed through Kane’s heart. He had done nothing to interfere. Why had the events changed?

Then he understood. Time consisted of many alternate histories, each representing a different possible choice or variable. In attempting to go back to the moment in which Charlie MacLeod killed Robin Striker he had somehow landed in an alternate history where Robin Striker killed Charlie MacLeod.

Eric knew he had to act quickly. Jack MacLeod had reacted to his daughter’s death with raw fury, attacking Striker with the power. Striker had managed to defend himself for now, but that would not last. With his daughter now dead MacLeod had nothing left to lose and this fact added to his unbridled rage led him to push his power beyond its normal limits.

Without revealing himself, Kane reached into the power and lashed out at Jack MacLeod with an invisible fist, sending him sprawling. Before he could recover, Kane presented himself to Robin Striker, grabbed him by the shoulder and concealed them both beneath the power.

Striker turned quickly and met Kane’s eyes with his own. “Who are you?”

“My name is Eric Kane.”

“What do you want with me?” Striker inquired. “Jack was about to kill me. Why did you stop him?”

Kane offered a slight smile. “Because I have a task for you.”

"I'm not interested in any task you would give me." Striker responded coldly.

"I disagree," Kane replied.

VI

Before Striker could argue any further, Kane reached into the power once more. Again he mustered every ounce of focus that he possessed. As had happened before, the slipping sensation returned together with incredible ecstasy that washed through him, mind and body, warming him to the core. Again, he cast himself into an invisible river that dragged him away as the beach at Fallow Point shimmered and then faded to white.

Kane fought hard to hold onto Striker with the power and at first, he succeeded. As the slipping sensation developed into the torrential river though, Kane felt his grip beginning to fail. Still, he never felt Striker completely slip away.

Kane felt himself weakening. The power raged and blazed nearly out of his control. He felt intense pleasure but also profound exhaustion. His body felt leaden, as if after a marathon session of intense sex. Kane's mind began to drift, pulled apart like warm taffy. Before he could understand what had happened, he found himself returned to that same beach at Fallow Point. This time he viewed the sands and ocean through strange eyes and as he did his mind melted into that of another man.

To his surprise and after only an instant Striker found himself returned to the beach. The strange man in black who had sought his aid had vanished as suddenly as he had appeared. Striker had no time to be confused or even to think as he had returned just in time to witness Charlie MacLeod incinerate an exact copy of him. He was fortunate to have turned away at the last second, or he would have been blinded.

Though mystified, Striker had enough wits about him to understand that it would not do to have Charlie recognize him when she thought she had just killed him using the power. Thus, he quickly concealed himself among the cliff face crags never taking his eyes from Charlie and her father.

Events here played out differently, instead of Striker killing Charlie, Charlie killed Striker. Sadly Charlie did not act fast enough to keep Striker from fatally shooting her father.

The rifle crack and heavy ammonia and sulfur scent of gunpowder still lingered on the salty sea air as Charlie crawled to her father, devastated.

Striker watched Charlie fumble in the sand for a few minutes before finding Jack's shoe. She began nervously feeling her way up his leg, her blinded eyes wide with obvious fear. Charlie continued up Jack's body until she blundered into the massive gunshot wound just above Jack's belt. Thick, crimson blood stained Charlie's fingers as tears spilled down her cheeks. Here she stopped, her expression registering sorrow and horror.

"Daddy?" Little more than a frightened moan.

"I'm here, Charlie." Jack's voice had been reduced to a harsh, slurred whisper. His hands closed on Charlie's shoulders and gently pulled her up to meet his eyes. Rivulets of blood ran from both corners of Jack's mouth and over flesh that had turned to pale death.

"Daddy, you're bleeding." More tears spilled from Charlie's grief-stricken eyes.

"I'm ok, Charlie." Jack lied. Even from a distance Striker could clearly see that Jack MacLeod was dying.

"Oh, Daddy, I'm so sorry… I killed him." She began to cry.

Even in her distraught state, she clearly still felt terrible guilt for having killed using the power. Striker's heart went out to her; Charlie had suffered terribly for a power she had neither asked for nor wanted. Though an innocent, guilt plagued Charlie terribly. She was a miracle never meant for this world.

"Shut up, Charlie!" Jack shot back at her. He gave Charlie's shoulders a gentle shake. "And listen to me. They're going to try to kill you now, and I can't protect you anymore. I'm dying Charlie." He spoke in little more than a whisper, and his tone was amazingly calm for a man facing his own mortality. "You have to get away if you can, and if you have to kill any of them to escape I want you to do it." Jack coughed up a fresh gout of blood. "They started this Charlie, and now it's time for you to finish it. This is war, Charlie. Make sure they know that. Burn it all down, and don't keep silent. That was my mistake. I want you to tell everything. Tell what they did to us. Make it so they can never do anything like this again."

"I can't…I can't leave you, Daddy." Charlie sobbed.

Striker felt his flesh flush. A strange queasiness that he had not felt in a long time stirred his guts.

"I love you, Charlie." Jack's voice was barely audible now. "You're the best thing I've done in my life, and I am proud of you. I love…" He collapsed backward and died.

Charlie rose slowly, her face a blank porcelain mask, her eyes red, and swimming with tears, her breath deep and shuddering. She cut a slender, still silhouette as she methodically plodded across the sand towards the stairs. The cool, salty breeze, now tainted with the scent of sulfur and fire gently lifted her hair from her shoulders.

Striker's heart went out to her and his flesh burned in a familiar but forgotten way. Charlie had lost *everything…* because of him. Oh, he had not actually pulled the trigger on her father; a mirror image of him had done the deed. And yet he knew he was at fault for Jack MacLeod's death. He had *wanted* Jack dead for his refusal to accept what was best for Charlie, and he had *wanted* Jack dead for interfering with his attempt to show the girl mercy.

Now that Jack had actually died Striker felt responsible. Something deep inside him ripped apart, a thing he thought he had long since left behind. Striker had intended to put Charlie down as an act of love and mercy, to protect her from a cruel world that could never understand her. Instead, he had compounded her pain. Thin tears streamed from his eyes as he watched Charlie slowly ascend the stairs and disappear.

Striker made no effort to follow her, not out of any fear of the consequences but rather because he felt unworthy. And so Striker remained on the beach as a cacophony of gunfire, explosions and screams filtered down to him. The cool ocean breeze grew heavy with the scent of gasoline, sulfur, and burning flesh.

After the passage of twenty or thirty minutes, Charlie appeared again on the cliffside. All at once the cool breeze became a hot gale, and then a searing wind, reddening his skin and raising a crop of white fluid-filled blisters on his exposed skin. On the water, ocean waves exploded into a furious boil, filling the air with scalding white billows. Striker retreated from the blank white cloud before it could envelop him, knowing somewhere in the back of his mind that the steam would be lethal. Nevertheless, Striker did find himself eventually swallowed by white. His vision obscured, Striker sat down and waited to die.

To his surprise Striker did not die and the steam eventually cleared. Once again able to see clearly, Striker set off for the stairs, part of him hoping that he would encounter Charlie. Upon reaching the top, Striker found a blasted hellscape with Charlie nowhere to be seen. Charred bodies littered an ashen white ground split apart by thick trenches of baleful orange and yellow flames. Burned out husks of vehicles lay scattered here and there about the grounds and among them stood the skeletal remains of trees. Several blazing piles of rubble marked the gravesites of outbuildings, while a massive smoking crater punctured the earth where the central tower had once stood.

Raw gasoline mingled on the air with diesel fumes, burning plastic, molten metal, and charred flesh.

Death, this place reeks of it.

Another man would have been horrified, Striker felt nothing for this horror scene. Only when he thought of Charlie did he feel that terrible rending sensation deep within his chest.

Striker carefully picked his way over the blasted remnants of the Fallow Point compound and left without knowing of or caring for any survivors.

Located near the North Carolina border, the majority of employees at the Fallow Point compound resided in nearby North Myrtle Beach, including Striker himself, who maintained a two-story Victorian in the Cherry Grove region. His car having been destroyed in Charlie's firestorm, Striker walked the twenty or so miles to his home.

Upon returning, Striker checked in by telephone with his handler, Vic, as if he were the same Striker that had burned to death on the beach.

Vic instructed Striker to remain at home until he received further orders, an instruction which Striker promptly ignored. Instead, driven by this new rending sensation deep within, he decided to seek out Charlie. He knew not what he would do if he found her, only that he must seek her out.

VII

Striker tracked Charlie to Wilmington, North Carolina and then from there to Richmond, Virginia where the trail went cold. Here, Striker learned that Charlie had used her power to rip off an ATM machine on Broad Street.

In his effort to track Charlie, Striker had called in several favors and made heavy use of his Activity, and underworld contacts. Now the time had come to repay those debts.

Approximately two weeks after the firestorm at the Fallow Point compound, a telephone call awakened Striker around two o'clock in the morning. The female caller, who identified herself only as Jane, spoke with a rich, smoky timber as she offered him her authorization code and then proceeded to inquire of Striker's progress in tracking Charlie. Striker truthfully advised "Jane" that he had no knowledge of Charlie's whereabouts though he withheld Charlie's theft from the ATM.

"Jane" ordered Striker to travel to the Portsmouth Sea Terminal, and target a man name of Ahmet Rafiq. Jane related that Central Intelligence suspected Rafiq of masterminding a plot to attack an American city with a nuclear weapon. Rafiq, a disaffected Pakistani nuclear scientist, had allegedly put his skills to work building a thermonuclear warhead for ISIS. At present, Rafiq had completed 60% of the warhead and had recently arrived on a return trip from Russia where he had allegedly obtained sufficient fissile plutonium to complete the warhead within a month. It was imperative that he die.

VIII

Striker left his room at the Fireside Motel in Richmond and drove to Chesapeake before entering the Portsmouth Sea Terminal. Upon arriving, he parked his car out of sight and carefully observed the security gate. Here, a single armed security guard stood watch. Striker reached inside his long coat and withdrew the scoped K98K that had once belonged to the Robin Striker who had died on the beach at Fallow Point. He then sighted the crosshairs on the place where the guard's throat met the top of his ribcage.

A young man of maybe twenty-six or twenty-seven, the guard's expression showed focus and a slight hint of youthful bravado. This young man enjoyed his job. Striker carefully squeezed the trigger.

-CRACK-

The sound echoed in the cool night air, and the young man went down as if struck by a baseball bat.

Striker remained still for a few minutes, listening for sirens. There were none, so he carefully approached the gate. Seeing no other security, Striker bypassed the corpse of the young guard and entered the port. "Jane" had advised that he would find Rafiq in a passenger stateroom aboard the *Hauptstadt,* a German container ship. Rafiq would be protected by several bodyguards and was known to carry a Colt Python.

It took little effort to find the *Hauptstadt;* however, Striker dared not approach directly. Instead, he hung back to watch the ship from the shadows. Here, two merchant marines stood guard at the gangway. Though obscured by shadows, Striker discerned the movements of several more guards on board. Striker saw no visible weapons, but he knew instinctively that they would be armed with pistols. Striker still held his rifle hidden under his long coat but decided against its use.

Too loud. I would alert the entire ship.

Instead, he sidled up to the ship, taking care to remain in the shadows. As he approached the two guards, Striker reached inside his long coat and withdrew a suppressed Walther PPK. Without pausing, Striker shot each guard in the forehead. The first pitched forward onto the concrete, while the second fell backward and tumbled into the harbor. Striker then moved onto the gangway and crept aboard the ship. He remained calm and collected despite the extreme danger. Instinctively, Striker reached out with the power and swept the deck in front of him for guards.

A single hot dagger planted itself in the middle of his forehead. Striker gritted his teeth and suppressed the pain by force of will. Two guards patrolled directly ahead, another had turned towards the stern at Striker's right while a fourth headed to the bow at Striker's left. Striker managed to avoid all four guards and locate Rafiq's stateroom just below the bridge. As he had with the gangway, Striker approached Rafiq's stateroom with care. As expected, Rafiq's bodyguards stood watch outside the door.

Striker dispatched both guards with his suppressed Walther and silently entered Rafiq's stateroom. He found the small chamber darkened and filled with soft, steady breathing and faint groans of deep slumber. Striker holstered his sidearm and withdrew the thin stiletto he had used to *kill?* Charlie. Her blood still stained the bade. Except she was no longer dead and he did not understand why.

Striker turned the blade over in his hand as he approached the rack on the left-hand wall. But for his enforced, stoic manner, Striker would have snarled a curse for "Jane's" briefing had left out a significant detail. Rafiq had not traveled alone. Here, lay a woman of approximately thirty years of age and ten years Rafiq's junior. This woman, being of Greek descent, possessed classic Mediterranean beauty complete with cinnamon-brown skin and raven black hair. For his own part, Rafiq was a man of middle age and unremarkable looks. He wore his dark hair close-cropped and had caramel skin and wide-set, heavy-lidded eyes. Striker approached the rack with great care, raised his stiletto and thrust it into the side of Rafiq's head with such care and gentleness that the woman remained deep in slumber.

Then he withdrew the stiletto and wiped the blade clean before turning and leaving.

All at once Kane found himself yanked back into his own mind. For a few moments, he drifted in agonizing darkness, his head throbbing and a thousand white-hot needles piercing his flesh. Then his vision returned, and he found himself lying on the floor of the royal suite, coated in thick, oily sweat. The hot needles had subsided to a dull ache that penetrated to the soul. His head continued to throb, but with slightly less insistence. Kane attempted to drag himself to his feet but found that he could only get to his knees. Terrible exhaustion had taken its toll upon his body, and his muscles refused any further effort. Kane remained like this for an unknown span of time before finally managing to drag himself onto the bed. Once his head hit the pillow Kane became dead to the world.

IX

After passing out, Kane slept for seven hours before awakening still feeling drained. It took little effort to locate Striker as he had voluntarily surrendered to NSA agents following the destruction of New York, but the damage had already been done. The woman that Striker had found in bed with Rafiq turned out to be his wife, Murial Rafiq. Rafiq had indeed been working on a thermonuclear warhead with the intent of detonating the device over an American city and Murial had recently learned of his plan. In her horror, she begged him to relent, and he had for they were deeply in love. That love had mattered more to them than anything else in the world such that when Striker killed Rafiq, it destroyed Murial. She too had a background in nuclear physics. Following her husband's murder, Murial devoted her talents and will to completing the warhead. Then having finished her deadly gift, she sought out men willing to deliver it to the only target she felt appropriate: New York City.

Once again, tampering with the timeline had led to disaster. Worse than the destruction of New York though, the bombing had catalyzed a lack of faith in the police state Kane's followers had carefully established in the United States and over most of the rest of the Earth's people. This lack of faith would later birth the Resistance movement, the same Resistance movement that had now set the Earth aflame.

As he remembered this, Kane took a long, slow sip of water, finding himself wishing that it were brandy.

Until that night, Kane had known only of the identities of the suspected bombers. Somehow his sources had overlooked Murial Rafiq's involvement and Striker's connection. Almost as if by design.

Kane downed the rest of his water before finally turning towards the crystal decanter of brandy on the sidebar near the bedroom door and pouring himself a snifter.

The timestream is off the table. Too dangerous, too unpredictable.

He would find another way to quell the flames of rebellion; another means by which to gain Charlie MacLeod's allegiance.

Chapter 8
Embracing the Inescapable

I

In the days that followed her arrival at the Black Hills Hotel, Charlie found herself haunted by creeping, terror soaked flashbacks to her time as a captive of the Black Empire. Until now these memories had remained mostly hidden just outside of her awareness, sublimated at first by pain and suffering from her shoulder burns and then later by immediate survival needs and the threat of capture by the Resistance. Now that her wounds had healed to the point where they no longer seriously troubled her and she and her family had found relative safety at the Black Hills Hotel old images began to boil to the surface and with them came that old, familiar feeling of *Hate.*

In her dreams Charlie found herself dragged back to that first horrible day after she and David and Catherine had been captured by the Black Empire.

She had awakened in a small, mostly featureless black cell. The far end of the cell appeared open, though a slight blue flicker and the scent of ozone told her differently. Charlie wanted to scream and collapse sobbing at once, but before she could do either, two figures in heavy blank-faced, black armor appeared and dragged her from the cell.

These men and women comprised the Black Empire, and served Lord Beathach and his Emperor Eric Kane, and at their hands, she suffered horrible physical torture, emotional torment, and crushing humiliation. Kane himself had forced her to face the darkest side of her own heart.

Kane had also offered Charlie the opportunity to use the power freely and without guilt. And yes, she had been tempted. Charlie had *enjoyed* the freedom to use the power as she wished and event to this day she missed that freedom. David and Catherine had never forbidden her from using the power as her father once had, but Charlie understood that to use the power on Earth, among Outsiders, would be dangerous. To most people, Charlie represented either a grave threat or a potent weapon. Thus, by using the power she would risk death, imprisonment or exploitation.

As she recalled her time in the hands of the Black Empire, Charlie understood, though it hardly constituted a sudden revelation, that she *Hated* Eric Kane and Lord Beathach. Lord Beathach had personally tortured and humiliated her without remorse and while Kane had never personally involved himself in her torment…

In truth, he had treated Charlie kindly and with something like compassion whenever he had personal contact with her. Nevertheless, though Kane had never personally participated in her torment, Charlie understood that Lord Beathach and his minions would not have brutalized her without Kane's express approval. And for that, she *Hated* him as much as if he had wielded the needles, the electricity, the gas, the drugs, personally. With *Hatred* came that old, familiar wish for revenge.

The Black Empire had taken her away from David and Catherine, they had humiliated her, tormented her. Kane and Beathach had done these things to her, and they deserved to suffer for it. The NSA had killed Daddy and Mommy, and they deserved to suffer for it.

But it's wrong. I murdered Robin because he murdered Daddy, I'm no better than he was and I don't even feel better. I shouldn't want revenge.

And yet she did, deep inside she desperately wanted to take revenge, to do something to sate the quiet, black flame that had erupted from the deep bloodstain of *Hate* seared upon her heart and soul.

Though she fought against it, understanding that hatred and vengeance are dangerous, that they only led to further hatred and vengeance, to ever-escalating violence, the black flame drove her to begin practicing with the power.

David told her again and again that they should keep to themselves and not have contact with the other residents of the Black Hills Hotel and Charlie knew that it was far too dangerous to use the power inside the building. Thus, Charlie spent her first day at the hotel locating a way to get outside unseen.

She quickly found an emergency stairway and then a secluded pasture beyond a stand of trees to the north of the hotel. Here, Charlie practiced with the power daily and for many hours, taking care to keep her activities secret even from David and Catherine.

Though Charlie never spoke of it to either, she sensed that David and Catherine both feared that she would one day lash out in revenge for the deaths of Daddy and Mommy, that she would one day become 'corrupted' by her anger. For this reason, David had stopped training her early on and would undoubtedly make her stop practicing if he knew.

II

Time passed slowly, winter eventually gave way to spring and Charlie' s birthday came. On that particular morning, Charlie awoke early, feeling both excited and more than a little sad. She turned ten today, and David and Catherine had promised to make her birthday special. But Daddy and Mommy would not be there to celebrate with her, they were gone, murdered by the hand the NSA.

As she slid out of bed and walked towards the bathroom, tears briefly spilled from her eyes before the burning bloodstain on her heart staunched any further mourning. Charlie felt her cheeks flush and her heart quicken before she pushed anger aside and forced herself to smile.

Today would be a good day, she felt sure of it. She would celebrate her birthday with David and

Catherine, they would do whatever she wanted to do to celebrate. Though Charlie had not yet decided how she wanted to celebrate her birthday the fact that she had been asked both excited her and touched her heart.

As she thought this, Charlie's smile widened a bit. They had not had to run for two months now, giving them the opportunity to be a real family. But for the fact that they lived in near isolation, frightened of discovery, life had almost normalized.

Still, she found it hard to find joy in her life as her heart remained consumed by the black bloodstain. Charlie had more time to just *be* with David and Catherine, and yet she spent much of her time alone, practicing with the power. She desperately *wanted* to spend the time with David and Catherine, but to do so would require that she let go, if only a little and that she could not do.

The horrible unfairness of it all made letting go unacceptable to her. To let go would mean accepting what the Black Empire and the NSA had done to her. It would mean smiling and accepting what they had done to her like a good little girl. The thought made her blood boil and her stomach churn. She would never accept what they had done to her and her parents, never.

With the passage of that last thought, Charlie went into the bathroom. Ten minutes later, she had dressed and headed into the kitchen. There she found David cooking French toast, one of her favorite breakfasts, while Catherine and Stephen sat at the dining room table chatting quietly.

As Charlie entered the room, David turned and flashed a crooked smile. "Good morning, Charlie. Happy birthday! How did you sleep?"

"Good." She replied in a bright tone. As she spoke the rich scent of cinnamon mingled on the air with eggs, butter, and frying bread. Charlie's mouth began to water.

"Good morning, Charlie," Catherine called to her in a sweet, motherly tone. "Happy birthday!"

"Happy Birthday Charlie!' Stephen added.

Charlie's heart warmed, and a smile spread across her face. "Thank you."

"Have a seat," David instructed. "I'll have your breakfast ready in a few minutes. Would you like some OJ?"

"Yes please." She replied.

David stepped away from the stove for a moment, opened the refrigerator and took out a glass pitcher of orange juice before pouring her a glass and setting it down in front of her.

Charlie picked up the frosted glass tumbler and gazed at it for a moment before taking a healthy slug.

Orange juice was a special treat she had not had in quite a while as juice of any kind had become a rare commodity. Charlie held the cold liquid in her mouth for a moment, savoring its sweet citrusy flavor before slowly swallowing.

As she enjoyed her juice, a new, and yet old and familiar scent greeted her nose.

Coffee?!

In an instant, the rich, nutty, smoky aroma thrust her back in time until she found herself sitting in her parents' kitchen once more. Mommy or Daddy always had a pot of Dunkin Donuts espresso brewing on the Kuerig machine. For a moment she saw her father and mother's faces as clear as if they stood before her. Both smiled at her warmly.

Good morning Charlie. Happy birthday!

Mommy and Daddy's joyous tones came to her as clear as if spoken just that moment. Their voices turned a slow knife in her chest, taking her breath away. A single, hot, and bitter tear spilled from each eye. The power, mournful, stirred within her, awakened by the terrible pain in her heart.

Charlie held onto the power as if it were an unruly dog on a leash. Her covert training had made it no longer necessary to fight the power as she had once.

She had last celebrated her birthday with both of her parents when she had turned six. As she recalled the day, the knife tore deeper through her breast, and her eyes blurred and stung with tears. She had been happy, Daddy and Mommy had thrown a big party for her with all of her friends and Mommy had baked her a triple-decker coconut cake, her favorite.

In an instant, the memory faded, and the knife in heart became the flaming bloodstain of *Hate* once more.

In that moment, she wanted nothing more than to taste the warm, smoky, bitter flavor of coffee so that she could remember and be with her Daddy and Mommy once more, if only for a moment.

"Can I have some coffee too?"

He turned and offered a somewhat surprised expression. "Of course, but I didn't think you liked coffee."

"I usually don't." She replied. "But that smells good, and I don't know when I'll be able to have it again."

"Ok, Charlie." As he spoke, David filed a mug from the coffee pot and set it down beside her now half-drunk glass of orange juice. "Careful its very hot."

Charlie took the mug by its handle and brought it up to her nose before taking a long sniff in the hopes that she would once again be carried back to be with Daddy and Mommy. She was disappointed.

Catherine's voice broke her attempts to reminisce. "You're the birthday girl Charlie. What would you like to do today?"

Charlie remained silent for a moment for she did not know. It had been years since she had been able to actually *choose* what she would do to celebrate her birthday.

After her sixth birthday, she and Daddy had been on the run necessitating a simple cake, card and a small gift for her seventh, eighth and ninth birthdays. No friends, no party, nobody but Daddy and her. She hadn't had any friends since leaving Taylor, Illinois anyway.

After a few moments of silence, Charlie had an idea. She had been by the resort stables and knew that there were a few surviving horses still quartered there. Charlie had never ridden a horse before.

"Can we go horseback riding?"

Catherine smiled warmly. "Of course, Charlie."

Charlie sensed some doubt behind Catherine's words as she would have to ask Ken to arrange it so as not to draw attention from the other residents.

Despite sensing Catherine's misgivings, Charlie smiled happily. "Oh goody!"

Though her expression did not change, Charlie could feel Catherine's concern deepen for she harbored uncertainty about the answer that Ken would give and desperately wanted to avoid disappointing Charlie.

For her part, Charlie remained uncharacteristically optimistic as she sensed that this would be a good day. As this thought passed through her mind, David came around from behind the counter carrying four plates piled high with French toast and set one in front of her.

"Bon Appetit!" He offered with a smile.

Charlie answered with a renewed smile of her own. "Thank you."

Her heart warmed even as the knife returned with a sharp twist that brought on fresh tears. Charlie looked away and quickly swept them aside with the back of her hand.

"Are you ok, Charlie?" David inquired in a concerned tone.

Charlie blinked back her tears, swallowed the thick lump that had formed in her throat, and turned back towards David, her smile renewed once more. "I'll be ok." She replied in a wistful tone. "I was just remembering my sixth birthday party, it was the last one I had with Mommy and Daddy."

David's expression fell a little, his brow furrowed, and his eyes turned down in regret. "I'm sorry they're not here Charlie."

Charlie retained her smile without falter. "I am too." She replied in a solemn tone before brightening up. "But I'm glad we're here together."

David's expression changed to a warm smile. "So am I."

Breakfast was delicious. Charlie ate six slices of French toast, drank two glasses of orange juice and two cups of coffee.

After breakfast, the four of them took the emergency staircase down to the second floor to visit Ken.

He agreed to arrange for them to go horseback riding in the same secluded pasture Charlie had been using to practice with the power for months.

From the moment she stepped outside, Charlie knew this would be a glorious day. Warm sunlight streamed from a flawless span of blue, while a gentle breeze, sprinkled with the scents of wildflowers and clover, stirred the grass beneath her feet. Off in the distance stunning, snowcapped mountains towered into the heavens. Charlie looked up at the sky and smiled joyfully, her sorrow forgotten at the sight of such beauty.

For a moment, she remained silent feeling the warm air dance through her loose, waist-length, blond hair. Then she turned to David and Catherine and spoke in a cheerful tone. "I've never ridden a horse before. I can't wait."

David and Catherine both returned her smile.

"Well, now you're going to get your chance," Catherine replied in a loving tone.

A short time later, Charlie sat astride a large, pure white horse, cantering gently through the hidden pasture. The man who kept the stables had explained that he was an American Quarter Horse and that his name was *Liberator.* As she rode Charlie forgot for a time, the events that had brought her to that moment and became just another little girl with her parents and friend. The power lay dormant within her, painful memory washed away leaving her heart cleansed of its stains. In those few hours, Charlie felt as though she had begun life anew, or perhaps that she *could* begin life anew if she so desired.

She chatted happily with David, Catherine, and Stephen about inconsequential things and simply lived. Sadly, the dream would not last. As the day grew late and the sun faded to orange, they circled around the abandoned pasture only to pass by a charred spot where Charlie had practiced with the power.

All at once memories of the past flooded back upon her and with them came the return of the black bloodstain and a new, nausea that nearly caused her to pitch forward and vomit upon *Liberator's* great neck. She had nearly forgotten, nearly allowed herself to walk away.

A familiar voice of a certain little girl spoke up in her mind. *How could you forget? How could you forget what they did to Mommy, to Daddy?*

No, please... She begged.

They died because of you.

Please...

Mommy died because of you!

Please don't! She pleaded.

Daddy died because of you!

Please don't say that!

And now you've betrayed them! The little girl hissed contemptuously.

Tears streamed from Charlie's eyes as she wept silently. The power stirred within her, awakened by her sorrow. Charlie held it firmly, and with little effort. Control came much more easily since she had begun to practice with the power. This was good for the power had grown so much stronger and closer to the surface, ready to leap out and destroy at any moment.

"Charlie? Is everything ok?" David's voice held concern.

"I'm fine." She lied as she swiped at her tears with the back of her hand. "I was just thinking about Daddy and Mommy."

David replied with something about how sorry he felt for the loss of her parents and how he and Catherine would be there for her but Charlie only peripherally noticed for her attention had returned to the voice of the angry little girl.

I didn't betray Mommy and Daddy. Charlie replied to the angry little girl's voice.

Really?. You were about to let go, to walk away!

To this, Charlie had no response for the angry little girl had struck upon a kernel of truth. She had, for those few hours of riding, let go of her sorrow, her anger, even her desire for revenge and *Hate.* For a moment, Charlie considered doing exactly that which the angry little girl condemned and simply letting go and walking away. Yet, she could not, for she felt that walking away would be a betrayal and it hurt too much. And so, instead, she renewed her commitment to revenge, and reembraced *Hate.* Deep inside Charlie felt the black bloodstain reemerge upon her heart.

Late that night, Charlie lay in bed, the iPhone that was her birthday gift in her right hand, and an earbud in each ear. Although the cell network had long since gone down, it still made a serviceable MP3 player and a precious gift. Music of any sort had become a rare treat. Charlie had nearly cried upon tearing away the pink paper in which David and Catherine had wrapped it.

David and Catherine had loaded the phone with old rock music by Journey, Bon Jovi, Guns and Roses, AC DC and Ozzy Osbourne among others, all music that Mommy and Daddy once listened to and all among Charlie's favorites. Now she gazed out the window by her bed, into the moonless night, as *If I Closed My Eyes Forever*, streamed into her mind.

The song seemed strangely appropriate to her feelings at that moment. The black bloodstain upon her heart blazed with an almost unsupportable intensity and yet part of her wished for an end to the anger and *Hate.* Another part of her asked if it would have been better if she had never been. Certainly, her parents would have been better off, the NSA would not have murdered them but for their desire to get to her. And David and Catherine, would they have made it out of Manhattan before the bombing? She felt sure that they would have; and that they would have been happier without her having come into their lives. And if she died that night? They would undoubtedly mourn her passing. But would they not still be better off?

These questions plagued her mind as she listened quietly to Ozzy Osbourn on that dark, moonless night.

III

Stephen Wolf too sat up late that night. He had said nothing, but he had observed the girl's sudden change in demeanor, and though she remained closed to him, Stephen understood that something clearly troubled her. David and Catherine McAuliffe, the girl's adoptive parents, had told him of the girl's history and for his own part, Stephen was amazed at how well adjusted the girl was. Though at times she acted depressed and withdrawn, overall the girl was friendly and acted like any other child of her age.

And yet Stephen remained wary of her, for she coped *too* well given her past. The girl had no outbursts of crying or anger, no acting out. And if she suffered from nightmares, then he had never heard her scream in the night, nor did she ever appear to suffer from lack of sleep. Stephen was unsure of whether the girl was in denial, or if something else was going on. However, he *had* noticed that Charlie seemed to disappear in the early afternoon at around the same time each day for several hours at a time.

Yesterday, Stephen had followed Charlie to the same hidden pasture as the one where they had gone horseback riding, and there he observed her practicing with the power. Stephen had known for some time now that Charlie was a pyrokinetic. Nevertheless, her power both intrigued and frightened him at once.

As he watched, hidden by a stand of trees and shrubs, Charlie carefully built several small pyres with loose branches she had collected from around the pasture. Then when she finished, Charlie stepped back and studied her handiwork for a few moments. All at once, her eyes narrowed and darkened, and her expression became cold and hard as ice.

Stephen felt the air come alive with invisible electricity. Then without warning the pyre furthest from him burst into orange flames. The scent of wood smoke ran thick and heavy on the cold, electric air. Without pausing, Charlie turned to the next pyre. As she did the electricity on the air intensified and the second pyre blossomed into orange flame. Without pausing, Charlie turned and swept the remaining pyres with bright yellow fire. Then she turned her eyes to the ground, and her expression tensed and reflected a slight hint of pain before she straightened up and set about gathering more sticks. As she did, Charlie turned her face toward his, and though she couldn't have known of his presence she flashed a hard, glacial smile of cold hate.

IV

Now, as he sat alone on the couch in his suite, the lights dimmed, and a crystal tumbler of scotch on the coffee table in front of him, Stephen came to a hard realization. Charlie was a sweet girl, and David and Catherine loved her dearly. And yet she was dangerous. Stephen recognized the expression she had had on her face after setting the pyres alight and knew it to be that of a person driven by raw anger and hatred.

David had once told Stephen that Charlie carried a great deal of unresolved anger over the deaths of her natural parents, and he feared that she would one day give in to that anger and seek revenge. It now appeared that she had begun preparations to do precisely that. Stephen knew anger to be both a powerful and dangerous motivation as it could easily lead one to justify evil in pursuit of revenge.

As that thought passed through his mind, Stephen took up his glass and drew a slow sip of scotch. For a moment, he held the warm, amber liquid in his mouth, savoring its smooth, woody flavor. Then he swallowed, took out a Prima and lit it with his silver Zippo lighter before taking a long, slow drag. As his lungs filled with smoke, and his tongue came alive with the flavor of rich, bitter tobacco, Stephen closed his eyes and laid his head on the back of the couch before allowing thick clouds to billow from his mouth.

Charlie MacLeod had power beyond anything Stephen could have imagined. In the grip of anger and lust for revenge, she would become incredibly dangerous. Stephen had only met a Dark Knight once in his life. The iron haired stranger, clad in leather, and armed only with a black cruciform sword, had slaughtered a dozen Spetsnaz before disappearing. That man had been frighteningly powerful and yet Stephen felt certain that even untrained, Charlie MacLeod was far more dangerous.

And she will not be untrained for much longer.

Stephen took another sip of scotch, followed by a long drag from his cigarette. He had no desire to kill Charlie, she was only a child, and he could hardly fault her for her anger or her desire to take revenge on the killers of her father and mother. Nevertheless, Stephen could not allow her to act on those feelings. He had to stop her.

Perhaps she could be redirected. David and Catherine have tried to convince her to let go, but they are her parents now. Kids only listen to their parents about half of the time anyway. Maybe she would listen better to a friend.

V

The following day, at her usual time of 1:30, Charlie discretely slipped out of the suite she shared with David and Catherine, down the emergency staircase and outside. As she crossed the resort property towards the northern line of tall pines that marked the edge of the pasture beyond, a familiar voice came from behind.

“Hi, Charlie. Where are you headed?”

She recognized Stephen Wolf’s voice at once. Despite being certain that Stephen could not know her intentions, Charlie’s heart leapt up in her chest, and she had to fight an urge to spin around suddenly.

Instead, she composed her face into a friendly smile as she slowly turned to face him.

"Hi, Stephen."

"Where are you headed?" Stephen repeated kindly.

"Oh, I was just taking a walk." She replied casually.

"Can I join you?"

Charlie did not want Stephen to accompany her, but off the cuff could not think of a good reason to refuse.

"Okay."

Annoyance nettled her. Resigning herself to the fact that she would not be able to practice that day, Charlie turned towards the gardens, all the while cursing herself for not being more discreet.

In an instant, Charlie became aware that Stephen wasn't buying her story. "Weren't you headed for those trees." He nodded his head towards the stand of pines concealing her chosen practice area.

Charlie remained silent for a moment while she contemplated whether to lie or tell the truth.

Before Charlie could answer, Stephen took her by the shoulder and crouched down to her level. "Look Charlie, I know what you're up to. You've been going to the pasture beyond those trees for months now to practice with your power. I saw you yesterday."

Charlie felt her skin flush and her flesh chill even as her heart dropped into her shoe. She looked away and slumped her shoulders, suddenly feeling ashamed of herself.

Stephen must have read her expression and posture, for she immediately sensed his concern and compassion. "Don't worry. You're not in trouble. I'm just concerned Charlie."

She turned her eyes slowly to meet his. "You're going to tell David and Catherine though, aren't you?"

He remained silent for a moment. "I think I have to, but I don't think they'll be mad at you, Charlie. We're all concerned for you, that's all. Why have you been sneaking off to practice alone?"

Charlie held his coral green eyes. "It helps me. When I practice I don't hurt as much."

Charlie sensed Stephen considering her words for a moment. "So, it helps with missing your parents?'

"It helps with everything." She replied softly. "I still miss Daddy and Mommy, but it doesn't hurt as much. I still remember what the NSA and Black Empire did to me, but when I practice, that doesn't hurt as much either. At least if I'm practicing I'm doing *something.*"

All of this was the truth though she withheld her desire for revenge as motivation.

For a moment, Charlie sensed that Stephen would tell her that she couldn't continue practicing, but instead he changed his mind and surprised her.

"Why don't we go practice together. We could spar with our swords."

Charlie smiled, feeling genuinely relieved. "Ok."

And so they walked to the hidden pasture again and upon arriving each drew their blade.

Stephen offered Charlie a teasing smile. "I'll take it easy on you since you're just a kid."

Charlie returned his smile with a slightly sardonic one of her own and reached into the power. She felt it flow through her in warm, pleasant rivers as her heartbeat picked up slightly.

"You don't need to."

With a cry she raised her sword, white flames licking up the blade, and brought it down hard, aiming for the notch where Stephen's neck met his collarbone.

In an instant, Stephen parried the blow with the flat of his blade and shoved her back in the same movement. Charlie quickly caught her balance, then before Stephen could bring a follow-up blow, Charlie swung her sword around in a sideways slashing movement that Stephen only narrowly avoided.

"You're good." He declared with a smile. "But I'm better."

And with that, he somersaulted into a scissors kick which Charlie had to leap backward to avoid. Then before she had a chance to retaliate, Stephen grabbed Charlie's arm and tossed her over his head while simultaneously stripping her sword from her hands. In an instant, the white flames surrounding her blade flickered out.

Charlie landed in a crouch, the power flaring within her, driven by her sudden anger at having been outwitted. If this had been a real fight, she would have incinerated Stephen at this point. Instead, she reached out with the power, snatched her sword out of Stephen's right hand and pulled it, hilt over tip, into her outstretched hand as if it were on an invisible fishing line. Upon landing in her palm, the blade once more ignited in white.

Stephen must have seen the anger in her eyes for Charlie sensed his concern resurfacing. He slid out of his fighting stance and drove his sword into the ground point first.

"I think that's enough, Charlie."

"Sure," Charlie growled, driving her own sword into the ground with more force than needed. As she did, the white flames were extinguished once more. "But I'm not done yet. I want to practice with the power."

Charlie sensed Stephen's concern growing, and yet he did not tell her she could not practice.

"Sure, Charlie, we can do that."

And so she spent the next few hours setting fire to piles of twigs that she had gathered from the pasture so that she could practice controlling the power. Stephen watched her carefully, his expression remaining neutral despite the growing unease she sensed in his heart.

After several hours Stephen suggested to her that she try a new exercise. “Let’s see how well you can move things with your mind.”

Charlie offered him an amused smile. “Ok.” She had to suppress a chuckle. Telekinesis came easily to her.

Stephen gathered a fresh pile of twigs and set them at her feet. “Let's see you pick these up one at a time using the power.”

Charlie renewed her smile, then reached into the power and carefully moved the twigs, one at a time and stacked them neatly a few feet away. When she had finished, she quickly restrained the power without difficulty.

“Well done, Charlie.”

“That was easy.” She replied. “You should give me something hard.”

Stephen raised an eyebrow slightly. “Okay.” His voice had a ‘you asked for it’ tone.

He then took out a pair of headphones from under his weather-beaten leather jacket and tossed them to her. “Here, put these on.”

Charlie slipped them over her ears, her smile broadening slightly for she knew what he had in mind.

After setting up a beer bottle for a target and slipping in a pair of orange earplugs, Stephen carefully withdrew his Glock 19 from his jacket pocket.

“I’m going to try to shoot that beer bottle, and I want you to redirect the bullet in flight so that bottle is undamaged.”

Charlie broadened her smile still further. “Sure, that’s easy.”

“Well let’s see it.” Stephen challenged. He took aim with his pistol and fired.

Time seemed to slow; Charlie reached out with the power, felt the bullet in flight and gently pushed it aside so that it curved off course and slammed into a nearby tree trunk.

Stephen inclined his head slightly out of respect. “Impressive. Your reflexes are very quick.”

Charlie renewed her smile and blushed slightly. “Thank you. Can I try that again?”

“Sure,” Stephen replied. He raised his firearm again, took aim, and fired a second round.

Again, time slowed to a crawl. Charlie reached out with the power and swatted the bullet off course. This time the little chunk of copper and lead slammed into the ground a few feet to the left of the beer bottle.

Stephen's expression became impressed. "Very good Charlie. You have been practicing."

The power continued to move within her. Charlie pulled it back forcefully, this time triggering a momentary stabbing pain in the back of her head.

Stephen must have seen her wince, for she could feel his concern renewed. "Are you alright Charlie?"

"I'm fine." She assured him brightly.

She did, in truth, feel very good. The use of the power flooded her mind and body with both euphoria and exhilaration as if she had just gotten off a roller coaster. Moreover, she felt accomplished, as if she had completed a difficult test or book report.

She sensed that Stephen had not been placated though his expression softened, and he smiled.

"Good. That was impressive. It took me a long time to learn to use the power that quickly and precisely."

Charlie smiled, feeling a certain, rare sense of pride in her power. "Thanks." She replied softly.

"Shall we head back?"

"Sure," Charlie replied.

She felt satisfied for the day, and more than a little hungry. A quick glance at her watch told her the time was six o'clock, David or Catherine would have dinner on the table soon.

Earlier that day, as Charlie wrapped up a page of trigonometry, Catherine had announced that they would be having pizza that night. Charlie understood that this meant frozen pizza. Yet as she thought of it now, her mouth watered in anticipation.

VI

Fifteen minutes later, Charlie had returned with Stephen to the club floor and was seated at the dining room table, two slices of pepperoni pizza lay steaming in front of her.

Stephen had not yet told David and Catherine what he and Charlie had been doing in the field that day, though she sensed that he intended to discuss the matter with them before leaving. Charlie took her time eating and made sure to ask for seconds. She feared how David and Catherine would react to her surreptitiously practicing with the power and wanted to delay the inevitable moment when Stephen would reveal what she had been up to.

After dinner, Charlie helped David wash and put away the dishes before sitting down on the leather living room couch between David and Catherine.

"There's something you guys should know about," Stephen began in a tactful tone.

David met his gaze steadily. "What's up?"

"I was out for a walk today and bumped into Charlie. She was on her way to the pasture to practice with the power alone."

David remained silent for a moment, and Charlie could feel him turning this fact over in his mind, uncertain of what to do. "Did you stop her?"

"No," Stephen replied flatly. "I went with her, and we practiced together."

David did not become angry but rather seemed somewhat unsure of how to react. Eventually, Charlie felt him decide. "Thank you for not letting her go alone."

"You are welcome," Stephen replied nonchalantly.

Charlie sensed something silent pass between them. Then David turned his eyes to her. "Charlie, could you go wait in your room for a few minutes?"

Charlie did as David asked, already knowing that she was not in trouble, though she did sense that David was angry with Stephen.

VII

After his daughter had left, David turned his attention to Stephen. "Why didn't you stop her?" He demanded in a low, harsh voice.

"She is your daughter, not mine, I felt it was not my place."

David took care to keep his aggravation out of his voice. "I appreciate your desire to not interfere but, in the future, I would appreciate it if you either stop her or let us know right away."

For a moment, Stephen remained silent and seemed to contemplate. His mind remained closed to David. "Perhaps you shouldn't try to stop her from practicing."

Momentary anger flashed in David's heart before he suppressed it.

How dare he tell me how to raise my own daughter. I didn't ask for his opinion. Anyway, doesn't he understand? She still carries around anger over the deaths of her parents. Letting her practice with the power will only fuel her anger and desire for revenge.

"I don't think that's a good idea," David replied in a measured tone. "She is still very angry over the deaths of her parents, and training will only teach her aggression."

Now Stephen's face showed momentary aggravation. "Perhaps she should learn some aggression." He replied coolly. "She will never have a normal life and as powerful as she is, someone will always try to exploit her. She should learn to defend herself effectively."

David wanted to argue for he feared encouraging Charlie to use her power would only fuel her anger. Moreover, though he would admit this only to himself, he wanted to give Charlie a normal life. Encouraging her to embrace the power would be an admission that Charlie was not normal and could never hope to be.

"I should not be the one to train her, though." Stephen continued. "You are her father. She should train with you."

David studied Stephen carefully for a moment but could not penetrate his mind. "Was she comfortable practicing with you?"

"She seemed to be, but you are her father."

"And you're her friend," David responded. "You're also better with a sword and with the power than I am. Perhaps we should both train her."

Catherine, who had been quietly observing the exchange between Stephen and David broke her silence. "Maybe you should both train her. She should train with her father, but she will also benefit from your skills Stephen."

Even as she spoke, David could feel Catherine's reservations.

VIII

Later that evening, after Stephen had left and Charlie had gone to bed, Catherine shared her concerns with David. The two lay side by side in bed, wrapped in each other's arms.

"I'm worried about Charlie." She began. "I know we agreed that you and Stephen would train her, but she's so angry and practicing with the power will only fuel that anger."

David shared her concern and feared that Charlie wanted to practice so that she might seek revenge.

"I know. It makes me uneasy too, but Stephen's right, someone will always be after her for her power, and she will need to be able to defend herself. And I think she will continue to practice regardless of what we do. At least if Stephen and I work with her, we can try to help her overcome her anger."

"Maybe your right." Catherine agreed reluctantly, her concern still palpable. "It's just…she's such a sweet little girl. I don't want her to lose that."

"Neither do I," David responded.

IX

Over the following days, Charlie spent many hours with David and Stephen honing her control over the power. During this time, she felt herself growing close to both men. While David had long since become a father to her, Stephen became something else entirely. Neither a father figure nor a big brother, Stephen became a close friend and confidant to Charlie. After a while, she found herself confiding secrets to him that she hesitated to share even with David.

Then on a warm afternoon, two months after her birthday, Charlie opened herself to Stephen completely. It was late in the day, and the sun had become a golden coin in a vibrant, orange sky. A soft breeze of balmy air stirred the tall pasture grasses. Charlie and Stephen had been sparring for several hours so that David and Catherine might have some time as a couple. Now she sat on a large, mossy rock sipping lukewarm water from a weathered canteen. Stephen sat on the ground a few feet away, mopping sweat from his brow with the back of one sleeve. They had been discussing swordplay techniques and how Charlie had improved dramatically over just the last two weeks.

As she chatted with Stephen, Charlie found herself swept with deep burning anger, as her mind flashed back to that last day at Fallow Point. She had been seated upon a similar, moss-covered rock on that day, talking to someone she would have once called a friend.

In that moment, Charlie felt terribly alone for she habitually kept the black fire in her heart to herself. She loved David and Catherine intensely, and the thought of disappointing them by revealing her *Hate* crushed heart.

Still part of her wanted desperately to tell, if only to not feel alone anymore.

But what will David and Catherine think?

This thought usually kept her silent for she feared hurting them. Yet she had become so tired of feeling alone. As she met Stephen's coral green eyes, Charlie desperately longed to tell so that she would not be alone anymore.

Charlie felt Stephen's concern as he clearly sensed that something was bothering her, though he knew not what. Charlie took pains to keep her mind closed to Stephen even as she struggled with the desire to tell.

"Are you okay, Charlie?"

"I'm fine." She replied in a tone that she knew suggested otherwise. Charlie remained silent for a moment before drawing a deep breath. "I need to tell you something, Stephen."

"Yes?" Charlie could sense strong wariness in his mind and heart. "What's going on? You know you can tell me anything."

Though she felt that Stephen had been less than forthright, Charlie could no longer resist the urge to tell…*someone* and she could not bear the thought of hurting David and Catherine with her confession.

Charlie feared that Stephen might tell, but a further probe of his mind told her differently. Stephen feared her and suspected that she had begun practicing with the power in preparation for revenge. Her confession would only confirm that which he already supposed. Furthermore, he believed that David and Catherine had become too close to Charlie and could not be relied upon to take action if the worst should become necessary.

This revelation both frightened Charlie and earned her respect. Stephen did indeed care for her and dreaded ever having to harm her. Yet he would do so if needed for he understood, perhaps better than David and Catherine, the true danger Charlie could pose.

Charlie remained silent for a moment longer, steadily holding Stephen's penetrating gaze with one of her own.

"I want revenge." She confessed in a flat tone. "I want to make the NSA and the Black Empire pay for killing Daddy and Mommy and for what they did to me. I want them dead! All of them!" Tears spilled down her cheeks.

Stephen's face filled with compassion. "I know, and I understand why you would want revenge. But you must understand that I cannot allow that. You are probably the most powerful Enlightened alive and if you take revenge, if you act out of hatred, even if it is deserved, then you will be corrupted."

Charlie sensed the sincerity behind his words. "I understand." She replied through the tears streaming down her cheeks. "And I know it's wrong, but I can't let go. I just can't. They killed Daddy and Mommy, and they hurt me. They hurt me so much. I can't let them get away with it."

Stephen's compassion deepened. "I know Charlie. I know it hurts, and I know how hard it is to let go. I will help you."

He took her into his arms and gave her a fierce hug.

Charlie clung to him desperately as she silently wept. She no longer felt alone with her *Hate* and yet she felt deeply afraid, not of Stephen but rather of how David and Catherine would react when they learned of what she had revealed.

"Please don't tell David and Catherine." She pleaded. "I don't want to hurt them."

Stephen met her tearstained eyes with a studied gaze, and for a moment she could feel him considering his next decision carefully.

"I will keep this to myself." He offered. "So long as you are willing to work with me to let go."

For a moment Charlie remained silent, waiting for the angry little girl's voice to return. It did not. Charlie took great care to keep her thoughts from Stephen as she answered.

"I will." She replied with great sincerity. "I promise."

In that moment she meant it, a part of her desperately wanted to let go, for the black fire *hurt*. Yet she knew deep inside that there would be no letting go. The fire would remain regardless of her intentions or wishes. Charlie tightened her grip around Stephen's waist, realizing that she loved him. This love differed from what she had felt for her parents or David and Catherine. Instead, she loved Stephen like one might love a life-long friend.

As Charlie spent her afternoons training with David and Stephen, Charlie spent her mornings and evenings with Catherine, learning far more mundane things. On weekday mornings, Catherine taught Charlie mathematics, English, history, philosophy, and science while in the evenings and on the weekends Catherine taught Charlie to cook, clean, care for clothing, change a tire and dozens of other practical skills. They also spent a great deal of time just talking.

Catherine too sensed the immense anger Charlie carried in her heart and tried in vain to convince her to open herself up. For her part, Charlie wanted to talk about the black fire in her heart with Catherine, but she feared hurting her adoptive mother. Thus, Charlie kept her *Hate!* to herself, instead only allowing Catherine to know of her pain from the loss of her parents and the suffering she had endured at the hands of the Black Empire.

Charlie sensed that something had changed within Catherine. She no longer tried to keep her distance but instead desired to become more of a mother to Charlie. For her part, Charlie had wanted to be close to Catherine since they had first met in Central Park so many years ago and felt touched by Catherine's efforts.

Thus, Charlie took joy in the time she spent with Catherine, for she knew that their time was short. Deep inside Charlie knew that it would only be a matter of time before either the Black Empire or the Resistance would find them and when that time came they would be forced to fight and then run again.

X

Time flowed slowly. Summer gave way to fall, and then the holidays. This would be the first holiday season since Charlie had been six that she was not on the run or a prisoner. And though Daddy and Mommy had been dead for many years now, she felt their loss more keenly than in previous years. Charlie spoke of this to Stephen at some length.

"I miss Daddy and Mommy," Charlie told Stephen in a sad tone.

"I know Charlie." He replied softly.

The two of them had been sparring in the hidden pasture. A light dusting of snow lay upon the brown grass and frozen, hardpacked ground. Now Charlie and Stephen walked side by side, the frost-covered earth crunching with each step they took.

"The last Christmas I had with Daddy and Mommy was when I was six. Daddy and I never really got to celebrate Christmas much because we were always on the run or hiding somewhere. And I never had a normal Christmas with David and Catherine, the first year we were captured before

Christmas came and…" She broke off before the tears could come. "I spent several Christmases locked up by the Black Empire. Last year David and Catherine tried to make Christmas special, but I was in the hospital with a bad burn, and we were hiding again. This is the first Christmas since before Mommy died that we're safe."

Stephen nodded. Charlie felt an invisible, warm glow flowing from Stephen. "This will be the first normal Christmas you've had in years, and your Mom and Dad won't be here to celebrate with you. I'm sorry. I know that hurts."

Charlie dropped her head as big, hot tears spilled down her cheeks. "I miss them so much."

Stephen took her into his arms and hugged her tightly. "I know, and I wish there were something I could say to take away the pain, but there isn't, and I will not insult you by telling you everything will be alright. I don't know that it will be. All I do know is that David and Catherine love you very much, I love you very much, and we will be there for you for as long as we can."

Charlie looked up at him for a moment, eyes stinging with tears before burying her face into Stephen's chest sobbing uncontrollably. She felt Stephen's arms tighten around her and gripped him back fiercely.

"Have you told David and Catherine how you are feeling?" Stephen asked gently.

"No. I don't want to hurt them. They try so hard." Charlie replied between sobs.

"David and Catherine love you. I'm sure it wouldn't hurt their feelings to know that you miss your Mom and Dad. They would want to help you feel better." Stephen spoke in a voice more gentle than a summer breeze, and Charlie desperately wanted to believe him. In that moment she just wanted her Daddy and David had become a Daddy to her since Robin had killed her real Daddy.

"Ok, I'll tell them." She replied, feeling sudden, and immense gratitude to Stephen that she could not explain.

Later that night, after the dinner dishes had been washed and put away, Charlie asked David if they could talk in private. David readily agreed. Behind his casual demeanor, Charlie sensed deep concern.

Despite the night's cutting polar winds, David and Charlie decided to take a walk. Charlie's heart quickened as she walked at David's side. Snowflakes danced on the frigid air as the frozen ground crunched beneath their feet. Charlie intended to tell and yet she feared what David might say.

David broke the spell first. "What did you want to talk to me about?"

Charlie looked down and then met his gaze steadily. "I…" She broke off for a moment before beginning again. "I miss Daddy and Mommy. I'm sorry…" Before she could finish, Charlie's words caught in her throat and tears spilled down her cheeks.

David stopped and took her into his arms. "I know Charlie and its ok to be sad." His voice was hurtful in its gentleness.

“The last Christmas I had with Daddy and Mommy was when I was six. That was the last Christmas I got to celebrate until now. Daddy and I never got to celebrate Christmas because we were always running and hiding. When you found me, we didn’t get to celebrate it either because we had to run and then we got caught by the Black Empire. And last year I was in the hospital. This is the first Christmas I’ll get to celebrate since Mommy died.” Her chest tightened as she spoke those last words and her throat caught. A silent sob escaped her lips.

David’s face softened and became deeply compassionate. Behind his expression, Charlie felt his heart breaking from sadness. He loved her as if she were his natural daughter.

“I’m so sorry, Charlie. I know you miss your Mom and Dad and nothing I can say will bring them back, but Catherine and I are here for you if you need us.” As he spoke those words, David’s voice whispered in her mind.

You didn’t deserve any of this. It just goes on and on.

“And we can celebrate Christmas any way you want.” He continued. “If you want to keep things simple, we can do that, or if you want to have a big celebration we can do that too.”

A sharp knife lanced into Charlie’s heart as brief snatches of memory of happier times flashed through her mind. Her soft sobs brought the power to the surface. Charlie clamped down on it immediately.

NOT NOW!

For a moment, a hot dagger planted itself in the center of her forehead. Flames radiated outward from the dagger. Then the power went silent taking the physical pain away with it. Charlie didn’t want to celebrate Christmas at all, but she sensed that both David and Catherine wanted desperately to make the day special for her. They wanted to be a normal family, if only for a little while. Charlie felt that like her, they understood that they would not be safe here for much longer.

“Can we just keep Christmas simple?” Charlie asked despite dreading the actual holiday.

“Yes, of course, we can Charlie,” David replied gently.

“Thank…” She broke off.

All at once, Charlie's stomach lurched, and her blood ran cold. For a moment her vision changed and she found herself confronted by narrowed eyes, veiled in shadow. She understood at once that they were being watched by…*someone* though she did not yet know whom. Immediately following this knowledge came a sudden and potent sense of danger. Charlie did not yet know the nature of the threat, only that they were in peril.

XI

Unseen by Charlie and David and hidden by shadows, a man with a pair of hunter's binoculars stood watch from a darkened room on the 9th floor. Known as Karl Spender, this man had previously been a resident of Turner. A widower of approximately sixty, Spender's daughter, Ellen attended college at Montana State while his son Owen had chased a girl to Omaha where he had worked for a construction company as a welder before the world had gone to shit.

Karl had not heard from either of his children for many months, and he did not hold out much hope that they had survived. Radio broadcasts reported that Omaha had been subject to a devastating firebombing while Bozeman remained ablaze with ongoing riots, arson, and murder.

Though he had never been an ardent Resistance supporter, Karl felt sure that he had lost both of his children in the Great Civil War, as the conflict was now known, and the Great Civil War would not have been but for a laboratory freak named Charlie MacLeod.

Karl had paid little mind to the strangers on the tenth floor. He had always believed in minding his own business and letting others mind theirs. Nevertheless, Karl found it odd that two of the reclusive residents of the tenth floor had chosen to go walking around the grounds at seven-thirty on such a brutal winter night. Now as he watched the two strangers he had spotted from his window only minutes before, Karl felt confident that this blonde-haired girl he saw through his binoculars was indeed Charlie MacLeod. He felt confident that this was the same girl he had seen on the news reports from Castle Bruce.

Karl did not even consider taking his suspicions to Ken Greenewood as he knew that this girl and her family would not be on the resort grounds unless Ken had allowed it. Instead, Karl resolved to pass his knowledge on to the Resistance.

They'll know how to handle that little freak.

With this thought in mind, Karl took out a Morley and lit it with his silver Zippo. As the room filled with acrid tobacco smoke, Karl felt his heart go cold with hatred. After his wife Margaret died, Ellen and Owen had been his only joy in life. Now because of this abomination, he had lost them both.

Karl took a long drag from his cigarette and let the smoke slowly drift from his mouth in thin, vile tendrils. The Resistance would surely consign the girl to the electric chair.

She'll get what she deserves.

XII

That evening the nightmares returned to plague Charlie's sleep. She remembered only one. In it, she was out in the pasture with David, Catherine, and Stephen. The sun shone down from a flawless blue sky, as a soft, warm breeze stirred golden field tassels. They had just finished training and were walking together through the tall grasses. Behind them, Charlie's flames danced across several wooden pyres streaming thin fingers of gray and black into the otherwise flawless afternoon sky.

Charlie smiled, feeling in that moment, genuinely happy.

"You did well today," David told her with sincerity. "I'm proud of you."

Charlie, feeling something warm move within her chest, broadened her smile. "Thank you."

"I know you've been through a lot;" David continued changing the subject. "And that you're still hurting and angry and I know that you've been training hard because of that."

Before David could say any more, a low rumble rippled through the pasture and dark thunderheads blackened the sky. All at once, icy winds carried away the warm breeze, bringing a rash of goosebumps to Charlie's skin. She shivered as her nose detected the heavy stench of ozone mixed with burning damp wood.

David, Catherine and Stephen vanished, carried away in the storm winds. Blue-white lightning slashed across the sky. Far in the distance, outlined in the sky's dim glow stood a solitary, rough-hewn stone. With slow, trembling steps, Charlie walked in its direction. As she approached, Charlie realized that she stood over a grave, the rough-hewn stone, its marker. Though the face of the grave marker held no words, Charlie felt a sudden and terrible sense of loss. Tears spilled from her eyes, stinging her cheeks. A heartrending sob of guilt escaped her throat before she suddenly burst into tears.

From nowhere, a red-haired woman materialized. Her appearance was unremarkable, save for her eyes which were darkened with unreasoning madness. The red-haired woman approached Charlie slowly and with a look of almost *recognition* in her eyes.

"Aria?" Her voice was both confused and hopeful. Her wild eyes focused for a moment as her addled mind tried to retrieve hazy knowledge only half-remembered.

Charlie reached out to the woman with the power and found the woman's mind to be closed. She approached slowly as if she expected Charlie to disappear.

As the woman neared her, Charlie spotted a faint glint of purple lightning on bloodstained steel. Charlie's heart had become a living thing in her chest, forcing icy blood through frozen, shuddering flesh. She wanted desperately to run from this woman's crazed eyes, and yet her legs would not carry her away. David and Catherine were gone, Stephen was gone, and she was alone with this madwoman.

The woman took Charlie's wrist in a drowning man's grip, her scrawny hands painfully crushing the small bones within. Charlie tried to pull away and found that she could not. Terror nearly took her breath away.

The red-haired woman made no effort to comfort her. Instead, she tightened her grip upon Charlie's wrist and began leading her away.

"Come on, Aria." The redhead's voice had filled with relief. *"Let's go home."*

"I'm not Aria." Charlie protested. *"I'm sorry. I'm not your daughter."*

"Come on, Aria." The red-head repeated, either not hearing or not caring about Charlie's objections. *"It's time to go home."*

Charlie tried to snatch her wrist from the red-haired woman's grasp only to find, to her immense terror, that the woman's grip was iron. In desperation, she reached into the power only to find it had forsaken her.

Charlie began to scream and scream, finding herself suddenly ejected from sleep and upright in bed. David and Catherine stood over her, trying to comfort her in vain. Both spoke to her, though she could not hear a word either said over her own horrified cries.

Somehow Charlie understood that this had not been a mere dream, but rather a warning. After several minutes of hysterics, Charlie regained enough control of herself to stop screaming.

"It's ok, Charlie, you're safe." David was saying. "You just had a bad dream."

"No," Charlie replied. "It wasn't just a dream. I'm sure of it. It was a warning." Charlie drew a shuddering breath and choked back a sob. "Something terrible is going to happen."

Chapter 9
The Lawgivers Come

I

At approximately nine-thirty on the twentieth day of December a radio transmission went out from the Black Hills motel to the regional Resistance authorities in Malta, Montana advising of the presence of a suspicious young girl and her family, who the broadcaster believed to be Charlie MacLeod and the McAuliffes. In response, the Resistance operator advised the broadcaster to observe the girl and her family and report back.

II

In the days that followed Charlie's first nightmare, her sense of danger grew. Driven by fear and anger, Charlie trained harder, knowing that her opportunity was drawing to a close. Charlie also strove to make the most of her time with David, Catherine, and Stephen for she knew that her time with them was also coming to an end.

They were no longer safe. Someone was watching. Charlie could feel their eyes on her. More than a few times, Charlie reached out with her power but learned only that she was surrounded by enemies. She and her family would soon need to run again.

III

On the night of Christmas Eve, a group of men and women met in an abandoned office block in the City of Malta. At first, the group spoke only of mundane business; food had grown short, fuel was almost non-existent, they would need to ration electricity.

Then the conversation turned to a photograph of a little blond girl. The leader of the group, a middle-aged woman with iron-grey hair and hard beaten features that might once have been called beautiful listened intently, and without a word as the other six group members bickered and debated the identity of the girl in the photo and then what if any steps should be taken. Finally, unable to tolerate any more of their foolishness, she banged her fist on the table to call for silence.

"Shut up!" She barked before gently taking the photograph from the table and studying it with care.

The image was blurry and depicted a girl of approximately ten years old standing in the snow with her father. The girl's perfect blond hair hung loose to her waist, and she wore an intense expression. A bright orange fire blossomed at the girl's feet as her father, still more boy than man, looked on with a subtle hint of pride in his wolf gray eyes.

The photograph proved nothing, that girl and her father could have been anyone. And yet she felt confident.

“That girl is Charlene MacLeod, and I have an idea on how we can snatch her.”

A sandy-haired man, also of middle age spoke up in response. “Whaddya have in mind?”

The middle-aged woman, who went by the nickname ‘Betty-Sue’ explained her entire plan in detail. Only after she had finished did the sandy-haired man respond.

“That girl ain't some everyday Enlightened. Why don’t we just kill her and be done?”

Betty-Sue leveled her gaze and took a sip of Jack Daniels from the hip flask on the table in front of her. “Because that girl is worth a lot of money alive.

IV

Following the outbreak of the Great Civil War, the Resistance began developing and arming a paramilitary organization that would later come to be called the Lawgivers. While initially, little more than a disorganized militia, the Resistance later discovered the process used by the NSA to manufacture Assets. The Resistance lacked the laboratory resources and expertise possessed by the NSA, and so could not reproduce the same quality end product. Instead, the Lawgivers represented a poor man’s Asset. However, they ultimately proved to be an effective weapon against Enlighteneds when turned out in numbers.

V

Charlie awoke early on Christmas Day, feeling both excited and sorrowful. David and Catherine had promised her a special Christmas, and yet she could not help feeling the absence of Daddy and Mommy. The sense of danger felt strong too, but Charlie mostly ignored it for she felt too depressed to do anything.

Charlie entered the living room to find David, Catherine, and Stephen awaiting her. At the center of the room stood a huge Christmas tree surrounded by gifts wrapped in bright red and green paper. Upon seeing her, everyone smiled, and David invited her to open her presents.

Charlie remained still for a moment, taking it all in. Then she went to the tree and took a small box from the top of the pile. She tore back the shiny red paper to find a small heart-shaped gold locket. Inside were two photographs, one of David and one of Catherine. Charlie was so touched that she nearly burst into tears.

"Thank you." She whispered in a broken voice.

David returned a gentle smile. "You're welcome. I'm glad you like it."

"I do." She murmured through her tears.

The remainder of her presents contained a collection of beautiful girl's clothing, a large bottle of Cinnabar, and a case of Paul Mitchel shampoo.

She would later learn that David had traded a large quantity of venison and the Seiko watch his father had given him for her gifts. Charlie felt guilty, but David assured her that his father would have wanted him to use the watch to provide her with a good Christmas.

And it was a good Christmas, or as good as Christmas could have been. Still, she felt intense sadness for nothing David or Catherine could do would bring back Daddy and Mommy, and on this day, their loss cut deep.

After opening the last of her presents, Charlie went to the little liquor cabinet by the bar that separated the kitchen from the living room, took out the crystal decanter of scotch and poured herself a glass. She then downed the liquor quickly and poured another before gulping this down as well.

The amber liquor warmed her from within and slightly dulled the knife of grief in her heart. Though she still missed her parents, the scotch made her care a little less. In fact, it made her feel, slightly indifferent, and yet it also made it harder to hold back the tears.

VI

Charlie wept softly on and off as she set herself upon the task of becoming blind drunk. As the day crept by, David and Catherine sat with Charlie and tried in vain to comfort her. Though her heavy drinking concerned both of her adopted parents, neither made an attempt to stop her.

Sometime after dark, Charlie became sleepy and decided to go to bed. The moment she laid her head on the pillow and closed her eyes, Charlie's head began to whirl with nausea, and her stomach began to do hula hoops.

Ugghhh I'm going to puke!

As that thought passed through her mind, Charlie sat up quickly and marched to the bathroom. On the way, she felt her stomach clench, her throat tighten, and her mouth fill with the taste of bile. Charlie had eaten nothing that day, but her stomach demanded to empty its contents nevertheless. She barely made it to the toilet before puking green fluid into the bowl.

As she vomited, a sudden and powerful sense of danger washed through her body in cold waves. Someone was coming for her, for them all; she felt sure of it.

David and Catherine appeared behind her both looking worried.

"Are you ok, Charlie?" David's tone betrayed more than a hint of concern.

Charlie moaned softly. "I'll be ok." The words came out as little more than a pained groan.

David gazed at her with a combination of concern and mild surprise. "I didn't even know you liked scotch Charlie,"

Charlie did not reply. In truth, the scotch had been almost painfully bitter and had burned like liquid fire, but it also numbed her pain.

"I don't think you should drink like this anymore, Charlie. It's not safe." As he spoke, David swept Charlie's hair out of her face.

Charlie turned miserable eyes upon him for a moment. Without warning, he doubled and then trebled before his clones merged together once more. As they did her stomach locked in spasm and she dry heaved into the toilet, coughing and sobbing in misery.

The cold sense of danger renewed its urgency. Despite her severe intoxication, Charlie understood its import at once.

"Something's wrong." Charlie heard herself speak the words out loud without meaning to. "They're coming for us."

"Who?" Catherine inquired.

"I.." She broke off as her head began to swim once more with alcohol-fueled dizziness. "I don't know."

Both David and Catherine were silent for a moment. Charlie sensed their sudden fear. *They feel it too.*

A loud knock echoed through the suit nearly causing Charlie's heart to leap out of her chest. The three of them all turned towards the bathroom door. David was on his feet first.

“Wait here.” His voice was low and frightened. “I’ll see who that is.”

Before either Catherine or Charlie could respond, David left the bathroom. For a moment, there was silence. Then David’s voice filtered through the wall to her.

“Ken? What’s up?”

“I need to speak with all of you.” Ken’s tone was both regretful and deadly serious at once.

“Does it need to be right now?” David’s voice contained thinly veiled suspicion. “Charlie’s not feeling well.”

“I’m sorry, but this can’t wait.” Ken’s tone was inflected by genuine remorse.

“Ok,” David’s voice held mounting concern. The force of his fear flowed through the wall in an icy river adding to Charlie’s own.

Deep inside, Charlie felt that something was very wrong. Someone had come for them. The power stirred within her, awakened by her growing sense of danger and fear. Charlie hauled it back like a cur that needed to be brought to heel.

STOP IT!

The words rang in her head, and for a moment, she felt a hot dagger dig into her skull before the power became silent, taking the pain with it.

“Where are your wife and daughter?” Ken’s voice remained apologetic.

“They’re in the bathroom. Charlie’s been sick.” David’s tone was businesslike. “What is this about?”

Ken ignored him. “Go get them.”

For a moment, there was only silence; then David appeared through the bathroom door.

“It’s Ken. He wants to talk to us.”

David was unnaturally calm. Behind that calm, Charlie could feel both fear and guilt. David knew they were in danger and thought he had failed his family once more.

Charlie felt sorry for him. David tried so hard, and yet it seemed things rarely went his way. Like gasoline on hot coals, sorrow quickly ignited her anger.

Why can’t they just leave us alone?!

It’s always someone, and we just run and run.

I Hate! them.

I wonder how they would like it if I set them on fire.

At one time she would have been horrified and guilt-ridden by that last thought, but no more. Now she felt only cold contempt. She would make anyone foolish enough to come after her and her family sorry.

Charlie stood up with slow deliberation and headed for the bathroom door. As she passed Catherine, their eyes met, and something passed between them. A final, silent *I love you* between mother and daughter.

Catherine turned to David. "What does Ken want?'

"I'm not sure but…" He dropped his voice. "He looks upset, and something doesn't feel right."

"Then why aren't we getting the hell out of here?!" Catherine's voice was no more than a harsh whisper.

"And run where?" David shot back under his breath. "We don't know what's going on or who might be after us."

David's voice rang clear in Charlie's mind. *And someone is after us.*

Catherine glared at him for a moment but remained silent.

Less than a minute later, Charlie sat on the living room couch with David and Catherine flanking her on either side. Stephen sat on the lounge chair to her left looking on with silent, wariness while Ken had turned the lounge chair to her right to face them. Behind his calm exterior, Charlie could feel the force of his guilt and…yes fear. He feared them for he knew who they were and what they were capable of.

"The Resistance contacted me over the radio ten minutes ago. They are on their way. They'll be here in two days. They are asking for you by name." His tone had become apologetic. "I don't know how they found out about you, but you're in danger. You need to get the hell out of here before they arrive."

Charlie's heart chilled, and her stomach lurched, this time from fear rather than alcohol. She sensed that he was telling the truth though the sensation of danger seemed much closer and more immediate.

"Where do you suggest we go?" Charlie sensed David struggling to keep his tone even. "It's Christmas, and it's snowing like hell. I can't just take my wife and daughter out into that without having somewhere to go."

"I can give you a snowcat, two weeks' worth of food and water, rifles and ammunition, and some coats and blankets. Ken's dark skin was now dotted with sweat, and his eyes were creased and liquid with remorse. "You'll have enough to get somewhere safe."

David returned an arctic glare. "Are you throwing us out?"

Ken's expression registered sincere regret. "No. I want to help, but you're not safe here anymore. The Resistance will be here in two days. They'll bring Lawgivers with them." Charlie sensed Ken's fear and remorse mounting.

Lawgivers

The name echoed in her mind bringing urgency to her fear and sense of danger. Despite the alcohol encouraging her to panic, Charlie forced herself to remain calm.

"I think we can take care of a few Resistance if we need to." David's bravado was both out of character and entirely false. Charlie felt that behind his angry voice, David was terrified.

"I don't think you understand," Ken's expression and tone remained reasonable despite the growing fear in his heart. "The Lawgivers are like the Resistance's version of the SS. They are specially trained to deal with Enlighteneds, and they are very dangerous. You're risking your lives if you stay here."

David's face darkened. "We have nowhere else to go."

For her own part, unlike David, who had become angry, Charlie felt only sadness for Ken. He did indeed want to help, and yet he was afraid.

Charlie turned to David. "It's not his fault."

Beneath her compassion for Ken, Charlie felt the sense of danger growing. No, the Resistance wasn't just coming for them, they were already there. "We can't stay here. I think they're here already. We need to get away before they catch us."

David's eyes widened slightly. "Is it too late?"

Charlie reached out for the power and found it far away across an amber sea of scotch. She found no answers there.

"I'm not sure, but I know they're close."

"I can get you to the snowcat without being seen." Ken was saying. "There's an underground passage from the hotel to the storage sheds, but we have to hurry."

David looked disposed to argue with him, but before he could, Catherine silenced him with a gesture. "Thank you. We'll need a few minutes to get ready."

Ken's expression relaxed, and Charlie felt relief wash through him. "Sure. Just don't take too long. It won't be dark for much longer, and I don't want anyone from here to see where you went. I still don't know who turned you guys in."

"We'll be quick," As she spoke, Catherine touched David's arm with her fingertips and something silent passed between them.

It's too dangerous to stay and fight. Besides…it isn't fair to endanger everyone here just so we don't have to run and it would only be delaying the inevitable…

Charlie heard no reply from David in her mind, but she could feel his reluctant agreement.

VII

Ten minutes later, the four of them had packed their meager possessions and were on their way down the emergency staircase near the rear of the hotel. By now, the sense of danger had intensified to an icy river that cut through her flesh like razors. Charlie's body trembled with such force as to make it difficult to stand up straight and her stomach went from doing hula hoops to twisting and contorting itself painfully. She might have vomited but for the fact that there was nothing left for her stomach to expel. Like her guts, Charlie's head too was afflicted, weighing heavily upon her shoulders as if it were a ponderous boulder. Dull, throbbing pain radiated from temple to temple. In that moment she would have sworn off drinking forever, and she would have lied.

The stairs came rapidly, followed by a long, slate gray concrete tunnel illuminated in harsh white from overhead fluorescent bulbs. Each of her footsteps echoed like a vault door slamming inside her skull.

Never again… She thought miserably.

And yet even as the words passed through her consciousness, Charlie knew she would break her oath. Though the symptoms pained her, the pleasant, floaty feeling brought on by drinking was compelling, and the amber liquor's talent for washing away pain and care was irresistible.

For a short time, alcohol had given her a respite from her ravenous need for revenge. *Hate!* had gone to sleep, its burning flame hidden behind a deaf stone wall.

They had reached a concrete stairway now and were ascending. Each footfall slammed through Charlie's body like lightning. The sense of danger had grown and become more urgent. Charlie shook so hard that she could barely keep her feet. The Lawgivers were close; perhaps at the top of these stairs. She could not be sure for the power was too far away.

The stairs ended in a heavy steel security door. Ken fumbled in his pocket for the key before unlocking it.

Beyond the door lay a large, darkened warehouse. Ken disappeared into the warehouse for a moment before sickly yellow sodium lights began to flick on row by row.

All at once, Charlie sensed genuine surprise and then mortal terror from Ken before his mind went quiet. He was not dead but rather unconscious.

David must have felt it too because he suddenly turned to them. "Run! Don't stop until you get outside." Charlie could feel the force of his fear.

Before she could react, a tall black figure appeared through the now open security door and raised a little black pistol.

Charlie reached across the amber sea that separated her from the power, but she was slow. A sharp -***POP-*** echoed through the corridor and Charlie felt her body go limp as flaming agony erupted from her throat and ripped through her flesh. For a moment she lay on the ground convulsing in pure torment. Then the world fell away into blackness until all that was left to her was the pain.

Chapter 10
In the Hands Of Madness

I

Charlie awoke with a blistering headache and two hot needle points in her neck. She had no knowledge of how much time had passed since the man in black had shot her. Now, she found herself lying flat on her back in a truck trailer looking up into the frightened faces of David and Catherine.

"Charlie, are you alright?" David inquired in a husky tone.

A soft groan escaped her lips. "I think so." She rasped.

"We were so worried," Catherine whispered.

Charlie studied David and Catherine for a moment. They both had electrical burns at the base of their throats and looked to be in pain.

Charlie instinctively tried to reach out to them with the power only to find it silenced. Fear cropped up within her.

What did they do to me? Do they have drugs like the Black Empire?

As that thought passed through Charlie's mind, Stephen stood up from where he had been sitting and came over. "Glad to see you're up again Charlie."

She forced a smile. "I'll be ok now, I think." This was a lie, for she was still in a great deal of pain. "What happened?" The question escaped her lips though she already had some idea. They had been taken by the Lawgivers.

"After that guy shot you, we tried to fight back, but something went wrong. Neither Catherine nor I could use the power, and they gunned us down too." David's voice was husky with thinly veiled anger. "I'm sorry, Charlie."

Charlie felt bad for David, he always tried so hard. "It's not your fault." She replied gently. Then: "Where are we going?"

"I don't know Charlie," David replied in the same tone.

II

The truck ride was a long and miserable ordeal. It was bitter cold, and the pile of army blankets left to them by the Lawgivers was woefully inadequate. They had little water and no food.

After what had to be several days, the truck stopped, and the doors were finally opened to reveal a sunset over desert wastes. A pair of black-clad mountainous men appeared with AR rifles leveled.

“Get out!” The man to the right barked. “Move your assess! Let’s go! Let’s go!”

Charlie dragged herself to her feet, feeling weak and lightheaded from lack of food and chilled to the bone. David and Catherine stood up before quickly positioning themselves between her and the two Lawgivers.

“March, you fuckin’ assholes!” The right-hand Lawgiver snapped.

The four of them stumbled from the truck trailer and found themselves standing among countless frightened and ragged looking men, women, and children. Numerous black-uniformed Lawgivers patrolled among the prisoners, herding them into single-file lines.

Unbidden memory instantly carried Charlie back in time until she found herself standing next to Eric Kain at a similar prison camp watching lines of innocent men women and children marching to their doom.

At once, Charlie understood the meaning of this place to which she and her family had been brought. Terror exploded within her.

No please! Oh God no!

Though her psychic senses remained muted, Charlie understood that they were to be executed together with the prisoners amassed here. The Lawgivers were no different than the SS guards from the prison camp Eric had shown her so many years ago.

As Charlie watched, the Lawgivers herded the lines of prisoners away. Some went deeper into the camp while the majority trudged towards two massive, soulless brick slaughterhouses. Thick smoke enveloped these, and though many entered, none emerged.

Charlie’s heart turned to ice in her chest, and a horrified sob escaped her throat.

Please no! Please, not David and Catherine! ***PLEASE!***

The two Lawgivers who had ordered them out of the truck were now leading them to a small razor wire pen. Inside stood a motley collection of men and women with a scattering of children milling among them. Though the power remained absent, Charlie knew at once that these people had the power too.

No one spoke to Charlie and her adoptive parents or even seemed to notice their presence. Charlie looked up at David and Catherine with frightened eyes.

"They want to kill us. I'm scared." Her voice came out as little more than a choked whisper.

David bent down to her level and took her into his arms. "No one is going to hurt us. I promise. We're going to be fine."

It was a poor lie. Charlie did not need the power to know that David did not believe his own words. She had only to look into his eyes.

"Ok, David." She replied listlessly.

III

David took her hand and led her further into the pen. Here they waited for some time. As the hours dragged by, the Lawgivers returned again and again to remove prisoners. And once removed, the prisoners never returned. Thus, the numbers inside the pen dwindled until only the four of them remained.

Finally, after what seemed like many hours, two mountainous and irate looking Lawgivers entered the pen.

The first of these was a pale-skinned man with a square jaw, black hair, and intense, coal-black eyes. The second was a sallow-skinned man with a hook nose, sandy walrus mustache, and an angry, vertical scar over his left eye.

From a knife fight in high school. Charlie thought absently as a brief image of the sallow-skinned man as a teenager, and a brown-haired youth with a straight razor flashed through her mind.

"Let's go." The square-jawed man barked.

"Where are you taking us?' David challenged.

"I said *let's go.*" He repeated, this time deliberately over-enunciating each word. To punctuate his point, the man unsnapped his holster and placed his hand on the butt of his Glock.

Charlie reached for the power only to find it still silenced.

Shit!

Without a word, the hook-nosed man grabbed her arm and dragged her from the pen.

David's voice rang out behind her. "Let her go, you fuck!"

A dull thud rang out, followed by a grunt from David.

"I told you to move your fucking ass!" The square-jawed man's voice barked. "Are you people stupid as well as freaks?!"

For a moment, David look disposed to fight back, and Charlie felt afraid for she understood the danger. Then, seeing the fear painted upon her face, he complied without further argument.

The four of them were separated. The hook-nosed Lawgiver took Charlie across the dusty prison campgrounds to a large and squat, single-story brick building with high, steel-barred windows. This was one of a dozen or more identical barracks near the rear of the camp. A sign above the door read simply 'Children.' Inside, the barracks consisted of a concrete-floored, green tile corridor with identical rows of heavy steel doors on either side. Without a word, hook nose took Charlie to the last door on the left, opened it, and shoved her inside. Charlie turned just in time to watch the heavy steel door close with a loud ***-KERBANG-***. Now she stood by herself inside a tiny concrete cell furnished only with a steel toilet and a matressless steel loft.

All at once, the reality of this place came home to her. She was alone again, and the power continued to hibernate, thus preventing her from knowing the fate of David and Catherine. Though the cell's single window was open to the outside, the air in here somehow remained both dank and chilly. Charlie shivered despite herself.

All she knew for sure was that this place was like the Nazi death camp Eric had taken her to. This was a place of destruction, meant to effect the annihilation of anyone with the power. The Lawgivers would surely execute them all.

If they haven't already killed David and Catherine.

Charlie desperately reached for the power only to find it still lost to her. It was a terrifying feeling. The power had been a part of her for as far back as memory went. To have it taken from her was to be maimed, as if she had lost an eye or an arm. Charlie's heart chilled and bled at once. She no longer felt angry, only frightened and depressed. Tears spilled from her eyes in silence as she wept for the family that she had been separated from.

There was no force behind her crying, only defeated sorrow. They had been taken, and the people who had taken them, the Resistance, were not like the NSA or the Black Empire. In the past it had always been about exploiting her power, getting her to light fires, or join the cause. These people had no such designs for her. Instead, they hated and feared Charlie and her family. Their goal was not to control or use her but rather to destroy her and everyone else like her. Though she was young, Charlie understood that her time was short and David and Catherine's time was probably even shorter.

And so she stood in the center of the cell and wept bitterly, mourning the loss of David and Catherine as she had mourned the loss of Daddy and Mommy. After a length of time had passed and the shadows in the room had grown long, exhaustion took her, and Charlie climbed onto the steel loft and quickly slipped into darkness.

IV

The heavy bang of the cell door awakened her early the next morning. Charlie opened her eyes to see two Lawgivers, one the hook-nose, from the night before, the other a raven-haired woman of indeterminable age and case-hardened expression.

Without a word, the two Lawgivers hoisted Charlie out of her loft and herded her from her cell to the outside.

This time they crossed the prison camp yard to a large two-story, steel, and concrete office complex with numerous large windows. This facility was used for research and experimentation on captured Enlighteneds and other prisoners unlucky enough to draw the interest of the camp 'doctors'.

The two Lawgivers escorted Charlie to an institutional green-tiled and windowless laboratory deep within the building. Here two men and two women in white lab coats awaited her arrival with excited anticipation. Though the power still eluded Charlie, she did not need it to see their eager eyes and faint smiles behind calm, dispassionate faces.

The apparent leader of the four was a young woman with a dour face and gold, wire-rimmed glasses. "Charlene MacLeod?" The woman inquired in a tone one might expect from a clerk at the post office.

"Yes." The raven-haired woman replied in a flat tone.

The woman in the wire-rimmed glasses approached Charlie and looked her up and down carefully. "Funny." She mused. "You don't look dangerous up close. Such power in such an unassuming package."

The woman in the wire-rimmed glasses reached out and ran a finger through Charlie's hair. "You are a pretty little girl, aren't you?" Now her voice held a faint hint of contempt, as if this woman were jealous.

The woman's expression became cold and rock hard. "Up on the table please."

Nerves screwing tight, Charlie went to the center of the laboratory where a steel table stood and boosted herself up. As she sat down, Charlie momentarily found herself sitting on the Black Empire's torture table and could feel its cold steel against her bare skin. An icy shiver wormed its way up her spine as her blood froze in her veins. Charlie felt her heart become a live thing in her chest, threatening to burst through her ribs.

Oh please, not again…

She would be experimented upon and tortured. Though she was frightened, Charlie forced herself to remain calm. She would not let them see her break.

The woman in the wire-rimmed glasses turned to the further of the two male technicians, a rat-faced man of indeterminate age and scrawny build. "James, bring me a phlebotomy tray."

James went to the long steel countertop running along the right-hand wall, picked up a metal tray laden with several test tubes, a plastic-wrapped syringe, a clear bottle of alcohol, a jar of cotton balls and a piece of rubber flex tube and deposited it on the table beside her.

“Give me your arm.” The woman in the wire-rimmed glasses demanded.

Charlie held out her arm without replying, and the woman swabbed it with icy liquid. Then she tied the rubber flex tube around Charlie’s upper forearm before carefully probing the inside of Charlie’s elbow. After a moment, she found a vein and roughly inserted a need into Charlie’s flesh, sending a sharp flare up her arm.

Charlie drew a sharp breath over her lower lip but gave no other sign of pain. Blood rushed from her arm into the test tube at the end of the needle. Charlie watched this with fascination. She found the sight of her own blood slightly disquieting and yet could not look away. When the first tube had filled, the woman in the wire-rimmed glasses removed it from the syringe and inserted a second. This too filled quickly, and the woman then replaced it with a third before withdrawing the needle from Charlie’s arm.

“I’m ready for the lumbar puncture tray now.” She instructed James.

“Got it Chief,” James turned once more to the steel counter. A moment later, he returned and, Charlie’s heart turned to ice.

She had suffered through a spinal tap at the hands of the NSA many years ago, and the memory remained fresh in her mind. Cold tremors swept her body, and she had to fight back tears.

Please don’t make me.

James set the tray down with a clang that nearly made her jump off the table.

“Now, I want you to lie down with your back to me.” The woman in the wire-rimmed glasses instructed her. “And if you would like to continue walking, I suggest that you not move a muscle.”

Please…I don’t want to. Charlie’s mind begged though her lips remained silent. Charlie laid down with her back to the woman. After a moment, she felt the woman pull her shirt up to expose her back and smear icy cold liquid on her skin. Charlie shuddered hard, though more from fear than cold.

At first, nothing happened. Then Charlie felt a hot nail driven into her back. A cry of pure suffering escaped her throat before she could stifle it as her eyes flooded with tears.

“Don’t move.” The woman in the wire-rimmed glasses commanded in a stern tone. “I almost have enough for a sample, and you don’t want to be paralyzed, do you?”

Charlie remained still, even as silent tears streamed down her cheeks. She wanted so badly to be anywhere else. The pain was incredible, and though Charlie had suffered far worse, this carried her back to her time in the grasp of the NSA and so she was afraid. She wanted David and Catherine, needed them for in her heart she knew she would suffer further torment and could not face it alone.

A second cry escaped her throat as the blazing dagger in her back twisted. Charlie had to fight an urge to pull away as the woman in the wire-rimmed glasses withdrew the needle from her spine.

"You did well, Charlie."

The woman's praise was shallow and superficial. Though the power remained silent, Charlie needed only look into her eyes to see the woman's lack of concern. To her, Charlie was but a lab specimen.

"You're free to go for now." The woman turned to the hook-nosed and chestnut-haired Lawgivers. "Take her back to her cell."

"As you wish." The raven-haired Lawgiver replied in a crisp tone before taking Charlie by the arm and leading her from the laboratory.

V

Late that evening, the woman in the wire-rimmed glasses, a Dr. Elsie Coke, sat looking over test results, still unable to accept that which she now knew to be true.

The girl, Charlene MacLeod, represented a new species of human. It seemed inconceivable, and yet the DNA results were incontrovertible.

Dr. Coke reviewed the girl's genetic profile once more, still unwilling to accept the evidence before her eyes. *Who is this girl?*

Where did she come from?

There was precious little information about the girl's background beyond the fact that the McAuliffes had adopted her. The exact fate or even the identity of the girl's parents remained a mystery. Thus she had no information to explain the reason for the girl's mutation.

Unlike the Resistance leadership who feared and hated Enlighteneds, Dr. Coke found them fascinating. Before the outbreak of the Great Civil War, she had spent many years in the employ of Reagar Pharmaceutical and Research studying the biology and genetics of Enlighteneds. Dr. Coke had joined the Resistance as a matter of convenience and had volunteered for command of the Cordoba Flats camp so that she might continue her research.

As she finished her review of the girl's genetics, Dr. Coke allowed herself the first spark of excitement. This girl could represent the next stage in human evolution. Physically she was an amalgamation of recessive traits, from her blond hair and blue eyes to her pale porcelain skin. Less obvious was the girl's pyrokinetic ability, an exceptionally rare manifestation of the power that Dr. Coke had not seen in fifteen years of research into Enlighteneds.

Genetically the girl was beyond perfect. Her DNA strands were constantly rewriting themselves to make her stronger and more resistance to disease, and injury. Though she had the outward appearance of an ordinary little girl with better than average beauty, this girl was, in fact very tough and exponentially powerful. It had indeed been fortunate that the Lawgivers had brought her here.

And she will not be available to study for long.

This was a certainty. The girl had singlehandedly triggered the Great Civil War when she killed Hailey Suire. The Resistance leadership both hated and feared her. She would surely be marked for extermination, and Dr. Coke could not allow that to happen.

This girl was a rare and valuable specimen. Further study of her could lead to a greater understanding of Enlighteneds at large. Perhaps even the elusive secret of why some humans were born Enlightened while others were not And of course this girl most likely represented Dr. Coke's only opportunity to experiment on a pyrokinetic.

Pyrokinesis.

For her, the word itself held a primal fascination. In her mind, Dr. Coke saw the girl standing amongst a great orange inferno. The flames almost seemed to smile and wave, as if beckoning to Dr. Coke as they danced across the ground. She could feel their warmth deep inside, the sensation tugged at her heart, promising pleasure beyond any she had experienced.

In that moment, Dr. Coke knew she had to see the girl light a fire. She needed it as one needs a glass of water after a hard run.

VI

As Dr. Coke sat alone in her office fantasizing about Charlie MacLeod's power, David McAuliffe sat alone in a dark, cold cell, wondering if his family was alive or dead. He had not seen Catherine or Charlie since they had been separated the day before, and the power remained silent.

Worse, from his cell window, he could see an endless line of condemned men, women, and children on their way to the gas chamber, and he could smell the heavy, acrid stench of burned human flesh. The air hung heavy with smoke from thousands of cremated bodies.

He had been taken to the camp's research facility earlier that day for testing, and this had given him a brief ray of hope. It occurred to him that the Resistance scientists would likely have kept Catherine and Charlie alive long enough to perform the same blood and cerebrospinal fluid tests on them that he had submitted to. He wanted desperately to believe that Charlie would be safe. She was uniquely powerful, and her pyrokinetic ability was a rarity. Surely they would not want to kill her.

Catherine will not be so fortunate, though.

She was powerful but not anywhere close to the magnitude of their adopted daughter, and her telekinetic ability was far more common among Enlighteneds.

The thought cut his heart so keenly as to bring tears to his eyes. Catherine was a good woman and did not deserve any of this. Neither did Charlie. They both deserved to be happy, to have a home, to be safe. They had done nothing to deserve being chased, terrorized, locked away, and threatened with death.

And in truth, he knew Charlie was not safe either. The scientists here would no doubt have more than a passing interest in her, but David understood logically that the Resistance was surely not led by scientists. Eventually, the Resistance leadership, motivated by hate rather than scientific curiosity, would order Charlie's termination when they learned of her presence here.

David did not fear his own death, but he could not face life without his wife and daughter. And so he sat on his cot, sleepless, and terrified.

VII

A few cells down, Catherine lay awake in a similar state. She wanted desperately to believe that they would be ok. That somehow, they would escape as they had from the Black Empire, and yet she felt this was different. The Black Empire had wanted them alive, mostly they wanted Charlie alive so that they might control her. But their desire to control Charlie meant that the three of them enjoyed a thin measure of safety from execution. The Resistance had no such compunctions. They existed to kill Enlighteneds, and Charlie had caused the firestorm that brought the Resistance from the shadows.

Like David, Catherine felt both terrified and depressed, for she knew there was little she could do to help her husband and daughter.

Charlie and David don't deserve this. David tried so hard to give us a good life. To make things better. And Charlie...she's a good girl and she's suffered so much already.

Catherine wanted to cry but found that she could not. Crying would take energy that she just did not have. Catherine stood and went to the window. As she watched the last of the condemned trudge towards their doom, Catherine imagined she could see her husband and daughter at the end of the line. A soft sob escaped her throat.

Please, God, they don't deserve this. Take me instead.

Her only answer was the muffled screams of the dying.

VIII

Like her adoptive parents, Charlie too lay awake, troubled by fear, depression, and anger. The air in her cell lay heavy with the choking stench of burning meat while the night was punctuated by the horrified strangled cries of condemned men, women and children. Though the power remained distant and muted, the force of their fear struck her in an icy wave that no drugs could entirely suppress.

Charlie wept openly and silently, knowing that this would soon be the fate of David and Catherine, of Stephen, and ultimately of herself.

It wasn't fair. David and Catherine didn't deserve to die. Neither did Stephen. They would all suffer and die just for knowing her. At one time, she might have felt guilty for this, but now she felt only sadness, bitter anger, and beneath them both horrible, gnawing fear.

Charlie's vision changed for a moment, and she found herself within a long steel-lined chamber crammed to the door with men, women, and children. Stripped naked, they stood shuddering, their eyes wide and panicked. There was a loud thud as heavy, armored steel doors slammed shut, followed by two sharp bangs and the soft, bubbling hiss of chemicals boiling. The air rapidly thickened with white smoke tendrils. Charlie found herself unable to breathe. Her lungs begged for air as her ears filled with horrified screams and desperate gasps.

Oh God, please no…Please take me away. Please, it hurts.

Her chest had caught fire now as her lungs filled with poisoned air.

Please make it stop.

She knew this was the power and that she still lay in her cell, but that knowledge did not help. Somewhere far away in the back of her mind, she felt the power move with faint subtlety. Still, it remained elusive and would be of no help to her here.

The air had become hazy white now and choking. Charlie struggled to get air into her starving lungs. All around her, men, women, and children had collapsed to their knees, searching in vain for something to breath. Others lay motionless where they had fallen, their bodies having already given up the struggle for life.

Charlie felt her heart thudding against the inside of her ribs as she fought for each breath she took. She was dying, choking to death on the steel chamber's toxic fumes. Black butterflies fluttered before her eyes and opened their wings, blotting out her vision.

Then, just as she felt she could not fight for another breath, Charlie found herself returned to her cot. She coughed hard, bringing up a wad of bloody snot.

Tears streamed from her eyes as Charlie gratefully drew in lungfuls of clean air. She was sobbing as rippling shudders wracked her body. She didn't want to die, and certainly not in that way.

Charlie tried to reach out with her mind and found the power had once again left her. The realization terrified her for to her it felt like having her eyes plucked from their sockets.

Charlie stood and went to the window only to see the yard outside her cell deserted, save for a scattering of Lawgivers. It had been a dark, and moonless night but now the sky glowed orange from the camp's massive crematorium. Charlie's blood ran cold for in that orange glow she saw her future, along with that of David, Catherine, and Stephen.

Charlie turned slowly from the window and went back to her cot, where she laid down with her face to the wall. Despite the storm of emotions within her, sleep came quickly and brought with it terrible nightmares.

IX

Charlie retained only flashes of memory from her dreams, save for one that would stick with her long after that terrible night.

In this dream, she found herself alone in a dark and windswept field of dead grasses and barren earth. Green and black storm clouds filled the sky above as the low rumble of distant thunder echoed on cold gales. Charlie's heart quickened even before she realized that she was not alone. Lord Beathach stood to her left while the mad-eyed redheaded woman stood to her right. Each seemed to be calling to her though she heard no words. Beathach swept back his cape and extended his arm. The gesture, one of protection. In that same moment, the red-haired woman moved towards Charlie, her eyes wild and frenzied. Deep in her eyes, Charlie saw what might have been recognition. This was followed in a moment by sudden realization. Then came fixation. The woman suddenly rushed forward, as if driven by some desperate hope of things too good to be true.

As the woman scrambled towards Charlie, Lord Beathach extended his hand to Charlie as if to offer her rescue from this approaching mad woman. Each of the two differing figures gave off their own sensation.

From the redhead, Charlie felt a confusing jumble of aching, desperate hope, sharp withering grief, and fury that seared to the core. The sensation washed through Charlie with potency nearly sufficient to overwhelm her mind.

In contrast, from Lord Beathach Charlie felt only bitter hatred and icy malevolence. This was a man who had long since lost everything that mattered to him in life. Now all he had left was vengeance and violence. And he reveled in both. For Lord Beathach, power lay only in that which he could inflict upon others.

Charlie felt her flesh freeze and her heart race. Cold sweat broke out on her skin. In her heart, she understood that she would have to choose. The madwoman or the dark lord. Though she found him terrifying, Charlie at least understood Lord Beathach. Though his motives and actions were both fearsome and malignant, Charlie could logically grasp them.

The red-haired woman's motives, on the other hand, were a jumbled mess of fragmented thoughts, beliefs, and emotions. There was no comprehending, for the reason for any given action by this woman could change by the moment. This woman's mind was alien to Charlie. She had never touched another like it. And she had to use care for even the slightest contact fragmented Charlie's thoughts and flooded her heart with terrible grief, anger, guilt, and desperate hope.

The torment Charlie had suffered at Lord Beathach's hands had left her terrified of the dark lord. Nevertheless, Charlie turned towards him and took his hand. As she did an icy torrent flooded her body, sending cold shudders rippling through her flesh. His grip was iron and yet almost gentle at the same time. In that moment Charlie understood the choice she had made and nearly screamed out of sheer animal terror. She wanted desperately to pull away. And yet she did not. Though Lord Beathach's grip was not so tight that Charlie could not escape, a part of her rebelled against fleeing. She would not give Beathach the pleasure of seeing her fear and…

She was angry. No, not just angry but furious. She would burn Beathach up for the pain he had inflicted upon her.

But not just yet…

As that thought passed through her mind, the field fell away only to be replaced by the concrete ceiling of her cell. She was not screaming, nor did she weep. Instead, Charlie found herself gasping for breath, her heart racing as if she had completed a hard run.

Oily sweat coated her feverish skin, soaking her clothes through and through. Still, despite her intense fear, the power remained silent and far away. Whatever drugs they had given her saw to that.

Though she was petrified, Charlie's mind remained lucid and warned her that they were in danger. Something terrible was coming, though she knew not what.

Charlie gathered herself up and strode towards the window once more. The night sky had darkened once more, and the desert air had thinned. Aware, for the first time, of how cold her cell had become, Charlie wrapped her blanket tightly around her shoulders and shuffled back to bed.

X

As Charlie lay awake in her bed in Children's Barracks A, a middle-aged man with sharp, green eyes and a face that seemed perpetually angry sat in a long-abandoned University Park tavern sipping a rare glass of Seagram's gin. In a former life, he had been known as Dr. Karl Gebhardt, esteemed professor of biology at the University of Nevada, Las Vegas. Now he went only by the moniker, Doc, and was one of the council of nine that served as the Resistance leadership in the former western United States. Tonight, Doc awaited the arrival of the other council members to discuss the fate of Charlene MacLeod and David and Catherine McAuliffe. Two days ago a team of Lawgivers had captured the three of them together with another Enlightened and took them to the processing facility in Cordoba Flats, Arizona.

The head of the facility, one Dr. Elsie Coke, had petitioned the council for additional time to experiment on the girl.

As he sipped his gin, Doc, gazed impassively at a faded photo of the girl. In it, she was tossing a football with her adoptive father. She had just thrown the ball, and David McAuliffe had his hands out to catch it. Charlie's face had lit up with joy, her cheeks had flushed red from winter winds and her eyes seemed to twinkle from the washed-out image. David wore a big grin, and his wolf gray eyes almost seemed to smile.

Doc hated to think about it. He had a daughter Charlie's age. But he understood that the girl had to die. She was exceptionally dangerous, both because of her power and because of her genetics. She could easily pass on her mutation to others and pollute the human gene pool.

Doc knocked back the last of his gin and set his glass down on the glossy red oak bar. This had once been a charming college bar before the Great Civil War. Now it lay abandoned under an inch of dust. Overturned barstools lay like dead dogs on the floor while shattered fragments of red oak tables lay among broken bottles and beer mugs.

Glass crunched under heavy footsteps. Doc turned to see Lloyd Morrigan, a towering man with hard golden eyes, and straw-colored, greasy hair that hung below his shoulders. His face lay hidden behind a thick and equally oily beard. Before the Great Civil War, Lloyd had been a professional activist with the Resistance Party and before that with a number of left-leaning organizations. A consummate street thug, Lloyd believed in direct action without remorse.

Beside him stood Sasha Moreno, an olive-skinned woman who might have once called herself big-boned. In reality, she straddled the line between Pillsbury doughboy chunky and 'oh my God did she swallow a wrecking ball' fat. Sasha had a manner about her. She carried herself, head held high and like one of those self-important assholes who thinks everything and everyone should meet their approval and nothing and no one ever does. As she strode across the broken tavern, Sasha looked down her nose at Doc with an expression of thinly veiled contempt.

Doc greeted both Sasha and Lloyd with a curt nod. "And how are you both doing this evening?"

"I'm fine," Sasha replied in a flat tone.

"Rather be at home relaxing." Lloyd joked.

"Yeah, me too." Doc rejoined. "Hopefully, this will be quick."

"Yeah right." Lloyd quipped. "We're here to talk about that damned girl. Once that old fuck Herb gets started, he'll run his mouth for hours."

Before becoming a member of the council, Herb Brändle had been the district attorney for Lancaster County, Pennsylvania. His son, Blake, a liaison between the Ephrata Police and the Pennsylvania State Police, had been present at the Ephrata Police Station when Charlie and Jack MacLeod escaped. And had died in the resulting firestorm.

Herb had been a lifelong conservative Republican and had a bright political career ahead of him. Blake's death changed all of that. Following the Ephrata firestorm, and despite having benefitted from the existing police state, Herb wasted no time in joining the Resistance movement. Doc suspected that it was personal for him. Long before killing Senator Suire, Charlie MacLeod had burned Herb's son alive. And he had concluded, as others would later, that the girl had to be the product of some government laboratory. Herb's motives went beyond fear of the girl and what she represented. Instead, he blamed her for the death of his son and truly hated her. It wasn't hard to imagine what he would want to be done with her.

The old fuck liked to hear himself talk though, and would surely ramble on for an hour or more before voting to electrocute the girl.

Remembering his manners, Doc raised his half-empty bottle of gin. “Drink?”

“Fine,” Sasha grunted with disinterest.

“I don’t drink. You know that.” Lloyd protested as if the offer of alcohol was a personal affront. He then took out a small baggy of leafy greens and proceeded to roll a joint on the bar top.

Pothead.

As that last thought passed, the tavern door opened, and Carla Garafini entered. A statuesque woman of mixed Italian and Apache descent, Carla wore her long, raven hair in a ponytail that hung down past her shoulders. Carla was intelligent, but Doc found her constant feminist nattering and reflexive embrace of any leftwing position tiresome. How a bright woman could lay aside all good sense in such a way mystified him.

A few minutes later, the much dreaded old fuck drifted in, looking more pissed off than usual. Herb greeted Doc with a low grunt. Then he helped himself to a bottle of Jack Daniels from behind the bar. Over the next ten minutes, the remaining four members of the council drifted in and seated themselves at the bar. Once everyone had arrived, the Chairman, one General Norman McDaniels, called the meeting to order.

“To begin with, I move that we dispense with the formalities and proceed with the one item on our agenda.” The general intoned in a deep and measured tone.

His deep-set, hazel eyes drifted over the gathered committee members before lingering for a moment on Carla.

“Do I have a motion to open the floor for debate on what to do with Charlene MacLeod and David and Catherine McAuliffe?”

“Motion,” Doc replied automatically as he raised his hand.

“Second,” Lloyd added.

“All in favor, please signify by saying ‘Aye.’”

The vote was unanimous.

“Floor is open for debate.”

To no one’s surprise and everyone’s immense annoyance, the old fuck raised his hand.

“Yes, chair recognizes Herb Brändle.” The General’s voice held more than a hint of irritation.

“Thank you, Mr. Chairman,” Herb replied, clearly choosing to ignore the General’s aggravation. “I wish to remind the council that Charlene MacLeod is not a typical Enlightened. This girl possesses a powerful pyrokinetic ability and has demonstrated a willingness to use it. She has caused at least three firestorms that we know of and murdered numerous innocent people."

Doc had to suppress an urge to sigh and roll his eyes. *You only want her dead because she killed your son. Understandable, but let's cut the shit.*

"Moreover, she is still a young child. The little bit of information we have about Enlighteneds tells us that they grow more powerful as they get older. What happens when this child reaches adolescence or adulthood? As it stands, we have a child who is capable of setting fire to asphalt and causing medium-sized explosions. What if this girl grows up to be capable of creating a nuclear explosion just by the power of her will?'

"That's insane, Herb." The words escaped Doc's mouth before he could stop them.

Herb sneered in return. "Is it? This girl is a laboratory monster, not an Enlightened. We don't know the full extent of her power."

"Then perhaps we should learn that before we terminate her," Doc replied in his most reasonable tone.

"Give her to Dr. Coke?" The old fuck's tone held pure contempt. "She's obsessed with Enlighteneds. She'll never want to terminate the girl, no matter what the danger is."

"That girl took out a cybernetic mutate." As he spoke, thick clouds of marijuana smoke wafted from Lloyd's mouth. "I'd like to know how she managed to get that done."

"I would as well." Carla agreed.

"That's one vote to terminate the girl and three to allow Dr. Coke to experiment on her," the General announced. "Does anyone else wish to be heard?"

No one raised their hand.

"Do I have a motion for a vote?"

"Moved." Carla offered.

"And seconded," Lloyd added.

"All in favor?"

Eight out of the nine council members voted in favor of cloture. Unsurprisingly, the old fuck wanted more time to debate.

The General banged his fist on the bar top. "Motion for a vote is sustained. All in favor of allowing Dr. Coke time to experiment on Charlie MacLeod, please raise your hands."

Doc, Carla, Lloyd, and Roland, a man of unknown east Asian descent voted to allow Dr. Coke to experiment on the girl. Herb, Sasha, Fiona a freckled redhead and Devin a tanned, former meathead that had aged past his prime, voted to electrocute the girl.

The General cast the deciding vote to allow Dr. Coke to experiment on the girl. The committee next decided that Dr. Coke would be permitted a month to test the girl, after which time she would be required to report her findings to the committee. Then the committee voted to adjourn.

Doc remained in the tavern long after everyone else had filtered out. A fresh glass of gin lay on the bar in front of him. He had voted to keep the girl alive. Yet he felt that this was the most dangerous decision they could have made.

But we'll know what she is. No matter what the cost, we ***will*** *know what she is.*

Doc set his glass down, took out a Camel, and lit it with his Bic lighter. The mutate had been a laboratory creation like the girl. A group of soldiers led them to its stasis tube within the Groom Lake facility. While promised to be a game-changing weapon, the mutate proved to be a devastating liability killing many Resistance soldiers before they were able to get control of it.

Ultimately, the council decided to use the creature to hunt Charlie MacLeod as they calculated it was durable enough to resist her pyrokinetic ability. They had been mistaken. And their mistake had ended in a spectacular conflagration.

The creature's destruction raised the disturbing question of what exactly it would take to kill the girl.

Would the electric chair even be enough?

Doc took a long, slow drag from his cigarette. *Could we even kill her if we tried?*

XI

Hands roughly shook Charlie awake. Her eyes flicked open to reveal the hook-nosed and raven-haired Lawgivers.

"Get up." Hook Nose barked.

"Why?" Charlie replied simply.

"I said get up." Hook Nose repeated. Before she could argue, he took her arm, hauled her to her feet and shoved her towards the door. "Let's go."

"Where are you taking me?" Charlie inquired.

"Dr. Coke wants to do more tests." He responded. "Now, let's go!"

Charlie stood fast. "I'm not going anywhere with you. Where are David and Catherine?"

Hook Nose clamped his hand down on her wrist and yanked her towards the door. "I said move your fucking ass, you little bitch!"

Raven Hair took his shoulder. "Frank, she's just a kid, and I don't think Dr. Coke will want her injured."

Hook Nose or Frank briefly turned his eyes towards Raven Hair. "I suppose you're right." Then he turned back towards Charlie. "Let's go."

Charlie twisted her arm out of his grasp. "I *told* you I'm not going anywhere with you. Now I want to see David and Catherine."

For a moment, Frank looked disposed to react angrily. Before he could, Raven Hair stepped neatly into the breach. "Look kid. I don't know where David and Catherine are, but Dr. Coke might. If you're a good girl and ask nicely, I'm sure she'll let you see them."

Charlie detected the lie at once. "You're a liar."

"Maybe I am." Raven Hair replied in a reasonable tone. "But do you think you are more likely to get to see your parents if you fight with us or cooperate?"

Charlie stood her ground. "I'm **NOT** going with you." She repeated in a firm tone. "I want to see David and Catherine now."

Wasting no more time, Raven Hair scooped Charlie up and carried her from her cell kicking and fighting.

Outrage flashed in Charlie's heart. "Let me go!"

Raven Hair ignored her. Frank smiled in amusement.

Charlie fought hard against Raven Hair, but her grip though gentle, was forged steel.

"Fight all you want." Raven Hair offered with mild amusement. "Without your power, you're not getting away."

Against Charlie's will, Raven Hair carried her from the cellblock, across the yard, and into the research facility before depositing her in the same laboratory where the woman in the gold, wire-rimmed glasses had taken her blood and spinal fluid the day before. This same woman now stood behind the steel procedure table waiting patiently for Charlie's arrival.

Charlie felt her flesh chill, and her heart race as tremors rippled through her muscles.

Oh please no…

Her previous anger forgotten, Charlie found herself desperately wishing to be anywhere else. Her cell would have been fine. More than that even, Carlie wished for….no she *needed* David and Catherine. This laboratory was exactly like the one in which the Black Empire tortured her. She could not face that alone again.

"Put her on the table." The woman in the wire-rimmed glasses instructed.

Raven Hair complied wordlessly. As she neared the table, Charlie's struggles became more desperate, and she began to hyperventilate. "Please…" The words escaped her lips before she could stifle them. "Please, I just want David and Catherine. Please don't hurt me."

Tears streamed from her eyes in rivers, as little terrified sobs broke from her throat between desperate gasps for air. "Please…"

She felt the cold steel table against her back and calves. Raven Hair quickly drew heavy leather straps across her chest, arms, and legs. Now Charlie could not move at all. Her gasping breaths grew more ragged and desperate.

The woman in the wire-rimmed glasses looked Charlie over before meeting Raven Hair's eyes. "Wait outside please."

Both Frank and Raven Hair complied wordlessly. Once both had left, the woman in the wire-rimmed glasses returned her attention to Charlie. "It's ok. You don't have to be afraid, although I can understand why you would be after yesterday."

Charlie's breathing quickened still more as great, wracking shudders took her frozen flesh.

"I just want to talk today." The woman's expression became concerned. "You look terrified. Would you like something to help you relax?"

"Please.." Charlie rasped. The words hurt coming out of her parched throat. "I just want David and Catherine…"

"We can talk about that once you're calm."

Charlie fought against the growing panic and terror in her heart without success. Though the power remained silent, she was sure this woman was lying to her. Charlie felt strongly that this woman was about to do something horribly painful to her.

As if in confirmation, the woman in the wire-rimmed glasses went to the steel counter and took out a vial of clear liquid and a syringe. She then prepared the injection before returning to Charlie's side.

"I'm going to give you a shot of Valium. It will help you calm down." As she spoke, the woman probed the crook of Charlie's elbow for a moment before swabbing the area with Iodine and sliding the needle into Charlie's vein.

Sharp lancing pain radiated out from the place where the needle entered her flesh. Charlie drew a sharp breath over her lower lip.

"It'll only pinch for a few seconds, Charlie. Then you'll start to feel better." As she spoke, the woman depressed the syringe sending heat radiating up Charlie's left arm.

At first, Charlie felt nothing, then her heart and breathing began to slow, and her tremors became still. Though still afraid, Charlie found herself artificially calm. There were other things as well. She started to feel detached from the world and floaty, as if drifting on an invisible lake. Her mind had scrambled itself to the point where it was hard to hold onto a coherent thought. Suddenly everything became amusing, as if part of some great joke.

"Feel better now?" The woman asked after a few seconds.

"Can I please see David and Catherine." Charlie persisted.

"We can get to that, but first, I thought I would introduce myself. My name is Dr. Elsie Coke. You may call Dr. Coke. As to seeing your parents, you can see your father right now."

Charlie felt both excited and suspicious at once. *What's going on?* They had taken such pains to keep her separate from David and Catherine. *Why would she let me see David now?*

Without pausing, Dr. Coke went to the laboratory door, opened it, and called out into the hallway. "Bring him in."

A moment later, a massive, bear of a male Lawgiver entered wheeling a restrained David ahead of him in a wheelchair.

The moment she saw David, Charlie's heart turned to ice, for she understood at once that Dr. Coke intended to use him for something.

"David!" The cry escaped her lips before she could suppress it.

"Charlie!" David's voice was sharp with fear.

The Lawgiver behind him struck him in the back of the head. "Shut up."

"That's enough, Gary." Dr. Coke commanded before turning back to Charlie.

"Now, you and I both know that you're far from ordinary Charlie. I've spent many years studying Enlighteneds, and I've never come across a pyrokinetic before. You are literally a one of a kind." As she spoke, Dr. Coke went to the steel counter and took out a vial of blue liquid. "I'd like to learn more about you and perhaps give you the chance to learn more about yourself."

"Don't listen to her, Charlie." David's voice reflected growing desperation.

Charlie felt deeply suspicious. Despite the effects of the Valium, her heart began to quicken, and her skin rashed out in goosebumps.

She wants me to light fires for her.

This understanding came with instinctive fear, for she had not forgotten what had happened when she lit fires for the NSA and the Black Empire. Both times she had been deceived, and that deception had cost her, her father, and led her to kill many people. This would not end well.

"I hope you will cooperate with me willingly."

As she spoke, Dr. Coke took a second syringe from the cabinets over the steel countertop and loaded it with blue liquid before returning to Charlie's side once again. She held the syringe and vial up so that Charlie could see them.

"This is X-22. X-22 is a unique virus that causes mutation in anyone exposed to it. X-22 was used to create the monster you killed in Turner." She raised the vial of blue liquid to Charlie's eye level. "This sample came from the same laboratory where the monster was made. Did you know that that creature was once human? I wouldn't have believed it, but the laboratory records are clear. Still, the records indicate that the virus was only ever used on normal humans. I have to wonder what the result would be if it is used on an Enlightened."

Charlie's blood turned to ice, and her heart dropped into her shoe.

Please don't hurt David.

"I'll leave this one up to you." Dr. Coke continued. "You can cooperate with my tests, and I will pick an Enlightened from Barracks A and move your father and mother into one of the suites in this building, or you can refuse, and I will inject your father with the virus. It's your choice, a cushy suite, or a mutagenic virus. You decide."

Though she could see him only from the corner of her eye, Charlie watched David's face fill with fear. "You don't have to do this, Charlie. I'll be ok.

Tears spilled down her cheeks and caught in her ears. "I can't let her hurt you."

"It's ok, Charlie. You're all that matters. Don't worry about me."

In that moment, Charlie wished desperately that she had the power back. It would make things easy. "I'll do it. Just please don't hurt David."

Dr. Coke smiled brightly. "See. Now that wasn't so hard." She turned to Gary. "Take Mr. McAuliff to the guest suite on the second floor. Take his wife there too. And have a prisoner brought up from Barracks A."

"Male or female?"

"Doesn't matter." Dr. Coke replied.

Twenty minutes later, Gary returned dragging a boy close to Charlie's age. Surely knowing what was to come, the boy struggled hard in wide-eyed terror. Though her psychic senses remained blind, Charlie imagined how the boy must have felt. Tears stung her eyes.

"Please don't hurt him. I'll do whatever you want."

Dr. Coke smiled cruelly. "I know you will." She turned to Gary. "Put him on the table over there."

Gary hauled the boy over to the steel table next to Charlie's and drew thick leather straps over his body.

"Please…" Charlie wept. She couldn't bear the thought of this boy suffering for her.

It's my fault. She's doing this because of me. Charlie's cheeks flushed with shame as still more tears blurred her vision.

The boy's eyes, wide and frightened, met hers for a moment. Though he did not speak a word, the message was clear. *'Help'*

The boy had to know what was to come. Charlie didn't need psychic senses to understand that. She watched as Dr. Coke prepared a second syringe before slowly approaching the boy.

"What's your name?"

The boy returned a frightened and confused gaze for a moment. Then "George." In little more than a terrified whisper.

"And what is your power, George?" Dr. Coke inquired.

George returned a confused look.

"What happens when you use your power, George?"

George remained silent for a moment longer before replying. "I…I can make things move."

"Telekinesis." Dr. Coke corrected him in a feigned 'teacher' voice. "A fairly common ability among Enlighteneds."

"I'm going to give you a shot, George." Dr. Coke continued. "At first it's just going to be sugar and water. Then I'm going to add a virus called X-22. X-22 is what we call a mutagenic virus. That is, it will change you, turn you into…well, I'm not really sure what. But we'll see won't we?" She smiled and winked at him.

The boy struggled harder against his straps and began to hyperventilate. His efforts were futile as the table's heavy leather straps held him fast.

Dr. Coke began by inserting an IV needle into George's hand. She then attached some tubing and a plastic IV bag. George gasped in pain as the needle went into his flesh but made no other sounds.

Charlie's heart began to race, for she knew what was to come next. "Please just let him go. I'll do anything you want."

"I know you will." Dr. Coke replied in a cold tone.

As she spoke, Dr. Coke took up the syringe of blue liquid she had prepared earlier. "Because you will trust me when I tell you that if you don't do exactly as I ask, then the next person I turn into a mutate will be your father."

As she spoke the word 'father,' Dr. Coke approached the boy and injected the syringe's contents into George's IV tube. As the ice-blue liquid flowed through the tubing and into George's veins, Charlie's flesh grew hot with guilt. This was her fault. George wouldn't be here if it weren't for her. He wouldn't be about to lose his humanity.

I'm so sorry.

After the last of the blue liquid had entered George's body, his breathing slowed as he realized that nothing had happened to him yet. Dr. Coke ignored him, returning to Charlie's side.

"Now, before I let you off the table, I'm going to inject you with a dose of dextroamphetamine. It will restore your power within a few minutes so that we may begin testing. I don't think I need to tell you what will happen if you attempt to escape."

Charlie was silent. A moment later, Dr. Coke took her right arm, and Charlie felt the sting of a needlepoint followed by a warm burning sensation up her veins. Within a few seconds, she felt her heart rate accelerate and her mind sharpen and open up. Then, all at once the power returned, an invisible river moving within her.

Charlie reached out with the power and released her own straps. Then she sat up and slid off the table. "What do you want me to do?"

"Well, for starters, you can follow me."

X

Dr. Coke led Charlie from the laboratory and down a series of corridors to a steel elevator. Inside, it was cavernous, like at the hospital, and smelled of chlorine and other chemicals. Charlie's heartbeat picked up, and she felt her skin rash out in goosebumps. There were no buttons in here but rather a lock into which Dr. Coke slid a big brass key. A moment later the car lurched, taking Charlie's stomach down with it. As they plummeted an unknown distance into the ground, Charlie felt her flesh turn to ice. In that moment she found herself carried back to the NSA's dungeons. Charlie saw Dr. Barrister and that murderer Robin. She saw her father lying on the beach, his blood staining the sand red. And she felt her heart break all over again. The power came alive within her, wanting to rip loose and destroy. Charlie stifled it fearfully.

STOP IT! STOP IT NOW!

A hot knife planted itself in the center of her forehead. Charlie had to bite back a cry of pain. Instead of abating, the pain grew to a scorching fire that quickly swept through her body. She was in agony now. Her feet barely supported her.

PLEASE STOP!

Charlie forced herself to focus through the pain.

STOP IT NOW!

The power, once a blazing river, became an unruly dog.

In her mind, Charlie grabbed the dog by the scruff of its neck and threw it back into its kennel. As the cage door slammed shut, she felt her flesh cool, and the flames recede back to a low-grade headache. Then a few moments later, the headache too had passed.

Dr. Coke was watching her intently, her face set in an expression of fascination rather than fear. Charlie sensed something inside the woman that she didn't like. Inside, this woman looked at Charlie like one might look at an attractive member of the opposite sex. Except it wasn't Charlie herself that the woman was attracted to, but the power, her ability to light fires.

"That was it. Wasn't it?" Dr. Coke's voice was low and intense. "You almost set the elevator on fire. Didn't you?"

Feeling creeped out, Charlie took a step away from Dr. Coke.

Something's wrong with you.

The elevator stopped suddenly, and the door clanged open on a desolate concrete hallway lit by fluorescent track lighting. Down here, the air felt chilly and stunk heavily of mold. Charlie followed Dr. Coke through the corridor without speaking a word. Her heart was thundering in her ears now. Her flesh rippled with tremors so hard she could barely stand.

At the far end of the corridor, they came to a heavy steel door with a deadbolt. Dr. Coke took out her keychain once more, produced a shiny steel key, and opened the lock. Beyond lay a long, gray concrete chamber with a sloping ceiling. A single, plaster mannequin stood at the far end. To its right a cast iron bathtub filled to the brim with water squatted on rust tarnished claw feet.

Dr. Coke turned to her and smiled. "This should be easy for you. Just set the target on fire and then expend your power in the water."

Charlie met Dr. Coke's gaze evenly. "Fine."

Charlie stared across the room at the female figure impassively. Then suddenly she lashed out with the power. The mannequin did not so much catch fire as explode, sending flaming plaster comets hurtling through the air.

Beside Charlie, Dr. Coke gasped in excitement.

Charlie took passing note of this before thrusting the now spiraling power into the bathtub, which erupted in a geyser of steam.

STOP IT!

The power whirled within her mind for a moment, lighting up her body with searing fire and warm, tingling pleasure. Then it went silent.

Charlie turned to Dr. Coke. "What else do you want me to do?"

Dr. Coke remained silent for a moment, a delirious smile on her face, and her eyes wild and mad. "Nothing." She replied in a husky tone. "I'll take you back to your room for now."

The air inside the chamber had become steamy. Thick, oily sweat coated Charlie's skin. Yet she felt cold. Fresh tremors swept through her body. As she looked into Dr. Coke's eyes, Charlie understood the pure insanity behind this woman's calm exterior and felt deeply afraid.

XI

As it turned out, Dr. Coke did not return Charlie to her cell. Instead she took Charlie to a lavish private suite on the laboratory building's third floor.

"This will be your home for the remainder of your time here." Dr. Coke's voice remained husky, and there was something behind it that made Charlie uncomfortable.

"You'll find a plate of chicken strips and some fries in the kitchen." Dr. Coke continued. "Eat up. You'll need all of your energy for tomorrow."

Charlie felt sudden wariness. "What happens tomorrow?"

"Tomorrow, you're going to destroy a gasoline storage tank." Dr. Coke's voice had become low and mischievous. Behind it, Charlie sensed something like a *physical* attraction. Like a man would feel towards a woman. Except Dr. Coke's attraction was not towards her. That would have been creepy enough. No, her attraction was towards the power, or rather the fires it created. In those flames, Dr. Coke saw the promise of pleasure beyond description. An inward shudder rippled through Charlie's body.

What's wrong with you?

"Fine." The word escaped her lips without much thought or hesitation. She had no choice. Dr. Coke would inject David with the X-22 virus if Charlie did not cooperate with her experiments. "But I want to see David and Catherine."

Dr. Coke flashed a brutal smile. "You can see them both, Charlie. And if you do not do as I ask then you will see them both injected with a mutagenic virus."

Charlie met Dr. Coke's gaze steadily but said nothing. Anger flashed within her heart, awakening the power. Incinerating this woman would be easy. Charlie could reduce her to a pile of white ash in an instant. But she dared not.

What would they do to David and Catherine?

The camp was crawling with Lawgivers. There would be no easy escape, as the Lawgivers seemed to have the ability to make it hard to use the power. She did not yet fully understand this ability, but she had felt it when Frank and Raven Hair had first escorted her to her cell in the children's barracks.

For a moment, Charlie and Dr. Coke locked eyes, then Charlie turned away towards the bedroom. Once inside she shut the door and locked it. Charlie then laid face down on the bed and closed her eyes. She was not tired, but there was nothing else to do. The power remained active, rattling at the bars of its cage, wanting to get out and destroy. Charlie forced it down.

STOP IT NOW!

A sharp spike drove into the center of her forehead for a few, agonizing seconds before dissipating.

Charlie lay on her belly in silence, mind racing. There had to be a way to get out of this. She had to find a way. They were going to hurt David and Catherine eventually, no matter what she did. And then there was Stephen.

Is he even still alive?

Charlie reached out with the power. For a moment, she felt nothing, but then she felt the faint, warm touch of Stephen's mind. He was alive and unharmed.

Relief washed through her, though it was short-lived. Stephen too was in danger. If Dr. Coke learned that he was Charlie's friend, then she would hold him hostage as well. If she did not, then she would have him killed.

Guilt and fear washed through her. This was all her fault.

If it weren't for me, then David and Catherine would be happy and safe. Stephen would be happy and safe.

Charlie wanted to cry but found she could not. Instead, she only felt bitter guilt and icy fear. Sharp tremors rippled through her body as her skin rashed out in goosebumps and oily sweat.

I'm so sorry.

Charlie lay trembling for an unknown length of time before exhaustion finally took over, and she drifted into darkness.

XII

As Charlie slept, on the other side of the world, Loyalist Russian pilots climbed into cockpits of SU-35's. Within a few minutes, the fighter jets thundered down the runway of their Siberian base on their way to attack their target in Oymyakon. The small village was of no particular note except that it contained a massive Resistance detention and extermination facility.

At 1600 hours local time, the wing arrived and delivered their payload.

XIII

Angela was in the midst of compressing a 7.62 round when she first heard the sound of sirens and distant explosions. She was not frightened at first, only confused.

What's going on?

Another explosion echoed in the late afternoon air, this one much closer, and the other prisoners began to filter out of the reloading factory.

Angela stepped away from her workstation and headed for the windows to her right. Now she could hear the low rumble of jet engines.

All at once, understanding washed through her. *Oh shit! Air raid!*

Before she could react, there was a deafening roar, and the floor came alive beneath her feet, tossing her onto her side. Glass peppered her skin. Angela quickly crawled under the workbench as more explosions shook the reloading factory. Now the low rumble had become a loud roar.

Then, suddenly, everything went silent white. Something hard and heavy fell across Angela's back. She screamed, but no sound came out.

When her vision cleared, Angela found herself lying face down under a steel I-beam. Each breath sent sharp daggers tearing through her lungs.

"Owww!" The word escaped her lips almost unconsciously.

More explosions rang out on the late afternoon air. Thick, acrid-smelling smoke floated everywhere. Angela knew she had to get away before she was killed. Angela fought against the I-beam and with some effort, managed to shove it off herself.

The reloading factory was leveled save for a single wall. As bombs rained down around her, their impacts shaking the ground beneath her feet, Angela ran across the campgrounds towards the fence. Prisoners and Lawgivers milled about in blind panic. Though her ears remained muted, Angela imagined they were screaming.

Angela spotted a hole in the fence that no one had noticed yet. She sprinted towards it, as still more bombs dropped. One struck a large propane tank near the camp laboratory, sending a massive fireball skyward. The heat baked out at her, reddening her skin. Angela's nose filled with the smell of burning. She was only a few feet from the fence now. She felt the power move within her. Angela stifled it rapidly.

KNOCK IT OFF!

The power quieted down but remained active in her mind.

Angela had reached the gap in the fence and hurried through. As she passed the last ring of barbed wire, an iron hand closed upon her shoulder.

"Where do you think you're going?"

Angela recognized Ivan's voice at once. "I'm getting the hell out of here before I get killed."

Ivan's grip tightened. "We'll escape together."

For a moment, his voice echoed in her mind. *Have you forgotten? You're mine bitch!*

Elsie Coke lay awake in bed, feeling excited and content at once. In her mind, she still felt the girl's power and saw the mannequin explode. Flames danced across plaster as if waiving to her. They were beautiful, almost erotic. Deep inside Elsie felt something grow hot, warming her flesh and making her skin tingle

In the darkness, Elsie felt the heat of the girl's fire, smelled the sweet scent of burning. The girl's power was incredible, like nothing Elsie had ever seen before.

So beautiful…Her flames are so beautiful. How did someone so fragile come to possess such awesome power?

Elsie had studied Enlighteneds for many years out of scientific curiosity, but this girl represented something much more. She was truly god-like, like Jehovah come to earth. The girl's power was intoxicating. Elsie had to see the girl light more fires. She would explode if she could not.

XIV

The following day Charlie found herself standing before a gigantic, three-story fuel storage tank inside an abandoned tank farm that had once belonged to Obele Oil Company. Her heart fluttered and, her muscles felt tensed, ready to strike. The power, awakened by her emotions, stirred restlessly within her. Charlie held onto it but did not force it back. Rather, she forced herself to focus. Some part of her understood the danger of what she was about to do. Yet another part of her *wanted* badly to do it. A third part of her was surprised, for there was a time when she was younger that she would have been frightened, and yet she felt only excited anticipation.

Dr. Coke's voice broke through her thoughts. "You know the drill, Charlie."

"Yes, but you might want to take cover." Charlie dropped her voice. "Something might happen."

Dr. Coke's face paled a shade, but she did not move. "Go ahead."

Charlie reached into the power and held on for a moment. The storage tank was filled most of the way with gasoline. She could feel its cold, smell its choking aroma. Charlie stood approximately one thousand yards from the storage tank, and yet she was concerned that she was still too close. This would be a conflagration, there was no telling how far the fire would spread. All at once Charlie shoved the power out of herself in the direction of the fuel storage tank. In an instant, the tank vanished in a massive column of white. Seconds later the concussion struck as a hot wind, sweeping her off her feet. She felt the searing heat against her skin, the pain was exquisite and yet there was no damage. Her flesh remained pale, pink porcelain, undamaged, not even reddened. Rather than pain, Charlie's body felt alive, every nerve ending tingled with ecstasy. Her mind opened, and in that moment she felt like the most powerful person on earth. Intense joy flooded her senses.

The power was raging, fighting her to get loose again and destroy. A thousand yards to the left of the tower of blue-white flames that had once been the fuel storage tank stood a long, sausage-shaped, propane tank. Charlie got to her feet and without pausing turned her power on the tank, which immediately vanished in a second brilliant white flash. This time Charlie kept her feet through the concussion. The roar of this explosion set her ears ringing.

Charlie put her hand to her head. *Owww!*

The power continued to rage within her mind. Charlie fought it back fiercely.

STOP IT! STOP IT NOW!

Invisible flames enveloped her body. Charlie cried out but continued fighting the power. Her head felt as if some great, unseen sword had split it down the center like a melon.

STOP IT!

The words screamed in her mind even as the power continued spiraling up and up. Flames licked across the sand at her feet, instantly transforming it to glass.

STOP IT! Her mind screamed at the power, even as she tightened her grip.

The fire in her flesh grew to a great inferno as the invisible swordsman hacked away at her skull. Then, just as she thought she could not fight the power any longer, it retreated into the back of her mind and became silent.

Heat baked out at Charlie from blazing remnants of the two tanks, coating her skin in thick, oily sweat. Academically, Charlie understood she should feel frightened or at least guilty for what she had done.

These fires could get out of control. Someone could get hurt.

Still, Charlie's heart raced excitedly, and her mind reveled in the sheer joy and freedom of using the power. The destruction of the tanks seemed wasteful to her, yet no one was injured.

But those tanks belonged to someone, and I destroyed them.

This thought brought a slow, sick feeling to Charlie's stomach together with withering heat to her chest and cheeks. She had hurt someone, destroyed their property. It didn't matter that she had, had no choice. She had deliberately burned up someone else's property.

Charlie turned away from the towering yellow flames feeling deep conflict. Her eyes fell upon Dr. Coke. She sat on her butt on the ground like an overgrown child, a stupid grin plastered across her lips. Her skin had turned a deep crimson, and angry, white, and yellow blisters had cropped up on her face and the exposed parts of her arms. And yet her delirious grin remained. Her eyes, half-lidded and relaxed, remained transfixed by the two towering yellow infernos of Charlie's making. Charlie touched Dr. Coke's mind and immediately regretted it for what she found profoundly disturbed her. Dr. Coke's thoughts radiated intense pleasure and satisfaction and something resembling adult sexual desire. Charlie felt her stomach lurch, and for a moment she thought she would vomit. Instead, Charlie swallowed hard and started walking back towards the camp.

For a moment, Dr. Coke did not react. Then with palpable reluctance, she stood up and hurried to Charlie's side. "Before I take you to visit with your parents, I need to stop off in the lab." Dr. Coke's voice was husky and disinterested.

Charlie followed Dr. Coke wordlessly as she led the way back to the laboratory where she had injected the boy named George the day before. Now he lay on the steel table moaning softly. Heavy sweat soaked his skin, which had turned the same green-white as the inside of a cucumber. Sharp, tremors wracked his slender frame, and his eyes had become sunken and red.

"I'm so sorry," Charlie whispered.

The boy replied with a low groan. "It huuurts."

Charlie turned away, tears in her eyes. This too was her fault. She had chosen this for George so that Dr. Coke would not inject David.

"You have to help him," Charlie begged Dr. Coke. "He didn't do anything wrong."

"No, he didn't." She agreed. "But that's beside the point. I just wanted to remind you of what will happen to your father if you stop cooperating."

"I promise I'll do whatever you want." Charlie sobbed. "Just please help him."

"Actions have consequences Charlie," Dr. Coke replied in a cold tone. "I trust you understand that. You chose to have me inject George instead of your father. Now you must live with the consequences of that choice."

Behind her cold exterior, Charlie sensed a certain grim satisfaction in Dr. Coke's mind.

She's enjoying this. Bitch!

In that moment, a part of Charlie wanted to torch Dr. Coke, where she stood. *See if she gets off if I set her on fire.*

Charlie's flesh chilled at that thought, and she felt her cheeks flush with shame once more.

A cold voice spoke up within her. *It's murder, you know. Even after everything she's done. Even though she threatened David. If you kill her, it will be murder.*

Charlie recoiled from that thought. The power moved within her restlessly, awakened by her emotions. Charlie slammed it down hard.

NO WAY! I'M NOT DOING THAT!

As if to grind glass into Charlie's wounds, Dr. Coke took her face and turned her eyes back toward George. As she did, Dr. Coke led Charlie closer to the table. "Don't look away. I want you to look at what you have chosen and remember that this could be your father at any time."

Charlie's eyes ran with tears even as her heart ripped apart at the horror of what she had chosen. "I'm so sorry." Little more than a choked whisper. Charlie felt her breath catch in her chest and had to fight not to break down completely.

Dr. Coke held her, forcing her to look at the poor, suffering boy on the table for what seemed like an eternity before finally allowing Charlie to turn away.

"I want to see David and Catherine," Charlie whispered through the tears.

"Yes. I think it's time now." Dr. Coke replied.

XV

Dr. Coke took Charlie's hand and led her from the laboratory to the same steel double-doored hospital elevator that had taken her to the testing room the day before. The stench of chlorine and chemicals inside was stronger than she remembered from the day before, almost overpowering. Charlie wrinkled her nose unconsciously as Dr. Coke turned her key in the elevator's keyhole. Both steel doors closed with the loud bang of a vault door slamming shut. Charlie nearly screamed. Beside her, she could feel Dr. Coke's perverted arousal radiating out at her in hot, putrid waves. Charlie felt her stomach lurch and had to fight back the urge to vomit. Beneath her clothing, her flesh crawled.

The elevator shot upward rapidly before skidding to a stop several floors up. Another vault door bang and the elevator doors had opened upon a corridor that looked more like it belonged in a fancy hotel than a laboratory, complete with cheery off-white paint, faux wooden doors, replica candelabra sconces, and brass fixtures.

"Let's go." Dr. Coke commanded impatiently. Her voice remained husky, and Charlie could feel the dark intent behind Dr. Coke's words.

Charlie followed Dr. Coke down the hallway to the last door on the right. Without pausing, she reached into her white lab coat and produced an unmarked key card, which she proceeded to swipe through a scanner beside the door. A low click indicated that the door had unlocked. Dr. Coke reached for the door handle and opened it with deliberate slowness. She then gestured for Charlie to enter first.

"Go ahead. Your father and mother are waiting for you."

Though wary and disgusted by what she still sensed in Dr. Coke's mind, Charlie entered the small apartment behind the door. Inside David sat beside Catherine on a small cream-colored canvas love seat watching a DVD of *Inside Out* on the television. Both looked up and smiled as she entered.

"Charlie? Thank God you're ok!" David's voice blended relieved disbelief and joy. He took her into his arms and clasped her to his chest.

"Charlie!" Catherine's voice too was both surprised and happy. "I missed you so much." Smiling deliriously, Catherine went to David and Charlie and wrapped her arms around both.

"I missed you too," Charlie replied. Her heart leapt within her, for she had only seen David briefly the day before and had not seen Catherine since they had arrived at the camp. Charlie felt a weight lift from her chest to know that David and Catherine were ok and yet she understood that they were not safe here. Dr. Coke would not harm them so long as Charlie cooperated with her tests.

And as long as she is still interested in the power.

But Dr. Coke was crazy and unpredictable and…

She doesn't have the final say.

Charlie felt that there were others who actually ran the Resistance and they did not share Dr. Coke's fascination with fire. Eventually, they would decide that Dr. Coke's 'tests' were not yielding sufficient information to justify the risks. As this last thought crossed her mind, a brief vision of the inferno that had once been gasoline and propane tanks flashed through her mind. The two fires had merged into a single conflagration that threatened to consume a nearby abandoned neighborhood. No one had come to put it out. The sight of the lonely, abandoned homes threatened to tear her heart to pieces and made her cheeks flush with shame.

I did that.

Then after a moment, the vision dissolved, and she was back in David's arms. Her remorse remained for several minutes before being washed away by intense joy.

Dr. Coke's voice quickly intruded upon Charlie's happiness. "You have twenty minutes."

The three of them spent the time talking about unimportant things, wanting for that short interval to forget all that had happened.

As the last five minutes ticked away, David met Charlie's eyes with a gaze of gentle concern. "You don't have to do her tests, Charlie. Catherine and I will be ok."

"Yes, I do. You didn't see what she did after you left. She injected a boy my age with X-22. He's very sick." Before Charlie could anymore, her heart twisted, and she burst into tears.

David took her into his arms. "It's ok, Charlie. It's not your fault. None of this is your fault. And you don't have to do any more tests if you don't want to."

Except she did. Charlie had no desire to waste the last few minutes she had with David by arguing, but she knew he was wrong. She had to cooperate with Dr. Coke, or she would lose David and Catherine.

When Dr. Coke returned, Charlie burst into tears anew. She didn't want to be away from David and

Catherine anymore. She was so lonely and afraid, and she just wanted to be with her parents. "Please, can I just have a little longer."

Dr. Coke turned cruel eyes on her. "Tomorrow, perhaps. Right now, I want to talk to you."

Charlie dropped her head hopelessly, letting her long blond hair fall in front of her eyes. The power had awakened. Charlie pushed it aside absently before it could begin spiraling upward.

Once outside the cheery little apartment, Dr. Coke gazed down upon Charlie with brutal cold eyes. "Tomorrow I want you to try something new." Her lips curled into a twisted, insane grin. "I want you to set fire to a person.

Something in Charlie's chest shot up in her throat before dropping down into her shoe. "I…" Charlie could not finish, for she did not know what to do. She couldn't hurt someone who hadn't threatened or hurt her first. But if she didn't do as she was told then Dr. Coke would hurt David and Catherine. Fresh tears spilled from her eyes, onto her shame flushed cheeks.

What have I done now?

XVI

As Dr. Coke returned her to her room, Charlie remained lost in thought, unsure of what to do. She couldn't lose David and Catherine, and yet she could not imagine harming an innocent either. For once the power was silent, perhaps stifled by the guilt and turmoil in her mind.

Upon returning to her own apartment, Charlie went straight to bed. Sleep, however, remained elusive. Charlie lay awake, staring at the ceiling and struggling desperately to find a way out. She dared not defy Dr. Coke for fear of what would befall David and Catherine, and she could not burn an innocent. Escape was not an option either, for she felt the risk was too high.

A cold voice spoke up within her. *Why don't you just do what she wants? What do you care if you burn up some stranger?*

Horrified, Charlie tried to push the thought aside and found that it remained, stubborn and implacable.

Are you really going to let her hurt David and Catherine just to save some asshole you don't even know?

Why do you care? Nobody ever cared about you, except David and Catherine. The rest of them wanted to kill you or use you for your power. Why do you care if one of them dies?

It's wrong. Charlie insisted, feeling less confident in that moment then she had ever in the past.

Why? They all deserve to suffer. Even the ones who didn't hurt you. They let the NSA murder Daddy and Mommy. They let the NSA and the Black Empire hurt you. They supported the Resistance. It isn't wrong, it's justice.

It's wrong! Charlie shouted at the voice.

The voice seemed to shrug indifferently. *Whatever you say. But you know I'm right.*

Fresh tears streamed down Charlie's hot cheeks, for she understood that this was all her fault. If it weren't for her David and Catherine would be safe, and none of this would have ever happened. Now she was in a box, and she had no idea how to get out.

XVII

As Charlie lay sleepless that night, the leadership council of the Resistance gathered for an emergency meeting. The topic: the destruction of the fuel depot outside of the Cordoba Flats.

After everyone had gathered in the ruins of their usual University Park tavern. The General called the meeting to order and quickly dispensed with any formality, even suspending Robert's Rules of Order.

"Dr. Coke has clearly gone rogue," Carla spoke dispassionately despite the cold hand gripping her heart. "And that girl has proven to be just as dangerous as we all feared. The time has come to put a stop to this nonsense and terminate her."

Doc raised an eyebrow. "Perhaps." His tone was infuriatingly measured. "She destroyed a large supply of increasing rare fuel. But that little display demonstrates exactly why we need more information on the girl and others like her. Dr. Coke is the problem here, not the experimentation on the girl. I suggest that we remove Coke and bring in someone more trustworthy to continue working with the MacLeod girl."

"I warned you that the girl is dangerous," Herb interjected. "We should have eliminated her already. I could have told you something like this would happen." He turned an angry glare on Doc. "Are you suggesting that we wait for her to kill more people?"

"We have the girl's adoptive parents in custody." The General replied in a calm tone. "They're the only family that girl has left. I don't think she will risk their safety. She only destroyed the fuel depot because Dr. Coke asked her to."

Despite the tightening cold in her chest, Carla could not argue with the General's logic. "You may be right, but I fear that our control may be tenuous at best, and as long as Dr. Coke remains in control of the tests, there's no telling what harm the MacLeod girl might cause. If we keep the girl alive, then we must remove Dr. Coke."

"I agree." Doc concurred.

"As do I," Llyod added, speaking for the first time.

"Three votes to keep the girl alive and remove Dr. Coke and one against. " The General announced.

Once again, the vote split four and four, with the General reluctantly casting his vote in favor of keeping the girl alive and removing Dr. Coke from any further testing. For her part, though she voted in favor of continuing experimentation with a different scientist, Carla had grave reservations. This girl was indeed different from any Enlightened. They had rounded up, tested and terminated hundreds of Enlighteneds. None of them possessed a pyrokinetic ability. And none of them had power on the scale of the MacLeod girl. She was incredibly dangerous and had demonstrated a willingness to kill to protect herself and her family. Using David and Catherine McAuliffe to force the girl's cooperation was a dangerous game.

XVIII

At 2000 hours that night, mere minutes after the close of the leadership meeting of the Resistance, two wings of F22 Raptors originating from Andrews Airforce Base, successfully bombed a radio relay in Phoenix, Arizona, taking the station offline and severing communications between the Resistance leadership and Cordoba Flats. And so the order removing Dr. Coke as commander and lead scientist of Cordoba Flats never made it to he adjutant.

XIX

Hands closed around Charlie's shoulders and shook, jarring her from sleep. She groaned and turned over. "Go away. I'm tired." She had not fallen asleep until 3am and was exhausted.

"Wake up." A familiar male voice insisted. "It's time to go."

Charlie groaned again and moved away from the voice.

"Now." The voice commanded.

Charlie opened her eyes to see Frank. His expression was annoyed as usual. The tray in his hand held a stack of syrup-soaked pancakes, bacon, and orange juice. Charlie sat up with a longing gaze.

Frank set the tray down beside her on the bed. "Take what you want. Just get your ass up and don't take too long. Dr. Coke is waiting for you."

"Thank you." The words escaped Charlie's lips without much thought. Frank was a douchebag, and she hated him.

Frank met Charlie's eyes with a cold gaze. "Just don't take too long eating. When I get back, I expect you to be finished eating, dressed, and ready to go."

Charlie ignored him and began to pick at the food. Frank stood over her a moment longer before turning and leaving. Charlie dawdled over her breakfast eating very little. It wasn't that she had no appetite; in fact, she was ravenous, but to her frustration food held little appeal.

The rich smell of bacon and maple syrup that would normally have made her mouth water made her stomach churn with nausea.

After several minutes she pushed the tray aside and went to the red oak wardrobe by the bathroom door. Here she found an abundance of girl's clothes. Blouses, cammy tops, capris, skinny jeans, t-shirts, and several turtlenecks all waited for her choice. Charlie absently picked out a pink t-shirt with the slogan 'Justice for Girls' on the front, and a pair of light blue skinny jeans.

Not long after she had finished dressing, Frank returned. "Let's go."

Charlie's stomach dropped into her shoe, but she went with him anyway because there was nothing else to do. Frank led her through the science building to the laboratory where George remained strapped to his metal table. Once inside, Frank forced her forward to stand before George.

His face had turned bone white with little purple splotches, and he had begun to swell. His cheeks looked like a chipmunk's, and his arms had become fat and round like great sausages. He was no longer groaning. The only sounds that escaped him were heavy, raspy breaths.

A soft sob escaped Charlie's throat. All at once, George's eyes flicked open, and he lunged at her with a roar.

Charlie stumbled backward with a cry, the power suddenly awake and eager to destroy.

George fought against his restraints with frightening ferocity, but he lacked the strength to break free. *Not yet...* His mind had disintegrated into a cyclone of madness, fragmented images and emotions spinning and twisting as if taken by an invisible wind. It *hurt* to touch George's mind. His whirling madness threatened to sweep her sanity away. In an act of self-preservation, Charlie closed herself to him, pushing his ragged lunacy away.

The virus had infected his brain, stripping away the last of his humanity. Charlie looked down on the poor broken boy and burst into renewed tears.

"Just wanted to remind you of what will happen to your parents if you do not cooperate." Dr. Coke sneered from behind.

Charlie turned and met Dr. Coke's gaze with a hard, icy stair. Sudden, hot fire, kindled in her chest, quickening her pulse and breath. The power, already awakened, began to spiral upward. Charlie forced it back before temptation could override her better judgment.

STOP IT! STOP IT NOW! I CAN'T...

A hot poker buried itself in the center of her forehead. A sob escaped Charlie's throat as she put a hand to her head.

"It hurts to stop. Doesn't it?" Dr. Coke's tone had become curious rather than mocking. "That's the cost of trying to stop a cascading neural reaction."

Charlie glared at her through the red haze of pain, in that moment wanting more than anything to let the power go and burn this madwoman where she stood. Yet Charlie dared not for she knew the consequences.

Dr. Coke's face had turned a deep crimson, giving her the outward appearance of being enraged. In truth, Charlie sensed eager excitement as if Dr. Coke were awaiting…*sex?*

Oh, that's nasty! Not wanting to see any deeper, Charlie withdrew her mind from Dr. Coke's.

Still, the force of Dr. Coke's emotions and thoughts was pervasive. Like a crying baby, her desire was hard to ignore completely.

Dr. Coke could wait no longer. "Ready?"

Charlie remained silent, desperately wanting to draw out the moment as long as possible. Wanting more than that to be anywhere else. She was no longer crying, but her eyes still ran with bitter tears. She wanted David and Catherine. She needed them to tell her what to do because she could not decide herself.

And what if I do the wrong thing? There really was no right decision here, yet Charlie understood that of all the bad choices, a wrong one could have disastrous consequences.

"Let's go." Dr. Coke's brusque tone broke Charlie's concentration. "You're not getting out of this by stalling."

Charlie trailed after Dr. Coke, each plodding step echoing as if in a nightmare. The institutional green hallways that had once been frightening brought terrified chills to her heart. The overhead fluorescent lights seemed painfully bright, and the air heavy with the sickening smell of bleach.

Please get me out of here. Please God, I don't want to do this.

She could not harm an innocent, and she could not bear the thought of losing David and Catherine. *Mommy and Daddy are dead. Please don't take away David and Catherine too.*

They had reached the elevator now. Its stainless steel door threw shards of light into Charlie's eyes, forcing her to squint for a moment. The power remained a live thing within her mind, digging its claws into her skull and brain as she fought to keep it from escaping.

STOP IT PLEASE! I CAN'T…SHE'LL HURT DAVID AND CATHERINE!

The power continued to race within her, tearing deeper into her flesh with razor fangs. For a moment, Charlie swayed on her feet before catching her balance. Dr. Coke was watching her with an expression of eager fascination.

"How did they take someone as young as you and give you such power?"

Charlie did not reply, silenced by pain and the knowledge of what she faced.

They were on the elevator now, the car descending rapidly. Charlie's heart began to race, for she knew it would not be long now. She would have to choose. And she feared what her choice would be. She could not lose David and Catherine.

After an all too short descent, the elevator doors banged open, and Charlie found herself facing that same, cold, bare concrete corridor she had traversed only two days earlier to set fire to a mannequin. The musty stench of mold seemed stronger than she remembered, almost to the point of being choking. Charlie dawdled in the elevator for a moment before Dr. Coke took her hand and firmly led her from the car.

"As I said, you're not getting out of this by stalling."

Charlie made no effort to resist. Resistance would require her to split too much of her attention, and as it was, she was lost in her thoughts. Charlie walked the long, overly bright corridor with the slow, plodding steps of a condemned woman. Her heart thundered in her chest, as hard tremors rippled her flesh. She felt frozen almost to the core, and yet thick oily sweat coated her skin. In her mind, the power had begun to spiral upward just within her ability to control it. It took all of Charlie's will to maintain control as the power's razor claws had now become invisible flames that enveloped her body.

"It's ok." Dr. Coke's voice had become gentle and soothing. "You can let go in just a few minutes, and you'll feel better. I promise."

Except she could not. She couldn't harm someone who didn't deserve it. "Please…" Charlie began in a weak voice. "Please, I can't do this."

"I think you can." Dr. Coke replied as she reached into her lab coat for her keys. "You see, I know more about you than you think, Charlie. I know that you have killed people before to protect your father and your adopted parents. You've even killed to protect yourself."

They had reached the end of the corridor now. Dr. Coke unlocked a familiar dead-bolted steel blast door and held it open for Charlie. "That's all you're doing today, Charlie. Killing to protect your adopted parents."

Charlie looked up at Dr. Coke with icy eyes but said nothing. There was a certain logic to Dr. Coke's words, and this frightened Charlie still further, for she did not want to be persuaded.

Beyond the door lay the same concrete chamber, with the same cast iron clawfoot bathtub from two days ago.

Charlie's heart caught in her throat for across the room from her a young red-haired woman sat shackled to a straight-backed wooden chair. A half dozen Lawgivers stood guard near the door of the chamber. The woman recognized Charlie at first sight, her eyes widening, and her breathing quickening.

"Please. I didn't do anything wrong. I do whatever the Lawgivers want. I work hard. Please don't let her hurt me."

Dr. Coke smiled coldly. "I won't lie to you and tell you that this won't hurt. It will probably be the worst pain you'll experience in your life, but you can take comfort in the fact that you will be giving your life for science."

Liar.

Charlie knew that at this point, Dr. Coke was motivated solely by her obsession with pyrokinesis. Driven by her anger and fear, the power slammed against the cage that held it sending waves of invisible fire sweeping across Charlie's skin. Fresh tears stung Charlie's eyes and trickled down her hot cheeks. She wanted so badly to let go, just to let the power run loose and destroy. Dr. Coke more than deserved it. But she dared not for if she killed Dr. Coke, it would surely mean death for David and Catherine.

Dr. Coke turned her flame reddened face towards Charlie. "You know what to do." Her words were cold as ice.

The woman had begun to hyperventilate, her pleas silenced as the reality of her situation sank in.

Charlie froze, heart racing, muscles trembling with such force as to nearly take her off her feet.

I...I can't, but if I don't, she'll hurt David and Catherine.

Can't, but if I don't...

Can't, but if I don't...

The thought spun round and round in her head, accelerating the already upward spiraling power within her mind. The unseen flames engulfing her body grew and intensified until she felt as if she would catch fire for real. She faced a choice of horrors, and each pulled her in a different direction with such force that she felt her mind would tear apart. With each moment, the power grew stronger, driven on by the strength of her emotions.

Please, I can't hurt her. She didn't do anything wrong, but I can't lose David and Catherine either.

Charlie turned pleading eyes on Dr. Coke's flame reddened face. "Please, I can't do it."

Dr. Coke remained unmoved. "Yes, you can. And you will if you want to keep your parents safe."

Charlie's eyes ran with bitter, stinging tears. "No, I can't." She wept. The power was nearly out of control now. Charlie feared it would blow loose if she didn't do something. The fiery agony was almost insupportable.

Dr. Coke's expression hardened, and her eyes became ice-cold. "Last chance Charlie. You saw what happened to George. Is that what you want for your parents?"

Charlie shook her head "No.," her voice rising with desperation. "But I can't do this... Please!"

"Your choice, Charlie. Either she burns, or your parents suffer."

A sob escaped Charlie's throat as the power painted invisible fire across her flesh. Charlie's body trembled with such force that she could barely stand as thick, greasy sweat enveloped her skin. *I have no choice. I'm sorry...*

But she didn't do anything wrong. She's a prisoner just like you. She hasn't hurt you, and it's not her fault that Dr. Coke is threatening David and Catherine. You can't hurt her. It's wrong.

For a moment, all rational thought left her, and Charlie turned towards Dr. Coke and *shoved* all of the power out of herself, knowing that Dr. Coke would be killed instantly.

In that same instant, her mind fragmented, breaking her concentration. Instead of focusing on Dr. Coke the power sprayed out everywhere at once, setting the walls, ceiling, and floor on fire. By some miracle or stroke of dumb luck, the woman remained unharmed, but Dr. Coke was not so fortunate. Bright yellow and orange flames leapt from her white lab coat and frizzy dirty blonde hair. A cry of shock escaped her throat, and for a moment Charlie sensed, not pain or fear, but *ecstasy* from Dr. Coke. Then she collapsed to the concrete, and her mind instantly went dark.

At once, Charlie's heart turned to ice and dropped into her shoe. "Oh my God, I'm sorry!" She turned to Frank, the only Lawgiver whose name she knew. "Please, I didn't mean to do it! Please don't hurt David and Catherine!" Before she could say anything further Charlie's body lit up with agony, and everything went black.

XX

When she awakened, Charlie found herself slung over Frank's shoulder. Dull heat radiated out from the muscles in her upper left arm. The power had become strangely silent. "Please! I didn't mean it! The power just got away!"

"I don't care," Frank replied resolutely. "It's not my call what to do with your parents anyway. That decision is up to the leadership council. I can tell you that they're not Dr. Coke. They'll probably just order that the three of you be terminated."

Charlie's heart sank. "No! Please! I did everything you wanted!"

"You nearly killed Dr. Coke," Frank replied matter-of-factly. "She'll never be the same."

"Then kill me," Charlie whispered. "But don't hurt David and Catherine."

The words themselves turned Charlie's blood to ice. She had seen death once before and did not relish experiencing it again. But she could not allow these people to harm David and Catherine, even at the cost of her own life.

"It's not my call." Frank's voice was hard and cold as ice.

Fifteen minutes later, Charlie lay on the bed in her apartment, sobbing uncontrollably. She had burned Dr. Coke and hadn't been able to escape. Because of her, David and Catherine were doomed.

XXI

Within an hour of Dr. Coke's burning, Carla found herself sitting in the same tavern she had been in the night before awaiting yet another council meeting regarding Charlene MacLeod. As she sat sipping a rare cup of Dunkin Donuts coffee, Carla's mind drifted over the strange course of events that had led her to become a member of the Resistance leadership. Carla had spent the initial days of the Great Civil War hunkered down at home, trying to avoid looters. Unfortunately, she only had a week's worth of groceries on hand and a single case of bottled water. Thus, by the following Monday, she was compelled to go out to look for food and water. By this time, rioting had given over to full-scale rebellion. Carla found herself confronted by armed members of the Resistance and quickly declared her loyalty.

Though she was sympathetic to the Resistance's position, she had never before had any desire to become too involved for fear of the personal cost. However, the world had become a very different place. The Resistance had taken Ann Arbor within two weeks of the start of the Great Civil War and demanded declarations of allegiance from all residents. Those who refused were rounded up and shipped off to concentration camps. Cooperation had become a matter of survival.

As this thought passed through her mind, Carla took a slow sip of coffee from her mug. The warm liquid lit up her tongue with the flavor of rich mocha and hints of caramel. Carla smiled slightly. In her mind, she remembered the cold hate that had consumed her for the first few weeks following the death of Senator Suire. That girl represented everything that Carla had stood against. Now, old politics and values seemed unimportant. Survival was all that mattered. The Loyalists were ruthless and brutal, and their laboratory monsters dangerous.

Carla had witnessed first-hand what the so-called Enlighteneds were capable of. There was no doubt in her mind that these *things* had to be destroyed. And yet she had ultimately supported experimenting on Charlene MacLeod after the girl had incinerated a cybernetic mutate that had come under the Resistance's control. Above all, Carla was a scholar and strongly believed in scientific inquiry. Moreover, understanding this girl's abilities was a matter of survival, for there were untold numbers of others with similar talents that they would have to locate and terminate.

The other members of the leadership council began to filter in. Carla still could not believe she was on the council. She had never desired such a position and yet found herself elected for the Western Territories.

After the last of the council members filtered in, the General called the meeting to order and promptly suspended the usual rules of order.

"I think you all know why we're here." the General began. "Earlier today, Dr. Coke attempted to have the girl set another prisoner on fire. The purpose of this test is unknown. What we do know is that rather than cooperate, the girl set Dr. Coke on fire along with six Lawgivers, and attempted to escape. Lawgiver Frank Isaac Parker subdued the girl. We are now left with the decision of what to do with her." The General looked out at the remaining council members expectantly.

"Obviously, we can't keep the girl alive any longer. She's proven herself too dangerous." Carla spoke with care and in a reasoned tone.

"I could have told you that this would happen." Herb snapped. "But you fools just had to play with fire. You refused to see the danger. All you saw was a bright shiny toy."

Oh, shut the fuck up you old bastard.

Carla hated Herb. She thought probably everyone there hated the old fuck, but he had somehow managed to get elected to the council, so they were stuck with him.

The old fuck was still nattering on. "I trust that now you will support terminating the girl." His tone was thick with self-righteousness.

"I don't really see where we have a choice," Carla replied. "How quickly can we have Charlene MacLeod terminated?"

"It will take at least a day to transmit the order to Cordoba Flats," Doc answered. "And Cordoba Flats typically takes about two to four hours to prepare for electric chair executions."

"Then I would suggest we send the order immediately." As she spoke, Carla's mind flashed back to an image of Charlene MacLeod burning down Castle Bruce on the television in her classroom.

She's a monster. She only looks like a little girl.

Still, the -thought of electrocuting a child disturbed her. She knew well what went on a Cordoba Flats. Children were murdered there every day. But Charlene MacLeod's death would be on her direct orders. Carla did not know if she could live with that.

She only looks like a little girl. Inside she's a laboratory mutate just like the creature she killed.

"That's two votes to terminate the girl. Are there any of you who object to immediately executing the girl?" As he spoke, the General once again looked out over the gathered council members.

No one spoke up.

Carla downed the rest of her coffee, knowing what would come next.

"Then I will instruct Doc to transmit the order. Charlene MacLeod, the McAuliffes, and Stephen Wolf are to be terminated immediately."

Doc nodded silently as he sipped his own coffee. "I propose that we name Dr. Coke's adjutant as the new commandant. He's already up to speed, and he's a good soldier."

Carla wrinkled her nose. "Eric Rader is a dumb thug. Sure he can follow orders, but he lacks foresight. Are we really going to put him in charge of our Enlightened prisoners?"

"*Major* Rader is the only person in Cordoba Flats who is even remotely qualified to lead. If we send in someone from outside, then it will take weeks for them to arrive and weeks more to get them up to speed on camp operations." As he spoke, Doc took his rimless glasses from his face, polished the lenses with his handkerchief, and placed them high on the bridge of his nose.

Carla felt her skin flush. "Are you telling me that our only option to deal with that girl is a fucking thug?!"

"Rader is our best man on the ground. Unless you'd like to place Frank Parker in charge." Doc smiled at that last part.

Carla opened her mouth to retort, but the General cut her off.

"So we have one vote for and one vote against appointing Major Rader commander of Cordoba Flats. Does anyone else have something to say?"

"I don't like it, but I think Rader is our best option." As he spoke, Lloyd took out a bag of pot and began rolling a joint. Under other circumstances, Carla would have enjoyed a hit herself.

"I agree." Fiona chimed in.

"Anyone else?" The General's tone had become slightly impatient.

No one spoke up.

"So the vote is three in favor and one opposed. How does the rest of the council vote?"

Herb and Roland voted against appointing Major Rader while Sasha and Devin voted in favor. Following this decision, the council adjourned, and the members drifted out of the battered tavern. Carla wandered back to her penthouse at the MGM Grand. Her mind was awash with conflicting thoughts. The girl was dangerous and fascinating at once. Her power was exceptionally rare. It was a shame to put her to death. And yet Carla felt that this was the best way to proceed.

As Carla sat alone troubling over her vote, Doc made his way to the Stratosphere tower. From here he could transmit the order to terminate Charlene MacLeod and the McAuliffes. Upon arriving in the broadcast room, Doc's mind raced with a thousand questions.

This girl is by far the most powerful Enlightened we have come across. Should we really be terminating her? Will we be able to terminate her? Could this girl hold the key to learning where Enlighteneds come from? And countless others besides.

Though the girl's fate had been decided (Hell *he* had voted to terminate her), Doc was in no hurry to give the order. He felt strongly that the council had made a mistake, one that they would pay dearly for.

Doc picked up the transmitter, an old 1980s Motorola. Static crackled from the speaker. Instead of clicking the transmit switch, Doc turned and gazed out the window. Even after the destruction of the Great Civil War, the Stratosphere tower offered a spectacular view. From here he could see the entirety of the Las Vegas strip. Once a bustling tourist trap, it now lay quiet save for the occasional resident scurrying home after a day out scavenging. At night, the once brightly lit casinos, now lay shrouded in darkness, the cost of illuminating their many bulbs too high in a world where electricity was a rare and valuable commodity.

Thin wisps of black smoke curled into the sky from smoldering ruins all over the city. Las Vegas, once a hedonistic paradise, had become a war zone and now served as the capital of the Resistance. Doc had always seen a certain irony in this. The police state government that the Resistance had rebelled against had used the promise of shallow, base pleasure as a lure to keep the public in line. And here they were, occupying the one city that was the very embodiment of hedonism as their capital.

Doc lifted the microphone to his mouth for a moment before lowering it. In his mind and the minds of the other council members, Charlene MacLeod had always been a laboratory monster disguised as a little girl. That had been how he had rationalized consigning her to the Cordoba Flats facility and allowing Dr. Coke to experiment on her. It had been this same view that had allowed him to order the deaths of untold numbers of Enlighteneds. They were monsters, with human masks. Rabid dogs that needed to be put down for the good of humanity. He had never felt an ounce of guilt for spilling their blood.

And yet now, as he held Charlene MacLeod's fate in his hands, Doc saw the girl in a new light. She was no longer a monster disguised as a little girl but rather a *victim*, an innocent child subjected to the depredations of a corrupt government. This girl was no more at fault for her power than a child with cystic fibrosis is at fault for his disability.

But a CF child is no threat. This girl can start fires, cause explosions, and she has killed. She may not be at fault of her power, but she is responsible for misusing it, and....fault is irrelevant anyway. The girl is dangerous regardless. She has to be put down.

As that last thought passed through his mind, Doc's blood chilled, and his heart began to thud against his ribs. For the first time, he found that he hated his duty. And yet hate would not turn him from his course. Doc pushed all thoughts of victimhood, pity, and compassion for this girl from his mind and clicked the transmit button on the old Motorola.

"Mercury, this is Doc."

The speaker crackled in return for a moment before a low female voice responded. "This is Mercury. What can I do for you?"

"I need you to forward a message to Cordoba Flats." Doc paused for a moment, still reluctant to issue the order. "Tell them that the Council has voted. Major Eric Rader is now in command and…" He paused again. "Charlene MacLeod, the McAuliffes and Stephen Wolf are to be terminated as soon as possible."

"Electrocution?" Mercury inquired.

"Yes," Doc replied. "And this is high priority, so put everything else on hold until you get a hold of them."

"Ten-Four," Mercury replied.

Mercury, (Doc didn't know her real name if she still had one.) was located in the former broadcast facilities of KGME in downtown Phoenix. Phoenix had recently suffered an airstrike, and Mercury had only gotten back online two days ago.

As he signed off and set the microphone back on its stand, Doc felt a powerful sense of foreboding, as if he had signed his own death warrant.

Doc turned from the Motorola and went to a nearby derelict bar. Before the Great Civil War, whales and trust fund babies would pay good money to drink cheap liquor and look out on the Strip from these bar stools. Now the bar lay empty, it's bottles of Smirnov, Seagram's and Dewers abandoned, it's air heavy with the stench of stale cigarettes and long ago spilled beer.

Doc went behind the bar and helped himself to a glass of Hennessey and a Phillies Blunt. As he took the first mouthful of cheap liquor and puffed at his dog turd of a cigar, Doc's heart rate picked up slightly. It was a mistake to kill the girl. He felt sure of that much though he did not understand why.

XXII

As Doc sat alone, smoking and drinking, Lord Beathach waited outside the fence line of Cordoba Flats. A small campfire burned at his feet. He had known of the girl's presence inside since she had arrived four days earlier and had intentionally taken no action.

She must see what they are capable of.

Until today Beathach had sensed that the Resistance wanted to experiment on Charlie and would keep her alive. Now, something had changed, and he felt that she was in mortal danger. He would have to take action.

Charlie was no lightweight. Given the opportunity, she could probably rescue herself and her adoptive parents. But Beathach would take no chances. He had seen what the Resistance did with Enlighteneds.

As he thought that Beathach found himself unwillingly pulled back into memory long forgotten. In the days that followed their wedding, Beathach and Alana lived in Sir James' household as husband and wife. Those days were, without question, the most joyous in Beathach's life. He loved Alana more than anything in the world, and she would be the only woman he would ever love.

In those days, Beathach had allowed himself to dream. He imaged acquiring a small manor house with a few hundred acres. After a few years, he and Alana would have children. Sons, strapping and brave; and daughters, beautiful and sweet. They would be happy and grow old together. But it was just a dream. In his bliss, Beathach had forgotten about his father and mother.

Malcolm MacAlpin had ambitions of marrying Beathach off to an English royal. Those hopes were now dashed. Beathach had also forgotten that he had left his father's home ostensibly to collect rents from Sir James. That had been over two weeks ago, and his father had begun to worry.

XXIII

On Saturday evening, three weeks to the day Beathach had left his family home, his father arrived at Sir James's door with several of his retainers. Sir James greeted them and invited them into the great hall where Beathach and Alana sat eating dinner and drinking.

"Lucius." Father's expression reflected genuine relief. "I was concerned when you failed to return."

"Father, I am sorry for worrying you." Without thinking, Beathach took Alana's hand.

For a moment, Father studied Beathach and Alana in silence. Then his expression began to harden. "Who is this woman?"

Beathach drew in a slow breath. "This is Alana, my wife."

Father's face darkened and flooded with blood. "Your wife?"

"Yes, I have married Alana,"

This time Father's expression turned to stone, and his cheeks turned a deep crimson. "You would marry without my consent? And to a low born girl?"

"I don't care about that father." Beathach fired back. "I love her, that's all that matters to me."

"You are of royal blood!" His father thundered. "You don't get to fall in love and marry whomever you want! You have a duty to the kingdom!" Father drew his sword. "It does not matter. You will be a widower soon enough, and then we will marry you off to House Wessex as it should have been."

"My Lord, please…" Sir James began.

All at once, the power leapt up with Beathach. As his father advanced towards the dais, Beathach lashed out with the power. A blue corona enveloped Father, and he was frozen solid mid-stride. Then an invisible hand took him and hurled him at the far wall where he shattered.

Sir Kendal and Sir John, Father's two closest retainers, both took a step backward and hissed: "Warlock!" before drawing their swords.

"My God…" Sir James' voice reflected sudden horror.

Alana screamed. "Lucius!" Beathach could feel her combined surprise and fright.

Beathach drew his own blade and steeled himself for a fight. Unconsciously he positioned himself between Alana and the two retainers.

The power was swirling within him, and he could have easily slaughtered Kendal and John, but he had no desire to do so. These men had once been his friends. Instead, he advanced with his sword, intending to disable them. Before he could, a crossbow bolt streaked down from above and to the right. Beathach stepped aside without thinking.

Alana screamed again, followed by the thud of a body. Beathach turned, and to his horror found his wife lying on her back in a pool of her own blood, the crossbow bolt now embedded in the center of her chest. Tears streamed from her eyes as she fought for each ragged breath.

Beathach felt his breath taken away, and his heart lock in his chest. "Alana!" Her name passed his lips in a voice he did not recognize. "What did they do to you?"

Her lips moved as if to speak, but no sound came. Still, he could hear her voice in his mind. *I love you, Lucius, I have always loved you, and I will always love you.*

"I love you too." He whispered as he took her into his arms.

Alana took one final, shuddering breath and then went limp in his arms. Beathach reached out to her with his mind but found nothing but blank space. She was gone.

With slow, deliberation, he got to his feet, the power blazing. Before he could strike, the world exploded in white, setting his skull to ringing and throbbing. White rapidly faded to black until only the pain remained.

XXIV

When his vision cleared hours later, Beathach found himself tied to a vertical wooden post atop a massive pyre. He had somehow been transported to a field outside of Sir James's castle. A crowd consisting of Sir James and his household, together with a dozen peasants, looked on with darkened eyes. The force of their hatred and fear washed over him in alternating waves of fire and ice.

"He's awake." Kendal declared.

Sir James stepped forward from the crowd. "Lucius, son of Malcolm, for the crimes of murder and witchcraft, I hereby sentence you to be burned at the stake."

Blood thundered in Beathach's temples as his heart threatened to burst from his chest. Both Kendal and John advanced on him, armed with firebrands.

Oh, fuck!

The power stirred within him, Beathach reached out with his mind and attempted to release his own bonds without success. John lowered his torch first.

"Burn in hell. Monster!" There was a low ***-warrump-*** as the pyre beneath his feet caught. At first, the flames remained small. Then Kendal lowered his brand, and the fire grew. Deep inside, something broke, and Beathach felt his heart turn cold, even as it continued to leap against his ribs.

Beathach had not seen who had fired the crossbow that killed his wife, but it didn't matter. They were all to blame, all of them. Everything felt unreal as if he were dreaming rather than awake. Perhaps this was a dream. Flames licked up the logs at Beathach's feet and enveloped his legs sending an explosion of searing pain radiated up from his scorched flesh.

Not a dream...

Within a few seconds, the flames spread from his legs to his torso enveloping his body in blazing agony. Beathach wanted to cry out but found that he could not. The power was racing within him now, and he had no remaining reason to hold it back.

You killed my wife. You will kill me if I let you.

Beathach's heart burned with hatred even as the fire spread to Beathach's face, and he felt the skin, muscles, and fat of the left side of his face begin to melt and run like tallow before erupting into flame. The sensation of burning was so horrible as to be almost insupportable, and yet he felt every agonizing minute. Time slowed. The power raged within, driven to fury by his hatred and suffering. Beathach felt himself growing weak, his damaged body turning stiff and unresponsive, his tormented mind beginning to drift away. The world grew hazy and far away, as if viewed through thick fog over a vast chasm. Black spots began to appear before his eyes and multiply. He was dying.

Before his mind faded away completely, Beathach drew inward, to where the power lay and immersed himself within it. Then, without pausing, he unleashed the power in one massive, pumping shockwave. All at once Beathach felt the flames that had enveloped his body absorbed within like a sponge. The sensation was intoxicating. Beathach unleased more of the power and great, blue-white bolts of unknown energy streaked out across the green Scottish moors ripping through the gathered crowd. Men, women, and children cried out in agony and terror as their life force was suddenly and violently ripped away. Beathach felt his dying body suddenly energized. His flesh warmed and the flaming torment drifted into nothingness.

As he slowly descended the pyre that was meant for his funeral, Beathach let his eyes drift over the newborn hellscape before him. The ground at his feet was scorched black. Ashen remains of what had once been moor grasses crunched with each step. Charred skeletal trees dotted a landscape littered with burned-out, human remains.

With slow steps, Beathach approached the smoking remains of Sir James.

Such is the fate of traitors.

In his heart, Beathach felt only cold hate. They had taken *everything* from him. His wife, his family, his friends gone. And then they had burned him alive. The physical pain had left him, the agony in his heart had crystallized into iron hatred.

He had spent all of his young life hiding the power, trying to live within the rules of ordinary humans, trying to please his mother and father. As his reward they had murdered Alana, rejected him and tried to kill him. Never again. All that remained to him was vengeance, and he would seek it with all of his being.

Now, as he stood over the flames of his campfire, Beathach's blood ran cold. The fire danced mockingly, as if it knew what had been done to him so many years ago. Beathach swept the flames with his power, quickly absorbing their heat into his cold flesh where they would give him renewed strength.

The darkness was gathering, and the Lawgivers of Cordoba Flats were preparing for an execution. He would have to act now if he wanted to save Charlie.

XXV

After the sun had dropped below the horizon, Frank and another male Lawgiver Charlie had never seen before entered her suite in the science building. Both men were armed with tasers and steel handcuffs.

"It's time." Frank's voice was low and menacing. He reached into his leather long coat and produced a syringe loaded with clear liquid. "Before we head out to the courtyard, I have some medicine for you."

Charlie stared at him with cold eyes. "What is that?"

“Just some medicine to help you relax.” He replied in that same low voice.

“Where are you taking me?” She already knew the answer to this question but wanted to hear him say it.

“You know,” Frank replied. “I know you can read my mind.”

Although the power remained far away, she could. The apartment, once cheery, now seemed empty and surreal. The air inside, arctic cold. Charlie shivered and clutched her slender body. Her heart began to thump against her ribs, faster and faster. Her blood, now bitter ice, froze her flesh stiff as death.

Still, despite her mortal terror, Charlie resolved not to give this man the pleasure of seeing her break. So she met his gaze with a hard icy stare.

“Put out your arm, Charlie,” Frank commanded.

Charlie stood up from her chair but kept her arms at her sides. The other Lawgiver grabbed her arm and pulled her against his chest. Up close Charlie could smell shitty cigar smoke on his clothing. His hands were rough, his skin sallow and hairy. Charlie fought against him to no avail as he was impossibly strong. The man grasped her chin in his left hand and turned her face towards his.

“Stop it.” He instructed her as if she were a naughty girl teasing her little brother or sister.

His face was dark and weather-beaten from exposure to the sun and wind. Charlie redoubled her efforts, but to her dismay, the man was able to forcibly extend her right arm.

Frank swabbed Charlie’s arm with alcohol and neatly slid the needle into the vein in the crook of her elbow. Sharp stinging pain erupted from the place where the needle penetrated her flesh and radiated up her arm. Charlie bit back a moan.

The drug, whatever it was, did not make her feel any calmer. It did, however, put the power further out of her reach. Still, her psychic senses remained relatively sharp. And she could feel Frank’s cold intent. He would take her from her apartment to the camp parade grounds where several inmates had set up a portable electric chair. He would then strap her to the chair, shave her head and electrocute her. David and Catherine would be electrocuted too. Charlie felt they were outside already. Mortal terror exploded within her.

Please, I don’t want to die! I’m just a kid! Please!

The nameless Lawgiver tightened his grip on her arm and dragged her from her apartment. Charlie began to hyperventilate. The corridor outside her apartment passed by as if in a nightmare. The lights were too bright, the air too still and heavy with chlorine. The floor, radiant from recent waxing, clacked and echoed with each step she took. All too quickly she found herself in the elevator descending to the ground floor. Once there, the elevator slammed to a stop, and the doors banged open, nearly causing her to scream.

Not long after leaving the elevator, Charlie found herself outside. Frank and the other, nameless

Lawgiver led her towards the parade grounds at the center of the camp. Here two dozen Lawgivers stood at attention in two opposite rows. Between them sat the camp's electric chair, squat, ugly, and terrible; crafted out of red oak. Behind it stood a massive generator, already emitting its demonic roar.

At the sight of the electric chair, Charlie's legs collapsed beneath her, and she nearly wet herself. She had faced many horrors in her short life, and yet this seemed the worst of all of them. In her mind, she recalled those last moments of agony while she was in the grip of the NSA's poison. She remembered feeling her heart stop.

Please! Not again!

"Charlie!" She snapped around at the sound of her name to see David and Catherine standing at the far end of the two rows of Lawgivers. They both looked on stone-faced. The force of their terror struck her in an icy wave. Stephen Wolf stood behind them, his face blank and inscrutable. His mind radiating horror.

"Please don't hurt my family!" David begged. "If you have to kill someone, kill me. But please let my wife and daughter go!"

The Lawgivers did not respond.

"PLEASE!" He repeated. The force of his desperation nearly took her off her feet.

As if in answer, the nameless Lawgiver dragged Charlie towards the electric chair. Charlie's heart began to slam against her ribs as her flesh and blood turned to black ice. Flesh rending tremors ripped through her muscles. Charlie stifled an urge to cry out to David and beg him to help her.

David tried to run to her only to be restrained by a pair of Lawgivers. One of them struck David in the face with a rifle butt.

"Knock it off! Your turn will come soon enough."

"You mother fuckers!" David screamed. His icy fear turning to biting desperation.

Charlie's pulse was thundering in her head, sending white spots flashing across her vision. Tears stung her eyes though she did not feel like crying, rather she thought she might faint.

She had closed to within five feet of the chair when her legs would no longer support her. Frank took her left arm and hoisted her back onto her feet for the remaining distance.

"This won't hurt for long, Charlie," Frank assured her. "Once the power is turned on your brain will be destroyed, and it will be lights out forever."

Charlie fought back an urge to cry out in terror. Instead, she pulled her arms from both men's grip and walked the remaining distance to the electric chair under her own power before sitting down.

Lawgivers immediately swarmed her from all sides, drawing heavy leather straps tight across her arms, legs, and chest. It did not hurt, yet the touch of the leather bit into her flesh enough to send fresh tremors through her muscles.

Frank stopped directly in front of her, electric clippers in one hand. "I'm going to shave your head where the electrode will go. You can either cooperate or be restrained." Without waiting for her answer, Frank switched on the clippers and pushed Charlie against the chair back with his left hand before proceeding to buzz cut the top of her head.

Charlie's heart sank, even as it sent cold blood rushing through her veins. *Please don't… Please, I'm just a kid I don't want to die.*

Charlie reached for the power and found to her horror that it had deserted her. ***PLEASE! I DON'T WANT TO DIE!***

-Buzzzzzzzzzz-

The whirr of the clippers sent cold tremors up her spine and back, making it hard for her to sit up straight. Within a few minutes, Frank had finished with the clippers. A tall female Lawgiver with auburn hair and hard, golden eyes stepped forward and smeared the now buzz cut portion of Charlie's head with shaving cream before handing Frank a battered Gillette razor.

Frank tested the blade by slicing open his finger before beginning. The razor's touch was an icy sting. A soft moan escaped Charlie's lips.

"It'll be over soon, Charlie." Frank's callous tone shocked her.

Silent tears spilled from Charlie's eyes and cut hot rivers down her cheeks. She wanted to be somewhere else. Anywhere.

"It's going to be ok, Charlie." David's voice was artificially calm. Behind it, Charlie felt powerful desperation and grief, as if she were already gone.

He's given up. The thought plunged Charlie's heart into darkness. *Then there is no escape.*

Charlie bowed her head, resigned to her fate.

"Charlie, listen to me." David was saying. "Close your eyes. Don't pay attention to anything but the sound of my voice. You're going to be all right. We're far away from here. We're together. We're someplace far away where they can't hurt us anymore. Just hold that picture in your mind while they do this. Don't think about anything else, just picture us at that safe place."

The same words he had spoken the day she was first strapped to the Black Empire's steel table. David's words had done nothing to mitigate her suffering then, and she doubted they would help her now. Still, she was touched by his sweetness. She began to cry in earnest now. Not out of fear but heartbreak. She loved David and Catherine, they were her Dad and Mom now, and they loved her as much as Daddy and Mommy ever had. And now that time was over, and she would pass into whatever lay beyond.

Frank had finished shaving the crown of her head, leaving her with a bald patch on the top of her head. Under other circumstances, she would have been mortified. On this evening, her scalp felt cold, and she felt only frightened desperation. A slow, chilly breeze stirred the evening air. There was no moon in the sky, making for an exceptionally dark night.

Having finished shaving Charlie's head, Frank stepped in front of her once more. "Do you have any last words before we terminate you?"

"I…I'm scared." The words escaped her lips before she could stifle them. Frank nodded, and someone behind her placed something cold and wet on her scalp. Icy water streamed down both of her cheeks and mingled with her tears. Charlie's breath quickened until white spots flashed before her eyes. A few seconds later, purple haze followed. Now someone was placing a heavy metal helmet on her head and strapping it under her chin. Charlie swallowed hard, fighting a sudden urge to vomit.

"Please, I can't…I can't do this."

She could barely breathe now. Her heart threatened to burst from her chest. Painful shudders rippled through her frozen body.

Frank bent down and smeared her leg with something cold and slimy. Then he clamped a cold metal electrode to her calf. A moment later, a black cloth dropped in front of her eyes leaving her shrouded in darkness.

"Roll on one." Frank's voice came to her from nowhere. All at once, the generator's roar grew to a cacophony in the darkness. For an unknown period of time, Charlie sat there listening to the growl of the generator and the thumping of her own heart. Her breath came in short, ragged gasps, and her muscles rippled involuntarily. Hot tears streamed down her cheeks.

Please, I can't do this. I don't want to die.

Again Frank's voice came to her through the darkness. "Roll on two."

In an instant, Charlie's vision changed, and she found herself looking at the tall auburn-haired Lawgiver who had assisted Frank in shaving Charlie's head. Now she was standing over a large triple throw, knife switch, her golden eyes hard as forged steel. Her mind radiating cold malice.

As Charlie watched, the auburn-haired Lawgiver closed her rubber-gloved left hand over the knife switch and threw it closed.

All at once, the darkness lit up in a bright blue-white corona. Charlie felt herself carried into the coronal light until it was all she knew, all that mattered.

Chapter 11
The Broken and the Lost

I

Because no one has restrained her or attempted to interfere, the bereaved woman turns on a second bar patron. This one, a man of middle age and slight girth, wears an open-collared pink button shirt under a gray sharkskin suit. The bereaved woman suddenly lets out a cry of pure suffering and outrage. Her eyes wild with madness; she thrusts her knife into the center of the shark skin's abdomen and then rips it free, spraying blood across the barroom and spilling his entrails onto the hardwood floor.

The Gentlemen in white and black both look on with sorrow and horror, understanding at once that the now dying man in the sharkskin suit had earned his mortal knife wound but also confident in the knowledge that the bereaved woman had to be stopped. Before either gentleman can act, a monstrous revenant of a man appears from the shadows in the back of the tavern to confront the bereaved woman.

As the man from the shadows approaches the bereaved woman, the man in the red suit has begun to regain the initiative against the man in the blue denim work shirt and is landing blows about the second man's head and face.

The man in the blue denim work shirt stumbles backward and collapses into the table where the gentlemen in white and black have been playing their game. Chess pieces scatter across the tavern floor, some of them breaking apart on impact. In a fit of impotent anger, the man in the blue denim work shirt grabs up the white queen and whips it at the man in the red suit's face. The man in the red suit ducks and the white queen clatters off a support beam before landing somewhere in the back of the bar.

A rifle crack from outside punctuates the cacophony inside the bar, and for a moment, everyone freezes. Then the brawl recommences with increased fury.

"Perhaps we should put a stop to this." The gentleman in black suggests to the gentleman in white.

The gentleman in white meets the gentleman in black's gaze evenly. "No, we must respect their free will and allow them to settle this among themselves. We cannot interfere."

"You are right, of course, my friend. But it seems wasteful to allow them to tear the world apart like this, and they are threatening to kill the girl. Shall we allow them to do so when she is so vital to the game at hand?" As he speaks, the gentleman in black fills two draughts from the tap behind the bar and hands one to the gentleman in white. "Drink up my friend. It will be a long night."

The gentleman in white accepts the gesture. "Thank you. I would think that you of all people would be most in favor of leaving them to decide for themselves. Did you not say that they can only embrace the darkness willingly?"

"I did indeed." The gentleman in black replies as he sips his beer. "Yet, it seems a shame to allow them to cause such destruction to no purpose."

"It does indeed. But that is the price of free will."

II

Kane had long since learned that travel backward in time for the purposes of changing present and future events would produce dangerous and unpredictable results. Viewing the future though, now that was something else entirely. Here, time was a river delta where he could see and experience thousands of possible streams, eddies, creeks, and side branches, any one of which could come to be or not. As dangerous and unpredictable as it was to tamper with the past, was as enigmatic and confounding as it was to try to predict which version of the future would come to pass.

Nevertheless, Kane did his best to foresee likely future events, and pursued his goals as a chess master, always thinking six moves ahead. Several days ago, before the Resistance leadership council voted to terminate Charlie MacLeod, the power presented him with a clear vision of the girl all grown up and with a tow-headed daughter of maybe seven or eight. Beside her stood a tall, dark-haired man of middle age. His coral, green eyes shone with fatherly pride. The three of them looked happy, untroubled by the collapsing world around them. Though he knew not how this future would come to be, Kane felt strongly that this would be the future…*if*...

If Charlie and her family escaped from the Resistance *unharmed.* If they could escape to somewhere safe and Kane knew of such a place.

In the days that followed the outbreak of the Great Civil War, Australia had become a sanctuary for Enlighteneds and those who did not wish to be involved in the fighting. While there were Australian citizens with sympathies for both sides of the conflict, the people quickly resolved these differences more or less peacefully and decided to remain neutral, opening their island nation to all refugees from the conflict.

Charlie and her family would be safe there, increasing the likelihood of the future in which Charlie had her own daughter. And that child…

The murder of Charlie's parents nearly drove her over the edge…If she loses her daughter too then, it will break her…

A cruel smile played across Kane's lips. With a slow and deliberate movement, he slid his hand under the bowl of the brandy snifter on the end table to his right and carefully lifted it to his lips before taking a slow sip. As the bitter liquor rolled across his tongue and down his throat, Kane gazed out onto the cityscape of the Black Imperial capital, bathed in fading golden sunlight.

Following the outbreak of the Great Civil War, Kane had sent Lord Beathach to silently watch over Charlie and her parents and given him a free hand in how he carried out the task. Kane knew of the Rouge, Kira Morozov, and of Lord Beathach's plan to use her to manipulate the girl's adoptive father. This mattered little, Kane recognized the threat posed by the Rouge but cared little. Kira was not especially powerful and represented only a moderate danger. A danger that could be managed or eliminated at any time. And he doubted that David McAuliffe could be so readily made to abandon false morality. Like his daughter, David was committed to a strong ethical code and would not turn from it easily. Still, it would be amusing to watch David squirm, and if he did kill Kira Morozov then he would be eliminating a problem.

"The priority is that you bring the girl and her family to safety Lord Beathach." Kane had instructed the dark lord at their last meeting. "You may try to persuade the girl's father to kill the Rouge if you wish, but the girl and her parents must be taken to safety."

"As you wish, my Master." Lord Beathach had replied, in an emotionless bass.

There was little chance that the Rouge posed a significant threat to David McAuliffe. Though not as powerful as the girl, David McAuliffe was nevertheless stronger than a typical Enlightened.

And he wields Deus Irae. He'll easily kill the Rouge. If he even tries…

Kane took a long sip of brandy and set his snifter down before walking towards the northern floor-length picture window of the Grand Observation Lounge. The sun had begun to dip below the horizon bathing the sky in crimson.

Lord Beathach would do his duty. Of that, Kane was certain. And Beathach was powerful enough to rescue the girl and her parents from the Resistance and safely transport them to Australia. The chess pieces were moving into the proper positions, but he could not be sure. The future was always in flux, always changing. There was no way to know for sure that the image he had seen would come to pass.

III

Kira awakened suddenly from a deep sleep to the sensation of a dark stranger. Kira's eyes slid open to reveal the dim outline of her hotel room. Here was the white oak dresser, the matching table and two chairs, the long-dead flat-screen television and in the shadows near the door the black silhouette of a titan of a man. For a moment, the figure just stood there unmoving before crossing the room in massive strides.

"Who are you?" Kira's heart thumped against her ribs as the words left her lips. Her psychic senses told her only that this man, whoever he was, was not an Enlightened. Rather, he was something otherworldly and immensely powerful.

The figure stepped into the moonlight to reveal a deathly pale face with black, vacuous eyes and long, straggly black hair. The scent of death wafted from his massive frame. Kira reached out to the figure with her mind and found only a shadowy void. From this void radiated power beyond anything she had ever touched before. Kira had faced Dark Knights several times in her life, and this man's power was beyond even theirs.

"What do you want?" Kira's blood chilled at the high pitched fear in her voice.

"You know who I am." The figure responded in a low, gravelly voice. "And you know why I am here."

Kira's mind swam with a thousand shards of half-memory. Her daughter Aria, her husband Terry, Gary Volkov, Sergei Markovic, Aria's murder, her mentor Ashley Underwood. Ashley had taught her what it meant to be a Lightwarrior, the commitment, and rules which she would be pledged to live by.

"You have broken the Accord." The figure continued.

Suddenly several fragmented images fell together into a clear memory. The Accord required all conflicts between Lightwarriors and Dark Knights to be resolved in one on one combat using the sword. It further prohibited any use of the Power that would expose the existence of Enlighteneds to an Outsider. Violations of the Accord would be punished by the Arbiter.

"You are the Arbiter," Kira replied in a calm tone. Her heart was thundering in her chest now. "I have violated no provision of the Accord."

"You have used the power to seek revenge upon several Outsiders. You were careless and have allowed the Outsiders to learn of your activities." With each word, the Arbiter's power pulsed in the air.

Kira felt her blood suddenly catch fire, and her face flush. The power moved within her, threatening to break out at any moment. "Those men *raped and murdered* my child! They took away the only person I had left in this world! They deserved to die!"

"You are a Lightwarrior Kira Morozov. You are not permitted to take revenge, and certainly not when your vengeance exposes the existence of Enlighteneds." The Arbiter's expression remained emotionless as he spoke.

"Fuck the Accord then!" Kira screamed back at him. Before she could say anything further, a second, smaller figure stepped from the shadows near the door. Kira recognized it at once.

"Aria!" Her heart soared as she spoke her daughter's name.

"Mom, I tried to tell you." Kira could feel the force of her daughter's sorrow both in her voice and her mind.

"Tell me what, Baby?" Kira already knew the answer despite her wish to the contrary.

"I tried to tell you that if you took revenge on those men that you would be letting them hurt you. Now it's too late." A single tear trickled from Aria's right eye and ran down her cheek.

Kira felt her heart rip in two inside her chest. Tears streamed from her red, tired eyes. "I miss you so much, Baby."

"I miss you too, Mom but why couldn't you just listen."

"I…I couldn't help it." Kira sobbed. "It hurts so much, and I'm all alone now."

Aria ran to Kira and wrapped her arms around Kira's neck. "You're not alone, Mom. I never left you. Why couldn't you just stop?"

The Arbiter was watching her with blank eyes. Though Aria had appeared behind him, he did not seem to react to her presence. Instead, he waited patiently for Kira's attention to return to him.

"I love you, Mom," Aria whispered through her tears.

"I love you too, Baby." As Kira spoke the words, she realized that she was alone again. A painful sob escaped her throat.

"Kira Morozov, for your violation of the Accord I hereby sentence you to madness. You shall be haunted by the image of your daughter but shall never be reunited with her. Your daughter's image shall condemn your every remaining step in this life, and you shall live with the guilt of your actions. You shall have no escape and no relief until draw your last breath. You will see your daughter at every turn, and she will *damn* you."

With those last words, the Arbiter vanished, leaving Kira alone in her hotel room. For a moment Kira sat perfectly still, her mind reeling with fragmented memory and snatches of half-considered thought. Then she suddenly burst into heart-rending, wracking sobs.

Aria was alive, she felt sure of it. She still had clear memories of her daughter's death, and yet she *knew* that Aria somehow still lived. Kira needed only to find -her.

An image of a girl formed in the back of Kira's mind. At first, she recognized the girl as Charlene MacLeod, the little girl from the last news reports. The little firebrand who had burned down Castle Bruce. Then, slowly, the little girl morphed, her hair and eyes darkening, her face maturing until she became Aria.

IV

Cody Rochefort sat at the dinner table with his wife and son, eating the last of a meal of canned Spam and Bush's baked beans. The radio was on, and all three of them listened intently to the evening reports on the war. This had become a nightly ritual for the Rochefort family since the Loyalists had begun to launch a counter-offensive against the Resistance. In the initial weeks of the Great Civil War, the Resistance had successfully pushed the Loyalists as far east as the Appalachian mountains. However, more recently the Loyalists had successfully driven the Resistance west of the Mississippi and were attacking Resistance cities all along the river.

Tonight's transmission reported airstrikes on Memphis and Davenport and an army of Loyalist forces advancing through Shiloh to reinforce the existing Loyalist forces in East Saint Louis.

The Loyalists would soon storm Saint Louis, that much was certain, and Cody had no intention of remaining in the city with his family when the attack came.

As that thought crossed his mind, the female voice on the radio suddenly changed tone.

"Loyalist forces have been sighted crossing the Mississippi River into Saint Louis. I repeat Loyalist forces have been sighted crossing the Mississippi River into Saint Louis. All residents are advised to evacuate immediately. If you are unable to evacuate, then you are advised to shelter in basements and remain off the streets…" The female voice was cut off in a burst of static.

A moment later, air raid sirens rang out on the early evening air. Cody's heart leapt up in his throat.

"We need to go, now!"

Stephanie met Cody's gaze. "Where? This is our home. All of our family lives in Loyalist territory. Where do you suggest we run to?"

He shook his head. "I don't know, but we can't stay here. We have our collection of CDs and the boom box, maybe we can trade them for a hotel room somewhere in Kansas."

"Are you sure we can get that far, Cody. There's only a half tank in the car. That'll get us out of the city and maybe halfway across the state, but that's it. How are we going to pay for gas and a hotel?"

"We could trade some of our extra ammunition," Cody replied in a tone far more hopeful than he felt. In truth, he had no plan. Cody only knew that he had to get his family out of the city before the Loyalist's army attacked in earnest.

As that thought passed through Cody's mind, the ground shook under his feet as the first bombs struck the eastern side of the city.

Cody's heart quickened, and he felt his senses sharpening as adrenaline dumped into his blood. "We have to go NOW!"

Stephanie nodded as she stood up from her seat at the table and took their son's hand. "Come on,

Blake, it's time to go."

He looked frightened, though he maintained his cool. "We are we going?"

"We're going to head to Kansas, Kansas City to start with. Then maybe Wichita." Cody had to fight to keep the fear out of his voice.

"Okay, Dad." Blake's voice remained calm, but his eyes had grown wide, and his breathing quickened ever so slightly. Cody spotted the first dots of sweat on his son's forehead.

Ten minutes later, Cody was behind the wheel of the same '92 Jeep Cherokee he had taken the night the Great Civil War had broken out. Stephanie sat at his right while Blake sat in the back with all of the supplies the old Jeep could carry. The city had already descended into chaos. Hundreds of cars and trucks choked the roads, while pedestrians milled about between them. The rumble and boom of falling bombs had grown closer, and he was at a dead standstill on Lindell Boulevard.

The December sky had gone from black satin to baleful orange, set alight by fires close enough to terrify. Thick, choking smoke tainted the cold air, filling his nostrils with the acrid stench of burning plastic and insulation. Cody's heart thundered in his ears, his skin erupted in sweaty goosebumps. He could not just sit here with his family and wait for the bombs to drop in their midst. Cody quickly scanned the street and sighted an alleyway between two buildings. The passage was darkened, and he could not tell if it was a through road or not, but seeing no other option, Cody elected to try his luck.

"Cody, what are you doing?" Stephanie's frightened tone pierced through the growing haze in his mind.

"We need to get out of this traffic before they start bombing here. That alley looks clear, maybe we can get to a street with less traffic." Cody was amazed by how calm his voice sounded. Inside he felt wound tight enough to explode.

"Are you sure that alley is a through street?" Stephanie replied.

"No, but we can't just sit here and wait to be bombed." As he spoke, it occurred to Cody that if the alley turned out to be a dead-end, then they would probably die there. But then if they didn't get out of this traffic, they would die anyway.

Cody pulled the Jeep out of the line of cars and into the shadows of the alley. The headlight beams revealed a narrow passage that let out to what appeared to be a vacant street.

As he carefully drove down the street, a gunshot rang out, and a bullet slammed into the windshield. Stephanie and Blake both screamed. Blake ducked below the seat as Cody had taught him, Stephanie remained frozen in place. A red blotch appeared over her right shoulder. Cody stared at it stupidly for what seemed like hours, but in truth was probably only minutes before reality sank in.

"Oh my God, Stephanie, are you ok?"

She took in a shuddering gasp of air. "I'll be fine. Just get us out of here."

A second gunshot pierced the night air and shattered the driver's side mirror. This time Cody saw the shooter, a teenage boy, armed with a revolver almost as big as he was, stood at the end of the alley firing madly at them. Cody drew his Glock 17 from its holster beside his seat and fired several shots at the boy, striking him in the left shoulder, chest, and head. Blood pouring from his wounds, the boy dropped his revolver and crumpled to the street. Without pausing, Cody floored the accelerator and raced from the alleyway before any further threats could appear. The alley let out on Forest Park Parkway, which while not devoid of cars, was at least moving. Unfortunately, the street was also awash in armed looters and rioters and before long traffic had slowed to a crawl.

Cody's heart began to pick up again as his skin rashed out in fresh goosebumps. Dozens of hands thumped against the old Jeep's windows as he slowly drove along the roadway. Jets roared overhead. Moments later a series deafening roars punctuated the night air, each closer than the last.

Blake screamed. "Daaad!" Then everything vanished into blinding, muted white. When his vision cleared a moment later, Cody found himself hanging upside down in his seatbelt. Stephanie hung motionless beside him. Cody released himself and crawled to her. A touch of her neck revealed no pulse and her flesh had already begun to cool.

Dead...

The word slammed through him like a cold knife in the night. Before he could lose his mind to grief, Cody crawled into the back seat to look for his son. He found Blake hanging upside down from his lap belt, his head twisted and cocked at an unnatural angle. As he had done with his wife, Cody checked Blake's pulse only to find that he too was gone.

Broken neck.

Cody clenched his jaw, grabbed his Glock, and crawled from the wreckage of his Jeep. His family was gone, all he had left now was his own survival. And for a while survival was the only thought on his mind. Something, some switch deep inside him, shut down, leaving him cold and without feeling. The reality, the terrible pain, and loss of what had happened did not yet touch him for his heart had been temporarily shut down.

Operating mostly on autopilot, Cody fought his way out of St. Louis as bombs rained from the sky. As the sun peeked over the horizon, Cody took shelter in a battered doublewide trailer on the outskirts of the city. Sleep came over him quickly, and in his dreams, he was reunited with his family.

V

Cody would have been glad to never awaken, but after several hours had passed, cruel reality broke through his blissful dreams. Cody groaned and looked around the bedroom. He lay on soiled low thread count sheets covered by a ragged leopard print comforter. The mattress itself was a hard slab with several broken springs. Behind his head stood a black vinyl headboard. Several jagged tears revealed crumbling, time-yellowed foam filler, and particle board backing.

A sand-colored pressboard half dresser and nightstand rounded out the room's furnishings. Cody dragged himself from the bed and headed for the trailer's kitchen in the futile hope of finding something edible. Unsurprisingly, the cupboards were bare, and the refrigerator empty save for a jug filled a quarter deep with a suspicious grey liquid that might have once been milk.

Having found no food, Cody moved on to the remainder of the trailer, which he found picked bare of anything useful. Emptyhanded, Cody ventured outside to find that he had stopped for the night in Copperfield Estates, a trailer park near the airport in Chesterfield.

Cody searched several other trailers with little success before stumbling across a small cache of Campbell's Soups and Chicken of the Sea in a battered Winnebago. Suspecting that the Winnebago was most likely still occupied, Cody quickly fled the trailer park. After putting what he thought was a safe distance between himself and the Winnebago, Cody went shopping for a car.

Cody found an abandoned Ford Fiesta in the parking lot of a Trader Joe's. Upon approaching the car, Cody hesitated for a moment. He hated thieves, and he had already more than likely stolen the last of some poor soul's food. Now he was about to take a car that could belong to anyone, even a family.

A family like mine.

Cody's heart began to tear apart, and he had to push the thought aside before it could take root. *Better not think about that now. Just focus on the task at hand.*

But the thought remained. The little Ford could be some family's only escape from the advancing Loyalist army.

Before he could change his mind, Cody took out his sidearm and shattered the driver's side window before reaching inside and unlocking the door. Cody had only successfully hotwired a car once, but he remembered how to do it, and in fifteen minutes, he had the little car's four-banger engine growling to life.

As it turned out, the little Ford had three-quarters of a tank of gas, more than he would have dared hope for and enough to carry him at least halfway across Missouri. This discovery filled him with renewed guilt, for he felt certain now that this car had been readied for someone's escape. Now they would most certainly be trapped to face the Loyalist army.

The roads of Chester were quiet and mostly deserted save for a light scattering of abandoned cars. Cody headed for Interstate 64, all the while praying that it would not be choked off by stalled traffic. To his immense relief, Cody found the interstate passible despite a scattering of abandoned cars and trucks.

Cody spent the remainder of that day behind the wheel heading west. For a while, he listened to the radio broadcasts of the ongoing battle for Saint Louis. By three o'clock that afternoon, the reports indicated that Resistance forces had withdrawn to the city outskirts and were preparing for a tactical retreat further into Missouri.

They're not playing around.

As that thought passed through his mind, Cody glanced down at the fuel gauge and saw that he had only a quarter tank left. He would have to get off the highway to look for fuel.

Cody took the ramp for exit 78A and turned towards Marshall Junction as there was a sign indicating there were several gas stations in that direction. Cody hoped like hell that one of them would still have fuel. This time he was lucky. Cody found a 76 station with a substantial quantity of gasoline and several plastic gas cans. There was no electricity rendering the pumps inoperable, but Cody was able to siphon fuel directly from the gas station's underground storage tanks.

After filling the Ford and six gas cans, Cody set out once more. An hour later, he reached the outskirts of Kansas City. Cody found the city in chaos as the radio reports had indicated that Kansas City, too, had suffered Loyalist airstrikes. Now the Resistance had ordered the city evacuated in anticipation of a Loyalist incursion.

Rather than drive through the city, Cody decided to drive around, heading south until he had reached Harrisonville and then heading west into Kansas.

Cody stopped for the evening at an abandoned Motel 6 in Hays, Kansas. That night Stephanie and Blake visited him in his sleep once more.

VI

It was a warm summer day, and Cody had taken his family to Six Flags in Eureka. The three of them had reached the front of the line for The Boss. Cody boarded first with Blake, while Stephanie slid into the seat behind them. After a few moments the safety bars dropped, and a teenage ride attendant made the rounds up and down the train checking to see that everyone was secure. Once satisfied, the young girl signaled the ride operator. A moment later there was a sharp hiss of airbrakes being released, and the train lurched forward.

The warm morning sun shone down from a perfect blue, summer sky. Beside him, Blake let out a shout of excitement.

"No fear!"

Cody smiled. "I don't know that hill looks pretty steep."

Blake returned a reckless grin. "I'm not scared, Dad."

The train coasted onto the incline of the first drop, locking onto the lift chain with a sharp ***-clack-***

and then began to ascend.

Cody looked down on his son and smiled. Blake was a good boy, he earned excellent grades in school and tried hard to please his mother and father. He deserved to have fun today, and the expression of excitement and pleasure on his face brought joy to Cody's heart.

Cody returned a fatherly smile. "Are you ready?"

"Yep," Blake replied, still wearing that same reckless grin.

The train was nearing the top now. The low clack and rattle of the lift chain echoed ominously beneath them, warning of the sharp drop to come.

Cody and Blake both enjoyed roller coasters. Behind them, Stephanie let out a little cry of excitement and fear. She too enjoyed these rides though she often feigned fear. The train had now reached the top of the first drop. There was a low ***-bang-*** and the train dropped down slightly as it released from the lift chain. The track ahead turned a slight corner and then dropped precipitously. As the train accelerated down the first hill, Cody felt his stomach drop into his shoe beside, and behind him, his son and wife cried out in combined fear and excitement.

The ride was over quickly, and within ten minutes, Cody stood outside The Boss with Stephanie and Cody discussing which ride they would go to next. It was a perfect day, and yet he knew this could not be real.

Somewhere, in the back of his mind, a voice insisted that he was dreaming. Cody tried to suppress this voice. On this day, he did not care. He was with his wife and son; that was all that mattered. And yet the voice remained insistent.

This isn't real. You have to wake up.

Cody forcefully stifled the voice. *I don't care! I don't care! It doesn't matter! I don't care!*

All he wanted was to enjoy the time with his family, to be a husband and father once more. It didn't matter that this made no sense, that memory reminded him of the deaths of his wife and son. All that mattered was that they were here *now.* And so he intentionally lost himself in that day, allowing himself to live in that moment alone without regard for past or future.

Finally, as the sun became low and the shadows grew long, Stephanie took him aside behind a pizza stand near one of the park's steel roller coasters. At first, she just kissed him, then she met his eyes with a tear in one eye and a heart-rending expression of sorrow.

"You're dreaming, Cody." She began. "You know that don't you."

Cody met her gaze steadily. "I don't care. You and Blake are all that matter to me. I want to stay with you forever."

Stephanie's expression saddened still more. "I love you, Cody, Blake loves you. We don't want to be away from you, but you have to wake up now."

Cody's eyes began to sting, his heart torn in half. "I don't want to leave you. Please…"

"I know." She replied, her voice heavy with compassion and sorrow. "But we have moved on, and it's not your time. You have to wake up now."

"I don't want to go back. I just want to stay here with you." Before he could say anything further, the world rolled away, and he found himself sitting upright in his ragged and sprung Motel 6 bed.

VII

Cody slid out of bed and went to the mirror above the dresser. He wanted a drink, needed a drink, but had not yet found any alcohol. All at once, the sight of his pale, sleep-deprived, and broken face stirred a hot flame in his chest.

Too weak! That's why they died!

Impulsively, Cody drew back his fist and shattered the mirror image of himself with a single blow. Blood streamed from an impressive gash in Cody's left hand, but he hardly noticed. Instead, Cody grabbed the pressboard nightstand and hurled it through the motel room's only window. It was still dark out, but Cody no longer felt like sleeping, so instead, he plodded through the motel room door to the little Ford with the intention of putting this Kansas town behind him. Hot fire continued to blaze in his chest as Cody turned the little Ford onto the interstate. Having no particular destination in mind, Cody decided to head to Las Vegas, capital of the Resistance.

As he drove to the former desert paradise, the hot fire in Cody's chest turned black and became unbearably painful, encouraging him to wish for terrible destruction. In his mind, he saw the young, blond-haired girl who had lit the match that started this conflagration. A slow smile crept across her face as her eyes darkened and narrowed maliciously. The black flame in Cody's chest began to burn hotter and more insistently.

Logically he understood that the girl had no responsibility for the death of his wife and son. She had killed Hailey Suire sure, but how could she have known the horror that would follow. Still, in that moment it didn't matter. He needed a face to put to the Loyalists, someone against whom he could bank the black fires in his heart, someone from whom he could seek recompense. And this girl was as good as anyone. She would not be the only person to suffer for the loss of Stephanie and Blake, but she would be the first.

Chapter 12
The Firestorm at Cordoba Flats

I

Though Charlie expected the same agony she had experienced from the NSA's poison, she felt none. Instead, the blue-white light enveloped her body in warm, intense ecstasy. Every nerve ending sang at once in joy, and her blood, once cold with terror, had now become a warm, pleasurable flood. A smile drifted across her lips. She had died. Charlie felt sure of it, that is until she realized that she could feel the power moving within her, building in intensity.

As blue-white light filled her eyes, and her body sang with joy, her nose filled with an overpowering smell of a thunderstorm. This quickly blended with the familiar scent of burning wood and flesh.

"CHARLIE! OH MY GOD CHARLIE!"

David's voice came to her dreamlike from nowhere.

The power continued to build within her, lighting up every nerve ending with warm pleasure so intense she thought she would explode. A cry of pure joy grew within her before escaping as a great soundless scream.

"CHARLIE!"

Like David, Catherine's voice too seemed to have no source for Charlie could see nothing beyond boundless blue-white light.

Charlie screamed again as the power and the intense pleasure in her body continued to build.

This must be heaven. A passing thought quickly swept away in her growing bliss.

The power had built up to an intense roar, all at once, a loud ***-CRACKBANG-*** pierced her veil of silence, shaking the very ground beneath her. In that same instant, the intense blue-white light before her eyes cleared slightly, and Charlie found herself once more looking down from the burning frame of the camp electric chair upon a gathering of startled Lawgivers. Intense electrical energy crackled and snapped around her body in a bright blue-white corona. Charlie could feel it as it blended with her power. Charlie knew not what she had done or how she had done it. For a moment she sat perfectly still, her mind empty, awash in a thousand fragmented thoughts. Then several came into focus. Charlie found her psychic senses suddenly enhanced. Without effort, Charlie touched the minds of all of the gathered Lawgivers. At first, she sensed a scattering of shattered images. In short time these images took focus and formed into a single-minded desire to see Charlie, David, Catherine, and Stephen dead, and behind it, Charlie sensed naked, cold malice.

With this realization, the power surged still more, and with it, the blue-white corona around her body blazed. David, Catherine, and Stephen stood between her and the amassed Lawgivers. She could not strike out with the power without harming them. Without thinking, Charlie reached inside and found a strange *balance* she had never known before. With this *balance,* Charlie thrust out with the power, pushing the blue-white corona away from herself towards the gathered Lawgivers. In an instant, the corona became a blinding white ripple of twisting, jagged bolts of lightning before streaking across the ground at her feet. As the ripple approached David and Catherine, it parted and arced around them, leaving each unharmed. The remainder of the crowd was not so lucky.

The Lawgiver nearest her, a man of late middle age with iron-gray hair, was impaled through the chest, head, and stomach by forks of lightning thicker than her legs. His mind winked out instantly even as his body collapsed to the ground, smoking and convulsing.

Behind him, a young red-headed woman was swallowed by more lightning bolts than Charlie could count. A single cry escaped the woman's lips before her life was snuffed out. She lay on her side like a dead dog her body still trembling.

Beyond her, the remaining Lawgivers were swallowed by angry blue-white tendrils of electricity. Their death cries echoed on the cold night air.

The ripple of lightning coursed further across the campgrounds setting fire to nearby barracks and dancing over officer quarters and administrative buildings, setting each alight in turn. Without thinking, Charlie stood. It took her a full two minutes to be surprised by the fact that she was no longer restrained.

Charlie turned her gaze back on the electric chair to see that it was severely charred, the leather straps that had held her in its deadly embrace burned away. After a moment she turned back towards David and Catherine. Both were looking on with blank expressions of pure shock. Charlie could feel their minds reeling at what they had just witnessed.

David spoke first. "Charlie? Are you ok?"

"I'm fine, Dad." Her voice came out sounding calm and casual. She had called David her Dad without thought or hesitation.

David's expression softened. Charlie felt that he was touched. "Are you sure you're ok?"

Charlie smiled. "Really. I'm fine." All at once, her vision changed, and she saw a horde of Lawgivers approaching from the far side of the camp. Then an instant later her vision changed again, and she found herself facing a familiar and terrifying dark figure.

Lord Beathach!

The name turned her flesh and blood to ice.

"We have to get out of here now."

David's expression darkened. "What's wrong? What did you see?"

"They're coming," Charlie replied in as calm a voice as she could manage. "The Lawgivers are coming. Lord Beathach is *coming*!"

David nodded. "Then let's get out of here."

As he spoke, he took Charlie's hand and began to run. Charlie scrambled after him, her shorter legs working hard to keep up. Behind her, she heard Catherine and Stephen's footfalls on the hardpan earth. As they neared the blazing shell of the science building, a troop of twenty or thirty Lawgivers appeared in their path while a second troop of roughly the same number gathered behind them.

Instinctively Charlie lashed out at the Lawgivers in her path, sweeping them with towering blue-white flames. There were no screams, only the deep ***-warrump-*** of fire followed by an intense wave of baking heat. Sweat beaded up on her skin, soaking through her white cotton t-shirt.

"Charlie!" David's voice came to her from very far away.

An invisible fist collided with her head, breaking her concentration. The power leapt out of her and set fire to the ground at her feet. Rather than step back from the lily-white and electric blue flames Charlie turned towards the Lawgivers at her back and *shoved* the power out at them. A wall of white flames looming like a tower erupted before her and swept across the ground before consuming the second group with greedy fingers. Again there were no screams over the roar of the fire.

"Jesus…" Stephen's voice was hushed, and behind it, Charlie sensed only awe. "Where did you learn to do that?"

She did not reply. More Lawgivers were approaching from her left. Again her head rocked from an unseen blow so hard as to bring bright lights flashing before her eyes, and again the power spilled out, trailing random lines of fire across the ashen white ground beneath her feet.

This time David attacked before she could, extending his hands and sending jagged sheets of forked blue-white lightning cascading towards a crowd of fifteen Lawgivers that had appeared from behind a pile of flaming rubble that was once a prisoner barracks.

Screams rang out on the cold night air as the Lawgivers were hurled to the ground by the force of their own spasming muscles.

The air had become heavy with smoke, seared flesh, and that strange smell of a thunderstorm. An engine roared to life, and Charlie turned just in time to see a tan Humvee loaded down with uniformed soldiers. One of them sat in the gunner's seat firing an M60 in her direction. A single bullet painted thin fire across the back of her left hand while another lashed up the length of her right arm, trailing a single rivulet of blood. Charlie felt her skin flush, her heart quicken, and her blood grow hot.

Without hesitation, she lashed out with the power, eyes narrowing. The Humvee instantly shattered in a bright white fireball and the gunner, no longer a man, but a blazing human comet, was hurled through the air and into the flaming skeleton of a prisoner barracks.

A low ***-whup, whup, whup-*** of rotor blades warned of an approaching attack helicopter. Charlie's heart froze and dropped into her shoe.

Oh no… We're not going to get away.

The Lawgivers just kept coming. Charlie scanned the sky and saw a spotlight tracing its way across the desert hardpan. Below it, hundreds of Lawgivers advanced with leveled M4 rifles.

No, please!

David tightened his grasp on her hand and pulled her to the ground amidst the deafening crack snarl of hundreds of rifle shots. In that same instant, Charlie felt all of the Lawgivers strike out at once with the power. This time it did not come as an invisible fist but rather as a massive, soundless, concussion that impacted with such force that Charlie's vision filled with white stars for a moment. But this time, Charlie was ready for it. Despite the shock, Charlie held fast to the power, and when her vision cleared, she lashed out at the Lawgivers with the power.

As she did, Charlie felt David, Catherine, and Stephen each muster the power and strike out. Lightning danced across white flames, as men and women, blazing like scarecrows and speared upon forked and jagged purple electrical arcs, were cast into the air as if by the hands of an unseen titan.

Agonized screams rang out on the cold night as the air filled with the roar of fire and the crackle of arcing lightning. All at once, Charlie's blood froze as she detected the familiar clang of steel-shod boots on blackened desert hardpan and the snap and flutter of a black silk cape.

"Lord Beathach…" Little more than a frightened whisper.

And then from nowhere, the dark lord appeared, sword drawn, cape streaming behind him as the night's winds caught it.

"Charlie."

He spoke her name as if addressing a friend, his deep, metallic voice booming in the darkness.

"I come not as an enemy but an ally." As he spoke, Beathach threw back his cloak to reveal four familiar blades embedded in the ground at his feet. Charlie felt him reach into the power and send the swords spinning through the air so that each landed at its owner's feet.

"You will require these."

Charlie reached out with the power. Where Beathach stood, she felt only empty, cold blackness, and behind it unmitigated malice. Strangely enough, she sensed he had no intent to harm or take them. Rather, Beathach was there to help.

"What do you want?" Charlie inquired, more than a little confused.

"I am an ally." He repeated again, addressing her as if she were a friend. "And I do not have time to elaborate. If we are to escape, you must fight."

As he spoke the Resistance chopper swooped in closer, the ***-whup, whup, whup-*** of its blades growing to an angry roar.

Lord Beathach turned his gaze upward and raised a single, upward turned palm. He then slowly closed his fist and pulled it downward. In that same instant, the Resistance chopper crumpled and burst into flames before hurtling through the sky as if it were a toy tossed by an angry child. The wreckage of the helicopter landed among the surviving Lawgivers dismembering and mutilating several who were unfortunate enough to be caught in the path of its still whirling blades.

Charlie looked on with fascinated horror, her heart thundering in her chest. Without pausing, Beathach lashed out with the power. A ring of purple lightning arced around his armored form before surging outward towards the surviving Lawgivers. With each man and woman it struck, it tore through their body, ripping away life itself and charring the body beyond recognition.

A horrified cry escaped Charlie's throat, and she began to sob. Beathach had torn out their very lifeforce. She would not have imagined anyone capable of such an abomination.

"There is no time to cry, little girl." Beathach's tone had changed to one of cold indifference. "We must make our escape while the opportunity presents itself."

"What do you want?" David asked warily.

"I am here to save Charlie. Charlie cares for you, so I will save you as well."

David met Beathach's blank gaze with one of deep suspicion. "And I suppose once we're safely away you will return us to your emperor."

Beathach's blank, artificial eyes remained unchanged. "I have no orders to take you."

Charlie felt that David was not convinced. "Really? You chased us all over the world. You held us prisoner for years. And now you say you're not interested in capturing us when you have us in your grasp?"

"You may believe as you will," Beathach replied simply. "But right now, it is in all of our interests to flee before reinforcements arrive."

Stephen too remained suspicious. "I don't trust you, Dark Knight."

"You need not trust, but you would be wise to come with me now." As he spoke, Beathach motioned with his sword.

Warily Charlie took up her sword and turned in the direction Beathach had gestured. David took her hand once more. His voice echoed in her mind.

Stay close to me and be ready to run.

She touched his mind in return.

I will. Dad, I'm scared.

I am too, Charlie.

II

Elise Coke awoke in great pain, her face blazing as if still alight from the girl's flames. She opened her eyes to see the roof of a canvass topped Humvee. The air stunk heavily of smoke and burned flesh.

The girl. She must be loose.

Elsie struggled into a sitting position setting off a fresh eruption of fire across her body. She gritted her teeth to stifle a scream. She had to see. She had to know. Once seated upright, Elsie looked out the back window to see a blazing hellscape.

Charred corpses lay littered among the blazing skeletons of buildings. The flames seemed to dance, almost as if they were calling to her, or trying to seduce her.

The girl must have burned the whole place down. Incredible.

Something deep within her began to warm. Her heart beat faster, and she felt heat building in her chest and between her legs. Instead of burning, her skin began to tingle. The pain remained, but it became sublimated by an intense winnowing hunger, a yearning for more. And the fires seemed to fill that hunger. Even as they grew, and spread, towering into the night, the flames filled her and warmed her through and through. Intense ecstasy washed through her, and she felt a smile come to her lips. Then she began to laugh. And laugh.

Chapter 13
A Deal With Mr. Scratch
I

After walking for what seemed like hours, Lord Beathach stopped them and became very still. All at once, the air began to shimmer and *-bend-*. Then everything went white. A moment later Charlie found herself standing hand in hand with David, in a dingy, poorly lit warehouse. The air here was slightly cold and smelled of must and rot.

"You ask what I want from you?" Lord Beathach rumbled. "I wish to strike a bargain."

Charlie instinctively reached out to him with the power and sensed that behind his dark malice, Beathach spoke the truth. And yet she knew at once he could not be trusted.

"We have a common enemy." Lord Beathach's voice remained low and even, but behind it, Charlie sensed dark hatred. "An Enlightened named Kira Morozov. She was once a Lightwarrior before Outsiders murdered her daughter, and she took up her sword to seek revenge. Now she is no longer a Lightwarrior, but neither is she a Dark Knight. She has become a Rouge, beholden to none but herself. She is a threat to us all."

David turned towards Lord Beathach and slitted his eyes. "What do you want us to do?"

Lord Beathach met his gaze evenly. "The Rouge must die for all of our sakes. And I would have you find and kill her. In exchange, I will take you to safety."

Charlie probed Beathach's mind deeper and felt that he was telling the truth. From David, she sensed deep wariness. "And how long before you come after us again?"

Though his masked face remained blank, Charlie could feel Lord Beathach's mirthless smile. "You have my word that if you do this, we will no longer pursue you, your wife, or your daughter."

Again Charlie touched Beathach's mind with her own, and again she felt strongly that he told the truth, though there was another darker truth that lay beneath, and this truth turned her flesh to ice.

Charlie sensed deep conflict within David. This Rouge had not threatened them, and she was not a Dark Knight. Although she was not an innocent, the Rouge was a victim, and they would be hunting and killing her. *He* would be hunting and killing her for selfish reasons. Charlie reached deeper into David's mind and sensed intense love. Love for Catherine, love for her. She had truly become his daughter, and he would do anything, sacrifice anything for her. "Will you make the Accord and pledge to leave me and my family alone?"

Lord Beathach removed his mask and met David's gaze with his one good eye. "I will little Enlightened." Then he extended his hand.

David took him by the forearm, and the two men locked eyes. Each reached deep into the power, letting it flow through himself and the other in alternating white and black tendrils of lightning that enveloped both men.

"If I kill this Rouge, do you, Lucius Beathach, promise to leave me and my family alone forever."

Beathach intensified his gaze. "If you kill the Rouge Kira Morozov, then I pledge that no man or woman of the Black Empire or who serves the Black Empire shall pursue or attempt to capture you, your wife, or your daughter forever. I swear this before the Arbiter."

And with those words spoken, both men withdrew the power and released each other's hand.

David took a step backward. "Where can I find this Rouge?"

Lord Beathach replaced his mask. "She was last sighted in South Miami Beach near 3rd Street." Without speaking another word, Lord Beathach turned and strode silently from the warehouse.

II

This was how it began. David, Catherine, Charlie, and Stephen took up residence in a pair of suites at the largely deserted Riviera Hotel. Lacking any supplies, save for the clothes on their backs, and the swords at their sides, the four of them were obliged to steal, something none of them felt good about.

For his own part, David's heart gnawed at him, for he had seen the change beginning in Charlie back when they had lived in Turner. Though she remained warm and loving with David and Catherine, her manner had cooled. She had started to explore her power and, though she had closed her mind to him, Charlie's eyes betrayed a winnowing hunger for revenge. She was growing stronger too. Even now, David could not believe that she had not only survived the electric chair but had been able to control its power and direct that power as she willed. And she had done so while under the influence of drugs designed to suppress the power.

It troubled David that Charlie had said nothing in objection to his accord with Lord Beathach. There was a time when Charlie would have begged him not to harm this Kira Morozov, and not to enter into any agreement with Lord Beathach. She had once feared the dark lord. Now he could not be sure.

For his own part, David felt torn. He wanted desperately to protect his wife and daughter, and yet he knew deep inside that this was wrong. This woman had not harmed him or his family. She had killed out of revenge, but it was over the murder of her daughter. He had watched Charlie die of poison, would he have done any differently if she had not been revived? And if he killed this woman for seeking vengeance would that not call for Charlie's death as well if she were to take revenge for the murder of her parents? This was indeed wrong and yet he had to protect his wife and daughter. Charlie and Catherine were all that mattered.

Nevertheless, David was hesitant and spent several weeks "searching" for the woman, which in fact consisted of him aimlessly wandering the streets of Miami lost in his own thoughts. In the end, the matter was decided for him.

III

A visit from the Arbiter did nothing to deter Kira from her course, for her desperate hunger for revenge remained. As time passed, Kira lost track of the days, and Aria's visits became more frequent. During these, Aria would plead with Kira to stop hunting and killing her murderers, and Kira would tell Aria how much she missed her and beg her to stay.

Late one night, Kira cornered Hunter Birch in his mansion on Hibiscus Island. She found him in a darkened bedroom, a half-drunk fifth of brandy on the nightstand beside his king-sized bed. He was sleeping, but it would not satisfy her to kill him in his sleep. He had to know she had found him. He had to know the reason for his death. And so, heart thundering in her chest, she took the bottle and slowly poured its contents onto Hunter's sleeping form.

He started awake with a cry. "What the fuck!?"

In an instant, Kira had drawn her sword and nestled the point against Hunter's neck. "Do you know who I am?"

His eyes became confused. "What the fuck do you want?"

Hot blood slammed through Kira's veins. "My name is Kira Morozov. My daughter's name is Aria Morozov."

"I don't remember you or your fucking daughter."

Kira felt her flesh grow hot as her vision sharpened. "You raped and murdered my daughter, and you don't remember?!" She spat the words, feeling as if she would explode inside.

"What do you want?" Hunter's tone reflected the first edge of fear.

Kira gently parted the skin of Hunter's throat drawing forth a thin rivulet of blood.

"What do you want?!" Hunter's voice had become desperate.

"You raped and murdered my daughter! Admit it!" Kira screamed the words at him, as she fought the urge to drive her blade through his windpipe.

Hunter's eyes reflected confusion for a few seconds longer before they widened in sudden recognition. "The girl from *The Red Room*... You're her mother. She was a little slut, you know. She begged me for it, and I gave her exactly what she wanted."

Hunter's words were razors, cutting through her to the bone. Before she could stop herself, Kira screamed, raised her blade, and slammed it through Hunter's bare abdomen just above the navel. He let out a howl of pure suffering. Kira ripped her sword free and methodically severed both of Hunter's hands. Before leaving she brought her face close to his.

"An eye for an eye." Then she turned and left him to bleed out from his wounds.

IV

On March 1st Charlie awoke early. For the first time in a long time, she felt rested, her mind free of fear and anger. She remembered nothing of the night before, only peaceful, blissful darkness. In that moment, she had forgotten her anger over the deaths of Daddy and Mommy, her fear of the Black Empire and the Resistance, the black bloodstain that burned upon her heart. All of them seemed far away.

Warm sunlight streamed in through the hotel room window in golden bars. Charlie smiled. This would be a good day.

Charlie slid out of bed and went to wake David and Catherine. David had promised to take her on a supply run with Catherine and Stephen, and she was eager to get out of the hotel, if only for a few hours. Miami was a Loyalist controlled city far enough from the front line to be quiet if not one hundred percent safe. And, though the Loyalists were connected with the Black Empire, Charlie felt safer here than she had in a long time.

And yet, somewhere on the periphery of her senses, she felt the faintest touch of cold darkness. Charlie did not understand the meaning of this; she knew only that it was there. Charlie pushed the thought aside, for she wanted to enjoy the day with her family.

When she first tried to wake David, he groaned and turned away from her without opening his eyes. Charlie climbed onto the bed and began to shake him forcefully.

"Ugghh, Charlie?" Still more asleep than awake.

Charlie smiled. "Wake up, Dad."

David's eyes fluttered open. "Ok, I'm up." He nudged Catherine. "Wake up, sweetheart."

She moaned softly. "What is it?"

He chuckled. "Charlie says it's time to get up."

"Ok. What time is it?" She reached for the clock radio on the bedside table and then stopped as she remembered that the power was off. "Oh right…"

"What do you guys want for breakfast?' David asked.

Charlie couldn't help but smile, for this had become a running joke among them. The only food they had was canned soups and meats.

"Canned meat." She replied with a giggle.

He smiled in return. "Canned meat it is."

In truth, she had long since grown tired of canned meat and soups. The thought of another lump of gelatinous flesh turned her stomach. Still, she was hungry, it was food and food was hard to come by. So she would imagine that the pink block of Spam on her plate was a slice of pizza and quickly scarf it down before her senses could dispel the illusion.

After breakfast, Charlie changed into a pair of blue jeans and a pink cotton long sleeve v-neck before retrieving her sword from under her bed.

The blade glimmered softly in the warm, morning light, and as she turned it over in her hands, Charlie felt the power flow through its length. Pale yellow flames licked up the gray steel edge as the sword's crimson flaw began to glow with soft anger.

Like the day Striker came back.

In her mind, she saw his tall, dark outline, his silver eyes, and his crooked, weathered smile. *Hate* moved within her, setting her heart ablaze.

He's dead. He's dead and gone forever. Charlie repeated the words over and over again in her mind, desperate to stifle the growing black fire in her chest.

The power moved again within her, and with it, the flames upon her blade intensified to a brilliant blue-white.

David's voice came to her from behind. "Charlie? What are you doing?"

Charlie did not turn around. Instead, she slowly lifted her sword until it pointed at the ceiling. In that moment it was as if Striker stood before her. She could feel his twisted mind. He had always told her he cared about her and Charlie had once believed him. In the end, she had been able to read his intentions and understood that he had *loved* her deeply, in his own way.

The flames surrounding her blade brightened still further and began to change from white to blue-white as their intensity grew.

Striker had seen her suffer desperately because of the power and had wanted to put an end to her suffering. He had never meant to kill Daddy, but her father had gotten in the way. So Striker killed Daddy so that he could put her out of her misery. And she *Hated!* him for it. Even now, years after Striker's death, she still felt intense *Hate!* for the man who had taken her Daddy from her.

Her sword blade had begun to blaze brilliantly, and Charlie saw with perfect clarity the choice that she had before her. It was a choice she had been making again and again. Two roads diverging in a sun-drenched wood. Down one lay her adopted father and mother and the chance of at least some happiness. Down the other lay only darkness and the promise of revenge. She could walk away now and spend her life with her adoptive family, or she could choose revenge, and whatever price came with it.

Charlie wanted desperately to just let go and move on. It hurt to *Hate!* and yet she could not let go for that hurt too.

They killed Daddy and Mommy, they kidnapped me and hurt me. They tried to kill me. I can't let go. I just can't.

As that last thought passed through her mind, Charlie stared intently into the bright flames surrounding her sword and saw for the first time hints of crimson blood and raven black in the fire.

Charlie felt David and Catherine's eyes on her and quickly slammed down the power. In an instant, the flames surrounding her sword vanished, and the power went silent. Part of her marveled at this, for only a few months ago, she would not have been able to stop the power so quickly.

"Charlie? What are you doing?" David's voice was concerned.

Charlie turned face flushed with shame. "I'm sorry…I didn't mean to."

"It's ok, Charlie you didn't do anything wrong." Behind his voice, Charlie sensed both concern for her and fear. It was good that she had closed her mind to him. "Are you ready to go?"

"Yes." She replied brightly.

"Good. Then let's head out."

V

Fifteen minutes later, they were walking south on Liberty Street towards the Dorchester. David had seen some lights on at the hotel and thought they might be able to trade some alcohol from the mini bar in their suite for food. As she walked, Charlie felt a sudden chill. At first, she dismissed it as winter cold. But it was something more. This feeling came not from the outside, but from deep inside. With each step Charlie felt more certain; something wasn't right. An overhead sign indicated they were nearing Sally's Alley. Though they were still a few storefronts down, Charlie could already detect the acrid stench of cheap cigarette smoke and even cheaper beer polluting the otherwise salty beachside air. Charlie wrinkled her nose in disgust but kept walking.

As they neared the dive bar's entrance, a red-haired woman appeared from an alleyway beside the building. In the same instant, Charlie's heart turned to ice, for she knew at once that this woman was dangerous. Her red hair appeared disheveled, and her golden eyes were wild with madness. For a moment the woman stood frozen in shock as if she had seen a ghost. Charlie touched her mind and saw a thousand fragmented thoughts whirling as if caught in a windstorm. This woman was broken.

Then all at once, the woman's thoughts took form, and her face reflected sudden recognition. "Aria?! Baby?! Thank God! I thought you were dead."

Without a word, Charlie met the woman's eyes with an even gaze.

"Can I help you?" David inquired.

The red-haired woman ignored him, instead locking her eyes with Charlie's. "Baby, I missed you so much. I thought I'd lost you forever."

Charlie remained silent, unsure of what to do. This woman was crazy, and an Enlightened, a Lightwarrior, or at least she had been. Charlie was both frightened and saddened at once. Instead of drawing away, Charlie probed deeper into the woman's mind. The woman's name was Kira, she had once had a husband and daughter. Her husband had died of hantavirus, her daughter was…

Charlie sensed Kira's horror at her daughter's fate and tried to withdraw.

…her daughter was raped and murdered.

The words clanged in Charlie's mind sending her stomach into a lurch. Charlie swallowed hard, fighting an urge to vomit. In her mind, Charlie saw the very act, and her flesh crawled. She also saw what Kira had done in response and despite being frightened, felt a certain sick satisfaction.

Serves them right.

"Can I help you?" David repeated.

Kira turned and glared at David. "You took my daughter, Sergei. You stole her, and I want her back."

David's expression became confused. "What are you talking about? Who is Sergei?"

"You took my daughter." As she spoke, Kira drew a long sliver broadsword from a hidden scabbard. "I'm taking her back now!"

David drew *Deus Irae* and pulled Charlie behind him. "You are making a mistake. This is *my* daughter Charlie."

"We didn't take your daughter." As she spoke, Catherine too drew her sword.

"You did." Kira insisted, golden eyes glistening with madness. "And I'm going to take her home now." As she spoke, Kira raised her blade and slid into a fighting stance. David and Catherine moved into flanking positions.

Charlie understood the danger at once. Her heart leapt up into her throat and dropped into her shoe. Kira was fully trained. She knew the power in ways that David and Catherine did not. She could kill them both. And if she did not, if David or Catherine somehow prevailed… This woman was a victim too. She didn't deserve to die.

Kira truly believed Charlie was her daughter, Aria. And she would fight to the death to get her back. Sudden, terrible understanding washed through Charlie, for she knew the only solution. She would have to go with this woman at least for a little while to keep Kira and David and Catherine from killing each other. Charlie only hoped that she would be able to convince Kira that she was not Aria.

Charlie pushed past David and stepped between him and Kira. "Stop, please! I'll go!"

Charlie sensed sudden terror and hurt wash through David. "No. Charlie, you can't. It's not safe. You don't even know who this person is."

Charlie turned her eyes on her and offered him a soft smile. A single tear trickled from her left eye. "It's ok David. I'll be ok."

"Please…" David's voice was thick with tears and high with desperation. "I love you. I don't want to lose you."

"Please, Charlie…We love you so much." Catherine barely forced the words out between sobs.

"I love you too." Charlie's heart nearly broke as she spoke the words. "And I don't want to lose you either. This is the only way. I'm sorry…" With those last words, she turned away and walked towards Kira.

Kira's face lit up with desperate, ragged joy, and she burst into tears before snatching Charlie into her arms. "Oh, Baby, I thought I'd never see you again."

VI

David could barely breathe. As he watched his daughter turn away and walk back up the alleyway with the red-haired woman, Kira, the Rouge Lord Beathach had asked him to kill, his lungs failed him, and his heart ripped apart. The power was a living thing within him, and yet he dared not use it. Charlie had asked him not to harm the woman. Her voice still echoed in his mind.

Let me go. Please Dad, just let me go.

And Charlie was standing too close to the woman in any event. He would risk harming his daughter if he were to attack the red-haired woman with the power.

And so he let Charlie go, despite the terrible pain in his chest, David stifled the power and simply watched as his daughter walked away from him. Perhaps forever.

"Charlie!" Her name escaped his lips before he could stifle it. She did not turn, but her mind touched his one last time.

Please let me go. I love you, and I don't want you or Mom to get hurt. Please just let me go.

David turned away and clutched Catherine in his arms. Both husband and wife wept for their daughter. Each feared that they would never see Charlie again.

Chapter 14
Charlie Leaves

I

Charlie followed Kira back through the alley and down another alley to the right before arriving at the mostly deserted Dorchester Hotel. Here, Kira led her inside through the shattered front door and into the darkened lobby. The electricity was out here too, so they took the stairs to Kira's second-floor room. Once inside, Kira sat Charlie down on the bed and bent down to look at her.

"I still can't believe you're here." She whispered, voice thick with tears. "I saw you bleed to death. But here you are." She laughed. "I'm so glad to see you."

Before Charlie could react, Kira drew her into a desperate hug, clutching her in the grip of a drowning woman. Charlie painted a smile across her lips, for the moment having no option but to play along.

"I'm glad to see you too." In truth, Charlie wanted to cry. She did not want to be separated from David and Catherine, and this woman frightened her.

What happens when she figures out I'm not Aria? What will she do with me?

In her mind, Charlie saw the silver glimmer of Kira's sword, heard the low *-shriiiiik-* as the blade slid free of its scabbard, and felt the woman's desperate fury at having her child stolen away. She would have killed David and Catherine to get Aria daughter back. As she probed Kira's mind, Charlie saw flashes of memory and felt her flesh freeze.

An image of a man with dark, shaggy hair appeared before Charlie's eyes. A moment later, silver steel flashed, and the man cried out in agony. Kira's blade protruded from his abdomen for a moment before she ripped it free, trailing crimson behind. Charlie bit her lip hard to stifle the scream that was building in her chest. Sharp tremors rippled through her body.

She's killed before...

Charlie sensed that Kira had killed this man because he had been involved in Aria's murder.

Like the men from the NSA...

This thought awakened the black bloodstain within her chest and its flames. Charlie felt her heartbeat pick up slightly, and her skin begin to warm.

He killed Kira's daughter just like Striker killed Daddy.

As these thoughts passed through her mind, Charlie found that she could not condemn what Kira had done to this man. After all, she had burned Striker alive and then chopped off his head with her own sword.

And he deserved it!

The thought tasted bright and painty, like sour acid on the tongue.

Charlie felt sure that this man too deserved to die and that Kira deserved to have her revenge upon him.

But it's dangerous, and it doesn't help. It still hurts. The pain never goes away. It won't until I can let go.

This last part came as a revelation to Charlie, and yet she could not let go. The black bloodstain would not allow her.

What will she do when she finds out I'm not Aria?

The thought turned her flesh to ice. Kira was dangerous, and her mind was shattered. Grief and rage had broken her into a million pieces. Even the belief that she had been reunited with her daughter could not mend the damage. Kira was lost.

"We have to go now." Kira was saying. "Ivan will be looking for us. We need to get out of Miami."

Charlie's heart leapt up into her throat.

No! If we leave the city, Dad and Mom will never find me. I'll be alone with this woman forever.

Still, she could not fight Kira. So she helped pack a suitcase with clothing and a duffel bag with canned food before following the madwoman to a battered blue PT Cruiser in the hotel parking garage.

A short time later, they were on the road headed north. Kira had announced they would stop in Savannah, Georgia that night and then continue north until they reached Bangor, Maine, which was rumored to be relatively quiet and safe. Charlie did not bother to ask Kira where they would get gasoline from now that the majority of gas stations were closed down, and the few that were open would only trade gas for supplies.

As she watched the city speed by outside the car windows, Charlie began to weep softly. She was leaving David and Catherine behind and would probably never see them again.

Kira seemed not to notice. Instead, she babbled on about how wonderful their life in Maine would be.

Please, I'm not Aria. I'm sorry your daughter's dead. Please let me go back to my Dad and Mom.

Charlie wanted to speak the words, to cry out, but she feared what might happen and so remained silent. She did not want to be forced to use the power on this woman.

II

David waited only minutes after Charlie and Kira had disappeared into the alleyway before turning to Catherine and Stephen. "Let's go. I don't want to let them get too far ahead."

Catherine met his eyes. "How do you plan to get Charlie back."

"I don't know, Catherine." He replied somberly. "But we can't just abandon her to that crazy woman."

"You know she's only going to protect you two, right?" Stephen's tone held a subtle warning.

Catherine turned to face Stephen. "I know, but she's our daughter. We can't just let Kira steal her away."

"I'm not suggesting that you do," Stephen replied. "Only that you remember that your daughter chose to go with Kira and why."

"Are you going to help us or not?" David spoke in a level tone, taking pains to keep his anger out of his voice.

"Of course," Stephen replied. "I don't want to leave Charlie with that mad woman any more than you do. But I would suggest that we have a plan before we confront Kira again."

Without further words, David, Catherine, and Stephen hurried down the alleyway after Charlie and Kira stopping short of the entrance to the Dorchester. Twenty minutes after they disappeared inside the darkened hotel, a ragged electric blue PT Cruiser appeared from the hotel's garage. Though the car's dark windows prevented him from seeing inside, David knew at once that Charlie was within. The force of her fear and desperation nearly brought him to tears. David looked around rapidly and quickly sighted upon a black Ford Explorer. Without a thought towards either gathering supplies or being seen by Kira, David used the power to turn the Ford's engine over. Then, after Catherine and Stephen had piled in, David carefully pulled out onto the road and began following the blue PT Cruiser.

As he drove, unreality set in. Burned-out shells of buildings, skeletal cars, and ashen garbage heaps sped by on both sides. Amongst them lay a scattering of corpses in varying states of decay. David's heart began to beat a little faster with each passing moment.

Charlie! Oh God, Charlie! Why did you go with her?

David had touched Kira's mind for but a moment and had sensed only chaotic shards of thought and memory. Kira had somehow mistaken Charlie for her dead daughter, Aria, and had mistaken David for someone named Sergei. Charlie had to have sensed this woman's madness, had to have known she was dangerous. And yet she had chosen to go with the woman anyway.

Why?

He would have gladly fought and died to protect his daughter, and yet Charlie had chosen to leave with a stranger.

And she's dangerous. What happens when she figures out Charlie is not her daughter?

As that last thought passed through his mind, David felt his heart race as the first, leading edge of mindless panic threatened to carry away all reason. The blue PT Cruiser had pulled a little ahead of him now, David had to fight an urge to floor the accelerator. He had no plan, no idea of what he would do if he caught up with Charlie and Kira, no idea of how to get his daughter back. He knew only that he could not let her go.

I'm coming, Charlie! I'm not going to let her take you away.

At his side, *Deus Irae* glowed a soft blue-white, awakened by his growing terror and panic.

When that woman figures out that Charlie is not her daughter...

He dared not finish that thought for where it led was too terrible. David had lost Charlie once before, watched her die in his arms. He could not let that happen again.

I failed you last time. I won't fail you again.

David felt something deep and terrible ripping within his chest. The pain was horrific and yet familiar, for he had felt it once before when had stood over Charlie's poison ravaged body in the Chicago General Hospital morgue.

Not again...I'll never let anyone hurt you like that again!

The image of Charlie's slight body lying on the cold steel slab remained fresh in his mind, sending his thoughts reeling out of control and setting his heart to trip hammering.

I'm coming, Charlie... Wherever she's taking you, I'm coming. I won't abandon you.

Without warning, the engine sputtered, coughed, and began to lose power. "Oh fuck!!" David pushed the accelerator down hard as the blue PT Cruiser opened a wider and wider gap.

"Not now. For fuck's sake, NOT NOW! GO YOU PIECE OF SHIT!"

In defiance of his words, the Ford sputtered to a stop, out of gas. David smacked the heel of his right palm against the steering wheel.

"FUUUUUCK!"

Tears spilled from his eyes. David dropped his head in defeat as the blue PT Cruiser carried his daughter away towards the horizon before disappearing from sight.

III

As her adoptive father cried out in defeated grief, Charlie felt something sharp and hot rip through her heart and began to weep. Now she understood, she had chosen to leave David and Catherine behind forever and had closed a door she could not now reopen. Charlie tried to reach out with her mind to touch David and Catherine, even as they fell further and further behind. For an instant, she felt a familiar, warm touch.

Goodbye…I'm so sorry…I love you both.

And with that last thought, the touch was gone, and she found herself alone with her thoughts.

Kira was watching her with confused eyes. "What's the matter, Aria? Why are you crying?"

For a moment, Charlie did not respond. The pain in her breast took away all words. Then, "My name isn't Aria, it's Charlie. And you took me away from my Dad and Mom. I only went with you because I didn't want you to fight my parents. I don't want anyone to get hurt."

"It's ok, Aria." She continued not hearing or not caring about Charlie's words. "Your safe from them now. You're back with momma now."

Charlie shook her head in frustration but said no more. The power moved within her, and she immediately stifled it.

Not that way.

She could have easily used the power to escape, but she felt it would be wrong to do so. And so she sat and cried silent tears as Kira drove her away from David and Catherine.

After a while, Kira pulled off the highway at the exit for Vero Beach to look for gasoline and some food. They searched several abandoned gas without any luck before stumbling upon a large Wawa station near the beach with a line of cars parked outside. A sign indicated that due to limited supplies, customers were restricted to ten gallons each, while a pair of uniformed attendants, armed with AR-15s took payment in trade items and ensured that no one was stealing gas.

"We can get gas here and maybe some snacks." Kira told Charlie in a 'mom voice.' "Are you hungry?"

Food had been the furthest thing from Charlie's mind, but now that Kira had brought it to her attention, Charlie did feel hungry. Still, she remained silent.

As they pulled up to the number six gas pump, Charlie felt her heart quicken and her blood chill. Something was very wrong. In that same instant, she heard raised, angry voices. Charlie got out of the car and turned to see two middle-aged men, each with a wife and children, fighting over who would use pump number eight next. One of the men, an olive-skinned man with iron-gray hair, drew a sizeable nickel-plated revolver from a holster clipped to his belt and pointed it at the second man.

“I don’t want to kill you, but I will if you don’t back off. My family needs this gas, and I’m not going to let you take the last of it.”

The second man, pale-skinned with jet black hair, met the first man’s threat with a steady gaze. “There’s no need to resort to violence. There’s enough gas for both of us.”

The iron haired man returned a hard smile. “Then, in that case, you won’t mind if I go first.”

“Well, I was here first.” The jet-black haired man replied.

The first man cocked the hammer of his revolver. “I thought so. You’re full of shit. And if you think I’m going to let you take the last of the gasoline and leave me and my family stranded here, then you’ve got another thing coming. Now move that piece of shit, or I’ll kill all of you.”

Without waiting for an answer, the iron haired man took aim and drew back on his trigger. In an instant, Charlie reached out with the power and snatched the revolver out of the iron haired man’s grasp sending it skittering across the concrete.

“What the fuck?”

The iron haired man turned towards her, eyes wide with shock and fear. Then all at once, his eyes went blank, and a bright red blotch appeared in the center of his chest. In the same instant, a gunshot pierced the late afternoon air, and for a moment Charlie feared that she had accidentally set the iron haired man’s revolver off when she knocked it from his hand. Then she saw the black-haired man and knew the truth. He stood holding a black Glock, smoke still curling from its gaping barrel.

The iron haired man’s wife screamed as he folded to the ground like a dropped doll. Then she fell to her knees at his side and pressed her hand against his chest in a futile effort to preserve his already departed life. Behind her, the iron haired man’s two boys both looked on with blank-faced horror, as tears streamed from their eyes.

The black-haired man turned his gun and gaze upon Charlie now. “I know you. You’re that little girl from the news reports. Charlie MacLeod. The Loyalist council is offering a sizable reward for you.”

Charlie felt her heart pick up slightly. The power was moving within her, ready to break loose and destroy. Charlie knew that this was no place to start fires. A single flame could set off an explosion that would kill everyone there.

The man motioned with his gun. “Let’s go. In the car now.”

Before Charlie could react, Kira stepped in front of her, sword drawn. “You’re not taking my daughter!” She shrieked.

The black-haired man leveled his weapon, preparing to fire. Once again everything seemed to move very slowly. This time Charlie felt Kira strike out with the power, sending the man sprawling. Then, before he could right himself, Kira was on the man, blade flashing. The man screamed, and blood streaked through the air as Kira opened up the man’s belly with a well-placed slash. This man’s wife, a rosy-cheeked woman with jet black hair to match her husband’s drew a gun and took aim at

Kira's head. Before she could fire, Charlie reached out again with the power and slapped the Glock from the woman's hand.

Then, before the woman could do anything further, Charlie ran to Kira and tried to lead her back towards the car. By this point, the two armed attendants decided that the commotion near pump eight was a potential threat to their business and sauntered over, rifles leveled.

"There a problem here?"

The one who had spoken was a young woman with red hair cut into a bob. For a moment, Charlie wondered how she had managed to keep his hair so short and neat before fear swept the thought aside.

"We just want gas," Kira replied in a voice that was deceptively reasonable. "These men tried to steal my daughter away."

Both the young woman and her older, straw-haired partner looked Kira and Charlie over with broad disinterest.

"You're that girl from the news."

At the sound of the young woman's voice, Charlie tensed, and the power moved restlessly within her.

STOP IT!

To let the power out now would mean triggering an inferno.

Still, the woman's tone was mostly bored, and Charlie sensed no threat from her.

"I suppose those idiots were after the reward the NSA is offering for your capture." Having seen the edge of fear in her eyes, the young woman's expression became contemptuous. "Oh please. You don't seriously think I'm that stupid, do you? According to the news you burned up a dozen or more people. And if you don't kill me, then the Loyalist council probably will. Now do you two have something to trade for gas or not."

"I have some hard liquor cordials." As she spoke, Kira turned back towards the blue PT Cruiser. A moment later, she brought out a plastic grocery bag containing a dozen or more little bottles of varying colored liquors. Here were several bottles of Jack Daniels, several more of Seagram's Gin, and six or seven bottles of Smirnov Vodka. The young, redhead eyed them with interest, despite her feigned expression of indifference.

"That'll get you ten gallons, no more."

"Ten gallons and some food from the store." Kira countered.

"Fine." And with that, the young woman took Kira's bag of liquor and began fueling the PT Cruiser.

As the red-haired young woman pumped their gas, Kira took Charlie's hand and led her towards the store. Once inside they picked out four cans of Chicken of the Sea, four cans of Spam, a large bag of Lays potato chips, and a gallon jug of water.

By the time they had picked out their food, the red-haired woman had finished fueling their car and had pulled it into a parking space outside the store. Five minutes later they were back on the highway headed north.

They drove for the rest of that day and into the evening before stopping to rest in Savannah, Georgia. Here they found the Hyatt Regency deserted, and Kira announced that they would spend the night inside.

IV

Charlieslept in fits and spurts that night, any rest denied by forgotten nightmares. Early the following morning, Charlie awoke and found she could not go back to sleep. So instead, Charlie got up and went to the bathroom to dress for the day. She found Kira already gone and for a moment wondered if the madwoman had realized her mistake and abandoned her.

To her dismay, Kira returned after a few minutes carrying a bundle of blankets and pillows. "I couldn't find any food, but we should be able to trade these for something to eat."

Charlie met her eyes evenly but said nothing.

I'm not your daughter! I'm not Aria! Why can't you see that!

Charlie wanted to scream the words but dared not for fear of what Kira would do. So instead, she remained silent as Kira stripped the beds in their little room and added the sheets, blankets, and pillows to her already large pile. Then she went over to the desk where she had left their food supply and picked up a can of Chicken of the Sea.

"Tuna fish alright for breakfast?" Kira asked in an obliviously cheerful tone as if she and Charlie were sitting down to breakfast in some sun-drenched kitchen before beginning a typical day of work and school.

Charlie stared at the canned tuna fish, her stomach turning slightly in disgust. She hated tuna fish, and there was no bread, so they would be obliged to eat it straight out of the can. Yet Charlie had lived through too many years of deprivation to be a picky eater. Any food was better than no food.

"That's fine." She found herself saying absently.

In truth, she was not hungry and did not care about food. She wanted to be back with David and Catherine, that was all that mattered to her.

Several minutes later, Charlie found herself sitting in front of an open can of tuna, fork in hand. Kira was babbling away about the drive ahead of them. Charlie ignored her, instead focusing her mind on the tuna. It was cold, clammy, and tasted like the can. Still, Charlie ate it, not out of any enjoyment, or even hunger but rather because it was something to do. Her heart bled for her lost adoptive parents. She desperately wanted to be back with them but feared what would happen if David and Catherine confronted Kira. While she felt that both David and Catherine were considerably stronger than Kira, she also understood that Kira was trained whereas David and Catherine were not.

What if she kills David and Catherine?

Charlie quickly banished the thought before it could blossom and sweep away all reasoned thought and control in a painful icy wave. The NSA had killed her Daddy and Mommy, she could not face the death of David and Catherine as well. Even if it meant being separated from them. It occurred to Charlie that she could easily kill Kira, but that too seemed wrong. This woman had lost her daughter, and that loss had broken her utterly. Charlie would have to keep trying to convince Kira that she was not Aria and that Kira needed to return her to David and Catherine.

After they had finished eating, Charlie helped Kira pack the car, and they set off once more. Before leaving the room and after taking care to ensure that Kira wasn't looking, Charlie flicked out at the little trashcan by the window, immediately setting it ablaze. She felt a slight pang, and her skin flushed warm, for she knew that this was wrong. Yet she had to leave something behind for David and Catherine to find, something to tell them that she was alive and safe.

Never mind. The hotel's deserted. Nobody will care.

It didn't matter, Charlie still felt sick to her stomach over what she had done. Impulsively, Charlie slammed the hotel room door shut before any smoke could escape. Not that it would make any difference, Kira would never notice. She seemed oblivious to everything except Charlie and the drive to Maine.

As they were pulling out of the hotel parking lot, several windows on the third and fourth floors blew out; and flames and smoke streamed out into the clear blue morning sky. No sirens rang out. No one seemed to care. It was a strange sight, as if the entire city were dead. And for all she knew, the whole city might have been dead.

V

After watching Charlie disappear over the horizon, David flew from the Ford Explorer in search of a vehicle with gas. Catherine and Stephen scrambled to keep up. The three of them searched frantically for a car with gas for the remainder of that day and into the evening before giving up for the night and bedding down in the back of the Ford Explorer.

The following morning, David stumbled across a battered nineties era Buick Century with a full tank of gas. The car's engine chugged and sputtered, but David couldn't care less, all that mattered was catching up with Kira and Charlie.

After starting the engine with the power and waiting for Catherine and Stephen to pile in, David turned the ramshackle Buick north on Interstate 95 and punched the gas. The image of Charlie turning and leaving with Kira repeated in David's mind over and over. They had lost a day, and the Buick was far from fast. They would be hard-pressed to make up the time.

Catherine's voice interrupted his thoughts. "How do you know this is the right way? They could have gotten off at any of these exits?"

David kept his eyes locked on the road.

"David!" Catherine insisted. "Are you sure they went this way?"

"No, but this is where they were headed when we saw them last," David replied. "I don't know what else to do."

"That woman thinks we took her daughter," Stephen interjected. "She will try to get away as far and as fast as she can, and she will not try to cross into Resistance territory. They're headed north."

Impulsively, David reached down and switched on the car radio, expecting nothing but a burst of static. Instead, he was greeted by a young woman's southern drawl.

"A mysterious fire has broken out in the Hyatt Regency Hotel in Savannah, Georgia, and is now spreading throughout the city. Government spokesman, Harold Davis reports that because Savannah has been evacuated due to ongoing civil unrest from Resistance sympathizers no action will be taken to put out the fire."

David switched off the radio, his heart suddenly thumping hard against his ribs. *Charlie!* She had been in Savannah. She had lit that fire. Though he had no evidence to prove it, David felt certain that Charlie had started the hotel fire. Blood racing through his veins, David pushed the old Buick a little harder, bringing their speed up to sixty-five. They were fortunate that someone had taken the time to clear the road of abandoned cars.

"She was in Savannah," Catherine stated in a voice that was cautiously hopeful. "Charlie started that fire."

"Yes, I think so," David replied.

"How do you intend to deal with Kira when we catch up with them?" Stephen inquired in a wary tone. "That woman is a fully trained Lightwarrior, or at least she was. How do you intend to get Charlie away from her?"

"I'll do what I have to," David replied. "If she won't give Charlie back willingly, then I'll challenge her to fight me to the death. Charlie is my daughter, and I'm not going to let some woman steal her away!" Though David intended a resolute tone, he only managed to sound defensive and petulant.

"So you will challenge her to one on one combat," Stephen replied. "Have you ever faced a fully trained Enlightened?"

"Yes." As he spoke, David's mind flashed back to his battle with Hardliner on the Black Imperial capital world. Hardliner had shot Charlie, and David had been overtaken by such rage that he had finished the Dark Knight with a blow powerful enough to split the man from crown to collarbone. He had hated Hardliner for what the Dark Knight had done to Charlie. David was unsure that he hated Kira nearly as much, even if she had taken Charlie.

Kira thinks Charlie is her daughter, and Charlie went with her willingly.

Kira was clearly disturbed, but she meant Charlie no harm.

A familiar bass echoed in his mind. *If you kill the Rouge, Kira Morozov, then I pledge that no man or woman of the Black Empire or who serves the Black Empire shall pursue or attempt to capture you, your wife, or your daughter forever. I swear this before the Arbiter.*

Lord Beathach had asked him to kill Kira in exchange for guaranteeing his family's safety. He had claimed that she was a danger to everyone and had to die, but that was not the whole truth. Beathach had hoped that David would kill Kira for selfish reasons the thus be corrupted, if only a little. David had become a father to Charlie and was closer to her than any other. If he could be turned towards the darkness even just a little, then he would take Charlie with him.

She took Charlie. This fact remained, and David knew that Kira would never give Charlie up willingly. Not so long as she was under the delusion that Charlie was, in fact, her dead daughter Aria. He would have to face her and kill her if he wanted Charlie back. That was why Charlie had gone with Kira willingly. And *that* was why Charlie had begged him to let her go.

The miles passed with agonizing slowness, and before long the sun had dipped below the horizon, shrouding the world in darkness. Still, David pushed on, not wanting to stop for anything. Gasoline was an ongoing difficulty. David had to stop three times; twice he was lucky and found abandoned gas stations with remaining supplies of fuel. The third time he found a manned gas station where he was forced to trade some of their food for fuel.

Not long after their second stop for gas, they reached the outskirts of Savannah. Though it was well past sunset, the night sky glowed orange from Charlie's fire. She had been here, he felt sure of it, almost as if some piece of her essence had been left behind in the blazing city.

In a frustratingly short time, the clock ticked over to midnight. David glanced at Catherine and Stephen and saw that they were both exhausted. As that thought passed through his mind, David's vision doubled, then trebled before sliding back into focus. According to the highway signs, they were approaching Elkridge, a suburb of Baltimore. Another sign advertised several hotels, gas stations, and restaurants. Though he could not be sure, David felt that Kira and Charlie had passed through here several hours ago.

David pulled off the highway and followed the signs to an abandoned Holiday Inn. Fifteen minutes later, he lay in bed, exhausted but unable to sleep. In his mind, the image of Charlie leaving with Kira played over and over, pushing sleep further and further out of reach. Finally, as the sky turned from black to purple, exhaustion took him, and he slipped into unconsciousness

VI

As David, Catherine, and Stephen made their mad dash up the east coast after them, Kira and Charlie took a much more leisurely pace, stopping in Nottingham, Maryland a few hours after dusk. That night, Kira got them a room at the Hilton Garden. As with the previous night's hotel, they found the Hilton deserted and mostly picked clean save for some bedding. Charlie slept better that night than she had the night before. This was more a function of exhaustion than any real relaxation though, for inside Charlie felt torn apart. Her heart bled from a thousand invisible wounds that had opened when she walked away from David and Catherine. She was alone again, her parents lost again. And she had left them behind by choice because she had feared for their safety and…

I didn't want them to hurt Kira.

Charlie had felt Kira's grief and pain from the time she first met her and felt her heart rip apart. Like Charlie, Kira had lost her entire family, her daughter had been brutalized and murdered right in front of her.

Just like what Striker did to Daddy!

This thought set her heart ablaze. Deep inside, the black bloodstain swelled with baleful flame.

Why are people so mean?

The question whispered in her mind, answerless, for there was no answer. This was her life, to suffer at the hands of cruel men, for reasons beyond her control. And so it seemed it was the life and fate of *anyone* with the power. Kira too had lost everything because of the power, and David and Catherine... Well, they had lost everything because of *Charlie's* power.

As she lay in bed, a dinner of canned sardines sitting in a lead lump in her stomach, Charlie's eyes burned with unshed tears of bitter grief. Her chest felt crushed, weighed down by a thousand pounds of cold cast iron sorrow. It hurt to breathe, hurt to move, hurt to remember, hurt more to try to forget. She wanted so badly to be back with David and Catherine at the Black Hills Hotel. A faint smile played across her lips even as the tears flowed down her burning cheeks, and fell into her ears. As fleeting and few as they were, those had been good days. She had felt something almost like happiness, like it had been before…

That was how life felt to her now. In truth, as she admitted it to herself, how life had felt to her since leaving Taylor. Before and after. Before the NSA and the Black Empire came into her life and after. Before she lost her Mommy and Daddy and after. The before days, days so far away now that they seemed another lifetime ago, or a dream. All she had left of the before days now were hazy, half-seen fragments and long faded vague memories. She recalled that last day, once bright and happy, now a haunting dream of what might have once been.

The tears came now in rivers, terrible and burning, they stung her eyes, cheeks, and ears before collecting in the soft porcelain shell of her right ear. Behind her, Kira snorted in her sleep and mumbled something intelligible.

Rather than recognizing that Charlie was not her daughter, Kira was becoming more detached from reality. That night before bed, Kira had read Charlie *Oh The Places You'll Go* and sang her a lullaby as if she were still a little kid. Then a few minutes later, her face went blank, and her eyes glassed over into vacant marbles for a moment before her expression softened into a warm smile.

"I am so proud of you, Aria. I remember when you were a little baby in diapers. Now you've grown into a little woman." She paused, and for a moment, her eyes swam as if they would spill tears down her hollow, wan cheeks. "How would you like to drive tomorrow?"

At the time, Charlie had been nonplussed. It wasn't until later that the import of what had happened occurred to her. Kira's mind was crumbling, what was left of her sanity rotting away.

A soft sob escaped Charlie's aching throat.

I'll never convince her I'm not Aria. I'll never see David and Catherine again.

The thought nearly broke her completely. She dared not allow herself to openly weep for fear of Kira's reaction. She did not feel that Kira would harm her, but she feared what else tears would drive the madwoman to do.

What if she tries to face David and Catherine?

Except Charlie knew the answer to that question. If Kira were to confront David or Catherine, someone was going to die. Her adoptive parents would fight to the death for her and Kira…well she thought Charlie was her dead daughter Aria. Surely she would kill for her daughter.

And so Charlie bit back her sobs and lay there facing the drape shrouded window silently weeping until the sun's baleful orange disk peaked over the horizon.

VII

Time to leave again…

The words echoed in her mind in an unfamiliar voice. As that thought passed through her mind, Charlie became aware that David and Catherine were close.

They might as well be a million miles away. I'll never see them again.

And with that last thought, a fresh flood of hot, stinging tears trickled down her cheeks to catch in the conch of her right ear where they collected in a warm pool.

Without a word, Charlie eased herself upright and slid to the edge of the bed. The carpet felt hard and prickly beneath her bare feet. Taking care not to make a sound, Charlie crossed the hotel room to the bathroom, and what she hoped would be a hot shower. The hotel had no electricity, and she thought it unlikely. Still, with only another long day of driving and loneliness, of grief for the loss of David and Catherine to look forward to, a hot shower would be a rare treat. It would perhaps, if only for a few minutes, help her feel better, even if she could not forget.

Charlie turned on the water and undressed quickly while she waited and hoped for the water to get hot. To her surprise and mild pleasure, the spray did indeed get warm, though not hot. When she was satisfied that the shower had warmed as much as it would, she drew back the curtain and stepped into the spray.

The water encased her in a warm cocoon, washing away, at least for the moment, all of her worries and cares. Charlie stood under the rushing stream feeling, if only for the briefest of times, almost normal, as if all of the fear, all of the horror, all of the terrible things, were gone and had never happened.

Except they did! A cold voice reminded her. *Daddy and Mommy are gone, David and Catherine are GONE! And you're alone. You'll always be alone.*

Charlie closed her eyes and dropped her head, letting her golden blond hair fall before her lidded perfect blue eyes.

I know. But can't I just have a few minutes. Can't I just forget for a few minutes and feel…normal.

Except she couldn't. Now that the thought was here, it would not be banished. Her parents were gone, David and Catherine were gone. She was alone with this madwoman, probably forever.

Or at least until she gets old and dies.

Yes, Charlie hadn't forgotten that either. *Deus Irae* had made her immortal. She would grow up, but she would never grow old, never die. She would live on, alone forever.

The water was growing cold now. It didn't matter. The shower had lost all pleasure for her now. Charlie turned off the water with a savage twist and stepped from the stall. She was not crying, crying took energy, and her body felt heavy and leaden, so thoroughly drained of energy as to plunge her into a coma or drag her down to death.

With slow, plodding steps, Charlie walked from the bathroom wrapped in a towel. Ten minutes later she was dressed and sitting on her bed watching the morning sun rise over the silent, haunted homes and businesses of a town, long since abandoned.

Kira had not yet awakened, every now and then she would grunt or snort in her sleep before resuming, steady, rhythmic breathing.

As she looked out over the town of Nottingham, Charlie could not help but wonder at how quickly the world had changed. Only a few months ago, Nottingham would have been alive with activity at this hour. It was a Monday she thought (Keeping track of the days of the week had become more difficult since everything had fallen apart.) the town would already by bustling with men and women on their way to work, kids on their way to schools. Moms in minivans, dads in SUVs, teenagers on crotch rockets and in second-hand cars, douche bags in convertibles, all jockeying for space on the interstate and the roads of Nottingham. All vanished and gone, scattered to the winds by war and the deprivations that follow.

Charlie let her eyes drift over darkened homes, stores, here a school, there a church and felt only black desolation.

All gone... Because of me.

Behind her, Kira stirred and awakened. "Aria?" Voice thick, still more asleep or awake. "Are you up?"

Charlie remained still, not taking her eyes from the window. The sky was a near-flawless span of blue save for a few white wisps of cotton on the horizon that promised the possibility of future flurries. It was going to be a beautiful day.

A woman's lithe footsteps trod on the shag carpeting. "What are you looking at, Baby?"

Charlie was silent for a moment. Then: "Nothing. I was just watching the sunrise."

My name isn't Aria; it's Charlie. Please, my name is Charlie, and my Dad and Mom are David and Catherine McAuliffe. Please, I just want to go home.

Kira looked at her carefully, and for a moment, Charlie imagined she saw the clouds pass from the mad woman's eyes to be replaced by fleeting recognition. Her lips moved as if to speak, yet no sound came forth. Then the clouds closed, and she grinned a stupid, deliriously happy grin. "Are you hungry? Would you like some breakfast? We have sardines or sardines."

Charlie wrinkled her nose in disgust but said nothing. She was *so* tired of eating canned fish, but of all the shitty things that had happened to her in the past few weeks, lousy food seemed to be the least important.

Seemingly oblivious to Charlie's misery *or identity,* she thought dejectedly, Kira offered Charlie a gentle smile.

"I know, Babe. I'm tired of fish too. I saw some vending machines down the hallway. Maybe they'll have something better. You wait here. I'll go look."

And with that said, Kira turned and headed for the door. It occurred to Charlie at that moment that she could easily sneak out and run away while Kira was plundering the vending machines. But where would she go? Charlie sensed that David and Catherine were close by, but she had no idea where. If she ran, Charlie had no idea where she would go, and that seemed unacceptable. So she remained and waited, watching as the yellow-orange winter sun climbed into a royal blue sky.

Below Charlie spotted what looked like a stray dog picking through a heap of garbage next to an abandoned crossover. For a moment she felt something like pity for the poor animal. Charlie and Kira had had to scrounge and trade for food. She could only imagine how much harder it was for an animal that could only forage or hunt for its dinner.

The hotel room door banged open behind her, and Kira came in carrying an armload of pillaged snacks. Here were two Butterfinger bars, a Milky Way, three bags of Lays chips, two blueberry muffins, and a package of chocolate-covered mini donuts. To Charlie, it looked like heaven. Kira set the bounty down on the bed before Charlie.

"Well, these aren't exactly pancakes and maple syrup, but I'll bet they're better than sardines."

Charlie smiled slightly, mouth watering. Kira produced a single bottle of Pepsi, cracked it, and handed it to Charlie.

"And this should wash it down nicely." She gave Charlie a gentle smile.

"Thank you," Charlie replied, feeling genuinely grateful that she would be able to eat something besides canned fish.

Charlie ate the donuts and one of the muffins. They tasted stale and dry. To Charlie, they were heaven. Charlie offered the second muffin to Kira, who took it and looked at it for a moment in surprise.

"Are you sure, Babe?" She asked with genuine concern. "We may not get any more of these for a while."

"Yes," Charlie replied with a smile. "You've gotta be sick of canned fish too."

Kira smiled and chuckled slightly. "I am, but are you sure you don't want to save this for later?"

Charlie nodded.

"Ok." Kira carefully unwrapped the muffin and took a bite. "Definitely better than canned sardines."

Kira and Charlie laughed, and for a moment, Charlie was able to forget that Kira had taken her away from her adoptive parents. For a moment she was just a young girl yucking it up with a young woman who might have been a teacher or a friend. And then Charlie's smile faded as the moment passed, and the reality of her situation sank in.

Though Charlie tried to hide it, Kira must have seen something in her eyes for her expression became concerned.

"Are you ok, Baby?"

Charlie blinked back fresh tears. "I'm fine." And to her relief, her voice came out steady and robust despite the thick lump in her throat.

"Good," Kira said. "We have a big day ahead of us. Today you're going to learn drive." Kira was positively beaming with pride.

Under other circumstances, Charlie would have been thrilled, but today she felt the salty sting of tears on her tongue and the weight of a stone in her gut. As she followed Kira outside to the car, Charlie's eyes burned with sorrow. She was sure now, David and Catherine were nearby, still sleeping, but nearby. And she would be driving away from them.

Before getting into the blue PT Cruiser, Charlie turned and swept an abandoned, Ford Mustang with the power. The little red convertible erupted into bright orange-yellow flames with a loud -***warrrump-***. Charlie fully expected Kira to be frightened or angry or both. Perhaps she would even realize that Charlie was not her daughter. And yet the madwoman seemed not to notice the blazing car at the back of the parking lot. Still, David and Catherine would surely recognize her hand in the fire.

The car turned over easily. Just a quick flick of the power and the engine roared to life. Charlie was in the driver's seat grasping the wheel with tentative hands. Though only ten, Charlie was tall for her age and could easily reach the pedals.

"Now when you're ready, step on the brake, push this button in" Kira gestured towards the button on the side of the shifter. "and put the car into reverse. Then look back to make sure nothing's in the way, take your foot off the brake, and the car will roll back. You'll need to cut the wheel to the right."

Charlie did as she was told, carefully shifting into reverse and removing her foot from the brake. The car lurched backward with sudden, unexpected speed. Charlie panicked and slammed her foot back down on the brake, causing the car to stop short. Kira offered her what was undoubtedly meant to be a reassuring smile.

"It's ok, Aria." Kira soothed. "You're doing fine. Now just ease off the brakes and cut the wheel to the right."

Again Charlie lifted her foot from the brake, this time carefully drawing the wheel to the right as she did. The rear of the car went in the direction Charlie had turned the wheel as it rolled backward. Once out of the parking stall, Charlie applied the brakes, this time a little more slowly, and shifted the car into D. For a moment she paused, flesh cold with apprehension, heart alive with excitement. She had never driven a car before today. The thought made her want to hold her head high with pride, for she knew only grownups drove cars but…

What if I wreck it? What if we get hurt?

A slight, cold smile played across her lips for a brief moment.

What if I do wreck it? We'd be stuck here, and David and Catherine could find me.

Charlie shoved the thought aside, horrified. She had only gone with Kira because she did not want David and Catherine to fight her. If she wrecked the car, then they would fight.

And someone's going to get killed.

Charlie slowly lifted her foot from the brake and let the car roll forward towards the mouth of the hotel parking lot. Beyond it, Derry Street loomed directly ahead, the distance closing far too quickly. Charlie let her foot rest on the brake, slowing the car's approach.

"You're doing great, Aria," Kira told her in an encouraging tone. She was seated beside Charlie in the front passenger seat, her hand resting gently on Charlie's hip. Kira's touch, though light, felt alien and sent worms crawling through Charlie's flesh. Charlie wanted to brush it aside, or at least ask Kira not to touch her, but she dared not for fear of the man woman's reaction.

They had nearly reached the mouth of the parking lot. "Now apply the brakes carefully and switch on your right turn signal. I know there isn't any traffic, but we should still observe proper driving habits, right?" Kira chuckled at her own joke.

To her surprise, Charlie found herself giggling. She had not seen a police officer since before the world fell apart, and she seriously doubted that anyone cared about enforcing the traffic laws anymore. Not when the world was at war and survival was at stake. As this last thought passed through her mind her smile faded and her giggles abruptly dried up. Charlie brought the car to a gentle stop at the junction between the hotel parking lot and the chipped asphalt of Derry Street. For a moment she fumbled with the control stick on the left-hand side of the steering wheel before finding the turn signal and signaling right.

"Good job, Aria." Kira praised her. "Now I want you to carefully take your foot off the brake and turn the wheel right."

Charlie obeyed mutely, her flesh crawling at Kira's touch, her heart racing with combined fear and exhilaration. Once out on Derry Street, Charlie positioned the car precisely two feet from the center of the road.

"Good. Now give it a little gas." Kira's voice held unmistakable pride.

Charlie lifted her right foot from the brake and lighted it upon the gas pedal. The car smoothly accelerated, more than Charlie had expected.

I'm driving!

The thought made her feel strong. Charlie sat tall in her seat and held the wheel in a casual grasp. In that moment, she had become a grown-up, if only for a time. A soft smile played across her lips as the car cruised down Derry Street towards Campbell Boulevard. A sign ahead indicated that a right turn would take her to interstate 95 while a left would take her to the hospital. Charlie carefully gave the car a little more gas, bringing the speedometer needle up to thirty-five. She felt as though she were flying, although she knew the car had attained only moderate speed. Buildings and trees slipped by on both sides, as if in a dream. If this were a dream, she would awaken now to find herself still with David and Catherine. Yet she knew this was no dream. Charlie removed her right foot from the accelerator and carefully applied the brakes, bringing the car to a graceful stop at the intersection of Derry and Campbell. Then she clicked on the right turn signal and pulled onto the wider boulevard. Within five minutes she was turning again to enter the northbound side of Interstate 95.

By this time her joy and exhilaration at being allowed to drive had dried up, and in its place, her chest felt hollowed out with desolation and sorrow.

I'm driving…away from David and Catherine…leaving them behind forever.

This thought cut deep, like a cold razor. Charlie had chosen this because she felt it was the right thing, the only thing to do to protect David and Catherine, her dad and mom. It was the only way, but knowing that did nothing to quell the deep, cutting pain she felt now. A single tear formed in her right eye and trickled down her cheek to fall on her bare chest above the V-neck of her baby blue blouse. The place where the tear fell tingled and burned as if touched by molten iron.

I'll never see them again.

As she thought this, Charlie pictured a heavy, wooden door slamming shut on an open, airy room in which David and Catherine stood, arms out, pleading with her not to leave them behind. Charlie felt the door's brass knob in her hand and felt herself push hard, sending the door whispering towards its frame, forever foreclosing any possible future she might have had with her adopted father and mother.

For a moment, Charlie felt she would break, a huge, meaty lump filled her throat, her chest tightened, and her eyes began to burn and water. Charlie swallowed hard and swatted angrily at the tears flooding her eyes. Crying wouldn't help. She had chosen this to protect David and Catherine. It was not easy. It hurt terribly, but then her life was never easy, and she had suffered pain for so long that she no longer remembered what it felt like to not hurt.

…not to Hate

The hurt had become a cancer with which she had lived with for enough years to make her forget what it was like to feel truly happy. Now she supposed she would never be happy again.

She had entered the interstate now. Trees, buildings and abandoned cars sped by her on both sides as she brought the blue PT Cruiser up to an even sixty miles an hour. She was crying now, though silently. Charlie no longer cared if Kira saw. In fact, a part of her *hoped* Kira would see and for once understand that Charlie was *NOT* her dead daughter Aria.

For the first time, Charlie felt something ignite deep within. This was not sorrow, or the black *Hate* she felt for the men and woman responsible for the death of her Daddy and Mommy. Instead, this was an intense, choking feeling, a burning anger directed at this stupid, madwoman for forcing her to leave the only family she had left. As miles rolled by, Charlie felt the fire bank and grow within her until she had to stifle an urge to reach over and smack Kira in the back of the head.

This anger also stirred the power which Charlie quickly stifled.

STOP IT!

STOP IT NOW!

To Charlie's pleasant surprise, there was no pain. It had once hurt her to stop the power, now it did not…most of the time.

After an hour, Kira offered to take over driving, and Charlie gratefully gave up the wheel at an abandoned Love's truck stop outside of Wilmington, Delaware. Before departing, Kira siphoned enough gas to refill the PT Cruiser's tank and scavenged a box of stale Twinkies and several cans of accursed Chicken of the Sea tuna fish. As she did, Charlie sat in the front passenger seat of the PT Cruiser with her eyes closed, allowing her mind to drift. She wanted to cry but found that she could not. Her tears had dried up and crystalized into black despair. This would be her future, running alone with this madwoman.

VIII

As she pulled away from the Love's station in Wilmington, Kira looked down upon her daughter's sleeping form and felt her heart soar with pride. Aria had handled the car expertly. She was truly growing into a young woman.

When she had first seen the young, slender girl accompanied by Sergei and Katya, she had recognized her at once as Aria. While initially unwilling to believe (after all had she not seen Aria die) Kira could not help but recognize her daughter. Aria had lost weight, and they had dyed her hair a golden tow, but it was her. Kira felt sure of it, as sure as her broken spirit could be sure of anything. Weight loss had made Aria's face younger and her eyes those of an old woman. Aria had changed, but she was still Kira's daughter.

Now, as she watched her daughter stir in her sleep, Kira felt her heart go out to her and with it the power. Aria had been born without the power, and yet now Kira felt a touch she had only ever associated with other Enlighteneds. Except this touch was more potent than anything she had ever experienced before. Had her daughter been Enlightened all along and just hidden it well? She must have, for this was indeed Aria. As this thought passed through her mind, Kira leaned a little harder on the gas feeling an urgency that came from the certain knowledge that Sergei and Katya were nearby and aggressively searching for Aria and her. They had lost a great deal of time resting in Nottingham and would need to fly in order to avoid capture. As this thought passed through her mind, the power stirred restlessly.

Kira stifled it quickly before the power could damage the car or harm Aria. A sharp dagger of pain planted itself at the center of Kira's forehead. Over the past few days, Kira had found her control of the power weakening, becoming less precise. It hurt to stop the power in a way that she had not experienced in many years. Not since she had completed her training with Father Maxim. It also seemed much closer to the surface, ready to spring out at any time and destroy. Perhaps grief had weakened her control, or perhaps it was something…*someone*…else.

The Arbiter

The name floated in and out of her conscious mind, detached from any memory or understanding. In that moment, all she knew, all that mattered was Aria. Aria was here now, and she needed Kira to protect her.

The day passed agonizingly slowly, and with each successive hour, Kira's nerves screwed a little tighter, for she could feel Sergei and Katya nearby. They pursued Kira and Aria doggedly as if Aria were more than a piece of property to them. As if they genuinely cared for Kira's daughter…

They sold her to be raped and murdered. Kira's mind reminded her. *They took her away and would have used her a thousand times over until she was burned out and broken. Until they had stripped away her childhood and innocence and scooped out her soul.*

Aria awakened as they were crossing the border from Pennsylvania into New York. Radio broadcasts indicated that parts of eastern New Jersey, along with all of Manhattan and the Bronx, remained contaminated with radioactive fallout, thus requiring them to detour far west of the hot zone.

For a while, Aria and Kira sat in silence. Kira simply enjoying her daughter's presence, Aria seemingly engrossed in watching the abandoned buildings and cars of southern New York State zip by. As Kira passed a sign for Port Jervis, Aria finally broke her silence. Her words would cut Kira deeper than any knife could have.

"My name is Charlie, not Aria. I'm sorry, but I'm not your daughter. Can't you see that?" Aria spoke in a voice that was both gentle and held more than a hint of frustration.

Kira glanced at her, eyes swimming with tears, heart bleeding out in her chest. She understood at once. Aria was disowning her for killing Gary and Hunter. "I am your mother, and you are my daughter." Kira forced the words out between sobs. "I love you Aria. I'm sorry for what I did."

Aria met her gaze with soft, sorrowful eyes, and a smile so gentle and wistful as to be a keen blade cutting into Kira's heart and drawing blood from deep within. "I'm sorry they killed your daughter, but I'm not her. My name is Charlie, and my parents are David and Catherine." Her eyes studied Kira for a moment before widening ever so slightly. "You killed them." She stated in a low, mournful voice. "You killed the men who killed your daughter. You took revenge." Her voice held no condemnation, only profound grief.

To Kira, Aria's words pronounced judgment greater than if she had damned her. "I'm so sorry. I shouldn't have, but…I hurt so much, and they hurt you. I thought they killed you."

Aria's gaze did not waver, nor did it lose its gentleness or compassion. "It's ok. Those men took away your only family. They deserved to die. I understand."

A sob escaped Kira's throat. "I'm sorry, Baby. It hurt so much, I couldn't help it." Her voice was rising with desperation as her heart raced in her chest. She couldn't lose Aria again. Not again. "Let's start over, Baby. I don't want to lose you too."

Aria shook her head sadly but said no more. Kira felt her withdraw and close her mind. The air inside the car quickly became stagnant and empty as death. Aria had already left her, mentally, if not physically.

IX

For her part, Charlie had to fight to hold her head up under the crushing weight of defeat she felt over her entire body. Suddenly, every part of her being became immensely heavy, taking every ounce of strength she had to keep from folding up into herself.

They were headed east now. The sky had turned iron-gray, promising a blanket of snow. Charlie shivered slightly despite the warm air streaming from dash vents directly in front of her. She was alone and defeated. Charlie could not make Kira see that she was not Aria. She would never be able to return to David and Catherine. Bitter tears streamed from her eyes. Charlie no longer cared to hide them. As the remainder of that day dragged by, Charlie sat in her seat and wept openly. Kira no longer bothered to talk to her or tell her how proud she was. She only drove on, making haste, no doubt, because she too could feel that David and Catherine were close.

Charlie stared out the car window watching as the sky darkened and began to drop the first flurries of what would become a blizzard. In less than an hour, the world had disappeared in a thick wall of white. Charlie found herself fervently wishing to stop. They could slide on the snow-slick road and crash, or become lost in the endless blizzard. Still, Kira pushed on, driven by fear of being caught. By seven o'clock that evening, they had reached the outskirts of Boston, and by ten that night they had arrived in Bangor. Kira pulled the car up to an old and creepy looking multi-story brick building off of Route 2. A burned-out neon sign nestled among the many gargoyles on the building's tile roof shared that this had once been Cecil's Tavern.

The snow was coming down in sheets now, and the air had grown bitterly cold. A razor wind cut through Charlie's clothes as she helped Kira gather up their meager supplies. Like the other hotels at which they had stopped, Cecil's Tavern was dark and deserted. The air inside was as cold as the outdoors. Charlie followed Kira through the shadowy lobby to a set of emergency stairs near the elevators. Woman and child ascended the stairs in silence. It was freezing. Violent shudders swept through Charlie's muscles, and she was forced to clutch at her arms for warmth.

For a moment, Charlie found herself carried back in time to the woods of Indiana, where she and Daddy had hidden from the NSA so many years ago. Those days seemed a lifetime away now. Fresh tears spilled from Charlie's eyes. She missed Daddy, even now, so many years later, she felt his loss as keenly as if he had died just yesterday. And now she had lost David and Catherine as well.

They had reached the second floor. The corridor here was pitch black and icy like a nightmare. Kira produced a small flashlight and motioned for Charlie to follow her towards an open door, two rooms down. Inside they found the place in shambles, sheets, and blankets strewn about, mattresses dragged onto the floor, the vanity mirror shattered into a thousand shards of twinkling glass.

"Watch your step," Kira warned. "I don't want you to cut yourself on the glass."

Charlie stepped over the pile of twinkling fragments carefully and went to the bed nearest the window. Without making a sound, she grabbed the nearest mattress and dragged it onto the box spring before setting about making the bed. Her body ached with exhaustion and was heavy with defeat, but Charlie had no desire to sleep on a bare mattress. When she had finished two minutes later, Charlie opened her ragged blue duffel bag and took out a worn pink flannel nightgown. She drew the drapes and then undressed down to her underwear before pulling the nightgown over her head. She did this automatically, her mind still preoccupied with old memories.

She and Daddy had nearly starved to death in that little hunting cabin in the woods. She *had* gotten sick with food poisoning. It had been a difficult winter, and yet at that moment, she would have given nearly anything to be back there with her Daddy.

She was in bed now, covered up to her shoulders by a white comforter, hotel sheets cool against her legs; the weight of the blankets against her chest mildly soothing. Charlie closed her eyes and despite the tearing sensation in her chest, quickly passed into darkness, carried away by physical exhaustion.

X

Two hours after Charlie drifted off to sleep, David and Catherine arrived in Bangor. As with Vic Garling, David too could sense when Charlie had used the power. It was as if she had lit a bright torch in a dark room, he would know exactly where she was. The car Charlie had burned up in Nottingham had confirmed that they were on the right track, and though she had not meant to, in fact, she probably wasn't even aware of it, Charlie had reached out with the power and led him north.

That same touch of the power also led David to Cecil's Tavern, a large Art Deco style hotel. It was late, two or three in the morning, he guessed, but despite the hour, David, Catherine, and Stephen began to search the darkened halls of Cecil's Tavern for Charlie and the mad Rouge who had taken her.

XI

Golden sunlight streamed through the windows of Father Jim's kitchen, splashing over the gray slate countertops, rich honey-colored cabinets and shelves, and brass fixtures. Charlie sat at the dark, red oak kitchen table with David and Catherine, a massive breakfast of pancakes, maple syrup, and thick-sliced bacon. This had to be a dream, it was too good to be true. And yet everything seemed so real. She could feel the hard, red oak seat of her chair beneath her bottom, could smell the rich, heady aroma of frying bacon fat, melted butter, baking pancakes, and warm maple syrup. Instead of feeling cold Charlie's body warmed as if submerged in a tepid bath. She smiled brightly.

"Good morning, Charlie." David's voice was bright and cheery. "How did you sleep?"

"Good." She replied brightly.

"I hope you're hungry," Catherine added. "We made your favorite, pancakes, and bacon."

Charlie licked her lips and broadened her smile. "Oh goody."

A glass of fresh-squeezed orange juice sat on the table in front of her. Charlie picked it up and drank down half its contents. The cool liquid soothed her throat and lit up her tongue with just the right amount of sweetness. A shadow played across Charlie's face as she remembered.

"But I left you guys behind in Miami and went with Kira. This can't be real. How did we get here?"

"We've been at my dad's," David replied gently. "You must have been dreaming."

Charlie's frown remained. She badly wanted to believe him, but she knew the truth. This was a dream, the fact was she was still at Cecil's Tavern with Kira freezing her ass off.

"It's ok, Charlie," Catherine added. "It was only a dream. You're safe here with us. Kira's gone forever."

Now she was sure she was dreaming for David and Catherine had never learned Kira's name, they knew her only as the Rogue.

Before she could reply to either David or Catherine, Charlie suddenly found herself sitting up in bed wide awake and feeling more confident than ever that David and Catherine were close by.

XII

The hotel room had grown lighter. Soft yellow sunlight drifted in from between heavy brown drapes, painting a narrow triangle upon white bedding and brown carpeting. Despite the cheery morning rays, the room felt colder and less friendly. Something was very wrong, Charlie felt it deep within. David and Catherine were nearby, they had found her, and they would confront Kira. Charlie knew as well that Kira would fight to the death for her, for the madwoman still believed that Charlie was her dead daughter Aria.

Please God...there has to be a way to stop this.

Except she knew better. Deep inside she felt that the die had been cast, now all that was left was to pay out the loss.

Hard, wracking shudders swept her body, as icy blood thundered in her veins. Heart in her mouth, Charlie sat up slowly and went to the pocket in her duffel bag where she had stashed the last of the box of Twinkies from the Wilmington Love's station. The little snack cakes were stale and tasted like sugar, cardboard, and lard, but they were an improvement over the metallic fish taste of canned tuna. And the sugar helped her feel a little more focused if not less frightened.

After eating Charlie dressed and took out the worn copy of *The Gunslinger* she had rescued from a Love's station in Boston. Only a year ago, she had read part of *The Stand* and found it far too dark and depressing. But now, Stephen King's bleak worldview seemed more real to her than the optimism of J.R.R. Tolkien. For a long time, *The Lord of the Rings* had been an escape for her, a brief respite from the harsh realities of her life. But now it felt like a lie, or maybe more like getting drunk to forget one's troubles. She would always enjoy reading about Frodo Baggins and his magic ring, but that enjoyment had faded and become tattered by the strong feeling that for her, the story had become a delusion and a lie. In the real world, nothing ever worked out as it did in Middle Earth. In the real world, the bad guys won, good people died, and innocents suffered for no reason. In Middle Earth, if you did all the right things and fought hard enough then good would ultimately prevail. In the real world, you could do everything right and still fail.

Charlie carried the battered paperback to the window and pulled back the drapes. Below she could see the snow-covered dome of the PT Cruiser. Beside it on the left and right sat two heaps of snow that had once been cars. Further down, she spotted something that nearly took her breath away. At the end of the parking lot sat a ramshackle purple Buick Century she hadn't seen the night before. The lack of snow covering told her the car had arrived recently. The power whispered to her that this was David and Catherine's car. A cold shiver of combined fear and excitement crept up her back, and her arms rashed out in goosebumps.

They're here... They came to get me.

A warm trickle built deep in Charlie's stomach, bringing a slight smile to her face. She *was* excited to see David and Catherine, and deep inside Charlie knew she would see them today. And with that knowledge, Charlie's flesh and blood froze with fear for she knew that David and Catherine would fight Kira to the death for her. Someone would die today, and she feared it would be her adoptive parents. Charlie turned from the window and climbed back into bed with her book. She intended to bury her nose there and forget the cold and terrifying thoughts that plagued her mind but found that she could not. Her mind continued to drift back to the sensation, no not just a sensation but a sure knowledge that David and Catherine were near and that they would confront Kira and demand Charlie's return.

And they'll fight her to the death for me. Just like she would do for her daughter.

After what felt like an hour of unsuccessful attempts to travel to Mid-World to join Roland and his Ka-Tet, Charlie finally gave up in frustration and put the book down. She didn't know what time it was, but the sun had moved further from the horizon, and the sky had cleared to a solid span of winter blue.

On the bed beside her, Kira snored softly; no doubt finally feeling relaxed enough to sleep peacefully. Charlie passed her with quiet strides and headed out into the hotel corridor. The air here remained as bitter cold as the night before. Charlie pulled her battered leather bomber jacket tighter around her shoulders and tucked her hands into her armpits as shivers took her. Her tremors could not be fully accounted for by cold though, for she was utterly terrified. She knew what was to come. She knew someone would die today.

As this thought passed through her mind, Charlie's vision changed, and for a moment she saw David and Catherine, followed a moment later by a flash of steel and splash of crimson. A body lay at her feet in a pool of blood, a terrible wound in its abdomen. Charlie could not see who it was or even if it was male or female as all but its outline was shrouded in darkness.

A cold shudder ripped up her back and down her arms as a soft moan escaped her throat.

No please…

Please don't let that happen…

Except she felt it was already too late. Charlie didn't know how or when, but she knew it was too late.

A door slammed behind her. Charlie turned to see Kira standing just outside their room and looking more asleep than awake.

"Aria." She yawned. "What are you doing out here?"

"Nothing, I was just looking around." The words came automatically, her voice surprisingly nonchalant.

"Are you hungry, Baby?" Kira persisted. "I could make you breakfast."

"No, not yet. Just bored." Charlie replied in that same nonchalant voice.

Kira stepped the rest of the way into the hallway. She was dressed only in a white terry bathrobe and a pair of white slippers. "I'll go with you. I don't want you wandering around this place by yourself."

"I'll be ok," Charlie replied. She didn't want Kira following her around, mostly because she felt more strongly than ever that David and Catherine were close. The battered purple Buick was *their* car. They were somewhere in this hotel.

We need to get out of here before they figure out we're here.

Charlie desperately wanted to see David and Catherine, but she feared what would happen if they crossed paths with Kira.

"Can we go look for a house today?' Charlie asked in what she intended to be a hopeful tone.

"You don't want to stay here?" Kira replied with a hint of sarcasm.

They were walking down the hallway towards the stairs. Charlie intended to descend to the lobby and lead Kira away from the hotel.

"No-oo.' Charlie replied, keeping up the act. "It's too dark and cold here."

Kira smiled. "Ok, Aria. We can go look for a house after I get dressed, and we eat breakfast."

Charlie's heart sank. "Ok." She had to force her voice to remain upbeat.

As the words left her mouth, Kira's hand closed on Charlie's shoulder and led her back towards their room. Breakfast consisted of cold canned tuna fish. Charlie ate without much enthusiasm. She had never liked canned tuna fish and was thoroughly fed up with it now. As she ate, Charlie's blood ran cold with imminent disaster. The sensation that David and Catherine were near grew stronger with each moment.

Charlie's vision changed several times, and again she saw the flash of silver and spray of crimson. Again she found herself looking down upon the unknown body as it bled out from a ragged abdominal wound. Several times Charlie felt her stomach clench and a meaty lump form in her throat. By some miracle, Charlie managed to stifle the urge to vomit.

After breakfast, Kira went into the bathroom to shower and change. Charlie tried again to read while she waited for the madwoman to return. She found that she still could not immerse herself in the novel and eventually replaced the book in her duffel bag in frustration. The sensation of *nearness* to David and Catherine was growing, building to a crescendo. They were in the building looking for her. She had little time.

Charlie reached out to them and touched David's mind with her own.

Please stay away. Please…I love you, Dad. I don't want you to get hurt.

Charlie! The echo of David's voice in her mind held desperate hope. *Thank God. I knew we would find you here. It's going to be ok. Just tell us where you are.*

In her mind, Charlie saw her room number, 317, outlined in brass, but kept this information to herself.

Please…I miss you, but I don't want you to get hurt.

Charlie, where are you? David's voice repeated with slightly more force this time.

I can't tell you. Charlie replied gently and then closed her mind before David could persuade her differently.

A short time later, Kira emerged from the bathroom fully dressed, bright-eyed, and with lips curled into a relaxed smile. "Ready to go, Aria?"

Charlie nodded, forcing herself to smile in return. "Yes."

"Good, then let's head out."

Charlie followed Kira from their hotel room and down the corridor. It was mid-morning, and the sun had begun to invade the darkened halls of Cecil's Tavern in narrow, haunting streams as if seen through the bars of a prison cell. Charlie shivered. The air felt colder than before and much closer as if the old hotel had been sealed up for years. As she approached the stairs, Charlie's heart rose, thumping in her throat. David and Catherine were very close, perhaps only a floor above or below. She had to get Kira away before David and Catherine found them.

Kira must have noticed something false in Charlie's painted on smile. "Everything alright?"

Charlie broadened her smile slightly. "I'm fine. Just looking forward to getting out of this creepy hotel."

Kira returned a knowing smile. "Ok, Aria." Her tone suggested that she knew there was more going on than Charlie had admitted to.

They were on the stairs now. Charlie descended the risers two at a time, eager to get away from impending disaster; desperate to protect David, Catherine, and Kira.

Charlie's footsteps rang off the concrete like gunshots, sending trickles of electricity rippling through all of her muscles. Upon reaching the ground, Charlie ran to the lobby fire door, pulled it open, and held it. Kira seemed to take forever to catch up. It was not that she was dawdling, rather time, as it always did in moments of crisis, had slowed to a painful crawl. With each passing second, Charlie's heart ramped up, and her mind raced faster, such that by the time Kira reached the lobby fire door, Charlie was nearly irrational with panicked fright.

As Kira passed by Charlie on her way into the hotel lobby, Charlie had to stifle an urge to shout at her for dragging her feet. The power had come alive, spurred awake by her building fear it moved restlessly within Charlie's mind.

She bit down on it hard.

STOP IT!

GO AWAY!

STOP IT NOW!

The power continued spiraling upward, driven on by the cold flowing in her blood. Hot, oily sweat beaded up on her skin and soaked through her clothes. Charlie drew in a slow, shaky breath and followed Kira into the darkened lobby of Cecil's Tavern. What had once been a pitch-black cavern, had now become a shadowy mausoleum. White marble trimmed in polished brass made up the floors and registration desk, below a vaulted ceiling clad in gold leaf and intricate square embellishments. The lobby's few furnishings, a few wingback leather chairs, and overstuffed leather couches lay untouched under a thin shroud of dust.

Their footsteps echoed off the polished floor, cannon shots in the darkness. Except there were more than two sets of footfalls. Charlie quickly understood this and turned to see David and Catherine standing at the back of the lobby near the entrance to the hotel restaurant. Behind them, mostly hidden by shadow stood Stephen Wolf.

Charlie felt something leap up within her sending electric joy surging through her body. This sensation was followed a moment later by a sharp chill of terror, for she knew already what was to come.

“Charlie!” David’s voice echoed hauntingly in the darkened lobby.

“Dad, no! Don’t come any closer!” But it was already too late.

XIII

"Sergei!" Kira hissed, eyes clouded with sudden, false recognition. "YOU WILL NOT STEAL MY DAUGHTER AGAIN YOU FUCK!"

"I think you're mistaken." David began in a calm voice. "My name is…"

"You stole Aria!" Kira hissed. "I'm not letting you take her away again."

David tried again. "I think you're mistaken, miss. My name is David." He gestured towards Charlie. "That's *my* daughter Charlie. I don't know your daughter, and I didn't steal her."

"LIAR!" Kira roared at him. In an instant, her sword was out, blade glowing a baleful turquoise.

Before David could draw *Deus Irae* in response, Catherine had stepped in front of him, weapon in hand, blade radiant in blue-white. "I challenge you." She spat.

A smile of pure madness played across Kira's lips. "I accept."

Her words echoed in the stale air of the lobby as if in a nightmare. Charlie's heart began to triphammer.

"No please…" She begged. "Please don't fight."

It's happening.

Just as she had sensed it would, it was happening. And there was nothing she could do to stop it.

Catherine slowly strode towards Kira, blade held at the ready. Kira changed her grip on her sword to a two-handed style. Her muscles tensed in preparation to strike.

Catherine struck first, targeting the crown of Kira's skull with a smooth vertical stroke. Kira easily evaded the blow, simultaneously attacking Catherine's throat with a horizontal slash. Catherine stepped clear of the blow, and lunged forward in a high sideways slash intending to sever Kira's head with a single stroke. Kira dropped under the stroke and rolled forward, simultaneously sweeping her blade around in a wide arc designed to sever both of Catherine's legs.

Charlie looked on, body trembling and aching with horror. It hurt to stand and watch, and yet she dared not intervene for fear of harming Catherine or Kira.

Catherine attempted to leap over Kira's glowing turquoise sword but stumbled slightly and caught the very tip of the blade in her left front thigh muscle. She let out a cry of pain but did not hesitate to retaliate with a low slash of her own that opened up Kira's abdomen along the hip, exposing glistening white bone and bright red muscle. Kira too let out a suffering cry.

Tears spilled from Charlie's eyes "Please stop." she sobbed, knowing in her heart that they would not. She was Catherine's daughter, and Catherine would fight to the death for her. She had also somehow become Kira's daughter, and Kira too would fight to the death for her.

Both women straightened up and leveled their blades. Their eyes locked for a moment, and then Kira charged forward with a cry, sword raised above her head. Catherine brought her weapon around in a hard, baseball swing. In that same moment, Kira brought her blade down. Blood flew on the stale lobby air as Kira's sword buried itself deep into Catherine's shoulder, and Catherine's tore open Kira's abdomen, just above the navel. Both women collapsed to their knees consumed with ragged gasps for breath.

"MOOOOOM!"

The cry escaped Charlie's throat without a thought. Her heart was tearing apart both from hurt and terror.

Please, I can't lose Catherine.

She had lost Mommy many years ago, and now it seemed she would lose her adoptive mother as well.

"I'm ok," Catherine replied raggedly. "Go to David." She turned her head. "David, take Charlie and get out of here."

David shook his head. "I won't leave you."

"There's nothing you can do," Catherine replied. "You know the rules. Now take our daughter and go!" She staggered to her feet and turned back towards Kira just in time for the madwoman to grab hold of her sword and rip it free of Catherine's shoulder.

Catherine let out a heartrending scream that brought fresh tears to Charlie's eyes. The power moved within her aggressively.

STOP IT!

The words screamed in her mind. Catherine had staggered backward as Kira leveled her blade. In an impossibly fast movement, Kira swung her blade in a wide horizontal arc at Catherine's torso. Catherine stumbled backward, but not before the tip of Kira's sword slit a jagged line across Catherine's chest just above her breasts. Catherine slashed wildly at Kira, who easily evaded the blow before crouching and driving her blade through the center of Catherine's abdomen. Catherine let out a terrible cry of pain and collapsed to her knees. Without pausing, Kira grabbed the handle of her sword, twisted the blade, and ripped it free, spilling a gout of blood and several loops of Catherine's intestines onto the white marble floor. A horrible smell filled the air and Charlie understood at once that Kira's blade had punctured Catherine's bowels.

Charlie screamed, "**NOOOOO!** Mom…**MOM!**" and ran to Catherine's side.

The power was a living thing within her. For a moment, Charlie found herself back on the beach at Fallow Point and very nearly burned Kira down to a pile of white ash and fused bone, as she had done to Robin Striker so many years ago. And then David stepped in the way.

STOP IT!

“I challenge you.” David’s voice was husky with rage and grief.

“David…” Catherine gasped. “Don’t…”

He drew *Deus Irae* and angled the point towards Kira’s throat. “I challenge you to face me to the death Rouge.” As David spoke the words, *Deus Irae,* lit up in intense blue-white.

Kira leveled her blade in response. Thick streamers of Catherine’s blood dripped from its point. “I accept.” She hissed, mad eyes narrowed with hate.

Then, moving with the grace of a ballerina, Kira strode towards David and swept her sword downward, intending to split him from crown to collar. David saw the blow coming and swept his sword upward, smashing Kira’s blade out of her hands and sending it clanging across the marble floor. Kira extended her left hand and Charlie felt her reach out with the power. In an instant, the sword flipped through the air and landed in her open palm. Without pausing, Kira again slid forward and slashed at David. This time it was a wide horizontal arc that he stepped under and answered with a low slash at Kira’s legs. *Deus Irae* drew a long, thin red line across both of Kira’s thighs, spraying bright blood across the marble floor. Kira let out a cry of combined pain and rage and charged forward, blade whirling.

David easily evaded each of her blows and shoved her backward with the flat of his blade. Then he turned quickly and slashed open Kira’s rib cage between her breasts. Kira let out a second shrill cry and swung her blade at David’s head. David managed to avoid the worst of the blow but had his cheek opened by her sword point. Before he could raise his blade to guard, Kira slashed again. This time her blade drew a jagged red line down the length of his left arm.

“Dad!” Charlie cried. “Please don’t hurt my Dad!”

Kira ignored her and pressed her advantage. The power was racing within Charlie’s mind, driven to frenzy by the cold fear and burning grief flowing through her chest. Charlie bit it back fiercely.

STOP IT NOW!

She would have killed Kira to protect David, but he was too close, the risk too high. She could only pray that he would prevail.

As Charlie watched, her flesh cold as ice, David and Kira hacked away at each other. Slash and parry, thrust and dodge, neither giving an inch. David smashed his blade against Kira’s intending to knock it from her hand, or so Charlie thought. Instead of disarming her, David was able to force Kira to lower her guard. Then in the same, smooth motion, he whirled around and slashed at her throat. This time Kira was caught unawares. Her face registered surprise for a moment. Then *Deus Irae* neatly sliced through her neck and severing her head with a neat ***-thunk-***.

Kira’s head fell from her shoulders, struck the ground with a ***-thud-*** and came to a stop next to Charlie’s knees. Kira’s eyes had become dull blue marbles, her face frozen in an eternal expression of shock. Blood streaked her long red hair and pooled under her slaughtered, decapitated body.

Charlie screamed, and before she could stop it the power leapt out of her and set the front desk and several chairs and couches ablaze. The air quickly became heavy with the acrid smell of smoke and the metallic stench of blood.

David strode over to Charlie and Catherine and crouched beside them. "Help me get her up."

Charlie complied, even as tears streamed from her eyes.

"D...David." Catherine's voice was little more than a pained whisper. "You need to get Charlie out of here before the whole place goes up."

"I'm not leaving you behind," David replied simply. "We're all getting out of here."

"Well, we'd better hurry," Stephen said impatiently. "This place is about to go up."

With some help, Catherine staggered to her feet. Blood and green bile leaked from a massive, ragged hole in the center of her abdomen. Charlie stifled an urge to scream. She was sobbing, but she managed to help David lead Catherine from the now blazing lobby.

Once outside, they dragged Catherine towards the PT Cruiser with Stephen following close behind. Five minutes later they were on the road, headed away from the now blazing Cecil Tavern.

"She's dying." Stephen was saying. "Blade went through her large intestine. She will either bleed out or die of infection."

"She's going to be alright." David insisted angrily. Charlie sensed that his words were more for his own denial than as encouragement to Catherine.

To Charlie, everything seemed immensely unreal, as if she were dreaming. The sun, now riding a noon-day high, seemed overly bright, colors seemed unnaturally vivid as if seen on a big screen TV with the Bright turned up too high. She could not yet fathom that this was real.

Tears streamed from Charlie's eyes though, as far as she was aware, she was not crying. "Mom..." She whispered the name to Catherine as she held her hand. "I love you, Mom."

Catherine returned a weak smile. "I love you too, Charlie. It's going to be ok. I promise you. Everything is going to be ok."

She was lying, Charlie could feel it even as Catherine spoke the words. Nothing was ever ok. Part of her thought she should be crying, and yet she did not. It was all too much too fast, the death camp, being taken by Kira, Catherine's wound, Kira's death. It was all too much to process. She felt like a computer that had been struck by lightning, wiped clean by shock. At some point, it would all come crashing in, and she would break, the computer would reboot. But for now, she felt nothing, even the power had gone silent.

They only drove a short distance before they had to stop. Catherine was moaning in agony, and the car had become saturated in her blood. David parked the car outside a large sandstone Victorian. The house was dark but did not look abandoned like so many of the other buildings that Charlie had seen.

Its brown wooden porch remained in good repair and free of clutter, its unbroken windows shone in the midday sun.

Stephen and David carried Catherine from the car and up onto the porch. Then David walked up to the Victorian's front door and knocked loudly. There was no response. Charlie felt him flick out with the power, and the door fell open. Inside, the house was dark and smelled of cinnamon and cloves. Charlie felt her nerves screw a little tighter. Someone was living here.

"Are you sure there's no one here?" Stephen asked.

"No, but Catherine can't travel any further," David replied.

"I'm fine." Catherine's voice was little more than a raspy, pained whisper. Her breathing had quickened, and her face was stamped with pain. "Let's get out of here."

David ignored her and began to search the house. After a few minutes, he returned carrying a bottle of whiskey, a roll of electrical tape, and a torn-up bedsheet. He then proceeded to clean and bandage Catherine's wounds.

Charlie would never forget Catherine's screams as David washed out her abdominal wound. Even as an adult, decades later, when she closed her eyes Charlie could still hear them, terrible, heart-rending.

After treating Catherine, David and Stephen carried her upstairs into the nearest bedroom and laid her out on the canopy bed within. Catherine was barely conscious now. Her eyelids hung heavy over hazy, half-aware eyes.

Charlie gazed at Catherine's face and forced herself to smile. "It's ok to go to sleep, Mom. We'll be here when you wake up."

Catherine groaned softly. "Ok.." Then her eyes fell closed, and her breathing became slow and even.

XIV

An hour after their arrival at the sandstone Victorian, familiar iron-shod boots rang on the hardwood floor of the kitchen. Charlie, who had been reading a copy of *It* that she had found on one of the house's many bookshelves, froze immediately at the sound, her heart leaping up into her throat.

Oh no...

She recognized the footsteps at once as belonging to Lord Beathach. They crossed the kitchen and foyer purposefully before ascending the stairs. David drew his sword with a low ***-shriiik-.*** Charlie reached into the power, preparing to strike. After what seemed like hours, but was most likely in fact less than a minute, Lord Beathach appeared, dark armor shining malevolently under the fading afternoon sun, black cape little more than a trailing shadow. David moved to strike. Beathach swept him aside with a simple gesture.

"You need not be concerned." He rumbled. "I am here to reward you, not to harm you." Though hidden, Charlie could sense Beathach's smile behind his death's head mask. "Congratulations, David, you have successfully slain the Rouge."

David met his blank gaze with hostile eyes. "You're not taking my daughter." His voice came out low and threatening.

"No," Beathach replied. "I have no intention. I promised that I would escort you and your family to safety if you slew the Rouge, and I intend to keep my word."

Charlie held the power at bay, wanting to burn down this walking nightmare but unwilling to kill Beathach in cold blood.

STOP IT NOW!

Her head began to throb. Charlie raised a hand to her temple and began to rub it absently.

Beathach approached the bed and regarded Catherine's sleeping form with cold eyes. "She is dying. She will not survive the night."

David glared at him but said nothing.

"I could save her." Beathach offered. "But it will come at a price."

Before he said anymore, Charlie understood. The power could not be used to create life, only to transfer life energy from one to another.

"Only life pays for life." Beathach continued. "I could use one of these wretched survivors. They are not Enlighteneds, and they are not your family. What do their lives matter to you?"

David's face darkened, and Charlie could feel him struggling with himself. He knew this was wrong and yet he believed Beathach and did not want to lose Catherine. Charlie too did not want to lose Catherine, but she did not want to see an innocent murdered either. Before either husband or daughter could speak, Catherine's eyes fluttered open.

"No. I knew what I was risking when I challenged Kira. I don't want someone else to die so that I can live."

Charlie wanted desperately to argue with her, to beg her to let Beathach heal her, and yet she found she could not speak. Instead, she sat in silence, tears streaming from her eyes.

"Where were you going to take us?" Catherine asked in a steady voice.

"The people of Australia have opened a sanctuary for all who would seek refuge from the Great Civil War," Beathach replied. "You will be safe there."

Catherine smiled. "I've always wanted to see Australia. Will we be on the beach?"

"I can arrange that." Beathach rumbled softly. Then he became very still. As before, the air began to shimmer and then *bend.* Then everything went to brilliant white.

XV

When her vision cleared, Charlie found herself standing on white sands looking out over azure seas on a perfect summer morning.

For a moment, Charlie thought she had died. Rather than fear, this thought brought on momentary relief. A warm breeze swept in from the water, carrying a with it the sweet, salty scent of the beach.

"Ughhh."

Catherine's groan brought Charlie back to reality. She was not dead. She supposed they were in Australia.

"God, it *huuurts.*" Catherine's moan cut Charlie to the quick. She remained in her bed, the legs of which were now half-buried in sugar-white sand. David and Stephen stood beside her. Lord Beathach was nowhere to be seen.

A sign near the edge of the sand advised that they were standing on Gunn Point Beach. There were no buildings or roads here, no signs of people, only mile after mile of pristine wilderness and perfect, white sand beaches. It was paradise, and a grave for Catherine, for there was also no help.

David, Stephen, and Charlie cared for Catherine as best as they could, but their efforts were futile. By midmorning, Catherine was running a fever and wracked by chills, and by that afternoon it became clear that her time was short.

Her breathing had become labored, and she was drifting in and out of consciousness. As the sun grew low on the horizon, David called to Charlie.

"Come here, Charlie.."

"Ok." Charlie approached the bed slowly. David was sitting on the edge of the mattress, holding Catherine's hand.

"Charlie…" Catherine's voice was hoarse and barely audible. "I love you, Charlie…" She took on a slow, shaky breath. "I wish we had, had more time…"

Something within Charlie ripped apart and all at once she began to weep. "Please don't….don't go."

"I'm sorry I've been so distant…because I do love you…I just…never knew how to show it." She was gasping for breath now.

David squeezed her hand tightly. "Don't talk, sweetheart. Save your breath. It's going to be ok."

“I’m dying, David.” Catherine admonished him. “You know it even though you won’t admit it.”

Thick tears trickled down David’s cheeks. “You’re not going to die. So stop the bullshit.”

Catherine smiled. “It’s ok David. I’m not afraid. You shouldn’t be either. We’ve had a good life together, the three of us. Even if it hasn’t been easy. We’ve always had each other, and that’s all that matters.”

Charlie began to sob. “Please, I can’t lose you. I can’t lose you, Mom.”

Catherine took Charlie’s hand with hers and squeezed it. “You’ll never lose me.” She touched the center of Charlie’s chest above her heart. “I’ll always be with you here.” Then she took one last shuddering gasp before her eyes went blank, and Catherine McAuliffe passed from this world.

Chapter 15
Catherine's Beach

I

The barroom is deserted, silent, littered with shards of glass and broken tables. The young woman in the green cocktail dress lies still in a pool of her own blood. She is dead by a bullet fired by the young man in the blue denim work shirt, from an unusual, toggle lock, handgun bearing a potent symbol of hate, its bullet meant for the young man in the red European cut suit. Both men have now fled together with the rest of the bar patrons save for the gentlemen in white and black.

The mid-thirties woman too lies dead, her blood growing tacky on the scarred barroom floor. She has taken on a man against whom she had no chance, a man who tried his best to avoid a conflict with her. Both women's deaths are tragic, and both the gentleman in white and in black are grieved by their passing.

No further sounds of violence drift in from the streets. A television above the bar that had once shown a rugby game now displays a black screen, the words 'No Signal' emblazed in white across its center.

The gentleman in white crouches over the remains of the two women and whispers an unheard prayer. "They did not have to die." His words are directed to no one in particular.

"No. They did not." The gentleman in black replies. "Men are fools..." As he speaks, the gentleman in black rights a table near the bar and begins to set the chessboard for another game. "But our game must continue."

The gentleman in white straightens up slowly. "I suppose it must." His tone is reluctant.

The gentleman in black approaches a beer tap behind the bar marked Pale Rider. "Care for another drink, my friend?"

"Yes." The gentleman in white responds as he wipes a single tear from his right cheek. "I think I could use one."

The gentleman in black pours two drafts and passes one to the gentleman in white. "Let us continue."

"Yes."

II

They buried her with her feet to the west so that she might watch the sunset over the azure waters of the Pacific, and far enough up the beach to ensure that the rising tide would not disturb her. A single stone, engraved by the power, with the words "Catherine McAuliffe.

Beloved wife of David McAuliffe, Beloved Mother of Charlene MacLeod" marked her final resting place.

Charlie and David stood over Catherine's grave hand in hand, both weeping softly, neither saying a word. A soft, cool breeze drifted in from the sea, gently lifting Charlie's perfect blond hair from her shoulders and caressing her tearstained cheeks, as if it were the silent hand of God comforting her, wordlessly telling her that it was ok to be sad and that everything would be ok. An old lie told to children by parents who know that nothing is ever ok.

Charlie stepped forward and gently laid her hand upon the chunk of granite that served as Catherine's tombstone. Suddenly remembering an old, familiar hymn from one of the few times she had attended the Taylor Presbyterian Church with Daddy and Mommy Charlie drew a slow, hitching breath and began to sing.

'Amazing Grace

How sweet the Sound

That saved a wretch like me

I once was lost

But now am found

Was lost but now I see.

And she sang in a voice more beautiful than she would have thought herself capable of. David's hand tightened around her hand as her high, thin voice flowed like water over lyrics only vaguely remembered.

'Twas grace that taught my heart to fear,

And grace my fears relieved;

How precious did that grace appear

The hour I first believed!'

'When we've been there ten thousand years,

Bright shining as the sun,

We've no less days to sing God's praise

Than when we first begun.,

As the last verse of *Amazing Grace* passed her lips, Charlie broke completely. Bitter tears streamed from her eyes, as she wept. As the soft ocean breeze ruffled her hair, Charlie mourned the awful unfairness of it all.

She had lost Catherine, her adoptive mother. Kira had died because of a desperate delusion, and she and David were alone.

As she watched the sun set over the Pacific Ocean, Charlie felt twilight closing upon the world, upon David and upon her. The darkness had fallen, and all that was left to them was sorrow and pain.

ABOUT THE AUTHOR

Brian L. Jackson lives in northeastern Oklahoma with his wife Melanie and two children. In addition to writing fiction Brian practices Domestic and Criminal law, is an avid reader and occasional gamer.

Brian graduated from Lock Haven University with a bachelors in English and went on to earn his Juris Doctor from Oklahoma City University.

www.ingramcontent.com/pod-product-compliance
Lightning Source LLC
Chambersburg PA
CBHW081134300726
48982CB00005B/962

* 9 7 8 1 0 8 7 8 1 9 4 9 5 *